Dance of Angels

I0606939

A Novel

by

Adrienne Lynn Rutherford

Copyright © 2017 Adrienne Lynn Rutherford

All rights reserved. No part of this book may be reproduced in any form or by any means, electronic or mechanical, including photo-copying, recording, or by any information storage and retrieval system, without written permission from the author. This excludes a reviewer who may quote brief passages in a review.

To request permission, please contact Adrienne L. Rutherford at imanifocus@gmail.com.

This novel is a work of fiction. Names, characters, places and incidents either are the product of the author's imagination or are used fictitiously. Any resemblance to actual persons, living or dead, events, or locales, is entirely coincidental.

Cover Design: Brittany J. Jackson

Published by G Publishing, LLC

Library of Congress Control Number: 2017952291

ISBN: 978-0-9985990-4-5

Printed in the United States of America

Prologue

Ma' me: Tulsa Oklahoma 1921

Ma'me rocked steadily in the old wooden rocking chair shaking her head and thinking to herself about the day that she and her brother Bufus hurried fast behind the tall Union Army Captain. He and his soldiers had proudly and victoriously escorted them along with the other children out of that old rundown plantation in Greensboro, North Carolina.

"Lawd, I thought heaven den opened up its gates of salvation on that day".

"I never knew my mama, my daddy said she run off a long time ago when I was just two years born searching for her freedom. In that moment, I thought freedom must be a precious thing for you to leave your children behind".

"My grandma Tullie told me that she just got right tired of massa and couldn't stand to see him sell off another one of her children. They later found her wandering in the woods talking to herself and hitting at the wind with anything she could find. She was never right again."

"Daddy, when he got the opportunity he went after freedom too. He and some of the other men folk found out about a ship that would take them back to a place called Africa, where he said we came from. I didn't know much about that at the time, but when I got older I learned. Yes, I learned about the land over there. A free life away from the only life I ever known and what my daddy called pure *hell*.

"He promised both me and my brother that he was coming back for us, but he never did. So, I stopped being sad over it and just kept on living. I grabbed only what I needed when the union army came, because I didn't wanna be weighed down you know."

"When the lord pushes you to move to better places you can't be taking no whole lotta stuff with you. It will just take you way too long to get there."

"When I could share my story with my daughter, she would shake her head and just remind me those days were behind me."

"I shake my head because, even though they are behind me, I remember them all too well, yes all too well indeed."

"You know why?"

"Because it was my life!"

Ma'me a faithful older woman full of memories of her and her brother Bufus and their departure from Master Conrad's Plantation in Greensboro, North Carolina. Freedom for her had been a painful reality, never really grasping its true meaning. It had torn her family completely apart long before she understood its value in the life as a young Black American woman in 1866.

"Shoot, me and my brother Bufus was tough, tough I tell you, we made our way west. I was barely fourteen and he was sixteen. We settled right her in Greenwood when it was just a small little old wooden plank store front community on the northside of Tulsa Oklahoma. I worked a while for two older white couples across the tracks on the southside cleaning and cooking, you know helping out, only now I was getting paid for it. Brother Bufus, well he thought he could do much better and he never had much patience with anything."

"Anyway, he married me off after a while, packed up and moved to Tennessee. He'd come back a few times with his wife and that baby girl of his, but after a time I didn't hear much from my brother Bufus or his wife no more."

"Dear Lawd, until that day them three girls walked up on my porch. I almost fell out my rocking chair. I knew whose they were from the pictures you know. Two of them looked just alike, but that oldest girl Queen she looked like me, built like me and when I looked into her eyes I could have sworn I saw my brother Bufus Sawyer starring right back at me. Right then and there I knew, my brother no longer walked this earth and them girls, well from the looks on their faces they were running from something or to something."

In the depth of the night, when the world is at rest. The stars spin forth to compliment the Moon to illuminate the night. But if you look really close in a blink of an eye you will see the Dance of Angels.

Chapter 1

Memphis, Tennessee 1921

Queen quickly gathered more of her and her twin sister's things. She'd forced them to go to the West Memphis train station in Arkansas, just five miles outside the Tennessee state line against their will without her. If anyone was going to sacrifice their life to cover the terrible incident that occurred in the beautiful two-story home her father Bufus Sawyer had worked so hard for, it would be her. Queen's father had done quite well for himself, almost too well in the eyes of many as a black man in the busy city of Memphis.

Skilled workmanship had always been a facet in the black community so, many of these talented men and women used their skills to provide services that were highly demanded in the growing town. It was because of these skills, passed down from one generation to the next, they could provide a decent life for their offspring just like Bufus. However, the great divide between the northern and southern states regarding the future and direction of the country's economy had been brutally settled by the Civil War. This brought about a racial tension that continued to grow and weigh heavy like a large tumor on the psyche of a now United States of America. Just like many other southern states, Tennessee was no different for Bufus Sawyer as he was constantly reminded that he would never be afforded the same opportunities as his white businessmen counterparts. This social and economic wall of racism would interfere with him along with many other ambitious black entrepreneurs and their ability to prosper as equals in the now United States of America. There were racial prejudices supported heavily by established laws in Memphis Tennessee, these laws limited any efforts made that would afford these black entrepreneurs the opportunity to compete with white businessmen in their community. This also limited the amount of property that Bufus could obtain, regardless if he could afford to purchase it or not. Nevertheless, Bufus along with many others would continue to risk their life to make a better world for their children. Their motivation came from the success of pioneers such as Robert R. Church, a freedman and the souths first black millionaire. Mr. Church mentored Bufus and many others early in their lives. Robert R. Church had acquired his wealth during the yellow fever epidemics in Memphis in the late 1870's as thousands of people fled the city. Mr. Church began to purchase real estate after the depopulation and founded the first black owned bank, Solvent Savings Bank. This was an unprecedented opportunity for many black people to establish businesses and mortgage homes, until the late 1890's when segregation was imposed. Although Bufus could not fight these segregation laws that festered in his community, he would come to one conclusion. If he could not use his wealth to build his empire, he would build the minds of his three beautiful daughters in hopes of a brighter future for his family's legacy.

As Queen rambled through the house for any remnants of letters, pictures or correspondences that could be used as evidence, she picked up her family portrait and added it to the rest of her things. She reminisced on those days and how happy she was. However, as she grew older she was forced to experience the pains of the time. Years before she was born, her father Bufus fell in love with a beautiful woman named Georgea. Life would have been good for the family, but Georgea's mother nor the segregated community would tolerate the relationship between her daughter and Bufus Sawyer. It didn't matter that he was intelligent, it didn't matter that he was a successful businessman, what mattered was the color of his skin. However, Georgea didn't care about her mother's wealth nor did she care for the life her family's wealth afforded her. In her own strength, she stood by Bufus. They secretly married and she gave birth to her first child and named her Queen. Georgea gave her daughter the name, in her mind to protect her from the evil she might endure from the ignorance of the world, so regardless of how people felt about her they would have to address her as royalty or don't address her at all. One day, Georgea took a chance and traveled back to the estate where she'd spent her entire childhood to show her mother their wealthy family's first granddaughter. When Georgea's mother seen that child she quickly had her removed from the premises and Georgea was disowned and discarded forever.

Adrienne Lynn Rutherford

This cruel treatment did not stop Georgea, as she continued to live happily with her husband and daughter. After the death of her mother Georgea gave birth again, but this time it would be twin girls and she named them Carolyn and Connie. Queen could remember how happy she was when her two sisters arrived. When word got back to Georgea's sister in all her evilness she plotted to destroy the humble Sawyer family. She loathed the fact that her sister had ruined her life and the family legacy. One child was one thing but twins were too much for her cold heart to handle. So, one day in the mid-morning when her children were in school and her husband at work, Georgea received a visitor at her doorstep. When her husband Bufus and his daughters returned home as usual that afternoon, Georgea was nowhere to be found. Bufus went to his sister-in-law's home to find answers. When he arrived, his life was threatened and Buford was warned never to return or death would surely befall upon him and the lives of his three daughters. Therefore, he spent many lonely and tiring years trying to find out what happened to his wife. Over time pneumonia and a broken heart had taken its toll on Bufus Sawyer and his three daughters were left to deal not only with the grief of losing both their parents, but also the responsibility for maintaining their humble estate. Queen, in all her efforts was unable to collect on most of the accounts receivable invoices from her father's business in the city of Memphis. Being the eldest, Queen knew for them to survive she would have to find a way to accumulate enough income to support her and her two sisters. Queen's main priority was keeping the twin's safe and above all well-educated, just like her father would have wanted it. Everything else she would lean on her faith in the Lord for further guidance and instruction after that.

Queen moved swiftly through the house to gather as many items as she could for both her and her sisters. She passed by her room once more and looked briefly in the open walk-in closet filled with many of her beautifully handmade costumes. She couldn't take them all, so she grabbed three of her favorites.

The art of Burlesque had been the primary contributor to their survival thanks to Madame Greta and as a result, Queen had become quite famous in the red-light district of Memphis. Now, because of the dreadful escapades of Rodger Quickman their lives would never be the same again.

It all had happened so suddenly, as Queen thought back on events that occurred only moments ago when she stood over him in a pool of blood. Her hand was shaking, but somehow her spirit relieved that she'd saved her little sister from a future of much pain and grief. It wasn't the first-time folks heard about *"the sick"* Rodger Quickman, heir of a very powerful and wealthy mining family in Memphis Tennessee. His mother had defended him on many occasions as he ventured into the segregated part of the city searching for his prey. Quickman had been watching the twins for a while and they would confide in Queen about his weird grins and uncomfortable looks when they found themselves in his presence. Therefore, for the protection of her sisters Queen decided to pay Madame Viola Quickman a visit. Viola Quickman out of curiosity allowed Queen in to see her. However, once she understood why she'd came, Viola was appalled by the accusations calling them hideous and branding Queen a filthy liar. Queen stood her ground as she provided names and proof of the lives that Rodger Quickman had ruined. She accused her of protecting him and turning her back on the madness. Viola then threatened Queen, reminding her of the power that she carried in the city of Memphis. Queen was then escorted off her property kicking and screaming. After that day, Rodger Quickman would keep a close watch on the Sawyer home waiting for an opportunity to arise. However, on this quiet peaceful night Quickman made the boldest move of his life. He'd known Queen worked evenings on Beale Street, so in his eager drunkenness he made his way without reservation to the Sawyer home. However, tonight Queen would return home earlier than usual. As she approached the back entrance of the house more closely she could hear the whimpering of her younger sister. When she opened the door, the anger arose in her like the hot lava of a volcano on the brink of eruption. Queen, in a brief moment of shock, observed her sister stretched out on the kitchen floor with a towel in her mouth while tears of agony ran down her face. Quickman had her dress above her waist and attempting to remove her pantaloons. For almost two or three seconds in his savagery, he did not even notice

Adrienne Lynn Rutherford

that Queen entered the room. When he did turn to Queen all she could see was all the evil that dwelled in him. His gruesome grin gave Queen chills while Carolyn struggled relentlessly to remove herself from his clutch.

Time had stood still in that moment for Queen as she reached for the largest butcher knife in the wooden cutlery holder and began to stab at him uncontrollably until his body laid limp and lifeless in a puddle of blood. Queen then dropped the knife out of her hand and it fell to the floor. She then reached down and untied her baby sister as she pushed the dead weight off her body. Queen held her tight as she cried uncontrollably. She then put her baby sister's face in the palm of her hands.

"Carolyn, are you alright?"

Carolyn still shaking from the unnerving event nodded a yes as she looked at the blood that covered her and front part of her sister's dress, she then grabbed her and held her as tight as she could.

"Oh Queen, I was coming home from the library this evening and I saw him standing near the corner of the block. I started walking faster, trying to make it home and he followed. I tried to run up to the house as fast as I could to get my key in the door but he attacked me."

Queen put her hand over her sister's mouth to silence her because she could see that it was about to take her to a dark place she didn't want her to go.

"He didn't hurt you, did he?"

While shaking, she responded, unable to conceive such a thought as she wiped the tears from her face.

"No, sister."

"Well then, we have nothing to be worried about, he is in our past now."

"Queen?"

"Yes, Carolyn."

Carolyn's fear soon turned to panic once she realized what had just taken place.

"Queen! What are we going do?"

"He's dead, they're going to come looking for us I know it."

"They're going to hang us for sure, I know it."

"Aren't they?"

Queen's mind began racing in every direction, she knew she had to figure a way out of this situation and fast. Once word got to Quickman's mother she would come after them with all the fury of the law. It didn't make any difference that Quickman attempted to do the unthinkable to her baby sister. The only thing that mattered was a white man dead lying in a puddle of blood in the middle of their kitchen floor.

Minutes later, Jonas and Connie had returned from the theatre. Both heard the disturbance coming from the kitchen as they entered the front door. Once they got to the kitchen Connie covered her mouth in horror and Jonas looked over at Queen in disbelief. Connie could not stand still as she made her way up the stairs to the bathroom. Jonas at that moment turned his attention to Queen.

"Queen, what the hell happened here?"

"Do you even know who that is on the floor?"

"Of course, I know who he is Jonas."

She then turned to Carolyn.

"Go see about your sister and the both of you grab only what you can carry and do it as quickly as you can, we have to get out of here."

"But Queen!"

"Go ahead now Carolyn, I don't have no time to be dealing with nothing else but this right now."

"We will talk about other stuff later, you hear?"

Carolyn went along as her eldest sister had instructed her and disappeared up the staircase. Jonas looked over at Queen shaking his head, but Queen paid no mind to his expression as she began pacing the floor.

"Jonas, Jonas! I must explain things to you later, you have to get the girls out of here and to the train station."

"Queen, are you crazy?"

"There is a dead white man in the middle of your floor, not just any old dead white man but the Medusa's first born, I can't leave you here either."

Queen shook her head at the thought.

"What was I supposed to do he's been harassing the young women on this side of town forever and no one, I mean no one seemed to care."

"Remember Aquila, Jesse's baby girl, he got hold to her and she hasn't been right since. Do you know when Jesse went to the authorities, they threatened to hang him if he stepped foot in the police station again."

Queen then began to manically pace the floor, but this time with an even more nervous energy.

"You know how this thing goes right Jonas?"

"In the daylight, they are the law and at night they become lawless nightriders."

"You know I can't risk staying here, me and my sisters wouldn't have a chance in hell in this town."

"So, as I look down at this piece of trash laying on my kitchen floor, I don't feel no type of way at all about it, you hear."

When Queen finally stopped pacing the floor, she grabbed a hold of Jonas with both hands and pleaded with him.

"Jonas please don't worry about me, you have to get the girls out of here."

"Where will you guys go Queen?"

Queen thought for a second, they hadn't lived any other place outside of their Tennessee home. Then she left the kitchen and went into the dining room and opened a drawer of the tall china cabinet. She pulled out her father's large black leather covered address book, inside held all the addresses of her father's personal acquaintances that he'd made correspondence with over the years. She flipped the pages and realized most were close friends in Tennessee and others were people she had never met. Queen continued flipping over and over until she came across the name Ma'me Black (sister). She then tore a blank page out and copied the address.

"Jonas, I want you to take the girls to the West Memphis Train Station now, you hear?"

There will be too many witnesses at the Memphis station, nobody will recognize us in Arkansas."

"Here take this, just in case I don't make it to the station in time you will have to make sure the twins get there safe, you hear?"

Jonas took the paper and read it.

"Oklahoma!"

"Who lives in Oklahoma?"

Queen looked down at the name in the book.

"It's my father's only sister and that makes her my aunt."

"Have you ever seen her before?"

"Yes, I remember her vaguely as a child, my father took me and my mother there a few times before the twins were born.

"Wow, those were happy times for me."

"I don't know why I never thought to go through this book and contact her sooner, so much has happened in our lives since then."

Jonas reached out and held on to Queen's hand.

"Queen you can't be so hard on yourself because you have done wonders for you and the twins. It takes a strong type of woman to overcome some of the things you guys were forced to deal with."

"Yeah you may be right, but that dead body in the kitchen is the worst thing ever."

The twins slowly came down the staircase well dressed and each carrying a piece of luggage and a small carry case.

"No Queen, we're not going without you."

Jonas nodded his head in support of the twins.

"Queen let's think about this, how do you even know this Ma'me is still at this address or even alive."

The twins spoke in unison.

"Who is Ma'me?"

Jonas continued.

"You just said yourself that you haven't seen her since you were a child, how long has it been?"

Adrienne Lynn Rutherford

Queen shook her head.

"Almost fifteen years, but it is a chance we must take and if she is there, and if she's anything like I remember they will be safe!"

"Go on now, all of you."

"That's an order and I promise I will meet you at the train station for the last train before dawn."

Jonas and the twins after much hesitation finally did what they were told and left the house headed for the train station.

Now alone, Queen knew it would be only a matter of time that their home would be a murder scene. Strangers would be rambling through their private life and it panged her that she nor her sisters would ever have a chance to plead their case. They would be found guilty in this part of the country and sentenced to death by hanging without remorse. After gathering her items from upstairs Queen went back into the kitchen and noticed that Quickman's blood had almost completely left his body. She looked at the pale shocked expression that laid like cement on his face. She then went into the cellar, kneeled into another doorway and crawled in. Inside was her father's safe, she opened it and took out her and the twin's life savings along with their birth papers and the deed to the house and slammed the safe door shut. When she returned to the dining room, she took one last look at her home. Maybe she would see it again or maybe not, but one thing was for sure she would protect her family at all cost. Queen then slammed the back door shut behind her and headed toward the garage.

Chapter 2

Tulsa, Oklahoma

The loud chimes of Greenwood's new and improved clock tower echoed at high noon once again. William Black stuck his chest out at another job well done. It had been almost two weeks since the chimes were silenced by the gusty dust storms that sometimes inflicted the Oklahoma Territory. Mayor Henry Watkins stood proud as he called for William to come down and join him in admiring his successful yet talented feat. Suddenly, Mayor Watkins was distracted by his youngest child and only daughter Cody Kay Watkins. She screamed out his name in excitement while running in his direction.

"Papa, papa, Calvin's home, Calvin's home."

Mayor Watkins suddenly found a lump grow in his throat, of all his children, Calvin had been the most talented and the most rebellious. To Mayor Watkins, his son's hopes and dreams seemed quite ridiculous and inconceivable and Calvin felt quite the opposite, which left their relationship on the brink of turmoil before he'd left.

Mayor Watkins had three children, two sons and a daughter: Calvin his rebellious middle child, Cody the apple of his eye and the eldest John who left home at seventeen years of age to serve in the U.S. Air force during World War I in the hopes of being a fighter pilot. Both of his boys were highly educated in their youth. However, as they matured so did their views of the world. To Mr. Watkins they were nothing like their father, or so he thought. Mayor Watkins, Cody was his only hope in leaving a respectable family legacy, now fourteen years old she would soon be attending college to become a "respectable citizen" and a credit to her race. Mayor Watkins thoughts were interrupted once again.

"Papa, did you hear me?"

"Calvin is home"

"He came only a few minutes ago and mama told me to tell you to come straight home when your business is done."

"Dear child, tell your mother I will be there just as soon as I can."

"You hear?"

"Yes papa, but aren't you glad Calvin is home it's been nearly ten years."

"Yes child, I'm sure we will talk more at dinner this evening, now run along and tell your mother I will be there by dinnertime."

William had descended the tower and noticed the look of confusion on Mayor Watkins face.

"You alright mayor?"

"Uhhh sure, sure how much I owe you Wil?"

"Same as the last time sir."

"Okay I will draw you up a note and you can come by the office and get it directly."

"Thank you kindly, I couldn't help but over hear that Calvin's home."

Mayor Watkins scratched his bearded chin and with a feeling of melancholy looked over at William.

"Yes, you two were quite close coming up, but it seems you took a more responsible route and didn't find the need to carpet bag all over the country looking for a dream you would never find."

"Now mayor I wouldn't say all that."

"Calvin was always a smart guy, he just seen the world a little different than you and I is all.

William begin to laugh.

"He was always more curious about the things of the world, I wouldn't have expected anything different than the life he chose."

"William that sounds ridiculous."

"Sir I beg your pardon, but respectfully I have to disagree with you."

"As men, we must be allowed to find our own way in this world, even if it gets in the way of the beliefs of those that we respect the most."

Mayor Watkins listened to what he considered only senseless noise coming from William. It was hard for him to be any other way. In the time he had come up, it wasn't about you just picking up and going about your own way. You contributed to the whole and you did what had to be done, not what you wanted to do. This philosophy kept Mayor Watkins at odds with both of his sons.

William, after leaving Mayor Watkins office made his last stop at the grocers for his grandmother and headed home. When he arrived, there was his favorite lady rocking steadily on the porch, his grandmother Ma'me.

"Hey Ma'me, got something for you."

She looked up at her only grandson and gave him a smile.

"You do?"

"Whatcha got for Ma'me?"

"I got your favorite, chocolate."

Ma'mes daughter Becky was standing in the screen door.

"Ma'me, you know you aren't supposed to be having no chocolate with your diabetes, Doctor Lacey told you that just yesterday."

Ma'me turned and looked up at her tall slender daughter, rolled her eyes and then looked back at her grandson.

"Wil, did you hear something, cause I ain't heard nothing."

"You say you got chocolate for me?"

William smiled and hunched his shoulders at his mother as he passed his favorite lady the one thing that he knew made her happy. He then kissed her on the cheek and followed his mother into the kitchen.

"Ma, you know a little chocolate isn't gonna hurt Ma'me, doc even said it."

"I know, but I don't want her to get too carried away with it."

"Everybody come by here brings her chocolate, if she eats it every time it won't be good for her."

"Son how was your day?"

"It was cool, finally finished the town clock."

"I know, I heard it this afternoon while I was shopping."

"I didn't realize how much I depended on that old clock until it stopped ringing."

William sat down at the table with his dinner plate piled high with his mother's turkey, dressing and collard greens then said his grace. He looked up at his mother after swallowing a hearty portion of dinner.

"Ma, you know when I was working on that clock, Cody came by and told Mayor Watkins that Calvin had come back home."

"Yeah, I heard and the ladies been buzzing around town something awful getting their daughters all dolled up and such."

"I tell you the gossip is thick in Greenwood son."

"Don't take long before word get around you know, and they are saying he's got a pretty penny too."

"He had an automobile shipped here all the way from Ohio."

"Well, Mayor Watkins didn't seem too thrilled, it's gonna get real interesting for the next few days, weeks or even months."

William began to laugh while shaking his head.

"Man, my friend still knows how to keep up uh ruckus."

Becky hit William with the kitchen towel.

"Now, now if I recall both you guys kept up a ruckus coming up, almost drove Mrs. Jordan crazy at that schoolhouse."

William thought back on the adventures of him and his good friend Calvin. He wouldn't go looking for him just yet because he knew Calvin had a lot on his plate, but when the time was right they would go out, have a beer and talk about old times. Becky stopped washing the dishes and turned her attention back to William.

"You know Wil, I don't know why Mayor Watkins is giving that son of his a hard time, he was always a good kid growing up, respectful and easy going."

"All of you were mannish at some point, but that's a part of being a boy."

"What happened between them son?"

"Well, all I know is that Calvin was supposed to go to medical school."

"Mayor Watkins had it all set up with a friend of a friend back east in Boston."

"Calvin, well he decided different."

William then shook his head.

"Ma, you know he hasn't forgave him for that."

"I told him sometimes we have to find our own way, but it didn't matter to him one bit."

"I don't think he heard anything I said."

"Well Wil, sometimes people feel compelled to live their lives through the lives of others and when it doesn't work out the way they think it should there is almost always conflict. I'm sure Calvin's coming home is the work of the Lord and hopefully they can mend their family once and for all.

"In the meantime, I need you to fix Ma'me a plate so that I can get myself together."

"I have to work at the Paradise tonight."

"It's amateur night and Gloria's gonna need me."

William smiled.

"Ah amateur night, anyone good?"

"Well, I have to say an honest no."

"I guess Tyler will keep this thing up until he finds some real talent."

"And besides, it's our biggest payday."

After William finished his meal, he did what his mother asked and joined Ma'me on the front porch.

Adrienne Lynn Rutherford

Chapter 3

As the sun begin to recede into its evening resting place Mayor Watkins sat behind his desk after completing his business at Greenwood's townhall. He'd spent the remainder of the day there after contemplating the return of his middle child. Mayor Watkins had no idea how this evening's dinner would turn out, but he was honest with himself as he felt a since of displeasure in his son's decision to come home unannounced after being away nearly ten years with very little contact with his family.

Calvin was strong willed and never saw eye to eye with him on certain matters of life as well as how his father conducted his business. Mayor Watkins, however loved all his children very much and felt that he'd done the best he could for his family. As Mayor Watkins closed the office for the evening, he looked at his picture of W.E.B. Dubois with pride on his wall. To Mayor Watkins, it was he who would become his greatest inspiration of his life. His philosophical understanding of educating the Negro race had a profound effect on how Mayor Watkins thought he'd raised his sons. Calvin had all that was required to represent the negro men of his time, distinguished in thought, handsome and intelligent in mind. He and his brother had been groomed to represent the very doctrine that W.E.B Dubois spoke of. That small group of men well trained and well prepared to take their race to the next level, to be looked at as the source of dignity and to be the epitome of the better part of the race. With a prestigious education, back east they would be an extension of the talented tenth. They would be admired and revered by their people, acknowledged and shown approved by the very system that had enslaved him, his father and his grandfather before him.

These were the desires in the heart of Mayor Watkins and they had been destroyed by the changing of the times, the new thoughts, and the new ideas of the young. He felt they were unexperienced and naïve to the world that he'd witnessed. None had known the feeling of a whip across their back, none had known the tearing away of families and the selling off husbands, wives, sisters, brothers, sons and daughters, many whom they would never see again. The never-ending fight for freedom that so many had risked life and limb for. For Mayor Watkins, it had been all worth it, every thought, and every struggle for him to be where he was today. He was a proud man, from a proud family who had overcame these atrocities and survived. None of his beloved children knew the tireless days and nights of plantation life and working from sun up to sun down, never having the ability to reap from the harvest of their hard work

The inhumane treatment and the unspoken horror of mental illness that plagued his people who day in and day out witnessed the ongoing raping, beating, and maiming of loved ones. Also, most importantly the inability to describe what you felt on paper or to read the thoughts of others. To Mayor Watkins, all he could see was the benefits of overcoming and acquiring the fruits of one's labor that would eventually free future generations from the effects of these very dark and gruesome times. Those strong men and women most, unspoken of, unacknowledged, uncelebrated, whose efforts forged in many years of sweat, blood and tears.

W.E.B. Dubois was his beacon, a bright shiny star that arose like a Phoenix from the depths of these dark times in the lives of the negro. Dubois had a plan, a solid plan that promised better days and peaceful nights. In the mind of Mayor Watkins, W.E.B. Dubois was his first-class ticket into the other world, the forbidden world and to him it was just that simple. He'd spent a fortune and pulled a lot of strings across the tracks on the south side of Tulsa to get the right books and special tutoring needed to prepare not only his children, but all the children of northside Greenwood for the world that he dreamed of. Now, after many years of grooming and schooling he was now only filled with hurt and disappointment. The night was calm as the mayor made his way toward his automobile, he glanced over at the town clock as it began to ring 6:00 P.M. *Dinnertime* he thought to himself.

The Watkins' home was a place of complete joy tonight for Mrs. Watkins and her three children. Cody their youngest set the table and prepared for dinner while listening to John play the piano. Calvin spun his mother around and danced her into a frenzy.

"Calvin, okay stop that, that's enough."

Adrienne Lynn Rutherford

"Your father will be home soon, and he will want his dinner."

"Calvin come into the kitchen with me please dear."

Calvin followed his mother into the large kitchen and assisted her as she attempted to pull the chicken out of the oven.

"Here ma, let me help you with that."

"Thank you, son."

"Calvin, I want you to be patient with your father tonight."

"Ma, I have no issue with my father, I just feel like I have the right to live my life the way I see fit."

"I'm a man mama, nobody told him how to live his life."

"Son, I understand what you're saying, but that was a different time dear."

"Life was much harder then and he had no choice in a lot of things." "You see, some of the things you think were tough choices were really no choices at all for your father, he didn't enjoy half the options you have today."

"So much grief and sacrifice son, it required your father to make some tough choices to better his life and it's made him who he is today."

"He, had no parents to turn to, and deep down he is a good man."

"He holds a lot of resentment for your choices and I know that, but just be patient with him dear."

"I don't want it to be another ten years before I see you again."

"Ma, I promise you it won't be, regardless of what you or other people think in this town, I didn't leave because of papa, I left because of me."

"Ma times is still hard, don't be fooled by this wonderful cushy town we live in. There is still a lot of work to do, life outside of Greenwood is still a struggle."

Calvin' mother took her hands and held him gently by the face.

"Son, I love you, Cody and John so very much, so much that I may have been naïve bringing you up here and not allowing you to see the ways of the world."

"But, who wants their children to feel pain and hurt if it can be avoided, you will understand when you have children of your own."

"Ma, but you have told me the ways of the world, every time

you sat us down and shared the oral history of your family, how they overcame adversity through faith and strength making it to freedom in Canada."

"That was my motivation to search for truth in who I am as a man, to find myself and my way in this world through my own experiences, not those created for me to experience."

"Do you understand what I'm trying to say to you mama."

"Papa wants to hide that from us, hide the struggle from us, he wants to paint this perfect picture of life after slavery that although we had a terrible beginning a new life as an educated negro is more than enough to gain favor in a community that really wants no part of him, you, me, John, or Cody for that matter."

"And let's be clear mama, as wonderful and independent as Greenwood is, we are still a segregated community, and none of us can be caught dead on the other side of them tracks after dark."

"Hell! I can't even get a shoeshine over there."

"Son, you watch your tone of voice when you speaking to me you hear?"

"Don't you show no ungratefulness here tonight?"

Calvin bowed his head in guilt of disrespecting his mother's wishes.

"Yes mama."

Soon the two of them heard the front door close and the piano cease to play, that was Calvin's que that his father had finally arrived home from his day. His mother handed him the chicken from atop the stove and asked him to take it out to the table.

When he went into the dining room there his father stood, still strong and prideful, but now his hairline had receded and turned almost completely white. Calvin sat the chicken on the table and greeted his father with a strong hug. At that moment, all the resentment that Mayor Watkins had, lifted from him as he grabbed his son and embraced him. His oldest brother John began playing on the Piano again.

"When the Saints come Marching In."

"Yes' were all together again one big happy family, let us rejoice and be happy then let us take a sip of some of that old faithful and catch up on good times."

He got up and poured himself a drink and turned it up and then poured another and handed it to his father. Cody grabbed a hold of both her brothers and held them tight, never in all her years did she have such an opportunity to hold them this close together at the same time. Mrs. Watkins began to cry as she watched her family embrace and love on one another. It was a moment that she'd hoped for and now seeing come to past. This was a heartfelt reunion for the Watkins family. Calvin had so much to tell them since he'd been gone, things he'd done and places he'd been. For him, things were looking up and he was so happy in this moment that his father had not passed any judgement on him.

"Maybe papa has changed?"

He thought to himself.

Soon they were interrupted by Mrs. Watkins.

"Okay dear, you guys go and freshen up, me and Cody will finish setting the table.

"Go on, hurry now so it doesn't get cold."

Soon after the men came and sat at the table, John looked around and smiled.

"Wow ma, everything looks delicious, you really out did yourself this time."

"Why thank you son, Henry will you say grace for us please." John then thought to himself.

"Am I the only one at this table that knows that papa saying grace is just a very bad idea?"

"Thank you, dear Lord, for the feast that my wife has so efficiently prepared for us this evening, thank you for the homecoming of our dear son Calvin."

"For it is with your power that he could finally see the error of his ways and return home, amen."

Calvin looked over at his mother with disappointment, but after seeing the look on her face he decided not to indulge in his father's comments and just enjoy a meal with his family. However, Mayor Watkins didn't let up.

"So, son what brings you home after all these years?"

"Have you been in jail?"

Calvin continued eating his meal not even looking up at is father, he knew once he laid his eyes against his, dinner would be ruined for the family that evening.

John interrupted.

"Come on pops, you know you raised us far better than that, Calvin here has been out in the world getting self-educated isn't that right brother?"

Calvin looked up at his brother.

"Yeah something like that, I been a few places, seen a few things."

"Had the opportunity to hear a man by the name of Marcus Garvey speak, great mind."

Mayor Watkins laughed out loud.

"Marcus who?"

"Garvey."

"Never heard of him, Gladdis have you ever heard of a Marcus Garvey?"

Calvin then turned and looked at his father with a long sigh.

"Well papa since you never heard of him let me be the first to tell you about him, he's a revolutionary and a man strong in his vision and his words."

"Ah I see, something like DuBois?"

"No nothing like your understanding of DuBois, Marcus Garvey represents the new negro one who wants to be self-sufficient, who embraces his identity as a black man and demands respect as such. He isn't interested in integrating into a society that doesn't respect him. He speaks of empowering the race and forming alliances with black people all over the world."

"He understands that the economic survival for the black man will be in him supporting and networking with other black people not just here in this country, but countries around the globe."

"Garvey's vision is large, much larger than Greenwood."

"Is that not what we have here?"

"Look around you son there is no other black community in this country as vibrant as northside Greenwood."

"Self-made negro businesses that stretch over thirty square

Adrienne Lynn Rutherford

blocks, where else can you see W.E.B. Dubois' philosophy so prosperous.

"This here is the place."

"Tell me son, where else in this country can you find such a paradise?"

"You have a lot to learn about this here world son?"

"Papa, no one is denying the magnificent success we have made on Tulsa's north side it's known all over the country as Black Wall Street."

"The accomplishments we have made here truly have set the precedence for other black communities in this country, so that they too may contribute to their communities and develop their own solid economic base of businesses and resources."

"You see *Black Wall Street* is just the beginning, a blueprint for the future of the race and that is what Marcus Garvey was getting at, self-sufficiency not just here, but globally."

"W.E.B. Dubois ideas are some of the greatest by far, but I can't give them all the credit for the success of Greenwood."

"What are you saying son?"

"We here in Greenwood are the first and we have flourished quite well."

"Many have come here from all over the country to reside in Greenwood, with much success I might add."

"I'm saying we don't have to be the last either and besides, it was more than just education that built our community."

"Have you forgotten the resilience, hard work and hope for a better life of those who fled harsh realities of the sharecropping plantations and nightriders of the south after the Reconstruction?"

"These hopes are shared in black communities all over the country papa. We are a beacon of light and a strong economic base, but we can also economically exceed thirty-six square blocks."

Mayor Watkins laughed aloud.

"What is this gibberish your speaking of son?"

It was now apparent Mayor Watkins was becoming frustrated with the ideas of his son. He was set in his ways and nothing had made him think otherwise up to this point. The Mayor made up his mind years ago that the leadership of the Negro were in the hands of him and others like himself in the Northside Greenwood District.

"I am a pioneer, a leader of the negro men and women of this community, they look to us, and many more will come here and we will show them how they will contribute to what we have built."

"See this is what I mean papa, your understanding of W.E.B. Dubois is far different from what many understand it to be."

"Your arrogant since of elitism has clouded your vision."

"Don't be fooled by the accomplishments that you see around you on Tulsa's Northside Greenwood District papa, we are still under segregated laws in this country."

It was obvious the Mayor and Calvin were getting angrier by the minute. Mr. Watkins felt his son was being disrespectful and Calvin was annoyed by his fathers closed way of thinking.

"That's ridiculous, who are you to come here after ten years and ridicule the accomplishments of negroes in this town?"

John then thought he should join the conversation to relieve the tension growing between his younger brother and his father.

"Papa, I don't think that's what Calvin is saying at all."

"It's not!"

Calvin shot back.

"The black folks in this town I'm proud to say are the reason I returned, but let's be clear this city of Tulsa is still as racist as it was when I left here ten years ago."

"Can you walk across the tracks after dark papa?"

"Can you papa?"

Furious the Mayor got up from the table, you get your things and you get the hell out of my house with your broke self, that is why you came home isn't it?"

"Because you're broke!"

Mayor Watkins then stood up at the table and pointed his finger in Calvin' face.

"I see that scar on your face, while everyone else just sits here looking crazy, scared to ask you a legitimate question."

"But me, I'm going to always give it to you straight son."

Calvin's mother stood up in frustration and interrupted.

"You stop it, stop it right now Henry!"

"That is enough!"

Adrienne Lynn Rutherford

Calvin also got up from his seat and his anger almost caused him to lose his self-control, but he remained calm out of respect for his parent's home.

"Is that what you think old man?"

"If I was broke, I wouldn't come to you for a dime especially because you are the only resident here in Greenwood that keeps his money in the white man's bank across the tracks."

"Get out!"

"I'm going, mama, Cody I'm sorry."

John grabbed his jacket and followed his younger brother out the door. They began walking in the chill of the night to the back of the house toward the stables.

"Man, he has not changed one bit, and just to think I actually believed that after all this time he would have some type of respect for the views of others."

"John, he is caught up in this small world, being Mayor of the north side has got him believing that the whole world is like this."

"Hell John, he even believes he's a real mayor."

"Yeah, okay your right, he's just a district administrator appointed by the real Tulsa Mayor who just so happens to live in a modest mansion on the south side of town."

Calvin then looked at his brother and smiled, while shaking his head.

"Yeah, and on top of that John, his misunderstanding regarding the views of DuBois, just burns me up."

John listened and when he had the opportunity he spoke.

"Shake that off man, you know how pop is, and you know he isn't going to change."

"Your beating a dead horse brother, so just let it go because he is not going to change."

"Let's grab the horses and take a nice ride out to my place, have a drink and give you both a chance to cool off a bit."

"Hell, why don't you just come stay at my place."

"That's a great idea, I'm not going back to that house while he's there."

"Tomorrow let's go into downtown Tulsa to pick up my automobile and maybe even consider a piece of property."

John smiled at the fact he was still able to calm his younger brother's hot temper with his sense of humor.

"Are you thinking about staying around here for a spell brother?"

"Perhaps."

"Pop may call me a lot of things John my brother, but broke isn't one of them."

Adrienne Lynn Rutherford

Chapter 4

The loud sound of the Chattanooga train bound for the west coast awakened Queen, her first instinct was to check for the twins. She watched as they slept quietly across from her. Queen stood and looked outside observing the fullness of the moon slowly taking its position in the night sky as it shined brightly over the vast Kansas plains. She had barely made the train early that morning. Sliding down in the corner of the baggage car with tears in her eyes she thought back on how she managed to start up father's automobile stored away in their garage. Queen had only driven it once, but she loaded it up and made her way to the Memphis Red Light District. As she drove cautiously down the partially lit black tar road in the warm summer night, thoughts of her father and how hard he'd worked for her and her sisters resonated deeply within her. When he'd passed on, it was Greta Funchess who befriended her that day at Memorial Hospital of the Saints. Queen had taken a job in the children's ward as a nurse's aide and was crying in the lady's room after she'd witnessed the still birth of a child. Greta was their visiting a friend, consoled her and informed her that this type of work was not for her. Afterward she asked Queen if she could hold a tune and Queen impressed her so much she invited her to *"Venus Alley"*.

Greta, who was born of Liberian and German descent, served as a writer for the *British Blondes Burlesque Group*. Burlesque were entertainment acts that consisted of highly sexual aggressive roles portrayed through skits combining dancing, singing and comedy. When the troupe arrived in the United States, Greta decided to use the knowledge she'd acquired to create an act that became part of one of New York's biggest burlesque theatrical sensations. Greta later retired and settled in Memphis, Tennessee with a prominent French-American gentleman and opened her very own Vaudeville and Burlesque Club on Beale Street and named it *Venus Alley*. Greta had taken a liking to Queen and her desire to give her best to her performance. She taught Queen everything she knew about the business and soon after Queen began writing her own skits as well as those of some of the other girls. But tonight, all this would change as she parked the automobile discreetly behind the building in the humid night. Greta was inside as usual fussing and directing the backstage area when Queen came in the backdoor. Greta had known Queen for quite some time, one look at her tonight and she knew that there had to be something serious going on.

+"Queen you alright?"

"Come, come with me, to the parlor my child."

Queen did not speak as she followed Greta up the narrow spiral staircase. She almost made it to the top before the events of the night began to turn her stomach and suddenly she became light headed and passed out cold. When she had awakened, Queen was in Greta's parlor on the third level of Venus Alley.

Greta sat next to her on the sofa while Jojo stood patiently at the door.

"Queen, Queen honey can you hear me?"

"Jo, pour me a glass of water for her please."

Jojo was Greta's bodyguard and he stood well over seven feet tall and an odd-looking fellow. Greta was known for saving people from the lives that she thought really didn't benefit them. So, when she saw him performing for P.T. Barnum, she could tell that he didn't like people gawking at him as if he was some odd creature in the zoo or some clown in a circus side show. She offered him a job that sunny day at New York's World Fair and he never looked back. He tipped his hat to Mr. Barnum and accepted the one-way ticket for Tennessee with Greta and the "Hearts and Kisses Burlesque Show". Now head of security he made sure Venus Alley ran smoothly and kept it rid of undesirables. Queen finally opened her eyes, frantically looking around until she realized where she was.

"What time is it Greta?"

Greta looked at the exquisite French grandfather clock that stood in the corner behind Queen.

"It's one o'clock in the morning, girl what is going on?"

"You left work earlier tonight, why did you come back?"

Queen looked over at Jo and then she looked back at Greta."

"Jo give us a minute will you."

JoJo opened the large wooden door and the sounds of the stage and the roaring and whistling of the crowd poured into the room for a moment as he closed the door behind him the room returned to

Adrienne Lynn Rutherford

silence.

"Queen, what's the matter dear heart, you look flushed."

"Greta, can you pour me a glass of wine please."

"I can't stay long, but I need to talk to you and I'm gonna need you to take me to the train station to meet my sisters."

Greta got up from the sofa and poured Queen a glass of wine, not taking her eyes off her for one moment. Queen grabbed a cigarette out of Greta's case and lit it. Greta looked on in disbelief.

"Queen what the hell is going on dear, when did you start smoking?"

Queen took a long drag, then a swallow of wine and sat the glass on the table.

"Greta, tonight I killed a man."

Greta stood in the middle of the floor motionless as she rechecked the expression on Queen's face.

"What do you mean you killed a man, what man?"

"Rodger Quickman."

Greta gasped.

"The Medusa's son?"

"Yes."

Queen picked up the glass and finished it off, she then got up and poured another. When she explained everything that happened Greta had literally sunk into the sofa.

"Oh dear, this is terrible, what's your plan honey?"

"Me and the twins, we gotta leave."

"That's why I came by here, I had to tell you."

"Jonas is taking the twins to the train station in West Memphis, I will be joining them and don't know if I will be back."

"If they catch us they will hang us."

Greta held Queen tight in her arms.

"You need money?"

Greta went behind the desk towards the safe.

"No Greta, I will be fine."

"I need you to take me to West Memphis to meet them, but you have to be discreet, you can't be seen because they will come here, I know they will come looking for me."

Queen began pacing the floor taking one more long drag from her cigarette and then pushed it deep into the ash tray.

"I need you to get rid of father's automobile, and promise me you won't tell a soul about anything we discussed tonight."
Greta looked at Queen with disappointment.

"Queen I will never speak about what was discussed in this office tonight."

She then went to her desk and looked at the evening schedule.

"Come on let's get out of here and get you to that station, I have a few hours before the last curtain closes. Queen grabbed her satchel and followed Greta thru the emergency exit.

Chapter 5

Memphis Tennessee

Viola Quickman looked down at her son's cold and lifeless body. The odor was too much to bare, as she covered her face with her handkerchief. Rodger Quickman's body was found two days later by the girl's maid Irene. She worked for the Sawyer home for many years after the disappearance of their mother and just like clockwork Irene arrived on Monday morning to assist the girls with the laundry. However, today she received the surprise of her life when she walked in the kitchen and saw Quickman's corpse on the floor. Irene screamed as she ran out of the house thinking to herself.

'What in the world happened that left Rodger Quickman dead on Buford Sawyer's kitchen floor?"

Captain Feldman, Chief of Police stood up next to Viola Quickman after investigating the body of her son.

"Looks like he's been here for at least forty-eight hours."

He'd had Detective Maximillian Torch taking information from the housekeeper who was still shaken up about what she'd witnessed when walking into the kitchen that morning. Meanwhile, the home was being flooded by police investigators just as Queen had suspected. They went through practically all the house destroying what they could to gather the evidence they needed to find out what happened to the heir of Tennessee's multi-million-dollar coal mines. Detective Maximillian journeyed to the second level with the other investigators to see what he could find for the captain. Captain Feldman looked over at Miss Quickman and took his hat off in protocol and gave his condolences. Although she had lost her dreaded son to such a horrific death, she kept the tears back, not out of strength, but a sense of relief that he had been taken out of his misery.

Meanwhile, Detective Maximillian returned to the lower level to give a report to the captain.

"Captain, got something."

"It appears whoever lived here, left here with no plans of returning sir, most of the drawers in the rooms upstairs have been emptied."

"There are things scattered all over the place."

"Something really weird though captain, there was a closet filled with lots of those girly costumes, you know the ones they use down in the red-light district."

Miss Quickman looked at the young rookie detective with disgust.

"Fool, you mean to tell me you don't know whose house this is, where you from boy."

"Captain where did you get this idiot that calls himself a detective, the cabbage patch farm?"

The young man didn't flinch at the words shouted out by Miss Quickman, he'd experienced what he thought was grief many times in a situation such as this, so he stood by and waited for the next instructions from his captain.

"Okay Max, get a written report started and gather the men up once they've finished searching the house, we'll meet back at the station and discuss more in detail."

"In the meantime, I will wait on the coroner."

The young deputy obeyed the instructions as they were given and after finishing up the investigation he and his fellow colleagues left the Captain and Miss Quickman in the house.

Miss Quickman was the eldest of two children, born and raised in a life that knew nothing of poverty. Her heritage was that of segregation, a generational curse which kept her mind and her heart insensitive to the pain that her son had caused many of the women on the eastside of Memphis. Her money, political power, and influence all which were passed down from one generation to the next had protected her son far too long. Now things had changed and Miss Quickman would make the city of Memphis understand both black and white that her family still held the influence established by her Grandfather many years before. Not long after, the coroner arrived. He exchanged information with the captain and removed the body from the home. The captain then pulled Miss Quickman to the side.

"You know this here house belongs to Buford Sawyer."

"People talk you know."

Adrienne Lynn Rutherford

"The one's that know the history around here, know them girls are your nieces and now the only heirs left to your estate, outside their mama, who is your sister and by the way just so happened to just up and disappeared from here without a trace hmmm, some years ago"

"Wouldn't that be about right Miss Quickman?"

At that moment, Viola Quickman's face turned beet red and although she had thought it to herself many times throughout the years, hearing it come from another person created an untamed fury that showed its evil intent as a resurrection of revenge. Viola tightened her lips as he continued.

"Now if you trust me with this I can make this thing go away for you, but it's going to cost you a pretty penny."

"I'm getting up in age now and I just don't see myself hanging on much longer here in Memphis, want to go down to the Florida Keys and enjoy that sunshine and maybe even catch some of that nice salt water snapper, if you know what I mean."

Viola Quickman pulled out her handkerchief and wiped the only single tear that she would shed from her face. She then grabbed the captain with both hands by the collar and pulled him close as if to place a kiss upon his lips.

"I will not tolerate my family's name being dragged through the mud by the likes of them."

"My mother didn't and I won't either."

"They killed my son and they will not have the pleasure of walking this earth much longer."

"I want you to find those three murderers and when you do, I want you to bring them back to me in three boxes."

"You hear me?"

"After all, I am the only next to kin left to give them a proper burial!"

The captain nodded his head in agreement as he slowly removed her hands from his shirt collar.

"I will start down over on Beale Street, where the oldest girl Queen worked......"

Viola put her white gloved hand up in the face of the captain and stopped him in the middle of his sentence.

"Mr. Feldman as of now you work for me, I don't care to hear any of the details of the job that you have been hired to do, I only wish that you do your job."

"Do you understand?"

"I will expect a daily report from you every afternoon directly after lunch."

"I take my lunch at noon therefore you should be at my house daily and promptly at 1pm."

"Also, I will no longer be addressing you as the captain, to me you are no more respected than a sewer rat looking in every little disgusting place to find a morsel to survive on."

"You will receive a weekly salary, enough for you to do what is needed to be done."

"Is that clear?"

At that moment in time the captain understood how she got the nickname Medusa. The captain regretfully observed the sudden change in her as soon as she discovered that he wanted something that she had. With him just like so many others, she would use that want as a tool the way she saw fit. Now, it was obvious he had made a deal with the devil and it would give her control of not only him but his entire police investigation. Captain Feldman could only imagine the request that would follow and the festering revenge that manifested only minutes ago when she walked into the Sawyer home.

"Mr. Feldman is that clear?"

"Uh, yes of course."

Viola then reached into her purse and pulled out a small bag of pure gold coins and placed them in Captain Feldman's top shirt pocket and patted him on the chest.

"There, that should get the ball rolling."

She then reached over and whispered softly in his ear.

"There is no price I wouldn't pay to avenge my son's death nor save my family's legacy."   "You do what I ask, I promise you, you'll spend the rest of your life a very rich man."

The captain nodded his head in agreement and watched Viola Quickman as she walked out the kitchen's back door.

Adrienne Lynn Rutherford

Chapter 6

Tulsa, Oklahoma

The loud sound of the Chattanooga train whistle startled and awakened Queen. She slowly stood up in the uncomfortable baggage car while cursing Jim Crow. Carolyn and Connie were already awake and excited as they took turns peeking out the small round window as the train came to a halt. Suddenly the porter slid the baggage car door open. He helped each of them down as they dusted off their garments and one by one handed them each their baggage. As he smiled at the ladies, Queen reached into her purse and handed him two silver dollars. He tipped his hat and smiled.

The girls took a good look around downtown Tulsa, Oklahoma. They were amazed at the extravagant brick buildings and the automobiles whisking up and down the dusty road. There were so many people, all appearing quite busy going on about their day. Connie also noticed in the distance, the large wooden pillars that moved almost in unison like huge strong arms pressing deep into the Earth's surface only to reach up into the sky again to repeat the process. These enormous tall wooden pillars were lined up side by side as far off as the horizon.

"Welcome to Tulsa ladies."

"What is your name sir?"

"My name is Peter."

Connie extended her hand."

"Hello Peter, my name is Connie and these are my sisters; Queen and Carolyn."

"Are the two of you?"

Carolyn stopped him in mid-sentence."

"Yes, we are twin sisters."

Connie smiled, but in her usual curiosity inquired about her new surroundings.

"Excuse me Peter, but what are those tall wooden pillars, if you don't mind me asking."

"Oh, them is what you call oil wells, you're in oil country now ladies."

"That is what we call black gold around these parts, yes suh it's the bread and butter of this entire part of the country and probably yours too, you just didn't know it."

"Oh, that's quite interesting Mr. Peter, I would like to know more about this black gold.

"You say your name is Connie?"

"Well, it's plenty to learn I tell you, stay awhile you gonna see a lot here in Oklahoma."

While Peter the porter was sharing a brief history moment with the twins, Queen went into her purse and pulled out the folded piece of paper and opened it. She then handed it to Peter

"Can you tell me where this is please?"

Peter took the paper looked at it and gave Queen a wide smile.

"I sure can, that's my side of town."

"Many call it Northside Greenwood District, but us folks who live there we call it our *Black Paradise* there is no place like our Greenwood District.

"It's the greatest negro community on this side of the country, built from the ground up by negroes.

"It's our place, our little space here in Tulsa."

He then pointed to another waiting area on the other side of the Tulsa train tracks.

"You can purchase your tickets for the northside over there at the Sands Springs Railroad. The train is owned by the Barber brothers, they're also residents of the northside.

"It runs the whole thirty-six square blocks of Greenwood out pass the airplane strip and a few more miles into dust country."

He then smiled.

"You won't be riding in no baggage car on that side of the tracks no suh, no more Jim Crow."

"Now you can relax in a soft cushioned passenger seat with nice windows for sight-seeing."

Queen and the twins were relieved, they all took turns complaining about the hardwood floors and how they had to sit on their luggage to keep from feeling each time the train's wheels hit a faulty rail on the track. The ladies bid Peter farewell and made their way to the west station as instructed and purchased their tickets. It

Adrienne Lynn Rutherford

would be ten minutes' time before the Greenwood train would arrive.

While they waited, Queen continued observing the surroundings. Somehow in a weird sort of way things were starting to become familiar to her. While glancing over one of the area, she spotted a place she recalled visiting with her father. Above the top of the modestly weather-beaten building read U.S. Post Office. Queen told the girls she would be right back and made her way over to the building. When she opened the door, Queen couldn't believe her eyes. There he was, the same big burly gentleman and there it was the very same glass jar filled with dozens of colorful giant lollipops.

"May I help you ma'am?"

"Uh, no sir."

Queen was amazed that the gentleman looked the same as she remembered him, only the dark brown whiskers of his beard had been replaced with an even tone of gray accented with red rosy cheeks.

"I just remembered this place as a little girl, I tasted my first giant lollipop right here."

The burly gentleman smiled at the beautiful well-dressed young lady and shook his head.

"You wouldn't believe this, but you are one of the many children who return here in their adult life and tell me that same story."

"What a wonderful world this would be if we shared with each other more lollipops."

"Please take one."

"Sir, may I have two?"

"I have two sisters out by the train station that have never experienced the joy of one of your giant lollipops and they could both use a little cheering up."

"Yes of course."

"Thank you, sir."

Queen reached in the large jar grabbed two and made her way back to the waiting area. When she returned, she handed the two lollipops to her sisters. They both looked at her, but before they could speak she stopped them.

"Say nothing you two, until we get to where we're going. I want you to enjoy that, trust me your life will never be the same."
They smiled, shook their heads at one another and placed their sister's gift deep in their bags.

Meanwhile, the smoke from a train pulling two rail cars could be seen in the distance. As it slowly stopped at the platform where the ladies stood, the smoke was complemented by a loud whistle signaling its arrival. When the ladies boarded, they noticed two conductors conversing with a tall gentleman wearing a brown cowboy hat, a cowhide jacket to match and a pair of hardly worn cowboy boots with shiny silver spurs. His back was facing the ladies, but when he'd noticed the Barber brothers stop the conversation mid-sentence he was tempted to turn around to see what was the distraction. To his surprise, he was graced with the presence of three very beautiful women. However, magnetically right away his eyes met Queens and a spark ignited in that moment between the two of them. It was as if their spirits had congregated in some far-off place many times before.

The gentlemen greeted the ladies, they returned the salutations and continued toward the passenger cars to find their seats. As Queen walked behind her sisters she was tempted to turn around to get another look at the gentleman with the large brim hat. Out of curiosity she did, and to her surprise it was as if he had been waiting for her to do so. As Queen walked behind her sisters she was tempted to turn around to get another look at the gentleman with the large brim hat. Out of curiosity she did, and to her surprise it was if he was waiting for her to do so. The gentleman tipped his hat and graced her with a smile as eyes met hers. He then graced her with a smile. Embarrassed by her curiosity, Queen quickly turned back around wide eyed, smiled and continued following the twins to their seats.

The ladies settled in and were thankful for the cushioned seats. The twins were excited as they smiled at Queen who claimed one of the seats directly across from them. Queen made every attempt to make things seem okay with the twins. However, in the back of her mind she knew the seriousness of their departure, legally they were

Adrienne Lynn Rutherford

on the run and although they had not faced the law they were considered fugitives. Queen had no other alternatives and hoped that her father's sister was still alive and even so, would she be kind enough to welcome them. Her thoughts were interrupted by the movement of the train as it began to slowly pick up speed headed for its first stop, North side Greenwood District. She looked across at both Connie and Carolyn and huddled them close to her.

"Listen, no word about anything and you talk to no one."

"Keep your conversations casual and strictly about current events, no personal things outside the fact that we're sisters just visiting our relatives."

"You got it?"

The twins nodded affirmatively in unison. Queen then sat back in the cushioned seat and closed her eyes.

Meanwhile, Carolyn was thinking to herself, she was looking forward to the change. The ladies had been in Memphis all their lives. Although the unconceivable circumstances back home had brought them to Oklahoma, to her in some twisted way it was by the grace of God that their lives had drastically changed overnight. Queen had worked hard sacrificing her freedom and above all a healthy life of love and romance to care for them and now she'd risked her very existence to save them all. Carolyn at that moment made a vow to do everything in her power to make sure her dear sister in her selfless nature would not regret a single decision she had made for their well-being.

Connie, on the other hand looked over at her sister and noticed it had not taken her long to fall into a deep sleep. Everything had happened so fast, she thought to herself. Yesterday she was at the theatre watching her favorite Shakespearean play *Much Ado About Nothing* with Jonas. He had always been there for the girls. Jonas was the only one that Queen trusted with her and Carolyn. She would miss his company and she never got the opportunity to let him know how she felt about him. He probably wouldn't allow it due to his respect for Queen and their father. Now, they were headed to see her father's sister, a woman she'd never met or even heard of until last night. Connie was looking forward to talking with her aunt. She was hoping that she could understand more about her father and

Dance of Angels

even find out about her mother, a person who was but a vague memory in her life. She wanted to know how Bufus Sawyer had become the gentleman that he was and what he was like as a young boy. So many questions filled her head as she remembered his constant response to her when she asked about her mother Georgea,

"When you're older my child."

Nevertheless, for Connie that time would never come. Bufus Sawyer had left them before he could fulfil her curiosity of the unknown that haunted the very depths of her soul. Who wouldn't want to know their mother she thought, who wouldn't want to hold and embrace the woman who gave them life. Queen and Carolyn had not been as emotionally devastated as Connie about the situation surrounding their mother. Both could channel their thoughts and energy in other places. Queen had known her mother's touch but less vaguely than the girls and she filled her void by caring for her dear father and her twin sisters. For Carolyn, she was a memory that only surfaced in her dreams and when she heard certain music from time to time. She learned to play the piano thanks to her father's persistence and would write music for Queen's performances. Her talent for writing and arranging musical compositions with Queen's creative comical skits would bring in a full house each time she went on stage. Now, things would be different for them all.

The sounds of the loud whistle once again filled the air. Now close to mid-afternoon the winds blew lightly lifting dust and clouding the vision of the plains as the smoking coal fueled train made its way to Northside Greenwood District. The weather was hot and dry something the ladies would have to get use to as they fanned themselves with papers they picked up at the station. Not long before the train's routine journey would come to an end, the tall gentleman that greeted the ladies while boarding reappeared as he made his way down the aisle way. When he got to the ladies' seats he noticed a seat on the opposite side of the aisle was empty and decided to sit there. He tipped his hat to the ladies and again expressed a high interest in Queen who did her best to ignore his friendly gestures as he shook his head while opening his newspaper. It was not Queen's intention to get close to anyone. She had not come this far to get caught up in a situation that would distract her

Adrienne Lynn Rutherford

from making sure that their future would be safe. Queen looked out the window as she thought to herself. She had serious issues to deal with and the flirtatious gestures of a man in a dusty old coat and hat with a large scar across the side of his face, although quite handsome he was not the type of problem she needed in her life right now.

Calvin browsed through the news reviewing events that were happening across the country. In California, ever since the gold rush of the 1880s many people were still taking a chance to head far west in the hopes of prosperity. For him money was not the most important thing in life. Calvin left home with the one thing that fascinated him the most, his intuition. Growing up in Greenwood had been a very fortunate thing for him as a child. His grandfather was one of the first to arrive and trade with the Creek Nation Native Americans, who was the primary population at the time. As time progressed, the talk of oil had attracted people from all over the country and the population of Tulsa grew. The demand for supplies in the area grew as well and the most popular place to get such tools was from the skilled craftmanship of grandfather Watkins. This made him one of the more well-off residence in the area, and as a result he encouraged others to come and open business and services. Soon, the little community of Greenwood grew into a successfully humble segregated area of Tulsa. Meanwhile, northern and southern whites also were acquiring land rights to oil filled soil and thus a very wealthy population emerged. This population required the services of maids, butlers and ground keepers. Most these jobs where taken by black people who lived in the township of Greenwood who settled here to escape the night riders of the deep southern states like Mississippi and Alabama. Although this population crossed the tracks to the south side of town to work for these wealthy families, they were not allowed to shop in their stores, attend their movie theatres, or eat in their restaurants without inhumane restrictions. Therefore, on payday at the end of the week these proud service workers marched back to the north side of the tracks with their earnings and patronized their very own community businesses. This would create a very lucrative economic base for the residence on Tulsa's north side of town.

Although Calvin and many other children who grew up on the north side were still surrounded by the poison of segregation, Greenwood District somehow provided a solace in the middle of the country that afforded them a proper education built on encouraging a sense of integrity for themselves and their race. Now, Greenwood District had become an economic power base. It was filled with successful black entrepreneurs, farmers, churches, doctors, pilots, lawyers, teachers and of course train engineers. Nevertheless, although highly prosperous the Greenwood community on Tulsa's northside created a deep-rooted resentment from their white counterparts on Tulsa's southside. Calvin loved Greenwood and felt proud to return and call it home. However, today after laying eyes on Queen for the first time in almost twenty years, his trip home had become that much sweeter. It was quite humorous to him that she hadn't noticed who he was. They were only children when she first arrived in Tulsa with her parents. Calvin then turned his attention back to the paper, he came across an interesting article about the famous Quickman Mining Family of Memphis Tennessee and the death of the family's sole heir. After reading the article he made a mental note to contact his partner's back in Montana and continued to browse the papers for other interesting stories that made the news.

Soon the train made it to the north side and the twins held their heads out the window, amazed at the tall brick clock tower that stood in the middle of the square in Greenwood District. The twins gathered their things and exited the train, as they sat their bags down they were in awe of the beauty around them. The brick buildings were finely made and they extended over a mile or more in each direction as far as the eye could see. Queen stepped off the train and was amazed at how things had changed. The humble town that she remembered had more black businesses in every direction. Northside Greenwood District was flourishing. Peter the porter was right, the girls had never seen a place like it. Greenwood was the best kept secret in the west, a uniquely prosperous city district filled with ex-slaves and descendants of ex-slaves. These resilient great men and women were able to build and maintain one of the first and largest economically prosperous black communities in the country. The

Adrienne Lynn Rutherford

racial tensions of segregation and the anti-voting laws that forbid blacks the right to vote in many areas of the country, none of these tactics could hinder the prosperity that resonated on Tulsa's northside. Greenwood District was a jewel and it was just as equally successful as the Tulsa City's south side, benefiting both directly and indirectly from the successful discovery of oil pockets that laid beneath the land of Oklahoma.

Suddenly Connie pointed.

"Look!"

All the girls smiled, but no one was quite as happy as Connie.

"It's a movie theatre."

Then Carolyn pointed to the left.

"Ice cream, and a dress shop."

The ladies would have never thought the place they chose for refuge would be so modern for the times. There were rumors about the west back home, describing it as a wild and untamed land of harsh elements and hard living for ex-slaves and their offspring.

However, what they were seeing dispelled all the rumors they'd heard. Black folks had successful businesses, even amidst the racial hatred that still festered in the country. The new look fascinated Queen, it was almost heaven to her eyes, a utopia of peace that was far away from the ills they faced back home in Memphis. As she looked around she noticed no intimidating police officers twirling their clubs. Queen took in a long deep breath and released it with a sigh of relief.

"Maybe this would be a good place after all to make peace with our past, only time will tell, first I must find Ma'me."

Suddenly her thoughts were interrupted by a deep concerned voice.

"You ladies waiting for someone?"

Startled, Queen turned around and couldn't believe her eyes it was him again. The scar along the side of his face was more prevalent now and his gaze caught hers in the mist of his question.

"Umm excuse me, what did you say?"

"I was wondering if you lovely ladies were waiting for someone."

Carolyn spoke up.

"Hello, I'm Carolyn this is my twin sister Connie and this is our sister Queen."

"Ah, twins, I should have known."

"And your name sir?"

"My name is Calvin."

Calvin waited for his name at least to ring a bell with Queen, but received nothing.

"And Queen, is it?"

"Yes, Queen it is."

Calvin extended his large hand and Queen gently placed her hand inside of his.

"It's a pleasure meeting you Queen.

"Likewise."

Calvin smiled at Queen and at that moment she knew it was something about this man that would require her to be careful about keeping her feelings in check. He was very handsome and had the whitest teeth she had ever seen on a man besides her dear father. Queen also couldn't help but notice the contour of his body structure even underneath all the layers of clothing he wore. His skin was dark and beautiful and the scar that extended from underneath his right eye to the end of his cheek gave him an alluring appeal. She imagined it was due to some wild adventure off the beaten path that required him to defend his life one way or another, something she only recently knew all too well. Nevertheless, although she was a very passionate woman, Queen's past relationships had been intentionally unemotional and this made it quite easy for her to turn down two marriage proposals. She had a difficult time trusting anyone after the passing of her father. Therefore, she never allowed herself to experience loving and above all being loved and cherished. Her main priority had been her sisters and as far as love was concerned, she'd accepted the fact that love would never again be a priority in her life. Queen hadn't noticed that her new acquaintance could see the cold dense expression on her face while deep in her thoughts. He tried to reconcile, but unknowing to him it wasn't him, but just her way of keeping her guard up.

"Forgive me if I have been rude, you just remind me of

Adrienne Lynn Rutherford

someone I use to know."

"Hmmm is that right, I doubt very much that you know me."

"Calvin, is it?"

Queen then looked at her sisters and begin to laugh and they joined in.

"It's been a long time since I've been in these parts, and to be frank I've never seen you before in my life."
Calvin smiled again as he thought to himself.

"This is going to be quite an interesting homecoming."

He then continued, not giving up on what he called nothing short of a miracle happening to him.

"Well, pardon my intrusion, I just thought maybe I could assist you ladies in some kind of way, maybe give you a lift."

"My automobile is just over there."

Calvin pointed proudly toward his convertible Patterson Automobile parked on the side of the mercantile.

Queen and her sisters smiled.

She then pulled out the small piece of paper and handed it to Calvin.

"I'm looking for this address, do you have any idea where it's located."

Calvin again smiled to himself, he never doubted his intuition and this time like so many other times it had served him well. It was that little girl from long ago the one he thought he would never see again. She had not changed a bit still witty and strong willed, only now she'd became the most beautiful woman he'd laid his eyes on. The small heart shaped birthmark on her left temple had given her away back in downtown Tulsa when they boarded the train. Calvin wondered what had brought her back to Greenwood District.

"Yes, sure I know how to get there, one of my best friends live in the area."

"I can take you there right now if you like."

Queen and her sisters were relieved and Carolyn grabbed his hand and shook it fiercely

"Oh, thank you, thank you so much."

"You have been a great deal of help, we didn't know how we were going to carry all these bags."

Queen then opened her satchel to give Calvin a pair of silver pieces and he threw his hands up to stop her.

"No, Queen, No, that won't be necessary."

"I'm going that way, and besides I couldn't take money from you ladies."

"Stay here, I'll get the automobile and bring it to you."

Calvin tipped his hat and left the ladies, while Carolyn nudged her older sister.

"You see that, I think that guy is soft on you girl."
Connie smiled.

"Yeah did you see how he was looking at her, as if he knew her."

"Oh, hush you two, that's absurd."

"Anyway, we have more important things to deal with than the flirtatious advances of an outlaw."

Carolyn laughed.

"You can't be serious right, I mean that's like calling the kettle black."

"Maybe so, but at least we don't look the part."

"Jonas should be getting in touch with us soon, until then we must be careful."

"Until we get to Ma'me, we're on our own and no matter what happens we have each other you understand?"

Both the twins nodded in affirmation, which took them all back to that uncomfortable place, that place that kept them fearful for their lives. As Queen looked at her sisters she grabbed each one by the hand and did what she'd done most of their life, provide encouragement in the mist of chaos.

"Don't worry"

"Like papa always said, this too shall pass."

Chapter 7

Memphis, Tennessee

Jonas was stretched out on his narrow cot in his small boarding room when he heard a loud knock on the door.

"Open up boy."

He jumped up, grabbed his shotgun and looked out the peep hole only to see the Captain and Miss Quickman.

"Shit!!"

He began pacing the floor while scratching his head trying to gain some type of composure.

"One moment sir."

He returned his shotgun to its hiding place and then slowly opened the door.

"Good morning."

Both murmured a salutation and then the captain pushed the door completely open looking over Jonas' shoulder.

"Well boy aren't you going to invite us in?"

"Oh sure, sure."

Jonas began moving clothing around grabbing his liquor bottle and sliding it under his mattress.

"What brings you to my humble doe step captain?"

Miss Quickman entered behind him and begin to look around the small room in distaste while the captain spoke to Jonas.

"Boy, I'm going to be brief, I'm looking for three friends of yours the Sawyer girls from Nottingham Court."

Then Miss Quickman spoke.

"We hear around town your pretty close to these girls is that true?"

Jonas thought it would be in his best interest to answer the Medusa first. Everyone in town knew that the captain was on her payroll.

"Yes ma'am, I use to do handy work for their father before he died and for them from time to time."

The Captain then impatiently interrupted.

When is the last time you had any contact with them girls?"

Jonas turned and looked at the captain.

"It's been a couple of weeks sir."

"They were having plumbing problems in the kitchen and Queen asked me to stop by and take a look at the pipes underneath sir."

"Finds out it was just clogged so I went on under the sink and…."

Viola Quickman impatiently interrupted.

"Enough of that boy, we do not need an explanation regarding the details of a clogged kitchen sink, the captain specifically asked you a question and I presume that you have no idea of what has happened."

"Don't you read the papers boy?"

Jonas looked at them both as if clueless to the events that recently occurred only a few days ago. Miss Quickman took a long sigh of frustration.

"I'm sure you heard that those girls lured my boy to their home, robbed him and murdered him in cold blood and to make matters worse they left him there to bleed out while they disappeared in the night."

"If you know something, Jonas is the name, right?"
Jonas nodded an affirmative.

"I suggest that you speak up now, because if I find out that you had anything to do with this or helped them girls in anyway, I'm coming after you and I want to be the first to tell you that my wrath is far worse than any lynch mob."

"You hear me?"
She then gave him a menacing grin.

"Of course, I did fail to mention that there is a five-thousand-dollar reward for that Queen woman and twenty-five hundred each for her sister's dead or alive!"

Jonas didn't flinch he held his ground. To him they both looked quite ridiculous throwing out threats about a man that everyone on his side of town wanted dead, especially the young women. So, while they were finding ways to intimidate him, Jonas was figuring out a way to get these latest details to Queen and the twins as soon as possible.

Adrienne Lynn Rutherford

"Boy, you hear what I said?"

"Yes, ma'am loud and clear."

The two then exited the door as they had entered and Jonas slammed it shut and went into a silent rage of anger. What kind of nerve he thought, to come into his place and threaten him about a sociopath whose behavior was ignored for years by the same captain threatening him for information on the girls. Jonas knew it would only be a matter of time before the Medusa would find her way to the girls. That type of reward money was sure to stir up even the devil himself.

Jonas would never let on where the girls were, but he knew that folks would be buzzing around town about the reward the Medusa was offering and five thousand dollars was a lot of money, enough for anyone to start a whole new life anywhere. To him it was a terrible situation that unfolded in their lives. Even though they were innocent and the death was one of self-defense, the Medusa had the money and the power to transform it into cold-blooded murder.

Jonas shook his head at the thought of never seeing the girls again, especially Connie. They had become quite close over the years but he would never risk his loyalty to Queen. His loyalty had cost him the opportunity to confess his love for Connie that night at the train station. His only hope was to do everything in his power to protect the girl's whereabouts until he could get to them himself.

Jonas grabbed his liquor bottle and started to turn it up, however this time he smelled the strong stench of *white lightening* and sat it down on the table. He would have to be sober for the girls. Since he'd left the train station that early morning Jonas had drowned his sorrows in the bottle, but now it was time to regroup and do his own investigating. Jonas knew the best place to get his information was on Beale Street. He also knew that now he would have to be more careful because after today he was sure that the captain would have his men watching him.

Jonas had been very careful leaving with the girls that night, they had taken the back roads. He was very good when it came to alternative traveling routes heading in and out of town without being seen. He'd used them often as a young boy traveling with his father in the dark of night to dodge the authorities while transporting his grandfather's famous *white lightening*. His father Oscar was a mountain man and his father before him. The family settled in the Rocky Mountains, after traveling many miles on foot along the Mississippi River after the Civil War. *White lightening* was a longtime profitable business for the family. The business was so profitable during the 1880s great expansion to the west, his father was finally able to stake claim on the mountain land that his parents had settled almost twenty years earlier. Jonas would listen to his grandfather and grandmother by the fire many nights under the stars atop his mountain home, intrigued by the many stories about their adventures on those Rocky Mountains in their youthful years. It was only a small group of them that decided to settle there with the Cherokee Indians. They had learned many things from the Cherokee's about the mountain way of life, like which mountain plants to use for medicine and how to set traps for small game. They also exchanged stories with the Cherokee regarding the quest for freedom and justice and how they were all able to rest well on the Great Mountain. Jonas was born a mountain man, he knew nothing but the mountain way of life until that fatal night that changed his life forever. His thoughts then drifted back to the girls, his past was not going to distract him, not now. He had people that he cared about depending on him and he wasn't going to repeat the same mistake, he was going to make sure he didn't fail the girls.

The humid breeze of the Memphis late spring night encouraged Jonas to pull out his handkerchief and wipe the perspiration from his brow. He only stayed a few blocks from the Beale Street Red Light district so he decided to walk. The streets were not as busy tonight, he thought to himself as he observed couples taking their evening strolls and the lantern keeper relighting those lamps along the street that required their wicks to be replaced. The large weeping willows that hung solemnly over the tar laid street leading to Beale was one of the many things that gave Memphis its unique character.

As Jonas approached his destination he could hear the loud laughter as well as the sounds of Blues music playing blissfully in the night. When he finally turned the corner, the lights were so vibrant, it was as if he entered another world. This street was never empty, but filled with many people and the one place in the city where

Adrienne Lynn Rutherford

segregation was only a word. Both black and white enjoyed the entertainment that stretched along the one mile culturally influenced Beale Street. Jonas had dressed in his finest after taking a cool shower. He slipped on a pair of grey slacks, black leather shoes and a white shirt with the sterling silver cuff links the girls had purchased for him as a Christmas gift. He'd caught the eye of some of the women of the night as they winked and blew kisses at him. He smiled mannishly at the attention they gave, but tonight he was on another mission as he continued his stroll. As the Blues band made its way down the center of the street, Jonas was taken by surprise by a pair of hands that covered his eyes from behind. He did not fill threatened because of the smell of the expensive French perfume gave her away as it always had. It was his childhood friend Manuela.

"Hey Jonas, what brings you out this evening."
Jonas smiled as he grabbed her hands.

"Just wanted to get out, thought I would listen to some good music and have a couple of shots of the good stuff, you know what I mean?"

Manuela always had a crush on Jonas, but somehow, he never thought twice about her. Manuela was the daughter of his mother's friend on the mountain. Her parents decided to leave the mountain so that she could go to school in the city. Since then Manuela spent most of her life living the life of a socialite in the segregated part of Memphis.

"Jonas, I know you heard about Mr. Sawyers girls, it's all over town you know."
My brother and his friends were over at the billiards just now talking about it."

"Everybody talking about that reward too, five thousand dollars is a pretty penny."

"Humph, that Quickman woman sure do know how to stir up mess around here, I mean everybody knows that son of hers wasn't wrapped to tight."

"Running around here attacking young decent black women."

"I know what happened, I can imagine it."

"That Queen is a spit fire you know!"

"He came sniffing around there and he got dealt with and it

serves him right."

"Folks say they proud of Queen and the twins, their heroes around here far as we're concerned."

"I hope they're safe wherever they are and never come back here."

"Because you and I both know they're some folk around here black and white that don't have any regard for decency, and greed is their soul motivation."

Jonas didn't say a word he took it all in as Manuela saved him a lot of trouble and time of going around inquiring about the events that occurred. Everyone knew how close he was to the girls, so him asking would have been suspicious and probably would have eventually got back to the captain. As always, Manuela had unknowingly with her gossiping nature been a great help by confirming a lot of what he'd already suspected.

"As long as that reward was lingering, things would get complicated really complicated."

Jonas smiled at Manuela as he thought to himself.

"It's a tense time in the town of Memphis."

Adrienne Lynn Rutherford

Chapter 8

Greenwood District: Tulsa Oklahoma

Calvin finished loading the car with the sister's belongings and they were on their way. Carolyn noticed many of the young ladies stopping and taking notice as they traveled pass them in the street. She smiled and from the back seat tapped Calvin on the shoulder.

"Looks like your rather popular around these here parts Calvin."

"Maybe."

"Guess I haven't really noticed."

"I do know, word gets around fast though."

He then looked over at Queen.

"I just got back myself yesterday morning, I knew it was going to be an interesting homecoming."

"But I didn't know it was going to be this interesting."

Queen didn't look his way she only looked straight ahead as they continued down the dusty road toward Ma'mes house. Soon the busy town was slowly left behind and another part of Oklahoma began to surface filled with lovely groves and beautiful streams that stretched across a wide plain. The ladies held on to their hats as the wind from the drive had attempted to possess them as its own.

"Wow it's beautiful out here."

"I was thinking the same thing, Connie."

Queen then turned around and looked at the girls.

"I remember that place there, that's the church house."

"My dad and mama use to bring me here for the annual cookouts and we would spend time with Ma'me, yes this place I remember."

Calvin stayed silent as he listened to the sisters. Suddenly out of nowhere a large aircraft swooped down above the Patterson-Greenfield automobile and the twins in the back seat began to scream.

"Oh, my God what was that?"

It then came around a second time, Calvin slammed on the brakes and the twins almost flew into the front seat area of the car.

However, they managed to restrain themselves as did Queen in the front
seat.

"Calvin!"

Queen shouted.

"What the hell is going on?"

"Ladies, my apologies, but that's my brother in his airplane and he must have noticed my car on the road."

"I'm sure he doesn't know I am in the company of you ladies." While he was apologizing, Connie and Carolyn were both getting up off the floor and grabbing their hats. Now, their hair was totally out of place as if they had been in a cat fight. Connie took her hat and shoved it in her bag and after watching her, Carolyn did the same thing. Finally, the large flying machine that swiftly flew over them and landed safely in the meadow not far from their location. John walked up to the car and once he realized what he'd done he began to laugh.

"Brother, I didn't know you had company with you, who are these beautiful specimens"

Carolyn looked at him in disbelief.

"Specimens?"

"Do we look like some type of specimen to you, birdman?"

John then leaned into the car and whispered to his brother.

"Oh, so you got a firecracker in your backseat brother?"

Calvin shook his head and smiled.

"Ladies this is my brother John, John this is Queen, and her twin sisters Connie and Carolyn."

John stepped away from the car and bowed gracefully.

"It's a pleasure meeting you ladies, I do apologize for the air show, I thought my brother was alone."

"He came in yesterday evening and no one has seen him since early this morning."

He then looked over at Calvin.

"You know you better not miss dinner again tonight, you're the guest of honor."

Calvin shook his head.

"Yeah right, I told you I'm not going back over there."

Adrienne Lynn Rutherford

"I have arranged to have dinner with Mama and Cody in town at Maggie's Place."

John begin to laugh.

"All come on man, you gotta have tough skin with pops you know that."

Calvin interrupted his brother.

"Man, this isn't a good time for this conversation."

"I'll meet you at your place in a couple of hours."

The girls patiently listened as the two went back and forth with one another and after a brief brotherly conversation John bid them farewell, but not before giving Carolyn a little special attention, a flirtatious wink.

"I like her man, she got fire!"

Carolyn leaned back in the back seat and unlike her older sister displayed an obvious expression of curiosity on her face.

John looked at his brother suspiciously.

"Brother, don't have me waiting on you and you don't show up."

"If it was me with these beautiful ladies, I would be trying to go where ever they're going."

"Brother, I'll be there, I'm going to drop these lovely ladies to Miss Ma'me.

John took another look in the car.

"Yawl some kin to Miss Ma'me?"

Queen then looked at him and smiled very sarcastically.

"Yes, she's our aunt."

"Oh, alright then, yawl staying for a spell?"

"We may, it all depends."

"Well welcome to Tulsa Greenwood District."

He then looked at Carolyn in the back seat.

"All of you."

As he departed Queen looked over at Calvin and then at his brother as he walked away. She then glanced back at Calvin as if contemplating a thought.

"Is there something wrong, Queen?"

"Oh, no there is nothing wrong, I was just wondering about something is all."

Calvin smiled as he started up the automobile and they all watched John take off into the sky.

Connie was excited to see the flying machine.

"Calvin your brother is a riot, were did he learn to fly that thing.

"He was in the United States Airforce during the 1914 World War. He was an aero mechanic, kept those U.S. fighters in tip top shape. Unfortunately, he and many other black men were not allowed to fly due to the U.S. Military segregation laws. So, he and some of his platoon buddies after the war spent most of the time designing and building their own airplanes."

"When you are denied certain opportunities for the wrong reasons, well it makes you creative. So, with help of some of his platoon buddies he built his own landing strip and hanger for his planes on his property. John lives a little further North of the Greenwood District."

"There is also another airfield with other airplanes built and owned by retired Black pilots on the Northeast side of Greenwood, not far from your Aunt Ma'me."

Carolyn smiled.

"That is amazing Calvin, I know that must require a lot of skill to create a machine that will lift off the ground and do the things he made it do."

"John has an amazing story to tell, he set the bar high for all of us, but I'll let him share his story with you, because something tells me you two will run into each other again."

Queen, while keeping her eyes on the road interrupted.

"I'm not quite understanding what you mean by that comment Calvin."

"We are not here to be entertained by the men folk, we're here to visit our aunt, I just want that to be clear."

Carolyn not at all amused by her sister's comment sunk back into her seat.

Calvin then turned to Queen and in a very inviting voice responded.

"Why can't she do both?"

The comment took Queen by surprise, she was not expecting that and turned an uncomfortable blush of red in the face. Queen

Adrienne Lynn Rutherford

knew her heart quite well and the feelings that she had were quite awkward for what she thought was a handsome and beautifully put together man. It was as if she had seen him before, but couldn't seem to figure out where. If she made eye contact now, all the hard and diligent work of not showing her attraction to him since their first encounter would have all been in vain. However, Calvin paid no mind to Queen's body language and was aware of her attempts to ignore his subtle gentleman like comments. He also thought it quite amusing how she blushed to his response and had no way of hiding it. Queen was no longer that little girl with the unique heart shaped birthmark on her cheek he remembered, but a full grown beautifully made woman. Calvin in that moment knew after all the years that passed by, it must have been a universal reason why they both ended back up in Greenwood at the same time. His thoughts were then interrupted by Carolyn

"Calvin, you think he can teach me to fly."

Queen turned to her sisters again.

"You can't be serious Carolyn, you wanna go up there."

"Sure, I bet the view is so beautiful from up there."

Queen then looked over at Calvin for the first time since they loaded up.

"Have you been up there?"

"Sure, lots of times and she's right the view is absolutely amazing from up there."

Queen thought for a moment and laughed to herself.

"Maybe it would be a good idea for Carolyn to learn to fly that contraption, it just may be their ticket out of here if they need it."

It wasn't long before Calvin pulled up in front of Ma'mes modest two-story colonial home. It sat in the middle of the Sassafras Circle, with a house across the vast meadow on each side in the distance. It was much more distinguished than its neighboring homes, because it had been one of the first brick homes built in the area with a cement porch and steps and raw iron railing from one end of the porch to the next. There was a lot of detail put into Ma'mes home thanks to her brother Buford and her husband so long ago. They were all freedmen that consisted of carpenters and bricklayers. Although they were long gone, the unique skills and talents of these men were unmatched and still admired by many of those who visited Ma'me and many other areas of Greenwood.

Ma'me stood up out of her rocking chair to greet her visitors.

"Calvin is that you?"

"Yes Ma'me, how's my favorite lady."

Ma'me smiled wide.

"Oh, my goodness come on up her and see Ma'me."

The ladies were still getting out of the automobile as Calvin walked up on the porch and gave Ma'me a hug.

"My goodness son, you sure is a sight for sore eyes around here."

"How you been doing?"

"I'm doing just fine Ma'me, how have you been?"

"Oh, I've been making it, one day at a time is all I can do, just one day at a time."

Ma'mes attention then went to the girls as they all stood silent at the bottom of the steps. She then walked to the top of the steps and looked at the luggage sitting on the ground and then directly at Queen.

"Queen, is my brother still walking this earth?"

Queen shocked that Ma'me had even remembered her couldn't say a word.

"Chile come on up here just don't stand there, Auntie Ma'me asked you a question."

Queen lowered her head.

"No, Aunt Ma'me he's gone."

Ma'me then pulled out her handkerchief and wiped her eyes.

"You mean to tell me my brother den left this here earth and nobody ever thought to contact Ma'me huh?"

"Did he suffer child?"

"Buford wasn't good at that, never good at that I tell you."

Queen fell silent because she was unable to say a word, her voice had completely left her.

Connie stepped toward the porch and spoke for her sister. In all the days of her life she had never seen her so vulnerable.

"Umm Aunt Ma'me, I'm your niece Connie and this here is Carolyn."

Adrienne Lynn Rutherford

Connie didn't want to tell Ma'me the heartache their father had experienced after the disappearance of their mother. The bouts with depression and then the onset of pneumonia that left him weak and feeble to the point that he had given up completely.

"Aunt Ma'me."

"Chile just call me Ma'me, everybody does."

"Yes Ma'me, but he didn't suffer and he left here peacefully."

"That's good then, yawl come on inside,"

"You hungry?" It's food on the stove."

"Calvin, you are coming in to join us?"

"I would love to Ma'me, but I got some traps to check, I'll be back to see you really soon.

"By the way, where is Wil?"

"Oh, you know he across the tracks working."

"He should be in this evening, hopefully before it gets dark."

"Calvin, you know things ain't changed much around here."

"This side of town is looking really good though Ma'me, I was sure proud when I got into town"

"Yes, it's nice, real nice all the businesses that they have put up, even an ice-cream parlor and a fabric store too, but them folks on the other side of them tracks is still mean and evil as a rattle snake I tell you, not all of them but most."

"Some of the folks around here who do cleaning at the homes of some of the white folks over there on the south side tells me about what them folks be saying about us over here on the north side of Tulsa."

They ain't taking too kindly to the progress that's going on over here in our community."

"Say we've gotten to uppity and living too much like white folks in all."

"What kind of craziness is that to say, just side talking is what it is?"

"Something deep down in my spirit tells me that negroes around here gotta be right careful displaying their wealth, right careful cause jealousy is uh ugly thing."

And we both know that white folks don't like to see negro folks living in peace and getting along good without any of them benefiting."

Connie and Carolyn followed Ma'me into the house listening to her truth sermon, while Queen stayed outdoors with Calvin.

"I just want to thank you for your kindness, and all that you have done by bringing us out here to my aunt's house, you didn't have to do that."

"Are you sure there is nothing we can give you for your kindness?"

Calvin thought for a moment.

"Oh, it was my pleasure, no worries."

"Would you possibly consider giving me the pleasure of spending a night out with you?"

"Excuse me, you're a little pushy, aren't you?"

"Pardon me, that didn't come out quite the way I wanted it to."

I would like to take you to dinner one of these days, not now of course, but when you get settled in, I would be honored."

"Honored?"

"Yes, Honored."

"Don't mind me this is an awkward moment, no one was ever honored to be in my presence before."

Calvin then bowed before her.

"Well shall I introduce myself to you again Queen."
She then smiled.

"You are really something else, yes sure I will have dinner with you."

Calvin was relieved as he tipped his hat off to her.

"In the meantime, if you girls need anything don't hesitate to get in contact with me."

"Yes, thank you very much Calvin, talk to you soon."
Calvin returned to his automobile as Queen watched him crank it up and then drive off. She then went into the house to join her family thinking,

"What an interesting visit this will be."

Adrienne Lynn Rutherford

Chapter 9

Calvin was deep in his thoughts as he enjoyed the drive in the warm breeze of the mid-afternoon. Ma'me was right in a lot of ways, it was hard being successful and black in this country. The world they were forced to live in wasn't ready to see a black community such as Greenwood District become self-sufficient and thrive financially. Not everyone paid attention to the consequences of success and how it could become dangerous politically and socially, overlooking the fact that most white business depended on the economic base of the black population far more than its own. Educating the negro was one thing, but seeing what education and self-sufficiency could do for the race economically was another. Calvin on the other hand, had taken the unbeaten path when he left home that warm summer Sunday afternoon eight years ago. He made his way to Canada and was able to land a job as a cowboy herding cattle across the Canadian border. His employer was an oil tycoon and cattle rustler by the name of Ira Stovall. Although completely out of the realm of what his father had planned for him, Calvin found solace in his own adventure. He befriended Mr. Stovall while playing chess in a small pub in Saskatchewan Canada. It was his way of earning money to pay his room and board at the time. Ira had taken a liking to Calvin and his spirit to win. Calvin smiled as he remembered what Mr. Stovall told him after he'd beaten the tycoon three times in a row and won over three-hundred dollars from his purse.

"The way a man plays chess, says a lot about that man."

Ira Stovall, an ex-slave had not experienced the path of most slaves, nor had the experiences that they were forced to endure after the Civil War. Ira Stovall was one of many African slaves of the Creek Native American Nation. After the Civil War, The Creek Nation signed a treaty with the United States Government in 1866 to emancipate their sixteen-thousand slaves and incorporate them into their nation as *"citizens"* to be entitled also to equal interest in soil and natural funds on the land in which the Creek Nation resided at the time. However, twenty years later the government reneged on this treaty and in 1887 *"The Dawes Act"* was passed. This act completely dismantled the physical unity of the five tribes that made up The Creek Native American Nation forcing them to live on individually allotted land no longer as a United Nation of people. Although their way of life had come to an end, over three hundred black children also known as *Creek Nation Freedom Minors,* were also allotted over one hundred and sixty acres of land that was deemed useless by the standards of U.S. government officials. Overtime, these same lands would soon be recognized for the valuable resources that were hidden underneath. Ira Stovall's life would change forever that day when governmental land surveyors came to his one room cabin asking him questions and requiring proof of his land deed. Later, he found that the black puddles of thick sticky substance that seeped from his land was crude oil and a valuable resource to the Government. This made Ira Stovall a very wealthy man as he collected over four-hundred dollars per day on profits from his land from his teenage years until now his late sixties. Ira Stovall could successfully purchase land in Canada, Montana and Colorado investing in cattle and horses. Calvin, over time while working for Mr. Stovall was soon able to invest in himself, purchasing his first ten cattle and that ten turned to twenty and before long Calvin would purchase his own cattle ranches with hired hands on a modest ranch in Montana. Calvin not only did well with the cattle, he was also intrigued with horses. Coming up with them as a child his father taught him well at distinguishing a good breed of horse. Therefore, it was second nature to him to breed them. As a result, he became known as one of the most popular Mustang breeders on the Canadian border. Calvin was grateful to Mr. Stovall for all the knowledge and support that he would give him over the years, so he took a vow to help him with his mission in life. After realizing the significance of the land allotted to The Creek Nation and its Freedom Minors, a law was passed that required full-blooded Indians, ex-slaves and their descendants who were citizens on Indian Territory with significant property and money to be assigned government guardians.

Mr. Stovall realized the hard way that these so-called guardians were not to be trusted when his soon to be wife, her brother and parents were murdered and their land seized for the oil rights. As a

Adrienne Lynn Rutherford

result, Mr. Stovall would never marry, but made a vow to track down any and every thief posing as legitimate government officials that would harm anyone in the Creek Nation and rob them of their legally allotted land and the natural resources that laid beneath. Calvin joined Ira in his quest to protect the Freedmen Minors and their families. It was events such as these that forced Calvin for the first time in his life, to take a life. However, not to save himself, but the life of a ten-year-old boy that was kidnapped and almost murdered for his family's rich oil homestead. It had been a battle to the death and he now owned a scar that covered the side of his face to prove it.

Now, although he didn't work for Mr. Stovall anymore they would still spend Sunday afternoon's playing chess for a handsome wager. However, one-day Mr. Stovall received visitors at his home. Oil was still a very lucrative commodity in the United States and continued to entice wealthy landowners to seek investors to invest in equipment and experienced oil field hands to release the rich resources from underground. These rich resources were known to guarantee astronomical profits. The gentleman Lou Garrison a longtime friend of Mr. Stovall, a wealthy mining heiress named Viola Quickman and her son Rodger would be the anticipated triad Mr. Garrison would put together. This powerful business collaboration would provide a thousand miles of oil pipeline from the United States all the way up into Canada. For Mr. Garrison, racism had not been a poison of his mind. His family legacy did not support it and for years while growing up he watched his family assist many slaves through the Underground Railroad to freedom across the border into Canada.

It was clear that when the Quickman family entered they observed Mr. Stovall sitting down in a casual game of chess with Calvin and were a bit taken by surprise to find themselves in the presence of two wealthy niggers contemplating over a game of chess. Mr. Stovall was very much use to dealing with people like the Quickman's and it was because of that he gave them no acknowledgement as he spoke to them without even looking up from his game. Calvin smiled as he thought back on that day, the day that Mr. Stovall changed his life forever. The Quickman businesses had been plummeting due to the economic turndown of the country and now they were very eager to invest in other avenues. Mr. Stovall had reluctantly considered investing as a third party with Lou Garrison and the Quickman family, but after meeting them that day he required one condition. Calvin Watkins would be allowed to invest as a part of his percentage. Garrison had no problem with Calvin because he'd did business with both him and Stovall many times in the past and it panned out well. However, the gasp made by Viola Quickman and the intense profanity used by her son made it clear that they would not have any business dealings with any Negros, regardless of wealth. Mr. Stovall was a fair man, but he had no problem putting them both in their place, reminding them that business was business and if they had a problem with the way business was done in the Oklahoma Territories they could take their business down to Texas.

Texas was not a place that Viola Quickman wanted to tread, the business of oil was vicious in those parts and the gun totting renegades, thieves and robbers that covered the small untamed country was a place she didn't want to venture. In need of this business opportunity to get out of debt with the banks back east, she had no choice but to sign the contract of partnership with everyone including Calvin Watkins. It had been well over two years since then. Calvin was now back home because he missed his family, even his father and the love and laughter that he once knew. He could go out into the world and did very well for himself and made some loyal lifetime friends. However, now Calvin was searching for something more in his life. He had an internal longing, Queen continued to resonate in his mind and it was just too coincidental that she would show up here after over twenty years. Calvin paid close attention to them all and from the looks of it, their visit just seemed far too rushed considering Ma'me had no idea they were coming. He was also surprised that Queen had no knowledge of her mother. Calvin knew it would be a matter of time before everything came to a head. It was one thing that he knew about Greenwood District, secrets were a rare commodity. If there was something behind the arrival to Greenwood District unannounced it was surely going to be found out. Nevertheless, Calvin felt a since of comfort in knowing that he

Adrienne Lynn Rutherford

had the opportunity to see her again and she also promised him an evening just the two of them. That was a moment that he was looking forward too. It was obvious these past years had made her a little rough around the edges considering the comments that she made to him when he spoke to her at the station.

"How in the world am I going to penetrate such a strong-willed woman, her skin tough as cowhide?"

Calvin smiled to himself at the thought. The challenge was something he would enjoy. The art of winning was no fun when the effort put into was too easy, so he adopted the quest of Queen. After parking his automobile Calvin headed into Maggie's Place.

"Calvin?"

"Calvin."

Calvin thoughts were interrupted by Damita Reynolds, she was a former class mate and girlfriend of Calvin's before he decided to leave.

"Damita?"

Calvin looked down at her huge belly in surprise and then gave her a friendly hug.

"Looks like you got a little something cooking in the oven."

She rubbed her stomach smiling with pride.

"Yes, I very well couldn't wait for you, now could I?"

Not long after the two exchanged greetings a gentleman walked up to them both while holding a little boy. They were both finely dressed in black tailored suits with bow ties and vests. It was obvious that the little boy and the man were father and son, they looked very similar with the only difference being the father wearing a pair of round rim spectacles.

"Calvin this is my husband James Lee Reynolds and this is my son James Lee Jr."

"James Lee owns the theatre over there, across the street."

Calvin extended his hand and James Lee Jr. turned away deeper into his father's chest while his father managed to extend the other.

"Calvin, is it?"

He looked at Calvin's attire as if he were dressed inappropriately for the casual conversation in front of Maggie's Place.

"I've heard quit an ear full about you Calvin Watkins and I must say your reputation is even far more exaggerated by my lovely Damita."

Calvin looked over at Damita as she looked at her husband and son smiling.

"Oh, James Lee you stop that."

"Don't mind him Calvin, he's just being a tad bit jealous."

"Anyway, what brings you back to Greenwood?"

"Well it is home."

Although Feeling a bit uncomfortable with the conversation Damita continued her small talk.

"Of course, of course Calvin, I mean this is home for us all right?"

Calvin then nodded.

"So, Calvin, you plan on staying?"

"For a while maybe, I'm thinking about looking at some homestead deeds out on the northwest side."

"Deeds?"

James Lee interrupted.

"The homestead is a pretty penny out that way Calvin."

"The lots are much larger than here in town."

"You would actually have to be into some type of high scale agricultural farming or ranching to even consider that area."

Damita smiled at her husband while admiring his extensive knowledge of the real estate on Tulsa's north side. She then looked at Calvin and smiled.

Calvin refused to entertain the comment that was made by this man. First, he'd never seen him around Greenwood District and figured that this James Lee must have arrived not long after he left. He obviously managed to successfully bid on and acquire a piece of business property in the district and was feeling very confident in himself. Secondly, Calvin didn't want to embarrass him in front of his wife and child so he held his peace.

"You know that's a good observation that you've made."

"James Lee, is it?"

"Fortunately for me I'm not really that serious just yet, I'm just checking out the area and the set up since I left."

Adrienne Lynn Rutherford

"Oh sure, sure, no worries man."

"If you need some advice at all on the real estate in the area just let me know, I've become quite friendly with the City Clerk on the south side of town."

"Will do, thanks man."

Calvin tipped his cow hide brim at Damita.

"It was a pleasure seeing you again Damita, I wish you guys well with the delivery."

"Oh, thanks Calvin, it was so good seeing you too."

She then nudged at her husband and he managed to go into his pocket while still holding the little boy.

"Oh, we're having a special showing at the theater next Saturday evening.

It's a special event honoring the Great Oscar Micheaux."

"He's the first Black American Film Maker, have you heard of him?"

Calvin once again did not have the heart to say something that would embarrass James Lee Reynolds, owner of Greenwood's finest Movie Theatre. So, he shook his head and responded.

"Vaguely."

Oh well then, let me be the first to enlighten you Calvin, he has two films that he's written and produced. The first was *The Homesteader* in 1918 and the newest release *Within Our Gates*."

"These here are two tickets to the premiere, we would very much like you to come."

Damita then smiled at Calvin while rubbing her stomach.

"Calvin, we really would very much like for you to come."

"Yes, we would, we are one of the very few theatres in the entire country that were given such an honor."

"Oh, and Calvin ummm, let me remind you that it will be a black-tie affair."

"Afterwards, you're invited to join us at our home with a selected few of course for coffee and sweet cake to discuss the films."

"If you were not able to experience the first, you will be able to comment on the latest release."

"Thanks, this is very kind of the both of you."

Damita then smiled.

"Oh, Calvin your always welcomed."

"I want you to bring yourself a date too."

"I don't want you coming alone, you here?"

Calvin knew Damita meant well, he also knew most of the young men in the area before he'd left thought she was the biggest catch on the north side. Calvin smiled, as she flexed that little-big ego of hers. It was one that he knew much too well.

"I will do my best, it was a pleasure meeting you James Lee and thank you guys so very much for the invite."

As the family strolled along down the side walkway Calvin shook his head. He wondered what expressive look James Lee and Damita would have had on their faces if he'd told them that he'd had Dinner with Oscar at the Canadian Film Festival in 1917 when it featured his first film. Also, that he'd met with him after a Marcus Garvey Fundraiser and Oscar had discussed with him and his lovely date at the time about his next project. It would a powerful yet discreet rebuttal to the racially controversial film of the time, Birth of a Nation. Now that Oscar had completed his project, Calvin was very interested in seeing what creative thoughts he put into his latest film and was very willing to find out. He then smiled as he thought of Queen.

"This is an opportunity to have Queen make good on her promise."

Calvin then went into Maggie's place and as usual the place was busy. Ever since he could remember, Maggie owned one of the most popular restaurant in Tulsa and from the looks of it she still held the title. People came from miles to taste her smoked Bar-B-Que pork and beef ribs. He walked up to the front counter and waited for the young lady to cash out another couple before attempting to place his order.

"Calvin is that you?"

Maggie came from the back of the restaurant wiping her hands with her waist apron."

"Oh, my goodness, look at you son."

She hugged him and then grabbed his face with both hands

"How are you, Miss Maggie?"

Adrienne Lynn Rutherford

"I'm just fine, we heard you were in town and I knew you would stop by."

She then began to laugh.

"You know gossip spreads around these here parts like wild fire."

Calvin looked around the small store front restaurant

"Yeah same ole Greenwood, but the place looks really nice Miss Maggie."

"Oh, business has been doing so good Calvin, thank you."

"Did you want something to eat?"

"Of course, I do."

Suddenly, a tall slender woman approached the two of them. The young woman was smiling and gave him a long hug of endearment, then bashfully placed a kiss on his cheek.

"Hello Calvin."

Maggie smiled as she noticed the confused look on Calvin's face.

"You don't know who that is do you Calvin?"

"Precious?"

"Yes, it's me."

Calvin tipped his hat.

"My have you grown up, and very beautiful I might add."

Precious continued to smile at Calvin while he and her mother continued their conversation.

"Precious is all grown up now Calvin, smart and she's a hard worker too."

"Isn't that right Precious?"

"Yes Ma'am, I'm smart and a hard worker."

Calvin didn't have any problems understanding where this conversation was about to go and he quickly changed the subject all together.

"Umm I was wondering if I could use your phone line, I have a business call that I must make."

"Oh sure, sure Calvin, what did you want from the kitchen dear?"

"I'll have a rib dinner."

"Sure, Precious can you direct Calvin to the back office to use the phone?"

"Yes, Calvin can you follow me please."

Once in the office Calvin pulled up a chair and placed a phone call to Mr. Stovall.

"Hello."

"Stovall it's Calvin, how are you?"

"Fine as cat hair man, how's the visit?"

"More than I expected, I called you because on my way back to Montana. I picked up a paper from back east at the train station and it had Rodger Quickman in there, said he was murdered."

"Yeah, I heard that too."

"I was waiting for you to call, that Viola Quickman contacted Garrison about her son, said she wanted to meet with her partners."

Precious returned with his meal and as much as she tried to get his attention Calvin's mind was on his business call. He thanked her while looking over his meal and continued his call.

"Oh, really about what?"

"Some type of re-negotiation in the contract."

"I don't like the sound of that man."

"I don't either, but it doesn't matter man that contract is legally binding"

"Calvin when can you get up this way."

"I'm in the middle of some important family business down here, I can leave out next Monday evening.

"Good, I will contact him and see if we can set up a sit down on Tuesday."

Calvin hung up the phone and went back to his meal and when he was done he returned into the main dining area of the restaurant and noticed Precious waving to get his attention in the front. As Calvin made his way to her, he'd noticed there were a few white folks from the south side sitting down having dinner. This was quite amusing to him considering that the black folks of the north side were not allowed to dine-in across the tracks.

"Here you go Calvin."

"A little something to go."

Adrienne Lynn Rutherford

Precious placed a large carry out bag in front of Calvin.

"No, I couldn't."

"Yes, mama insisted and I put a little extra sauce in there for you."

"Thanks Precious, that was very kind of you."

Precious blushed at the comment.

"Tell Miss Maggie, that was right kind of her."

Calvin reached down in his pocket and pulled out a twenty dollar note and handed it to Precious.

"Here that is for you."

Surprised, Precious stretched the note out to see what he'd tipped her was what she thought and then she smiled.

"Thank you, Calvin."

"No, thank you."

He then exited the door and headed out to his brother's place.

Chapter 10

Rocky Mountains, Tennessee Region

Jonas, did not have much luck on Beale Street the other evening. Nevertheless, he was fortunate enough to have ran into Manuela, who had provided him with the information he needed.

After leaving the mountains, Manuela's brother Coaster, pretty much ran the streets in the segregated area of Memphis. Any dirt that was circulating regarding the circumstances surrounding Quickman's death and the girls would continue to surface there first and that he was sure of. As he continued the climb up the long narrow trail to his place of birth the thought back on the tragedy that devastated his community. His parents had left him much too soon because of a deadly mountain fire that would wipe out most of the land that was owned by his parents and a few other families. Those who managed to escape the tragedy, fled to the mountain regions of Kentucky and never returned. Others who decided to return, overtime could work hard and re-build their modest mountainside community. Jonas and his family were not so lucky. He had been saved by Lone Wolf a Cherokee warrior. He remembered struggling to release himself from his grasp to go into the hot flames to find his parents, but as a young child he was far too weak to handle the strength of a warrior.

After growing up he left the mountain and although he still owned the land of his family, his heart still ached from the greatest loss of his life. So, Jonas as a young man went into town for work caring with him a guilt that resonated as spells of deep depression. These grief spells could take days or even weeks for him to come out of. Then one day he met Buford Sawyer, a successful black businessman who treated him like a son. He taught him the craft of bricklaying. Although he was well equipped to run his own business after the death of Mr. Sawyer, Jonas had no desire to do so.

For Jonas and many others, the passing of Mr. Sawyer was a sad day and it sent Jonas to his place of solitude in the mountains near the copper stream that faithfully trickled down into the Tennessee River. On that day, almost eight years ago to his surprise

Adrienne Lynn Rutherford

he was approached by a white woman. Although she was not a young woman, she possessed a youthful yet regal appearance unlike that of any other white women in the mountain region. Jonas was taken aback at first when she approached him. She was carrying what appeared to be her morning catch on a long branch across her shoulder and in the other hand a few small logs that could have been for a fire to prepare her evening dinner. To Jonas she didn't appear to be a happy woman but sad and warn as if life had taken the best of her some time ago. After talking with the woman, Jonas could not believe it when she revealed who she was. His first reaction was to help her gain revenge on all the heartache that her sister had caused the Sawyer family. After spending hours with her she offered him a warm meal and he dare not decline. Georgea spent most that day telling the story of her life as a wealthy heiress until she fell in love with a proud man that day at her father's Annual Freedom & Liberty Gala.

To Georgea it was like yesterday, love at first sight. She knew Bufus Sawyer, regardless of his race was the man that she would love for the rest of her life. His spirit of giving that day would penetrate her very being as they danced much into the night. Georgea had the heart of her father, a kind man who practiced embracing the human spirit and became good at it. He supported the causes that he felt would make the United States a great place. He believed in diversity and openly battled racial injustice that targeted the American Negro both free born and ex-slaves. These battles sought to support equal economic opportunity and a better life in a land that claimed to pride itself in providing liberty. He used his power and influence to politically support lobbyist in the nation's capital to establish bills that would develop into laws that would provide justice for all people. However, when he decided to run for governor of Tennessee, it was far too much for the segregated southern state to bare. As a result, Mr. Quickman would take his last journey east to the nation's capital in the spring of 1886 when an automobile accident would leave his body lifeless along with his driver on the side of a narrow road in Kentucky. That was the day Georgea's life changed forever. After her father's death, Georgea learned a very painful thing about her mother. All that her father was she wasn't, her heart was cold and she did not take kindly to mixing life or blood especially with Negroes. Mrs. Quickman had also trained up Georgea's sister Viola the same way and it was because of this that they were one in the same.

Viola, although she was the eldest had a deep jealousy of the relationship Georgea had with their father. The fishing trips that Georgea and her friends went on in the mountains with her father attested to that. Viola just didn't have the patience or the desire to explore outside of the privileged southern aristocratic lifestyle both she and her little sister had been accustomed to. Nevertheless, it was Georgea's adventurous spirit during those yearly treks into the mountains with her father that afforded her the knowledge of how to maneuver through the Indian routes she explored as a child. So, on that brisk fall day when her sister Viola sent mercenaries with a message of mercy to either disappear forever or find her daughters lifeless on any given day in their beds, she didn't think twice. She knew her sister Viola had a sickness that resonated as hate and misery on her demented spirit.

Georgea's quick wit led her to the sanctuary of the Smokey Mountains that cloaked the western skyline of Memphis. Although heartbroken and defeated for a time, Georgea had her father to thank for saving her life. The unconceivable sacrifice she would have to make to save the lives of her children left her sad and eager to take revenge on her sister. Patience, hope and faithfulness had kept Georgea's spirit at peace until that day she came across Jonas, an angel she thought heaven sent. She told him everything about her life and Jonas thought he had to be dreaming to have come across this legend of a woman who called herself Georgea. As much as he knew it would hurt he felt it only right to tell her about Mr. Sawyer and how he'd been sick and passed away. He watched as the tears filled her eyes and she moaned quietly as she sat down in the meadow like a little girl burying her face in her knees and hands. Jonas thought about his own mother, he knew what it was like not to have the love and tenderness that only a mother could provide. His mother was no longer in his life and to know that the Sawyer sister's mother was alive and they were being deprived of what they so very much needed didn't sit well with his spirit.

Adrienne Lynn Rutherford

Georgea had sworn Jonas to silence, not to speak a word of what she had told him especially to the girls. As long as her sister was alive they all would truly be in danger. Confused by the events that were taking place, Jonas explained he could not promise her what he would or would not do. It took him quite a while to accept the silence that Georgea requested of him. The Sawyer girls were his family and to hold this information from them and especially Queen, would be the end of life as he knew it for sure. However, Jonas eventually accepted the fate that he would have to face after that day and he understood his higher purpose for the Sawyer Family. Now, he was the life line for Georgea to the lives of her daughters and he brought her pictures and visited the mountain more sharing stories of their lives over the years and the beautiful women they'd become. She would smile with joy at the stories of her eldest daughter Queen. Georgea knew when she was a child that she would grow up to be a strong woman. She'd become proud of her twins as well their strength in the arts and thankful for the investment their father put into their education. Queen had become the rock, she'd grown up fearless and Georgea was proud of the strength she had to care for and love her younger sisters. Jonas kept his vow of secrecy for years concerning the girls, however after the recent events he thought it was necessary to speak to Georgea. The girls were in danger and they needed to talk.

Jonas thoughts where interrupted by the loud noise of children playing hide-go-seek near the entrance of the hidden community of the Cherokee Clan. He was greeted by Lone Wolf and both gave the other a heartfelt embrace.

"Home to stay young sparrow."

"Not this time, just visiting."

"How are things?"

"Things are good, the weather has been in our favor this year, and the land has been moist and providing good crop."

"Is Miss Georgea around?"

"Yes, she's in her cabin."

"Thanks, I will see you before I go."

Lone Wolf nodded as Jonas made his way over to Georgea's place. She moved to the small community upon the insistence of Jonas so that she would no longer be alone on the mountain.

He knocked on the door and slowly the door opened.

"Come in Son, I've been expecting you."

Jonas walked into the dimly lit cabin and notice Georgea sitting in the corner in her chair.

"Afternoon Miss Georgea, I was coming to see you and got so much to tell you."

"Yes, I know son, I know."

"Where are my girls?"

"They're gone."

"Far away from here, to Oklahoma."

Jonas then pulled out his pocket watch.

"They should be with Mr. Sawyer's sister by now."

Georgea raised up in her chair.

"Ma'me?"

"They are with Ma'me?"

"Yes ma'am."

"Thank you, dear God."

"Here sit down, you want some tea and sweet bread."

"No thank you."

"Jonas, what happened son?"

"Well, me and Connie weren't there we were at the theatre. When I brought her back home, we walked into the kitchen and seen your nephew, I mean Rodger Quickman dead on the kitchen floor."

"Queen stabbed him to death to protect Carolyn, he tried to rape her Mrs. Sawyer."

"Oh my God, sweet Jesus those poor girls."

"I have to go to them."

"I have to go to them."

"Ma'am I don't think that will be a good idea."

"Not just yet anyway, the Medusa has the whole city on edge and she's offering a king's ransom for the girls."

"Even has the police captain on her payroll, they came to my place snooping around asking questions about the girls."

Adrienne Lynn Rutherford

Georgea got up and went for her shot gun.

"I'm going to go down and see my sister, she has created enough havoc in that town."

"She's ruined the life of my husband and now she is trying to kill my children, God have mercy on my soul."

"I will take her life today."

Georgea then began to cry.

"Her and my mother, they have tainted my father's legacy, but

"I will fix it, I will fix it."

Jonas got up and grabbed the rifle's nose.

"No, Miss Georgea there is a better way, we can get you to the girls but we have to have a plan."

"You have to remember you and those girls are the only heirs left to your father's legacy."

"You don't want it to be left in her hands do you?"

"If you go down there like this, she will use you, use you to get to the girls and after that who knows what she may do."

"The girls are fine, I will go to Oklahoma to check on them once things cool down, but in the meantime you have to be patient."

"They haven't seen you in almost twenty years, so we have to approach this more sensibly."

Georgea slowly began to calm down as she sat down at the table.

"Your right Jonas, I'm nothing like her, nothing at all."

"God can handle people far better than we can son."

Georgea knew that Jonas was right, and besides she'd waited this long to see the girls, what would a few more weeks hurt. Her biggest concern was if they were safe and she knew if they were with Ma'me nothing could happen to them. She was also happy that her prayers all these years where finally being answered. The only thing that kept her sane in this world was the hope of seeing her babies again and now that she knew the day would truly come and come soon all was right with her world.

****

Although Mitchell Quickman had almost tripled the Dupree fortune after marrying Violette, it was no matter to his wife. His loving kindness would not be enough to sustain her after discovering secrets in her family that would turn her heart cold and ruin her forever. Viola was much like her mother and as a result after her father passed she vowed in all her bitterness to keep the traditions of the Dupree's and with full support of her mother. Never mind that the country was changing, never mind that the world was changing. The main thing that resonated with Viola regarding the Quickman estate, was to do everything she possibly could to hold on to what she thought was the *true* family legacy. The years had passed swiftly for Viola and now after the traumatic incident and loss of her only son, she had much to consider. The loans that she'd taken out on the Quickman Mines where not quite paid off and Viola was drowning in debt. She attempted to compensate through contracts with the state prison system to use inmates as a means of cheap labor, but it was not enough and eventually she would no longer be able to keep up her loan payments with the bank. Viola's only recourse now was a meeting with her partners out west to re-negotiate her contractual business agreement as soon as possible.

Not realizing the time, her thoughts were interrupted by the captain.

"Afternoon Miss Quickman."

"Good morning, you have anything for me today."

"We're still working on it, we've checked the train stations and ticket purchases for the last couple of days, thinking maybe they were here and waited for a clean break, but so far we've come up with nothing."

"If you didn't know, I am not paying you what I do to keep this thing within the realms of your law captain, sometimes you must think outside the box, if you know what I mean."

"Currently I have some more pressing problems and must put this investigation on the backburner, but that doesn't mean that you should not be resourceful and diligently continue to find out what it is you can."

"Somebody knows something and like my mama always said everything will come out in the wash, therefore I have decided to increase the reward to ten thousand for Queen and fifty-five hundred for each of her sisters."

Adrienne Lynn Rutherford

"I am planning a business trip and will be leaving this evening, you need not contact me, I will contact you when I return."

"By then you should have some type of lead for me, I would hate to come home and you have found nothing."

"If you're unable to fulfill the obligations you promised in a civilized manner, I do have people who can, although they will not be so civilized."

"That is all for now, you may leave."

The captain without a word removed himself from the chair and the presence of Viola Quickman.

"What a sad and lonely wicked woman."

He said to himself as he was escorted from her presence.

Chapter 11

Oklahoma, Northside Greenwood District

Ma'me sat at the dining room table with her family, Becky had come home to the surprise of her life later that evening when she seen her cousin Queen sitting on the porch with her mother. She had no reservations of who she was and hugged her endlessly and grabbed hold of her twin cousins as well, giving them the most tender embrace they'd had since their mother had left many years ago.

Queen at that moment realized all that she had been through growing up back home. She'd grown up too fast and it truly affected her memory of some of the very best times she'd had in her life. Although her reason for returning was a botched one, Queen was still grateful to have had the opportunity of returning to the place she'd had some of her finest times as a child. Those solemn days she'd experienced back home in Memphis had overshadowed and almost destroyed the softest part of who she really was. It was now in Greenwood that she could feel the joy and comfort of what love and family really was again.

Queen had not told Ma'me everything surrounding their reason for coming to Tulsa, but she would soon enough. Right now, she watched the laughter of her sisters as they became acquainted with a family they had never known. Therefore, she decided this time would be spent enjoying a little peace and solitude with loved ones. As they went through the family pictures, the girls could see their father in his younger years and their mother Georgea. Soon Queen came across a picture of her and two other boys.

"Who are these boys with me Aunt Ma'me."

"Give it to me, let me look."

Queen then passed the picture to Ma'me.

"Chile, you know who that is that's your cousin William there on the right of you and the other fella you know him that's Calvin."

"He brought you here this afternoon."

Queen was startled and snatched the picture out of Ma'mes hand. She then looked at it again more closely.

"Oh, my goodness, I remember now, oh my goodness."
Queen put her hand over her chest, then she put it on her forehead.

"Oh, I can't believe it, I just can't believe it."
The twins said in unison.

"Believe what?"

Carolyn took the picture out of Queen's hand and she and Connie looked it over.
She then pointed to Calvin.

"Okay sis let me get this straight."

"Is this the tall dark handsome man that had his eyes all over you at the train station. The same one who sat next to us in silence and I might add, waited for us to get off the train and offered us a ride."

Queen began to laugh.

"That rascal, he knew all along."

"And besides, how was I supposed to know who he was?"

"We didn't call him that, that wasn't his name, it was ummm Hannibal."

"He told me his name was Hannibal."

Carolyn and Connie spoke in unison again.

"What?"

"Yeah Hannibal, I was seven years old okay."

"I called him what he wanted to be called."

"Anyway, enough about him."

"Where is Wil?"

"We been here all day and he hasn't showed up yet?"

"Is he coming home?"

Becky's smile suddenly turned into a frown as she walked into the kitchen to the icebox and poured her something cold.

"He's playing with the forbidden fruit."
This time all the sisters looked confused at Becky

"Wil knows he should've been back across the tracks before dark, but some little young white woman over there has got his nose wide open and some days just like this one I think he just a little too risky for his own damn good."
Ma'me shook her head in agreement.

"I see that too."

Dance of Angels   85

"But, it's not her that worries me, shoot I don't trust them men folk in that family of hers."

"Addie Mae who works over at the McIntyre Place, well she told me about that uncle of hers, they got *the thirst* in them you know."

Carolyn looked confused at Ma'me trying to figure out what she was speaking of.

"Aunt Ma'me, what's the *thirst?*"

"Well dear, when I was coming up *the thirst* meant a yearning for the blood of a negro, see for some   of them the hate is so deep in them, the only way they can relieve that rage is tormenting negro folks in some form or fashion.

"It thrills them to just stand there watching a human being's body jerk and tremble until the life leave out of them."

Becky then shouted.

"Ma'me stop!"

Ma'me then shook her head.

"It's the truth I tell you, they have pictures to prove it!"

"Addie Mae says she hears the evil conversations they have on the south side, been that way for years I tell you."

"Humph, don't you dare shush Ma'me."

"Too many times I have seen that type of situation go just bad, just bad."

Them southside girls, they get pressured by their brother's, father's and the likes to leave these northside boys be and after enough coaxing they either runaway with them boys or turn against them."

"And if they decide to turn against them, lawd help em."

As if he'd heard them speaking his name William came through the door, and just like his mother he was surprised to see the house full of company.

"Hey Ma, Hey Ma'me."

"Who's these young beautiful women taking up space in my castle."

He then looked at them again."

"Q, is that you?"

"Good lord, come here girl, I ain't seen you in twenty years,

Adrienne Lynn Rutherford

look at you girl fine as wine"

"Who these other ladies with you?"

"Oh, goodness gracious William, you haven't changed a bit put me down with your crazy self, these are my sister's and your cousins."

"Twins uh?"

The girls said in unison

"Yes cousin, twins"

He then gave them each a big hug

William still feeling the effects of the few shots he'd had for his night cap began rubbing on his head.

"What the heck is going on around here, really though?"

"When yawl get in?"

"Where's Uncle Bufus and Aunt Georgea?"

Soon the room became silent.

"No, don't tell me, I know, I know."

"He then went over to Ma'me and held her tight.

She held on to him and for the first time since the girls arrived Ma'me let out a moan of hurt as if she'd been waiting on William to come home to console her aching heart.

William sat on the side of Ma'me and after she was about to pull herself together, she made no reservation about saying her peace to William.

"William, I don't like it, I don't like it."

William concerned with the look on Ma'mes face.

"What is it Ma'me, what is it?"

"You is what it is, hanging over across the tracks after dark, it's just dangerous son and you playing with fire."

"Ain't no women folk worth you losing your life for white or black."

William although he knew the concern that Ma'me and his mother had for him, he seen things a tad bit different.

"Listen, I am a man not no child, I don't care what those people say, I go where I want to go."

"Now I'm not gonna talk about it no more."

He kissed all the beautiful women in his family and went out the front door. Connie was impressed by her cousin's integrity as a man. However, she could not understand his foolishness for risking his life. Becky shook her head as she watched him disappear out of the screen door into the darkness.

"Where's he going?"

"Chile around on the side of the house is a duster cellar we use it for emergencies like twister weather, but that Wil has turned it into his very own personal lodge."

"He's so talented with the bricks among other things."

"I don't know why he insist on working over there across the tracks w for that watchmaker, been doing it for some years now. He could make a decent living working for himself right here in Greenwood District."

Becky got up and begin clearing the table of the coffee cups and remaining biscuits they'd shared.

"It's just a shame how things happened to Uncle Bufus like they did."

"And your mother, yawl don't know if she dead or alive."

"Queen you never got the story from your daddy about what happen?"

"It just doesn't seem right, her just up and leaving like that with no good bye or nothing."

"Georgea just wasn't that type of woman."

"Do you think someone took her or something."

"I just don't know what to think Becky, hell I didn't have time to think about nothing cause when daddy got sick I had to step it up, look after my sisters and care for him. There was no money coming in anymore because daddy couldn't work, and the people that he had accounts with who owed him money didn't wanna give us what was owed to my father. So, we just lived off Papa's savings for a while, but when he left us well, we were a few dollars shy of being evicted from our home. You know how the bank is about their money. The man from the bank was coming around every other day. I was working at the State Hospital at the time and soon I was just fresh out of ideas."

"Something told me not to give that man all my father's savings and I didn't."

"That's when I met Miss Greta aww man, she was a life saver I tell you."

"Who is she Carolyn?"

"She owns the *Venus Alley* in the red-light district back home in Memphis."

Then Connie spoke.

"It's of real French décor"

Carolyn laughed at her sister

"Yeah, Queen was performing there four nights a week and they absolutely loved her."

"She was making a lot of money."

Queen tried to distract the girls, but it was no use.

Connie agreed.

"Yes, she was known as the Black Butterfly and she was great wasn't she Carolyn.

"Yes, she still is."

"Everyone loved her, she's being modest right now, but that girl got some vocal cords on her and the skits she and Carolyn wrote made her one of the most popular entertainers on Beale Street."

"Ain't that right Queen?"

"Enough already you guys."

"I did what I had to do to make ends meet It just turned out to be a lucrative choice that allowed us to live a decent life without the threat of having to live on the street."

"I am quite grateful for the opportunity."

Becky stood and listened to the girls, but was not getting a full understanding of what this performance really was.

"Sooo…. Queen you perform, what do you do?"

Carolyn interrupted again."

"Burlesque."

Becky's eyes widened with surprise.

"You're kidding, no way, how?

"What?"

"Hush yourself."

Queen began to laugh.

"Yes, cousin I am a *Burlesque.*"

Then Connie interrupted.

"She's so good too."

Becky didn't hesitate to offer her idea to Queen.

"Queen, right now I'm managing the Paradise Club down near Greenwood Avenue. It's a quaint little place very modest yet edgy and the band is great, but keeping good talent has been such a struggle."

"I'm always looking for performers."

"Would you mind, I mean I know your here on vacation and all, but it would be just sugar if you would perform for us."

"No problem, I would love to perform for you. I did bring a costume or two."

"I think it would be a good idea, I need to come and see your set up for the place."

Then Carolyn interrupted.

"I would like to come too, I want to see the piano."

"You do have a piano, don't you?"

Becky smiled.

"Instruments have never been a problem, we have a full band, they are the one thing that's keeping us open right now."

"But, a surprise like Queen down at the Paradise is really going to get a good time going."

Becky, what about props is there something that I could use in my skit?"

"Chile it's so much stuff in the attic of that place, you can help yourself and come on down and peek at whatever you want up there."

She then smiled.

"Hopefully I can get you to stay for a spell huh?"
Queen returned the smile.

"We'll see cousin, we'll see."

Ma'me slowly raised herself up from the table and reached for her walking cane.

"Well family, Ma'me is getting tired I'm gonna go on upstairs and get myself ready for the bed."

"Imma see you girls in the morning."

"Becky, can you get them settled in and show them the guest room where they can sleep."

Adrienne Lynn Rutherford

Later that evening after everyone was settled in a space, Becky made her way into Ma'me bedroom. Ma'me was up reading her Bible and looked at her daughter over her glasses and smiled.

"Chile what took you so long get in here and shut that doe." Becky came in and slowly closed the door behind her, then she crawled up on her mother's bed liked she use to as a little girl and long sat up against the soft down pillows on the head board next to her mother.

"Chile, I know you knew I was shocked when Calvin brought them girls to my door step unannounced."

"What happened Ma'me?"

"I didn't want to seem as though I was prying"

"They're family so they're always welcomed here."

"It's some strange things going on back there in Memphis and them girls is the only ones who know exactly why they're here and how long they plan on staying."

"I haven't heard from anybody in almost fifteen years, that oldest girl you know she was a child, now she a grown woman and she got two more sisters."

"Ma'me are you going to talk to her?"

"Of course, Imma talk to her."

"That Queen should know Ma'me and if she doesn't know. she will really soon."

"I gave them some room tonight to settle in, I'm sure it was a long journey from Memphis to Tulsa."

"But it's one thing you know Ma'me don't tolerate is bullshit."

"I don't take kindly to bullshit."

"Especially in my house, you should've seen them when they arrived."

"As much as that girl wanted to look like they were just coming for a visit I could tell her and them sisters of hers had gathered all of nothing and what they could and stuffed it in a carpet bag."

"I will get to the bottom of this and she gonna have to tell me what happened to her mama and her daddy."

"The truth!"

"Or else she'll have to get her narrow ass outta here, and I mean it."

"Ma'me don't want no bad news coming to my doorstep, that I ain't tolerating."

"But Ma'me you can't put them out, they may have no other place to go."

"I'm happy to see Queen, I always wondered why they never came back."

"And why didn't you keep in contact with Uncle Bufus anyway?"

Ma'me then bowed her head thinking briefly about the last time she would see her brother Bufus Sawyer. It was a day she would regret for the rest of her life.

"Ma'me, did you hear me, why didn't you reach out to Uncle Bufus and Aunt Georgea?"

Ma'me then grabbed her handkerchief and wiped her eyes.

"Reached out?"

"I did many times to my brother, but he never ever responded to my messages."

"So, I just gave up."

"Just want them girls to come clean with Ma'me is all, they my family, my only brother's children and my home is their home."
Ma'me then smiled at the thought of her older brother.

"To be honest I did think I would see him again though."

"That and he would come back home with that nice black top hat on his head in a clean suit with suspenders and that big grin to greet his baby sister at least one more time."

She then wiped her eyes once more as Becky gave her a comforting hug.

"But, he didn't and I will take the blame for some of that."

"At the same time, Becky, I still believe them girls is running from something and I'm gonna get to the bottom of it."

Chapter 12

Calvin got up early that morning thinking about the meeting that he and his partners would have with Viola Quickman, more interesting enough he was looking forward to hearing her story. The newspapers were hardly ever good with the details of such a high-profile murder in such a high-profile family. Whatever the reason for such a brutal death Calvin's intuition told him, knowing Rodger personally it was probably due to his lack of reasonable judgement. As he drove down the narrow unpaved road he thought about the progress that he was gradually making while back home. It was always good to have a piece of property in those places you enjoyed being in the most and Greenwood was no exception. Although there was nothing that interested him in Greenwood district, he was able to purchase a modest ranch about four miles further north of his brother's place in the town of Oakhurst. When he signed the agreement he also added his sister Cody's name to the deed. It would be his gift to her after returning from college if she so chose. If not, she could sell it and make a pretty penny. The wealth that Calvin had acquired over the years was a good thing, however him being able to present it to his family and the people he loved was difficult for him at best.

After stopping by to spend time with his mother and little sister, Calvin finally made his way back to his brother's place and to his surprise William had finally showed his face. They were both in the recreation room playing billiards with John.

"Finally, the eagle has landed."

"Wil man what's going on, how life been treating you."
Both men grabbed the others hand pulled them into their chest and embraced.

"Hey man I can't complain, same ole same ole, a little bit of this a little bit of that"

"What's going on with you."

"This is a surprise no doubt man, I must say it's been far too long."

"Welcome back man."

"I missed you at the house, but I ran into your dad in town and he told me you were probably staying out here with this old hound dog."

"Yeah, me and my pops... well you know how that go, man it's good to be back home and see my folks though."

John interrupted the two as he waited for William to take his turn on the table."

"It's on you man."

William turned around and smiled."

"You see that Calvin; your brother is anxious to get a whipping on his own pool table."

"Seven ball corner pocket."

William pulled the stick back and forth measuring softly where he would aim on the white ball and gave the stick a quick push through his fingers and watched it hit the seven ball as it fell swiftly into the corner pocket hole.

"Eight ball side pocket."

Again, with the precision of a professional he measured his target point on the white ball, this time softly hitting it up against the side of the table and watched as it bounced off and slowly tapped the eight ball into the side pocket."

He then threw his hands up.

"Game!"

John shook his head.

"You know what I don't understand, how this man can come into my house and beat me in three rounds of pool on my own damn table."

Calvin laughed.

"Because brother you probably hardly play."

"Your right Calvin he doesn't."

"You guys want a drink?"

"Got some of the good stuff."

The men nodded and continued catching up while John went over to his modest bar and poured them all a drink."

Calvin took a swallow.

"This is Canadian."

"Yeah, Oh I guess you had a taste on your adventures

"I've had a few bottles in my time."

William then turned his glass up and sat it on the table."

"Heard you bumped into Queen and her sisters at the train station."

"Yeah man, now that was a pleasant surprise."

"Well man, I got the surprise of my life when I saw cousin Queen."

"It had been years brother and she brought two more that look just like her."

John laughed.

"All of those girls got fire, you can tell they're well equipped to take care of themselves."

"Can't be fooled by them soft pretty faces they have, that's for sure."

"Something tells me a man will come up short if he crossed any of those three."

William nodded in agreement.

"You about right man, I remember Queen being a tough one.

Calvin smiled.

"Yeah she wasn't so tough that day she got stuck in the tree and was scared to climb down."

"Climbed up all that way to the top with William and was scared to come down at the church Bar-B-Que."

"Remember that?"

William shook his head.

"How could I forget it?"

Calvin laughed and looked over at John.

"Then Wil came and got me, because he didn't wanna get into trouble."

"Yeah only because you were the tallest cat I knew and Ma'me told me to stay out of the trees."

"That was the first time I saw her, she seemed like just a little girl then. I had to climb way up there in that tree and that girl still wouldn't come down."

"So, I had to tell her I was a Prince that came to rescue her and then she asked me my name."

Calvin shook his head and smiled.

"I knew Calvin didn't sound much like a Prince, so I told her to call me Hannibal and it worked."

Both men looked at Calvin and laughed.

"Hannibal?"

Calvin still smiling while thinking about the meeting at the train station and the day he rescued her shook his drink around in his glass and turned it up.

"I knew who she was the moment I laid eyes on her, although I was thrown back by her sisters. I knew that It was Queen from that heart shaped birth mark on the side of her cheek."

"I remembered it because I had never seen anything like it before. She grew up to be a fine-looking woman and I realized just a few hours ago, that I wasn't that much older than her at all."

"Man, we were just kids then, but you, you were a big kid."

William and John begin to laugh as Calvin shook his head at them both.

After listening to Calvin's conversation about reacquainting with his childhood friend, William shook his head and smiled.

"Man, you got a thing for Queen, don't you?"

Calvin nodded in agreement as he leaned down to the table to take his shot.

"Man, I been thinking about that girl since I dropped her off at Ma'me."

"I don't know but it's something about her man, she got this energy man that draws me to her." I don't know, it's crazy man."

"I haven't felt this type of way about no woman."

William shook his head at his friend.

"Jesus man, you just got back, you ain't even got your feet wet yet and you falling in love with the first woman you see."

"I had plans for us this Friday night at the Paradise club."

William wiped off both his shirt collars.

"I'm getting suited up all nice, you know how I do it."

"You gotta spread yourself around some man."

John laughed at his dear brother, he'd never seen him so vulnerable when it came to the ladies.

"Well fellas, its first Friday for me out here and I got friends flying in with Tequila."

Adrienne Lynn Rutherford

"The house will be open Friday night, yawl can come here after you leave the Paradise and stay overnight there's plenty of room." William smiled, it's that time again?"

"Yep."

Calvin looked confused, what's first Friday?"

"Just be here man."

The men spent the remainder of the night talking about old times. Calvin although he wanted to share his success with his brother and best friend he would do it at the right time. One thing he didn't want to do is overwhelm anyone with the fact that they would no longer have to work again for anyone the rest of their lives. This news would have to be a gradual introduction one he would present to them soon enough. In the meantime, Calvin's thoughts went back to the lovely Queen. She'd blossomed into a beautifully sensuous woman. Calvin knew that he'd fallen for her, he only hoped that he could get the opportunity to spend time with her. He wanted to know for himself if she felt the same energy that had captivated him. He smiled to himself as he thought how innocently she did not remember Hannibal the prince that rescued her so very long ago.

Chapter 13

On Friday afternoon, while Ma'me took her favorite place on the front porch, Queen and her sisters went down to the Paradise Club with Becky. Queen wanted to check the club out along with the stage and the props that Becky spoke of. When she entered the small but quaint place, Queen was amazed at the solid red brick and mortar walls that gave it a unique appeal. She was somewhat familiar with the fine masonry and carpentry that went into the unique foundation thanks to her father Buford Sawyer. However, it was something different about this building with its tall lean appearance and historical uniqueness. The floors were a cedar wood of a finely tempered richness. Carolyn right away could easily compare them to the photographs of those wealthy New England homes back east. However, what stood out the most would be the master carpentry that went into the beautiful woodwork along the sides of the wall and the newly fixtured stained glass lanterns that lined them all which made for what Queen imagined as a classy yet eloquent atmosphere. The bar took up the entire north side of the wall and the stage the west side. The curtains were dark and weathered as if they had been hanging since its first grand opening, possibly quite some time ago. Queen stepped up on the stage and walked back and forth trying to get a feel of its sturdiness.

"This is a good performing stage, I think I can manage."

Carolyn after noticing the piano went over and begin playing with the keys to check for tuning. She then sat down and began playing the tune of one of Queen's more popular skits, *To Crazy, Too Cool.* Becky, smiled as she sat on the stool next to Connie as Queen began her dance.

She hiked her dress up showing her pantaloons and strutted fiercely across the floor. She then stopped in the middle and put her hand on her hip and blew them all a big kiss

"Yawl ain't ready for this."

Becky began to laugh with her cousin as she shook her head in amusement.

"C'mon, don't stop now, why don't you show us what you got."

Adrienne Lynn Rutherford

Becky was amazed at Queen's voice and her act as she performed flawlessly while even wearing a waist dress and shirt.

After she finished there was a loud clap from high up in the shadows of the second floor. It was Tyler Parker, owner of the Paradise.

After he made his way downstairs to the bar, he took a drag of his cigar and smiled.

"Well what do we have here?"

Becky approached him.

"Hey boss, these are my cousins from back east this is Connie her twin sister Carolyn is on the piano and on stage performing one of her many skits is the dance extraordinaire Queen.

He then nodded to both young ladies.

"Wow you guys sounded really good from up there, so I had to come and see what was going on."

Queen jumped off the stage and went to join them at the bar and extended her hand to Tyler.

"Hello nice to meet you sir."

Tyler took Queen by the hand and brought it close to his chest near his heart.

"I think I just met my guardian angel, I've been waiting so patiently for you."

"Oh really?"

"Well this angel sure ain't no guardian honey so, you best be finding another tour guide on this here trip through life, because I can barely find my own way right about now."

Tyler began to laugh out loud.

"Ah, a sense of humor too."

"Hey Becky, I like her, I like her a lot."

"Queen you got talent, do you plan on gracing my stage this fine evening."

"Well that's what I came her for, to check it out, Becky said you have some costumes in the attic."

"Well I do, I had some fine ladies come through here and left some fine things over the years, your welcomed to any and everything that is there."

Queen smiled.

"I must let you know my show doesn't require a lot of costume only in the right places."

"Of course, of course"

"Burlesque, is it?"

"Yes, how did you know?"

"Been in this business a long time and seen a lot of things, I know the difference between a simple show girl side show and the art of Burlesque, that was Burlesque."

Carolyn joined them.

"Your absolutely right sir, and my sister is the best."

"Are you interested in booking her for this evening show?"

"We would have to make financial arrangements of course."

"Wow, Carolyn is it, you don't waste much time on the business flip side."

"No sir I do not, especially when there is money on the table."

"Okay that's fine, I can live with that."

"Becky, can you get word out about this rare gift that has adorned us with her presence?"

Becky smiled.

"I'm already on it boss."

"Good then, ladies until this evening."

Tyler tipped his hat to the women and retired back to his office.

After stocking the bar for the night Becky led Queen and the girls to the attic. Once they made it to the top she felt along the wall and flicked on the switch. The first thing to catch their eye was the large trunk that sat alone in the rear of the small room. Queen didn't hesitate as she opened it up and inside she found many beautiful feathered head pieces of all colors. Carolyn right away picked up one and placed it on her head while the other girls laughed. Connie went for one of the smaller trunks against the wall and inside she found beautiful fans and gloves and a two-piece outfit.

"Queen come over here I think you're going love what I found over here."

She pulled out the beautiful white set embroidered with pearls and rhinestones. The two pieces where connected by thin chains that draped in three layers on each side of the brassiere.

Adrienne Lynn Rutherford

Queen looked at the piece while Connie held it up to the light, she then walked over to inspect it more closely.

"That is a very beautiful piece, it's absolutely amazing Connie." Connie agreed.

"Yeah, it needs a little cleaning though."

Becky joined them.

"That won't be a problem at all, we can take it over to Maxi's Cleaners and she'll have that cleaned up in no time."

"She's good at what she does."

Queen smiled.

"That would be great!"

"I love it."

****

While the ladies where contemplating the night to come, Tyler Parker sat behind his desk in his beautifully adorned oak wood office going over his bank statement and adding up all that he'd acquired these past eight years at Paradise Club. Although his plan was a far greater success than he anticipated, he still felt like he was in prison.

Tyler was born to a family of freedman who had the opportunity to escape slavery before the Emancipation Proclamation. He'd travel many places with his parents and was afforded many opportunities than most of his peers. However, a tragedy struck as his parents would lose their lives to a deadly disease that left him alone at eight years of age in St. Louis Missouri. Fear of being subjected to the harsh life of being a negro orphan, he and several other peers would be successful at escaping this life and took to the streets of St Louis. It was here he learned how to survive on his own, as he quickly developed the skill of pick pocketing as his primary means of survival. Overtime, he became anxious and very bitter inside about the circumstances that he felt forced to live in. Nevertheless, his fate would soon change after pick pocketing a very distinguished gentleman by the name of Dorian Francoise. Dorian was a wealthy merchant and ship captain from the country of Haiti. He owned a modest fleet of six ships that imported a variety spices well as rum to the United States. Also, thanks to the interest of foreigners from many distant lands and his influences along the coast of Central America he could acquire some of the most exotic fineries from all over the world for sell and trade. After Tyler was seen by Mr. Francoise's distinguished Butler Sabastian stealing his employer's wallet he quickly snatched him up by his trousers.

Tyler fought the best he could to escape the grasps of the well-built gentlemen, however his efforts would be futile. Dorian was quite amazed at the young man's skill, as he himself had also been a professional pick pocket in his youthful days back in Haiti. Tyler thought for sure his life was over as he had known it, however to his surprise Mr. Francoise offered him and his friends a job aboard his ships traveling abroad. He promised Tyler he would see the world and he didn't turn back on his promise as Tyler sailed to places as far off as Europe and Morocco as a shipmate. After overcoming seasickness, he would acquire a love for the ocean and the adventures that it afforded him in their journeys. Dorian had grown to trust Tyler raising him like a son of his own. Soon Tyler would become a man and on his twentieth birthday Captain Dorian Francoise gave Tyler the surprise of his life. A smaller ship in his fleet named *The Essence*. His crew would consist of the very young men that he ran the streets of St. Louis with many years before. Captain Francoise was very impressed by Tyler and his business savvy and reared him with profitable returns. Everything was well in his life until the day he would meet Macia, a beautiful young woman from Barbados. Tyler would see her near the Pub on the docks when he came in with his monthly shipment. To Tyler, her looks were captivating and overtime he fell in love with her. Each time he stopped in Port Barbados they would spend intimate time together. Soon Macia would join him in his travels. Tyler introduced her to his life and eventually entrusted her with his manifest and business dealings until one day she would betray him and make his heart cold. Her betrayal resulted in Tyler losing his most expensive cargo of the season.

Although Tyler and a few of his crewman managed to survive, he knew he would have to answer to Mr. Francoise. He'd broken the number one rule; never mix business with pleasure, especially the pleasure of a Caribbean dock girl. Once Mr. Francoise found out about the turn of events and Tyler's lack of insight and judgement he became frustrated and angry with Tyler. Therefore, like any father

Adrienne Lynn Rutherford

aiming to discipline their son for irresponsible behavior he took his ship and vowed not to return it until he paid back all that was owed on the shipment that was lost. Tyler like a man accepted his consequences and vowed to pay Captain Francoise every penny that he owed him. However, admittedly ashamed of his irresponsible acts he found solace in the most prestigious Negro community of "Northside Greenwood District"of Tulsa Oklahoma. Tyler, was allowed a small fortune to live on and established a means to increase his wealth. He purchased and opened the Paradise Club with the hope of generating enough income to support him paying off his debt to Captain Francoise and set sail as the Captain of *The Essence* once again.

After choosing a couple more costumes from the trunk Queen and the ladies made their way to the dry cleaners and then went back to Ma'mes. When they got there, she was in her favorite place on the porch and this time she had the gramophone and she was listening to some of her favorite spiritual hymns from the Fisk University Jubilee Choir.

"Evening girls, where yawl been?"

"Yawl left Ma'me here asleep and didn't wake me up."

"Thanks for the breakfast though and that fresh coffee Becky."

Becky smiled at her mother and placed a kiss on her cheek.

"You always welcome Ma."

"I took the girls down to the Club and let me tell you that Queen sure knows how to put on a show I tell you."

"Ma, you should come on down to the club with us tonight and watch her perform."

"Mr. Tyler was very impressed, and you should have seen the look on his face."

"He hired her right there on the spot, no questions asked."

"He must have been awfully impressed, because he is a hard nut to crack."

Becky then started dancing the two-step in the middle of the porch.

"I can't wait for tonight, girl you gone have them fellas here in Greenwood District in a frizzy."

Ma'me looked over at Queen, impressed.

"That's good to hear girl, you come right here and got yourself a job, just like Ma'me, you don't waste no time."   "I think I will just hangout around here tonight and wait for you to come home and tell Ma'me all about it, how's that."

"Aw Ma, just think about it, you hardly go anywhere."

"It won't be long, I promise I will get you home directly as soon as Queen finishes her act.":

"Okay, okay, I'll see how Ma'me feels later."

Ma'me then turned her attention to Queen.

"Queen, I wanna speak with you for a minute or two, you girls go on inside and let us be."

"I made some nice fresh ice tea with a splash of fresh lemon in the icebox."

"The others went on inside and Queen went to the swing chair and sat next to Ma'me."

"Chile, you are sitting next to an old woman, a woman who have seen many things and been through many things; I'm telling you da truth."

"I love you dearly, just like you were my very own, but you and me both know that your surprise visit to see old Ma'me somehow has a trail of tears behind it."

"Now my thing is to make sure them trail of tears don't affect the life we have here girl, you understand what I'm saying."

Queen nodded her head in confirmation.

"Yes Ma'me."

"Good then, so you wanna tell me what's going on with you and them sistas of yours?"

Queen didn't have the heart to lie to her Aunt and she had so much built up in her since they all left Memphis. She wanted to talk to someone about the tragic events that occurred back home. Although she had been strong for her and her sisters up to this point, the burden was weighing heavier on her by the day.

"Well, I guess at this point, the only way I can start off is to just start."

"Go ahead girl, I'm listening."

"Ma'me since we left here the last time when I was just a girl so much had happened. Mama got pregnant with the girls and things where so happy for all of us, but after a few years she became so sad."

"Then one-day papa brought us all home from the school house and she wasn't there."

"Just up and left disappeared into thin air."

"It really hurt me, and my sisters would cry nights at a time."

"It was awful for a long while, and it never got better. Watching papa, it was if his soul had been snatched right out of him."

"He spent so much money and time looking for mama going this place and that place always coming up empty handed."

"The last time he came back home he was sick with pneumonia, it was like he'd given up all together."

"A month later he went on to be with the Lord, and as for mama we didn't talk about her no more, we just made up in our mind that her and papa were together."

"I didn't mean no harm in not calling you and telling you what was going on, I just didn't think about it."

"We managed and was able to stay in our home until two days ago, something very bad happened and we had to get out of there. A man, a very sick white man."

"Well he tried to rape Carolyn in our home, in our goddamned home!"

Queen began to cry and Ma'me passed her the handkerchief from her apron."

"I walked in and seen my sister lying on that floor with him in between her legs trying to violate her very soul, I didn't think about it, I didn't think Ma'me."

"I went to the cutlery holder on the kitchen counter and I grabbed the biggest sharpest butcher knife I could find and I stabbed him."

"I killed a man Ma'me, I killed a man!"

"Ma'me grabbed hold of Queen and held her really tight, she then started humming her favorite spiritual to her. She rocked and rocked her until she could get a hold of herself.

"You ain't gotta worry about nothing now, you hear?"

"You are safe here with us, you can stay long as you like"

"You here?"

"Yes Ma'am."

Queen wiped her eyes and pulled herself together, she didn't want the girls to see her this way.

"Thank you so much aunt Ma'me, as bad as the situation was that brought us here, I am so glad I was able to reconnect with my family and come back here."

"It was like soon as I got here I could remember all the wonderful times I had down at the grove near the church house."

"I had no worries then, no worries Ma'me."

"Anyone know you here girl?"

"Only Jonas, but he's a loyal family friend, he drove the twins to the station in Arkansas just outside of Tennessee and he knows the backroads well, and also my employer Miss Greta."

"You sure you can trust these folks?"

"Yes Ma'me, I can."

"Okay then, well we ain't got to worry about no trail of tears then, now you go on in the house and clean yourself up, you got a big night tonight and I think I just might join you ladies tonight."

"I wanna see just what you got."

Queen smiled, gave Ma'me a kiss and went inside.

Chapter 14

That evening the ladies and Ma'me couldn't wait as they prepared for their night out. They all made it to the Paradise Club with time to spare thanks to Becky. It wouldn't be long before the residence would enter the door creating an intriguing ambience that would set an alluring tone for the evening.

Friday nights at the Paradise on the north side of Tulsa was a ritual in this prosperous town as Black folk. Entrepreneurs as well as those who worked across the track on the south side all week would indulge themselves in the opportunity to relax and enjoy the weekend. Just like their African ancestors, they adorned themselves in their finest clothing and jewelry and relished in one another's company with a backdrop of good food, dancing and soulful music. This was the formula for the weekday woes or burdens they carried. This was a great joy and if it only lasted for one night they invited it with no sorrow added to it.

They were like warriors, capturing Friday night in a quest to conquer it for surviving another week in a world that brought predictable and most often unpredictable circumstances. A world not of their chosen a world where they were far too long found to be misunderstood. Queen and her sisters were no strangers to this ritual. Friday night in the black community was a universal indulgence for the Soul of Black Folks. With a few coins in their pockets black folks attempted to cleanse themselves from the stress and frustrations of the work week. From the big band clubs in the big cities to the back-wood juke joints of the country, by any means necessary this temporary attempt at joy would surface in the lives of these resilient people in preparation for the insane attempt to do it all over again. This secretly intrigued many of the same white folks who employed them as they eavesdropped on their employee's listening while they swapped stories about the weekend which most often left them quite intrigued, why? Because as much as they would like to, they could never understand how black folks could be so happy with what they assumed was so very little. Nevertheless, this same intrigue led many white folks to imitate this same weekend ritual in their own communities. They came to be enchanted by a world of Big Band houses, Juke joints and speak easies, many times never quite able to capture the true essence of this inner rhythmically spiritual ritual of Friday night's in the Black Community. Many of them with their high-strung curiosity it had become almost mystical and for others sometimes even whimsical. As a result, their attempts were only mere imitations. However, for black folks on the northside of Tulsa in the Greenwood community and many other communities around the country it was a way of life. The girls sat at the bar while Queen prepared for her introduction in the dressing room.

"Ma'me you want something to wet your whistle?"
Ma'me looked at her daughter and shook her head.

"You ain't gonna give me what I really want, so why you even asking?"

"Ma'me now you know that you can't have that, it's not good for your diabetes."

"I was offering maybe some nice cold honey and lemon tea."
Ma'me turned her nose up at Becky and waved her hand while she turned herself around in her chair toward the stage. Becky put her hands on her hip for a moment then shook her head as she continued stocking the bar for the night.

Carolyn smiled.

"Ma'me she is only doing what's best for you is all."

"I know that, I know that."

"Carolyn, you ready."

Connie, you know I'm always ready."

"Will you stay up here with Ma'me?"

"Yep, you guys go head, we have a good seat right here."

Queen and Carolyn went backstage toward the dressing room and ran into Tyler.

"Ah, so we meet again beautiful, are you ready to grace the people of Greenwood with your unique expression of art."

"I am, I'm really looking forward to it."

Tyler then took Queens hand and gently kissed it.

"I am as well, perhaps after the show you will join me and have a drink at my table."

"Perhaps."

Tyler smiled and made a pathway for Queen and her sister to pass and headed to the front of the house. It wasn't long before the Paradise Club was standing room only as the crowd cheered the band leader's rendition of Cab Calloway's famous:

"Hiedi Hiedi Hoe."

The ladies smiled as they watched some of the men and women dancing athletically in front of the stage on the dance floor twisting and flipping their partners to and fro, while keeping up with the powerful sounds of the band. Becky tapped Connie and pointed toward the front door as she watched Calvin and William enter the building like celebrities. The two-tall eligible handsome bachelors turned the heads of many of the women in the building. Calvin came in like the cowboy renegade he was, only tonight he'd had on a quarter length cowhide jacket with a hat to match, Levi Strauss jeans, white dress shirt with white gold cuff links and pair of cowboy boots. William had spent most of his day on the other side of the tracks and when he saw his friends outfit he insisted on going home to change. He walked in dressed the opposite of his best friend, wearing some black vest and slacks with a white crispy shirt, gold cufflinks and tie to match. His black animal skin shoes shined like a new nickel as he strolled in the building. A few of the women, and childhood friends without hesitation walked up acknowledging them with hugs of affection. After a few minutes of distracting conversation and tempting propositions the two eligible bachelors finally made their way to the bar. William smiled when he seen his grandmother sitting in her finest clothes.

"Look at you Ma'me, you look beautiful."

"What den brought you out here to the Paradise, must be something really special to get you away from that rocking chair of yours for sure."

Ma'me smiled at her grandson.

"Aww something like that."

She then gave him a hug of affection.

"How you Calvin?"

Calvin bent down to give Ma'me a kiss."

Ma'me smiled at him and looked them both over.

"Yawl sure do clean up nice, got these young girls wooing all over yah."

"Look they can't even keep still in their seats, it's a shame the two of you had to be cursed with such a life-long problem."

Ma'me then started laughing, while Calvin and William greeted the others.

Hello Connie or Carolyn?"

"I'm Connie, hello Calvin."

"Just making sure."

"You did good."

"Hey Wil."

"Hey cousin, where's everybody?"

Connie smiled.

"Everybody like who?"

"Your sisters silly."

"Oh, their preoccupied now, but they should be around shortly, here you two can sit in their seats until they return."

The gentleman sat down and not long after the room became silent and the lights were dimmed as if the night had been waiting for them to walk through the door and settle in. The spotlight was huge and to their surprise lit up the entire center part of the dance floor. The band leader smiled as he walked into the bright light at the center of the stage and bowed to the crowd. William curious, looked over at his mother behind the bar.

"Hey Ma, what's going on?"

Before he could say another word, his mother tapped him and put her fingers up to the center of her mouth as if to keep him quiet."

Calvin had noticed that Carolyn had taken the place of the piano player in the corner of the stage. Then the band leader spoke and everyone in the club gave him their undivided attention.

"Ladies and gentlemen, I have the pleasure of introducing to you a unique talent that has crossed the path of the Paradise this evening, a very beautiful creature that will woe you into a seductive space in time."

"Please welcome the beautiful...*Black Butterfly*."

The audience began clapping their hands as Queen walked out on stage strolling with the grace of a peacock, hands straight down and head in the air with the silhouette of an empress. She wore a

110   Adrienne Lynn Rutherford

beautiful black feathered head piece layered in rhinestones that hung gracefully along her front hairline. Her makeup was tribal and creatively done, displaying the look of a beautiful enchanted being. Her beauty so alarming, both men and women starred and begin whispering to one another of this unique exotic beauty that reminded them of North Africa's ancients. Her body custom sensual in all aspects of the word, complimented by a brassiere covered in black lace and feathers with beautiful silver chains encased with shiny rhinestones. All strategically layered, attached and connected to her sexy bikini panties with beautiful pink and black feathers trailing behind her.

The Black Butterfly crossed her hands over the front of her chest and waited for Carolyn to start playing. When she did this beautiful being began strutting across the floor back and forth as the other band members joined in. She then started talking to the crowd musically.

"So, you think you can handle this?"

In no time, the crowd went crazy. Calvin stood up out of his seat as did many of the men in the club, they were in awe as Queen gave them a Burlesque event that would follow them well into their old age. Calvin could not believe his eyes as Queen created a sensuous atmosphere that had never been seen in Greenwood District. Moving her body rhythmically to the tunes that were played, it was as if she and the music where one, as her footwork fell on ever note, a poetry in motion from head to shoulders and then to hips. Black Butterfly no doubt stole the hearts of many in a matter of minutes. Calvin smiled as he thought to himself.

"This woman is full of surprises."

Queen received a standing ovation, even the ladies in the crowd who had never seen such a show were even intrigued by the artistic creativity of Burlesque. After the performance, the band returned to entertaining the crowd and Queen went to change and was escorted directly to Tyler's table. Tyler was quite amused to say the least by the turn of events that were occurring in his place. Queen knew how to work the crowd and the stage quite well.

"Queen would you like a drink?"

"Sure, I'll have a bourbon on the rocks please."

Tyler gave the waitress their order and continued his conversation with Queen.

"That was some performance you gave us Black Butterfly, look around you the men have lost all sense of themselves."

Queen jokingly smiled.

"It's only a temporary, but normal thing."

"The first time anyone attends a burlesque show it creates one or two things, a sensual urge to be a burlesque or make out with one."

Tyler began to laugh and then gracefully took Queen by the hand and gently began rubbing his finger inside of her palm. Queen seeing the advances that Tyler was attempting to make slowly removed her hand out of his reach and folded them gently together in front of her on the table.

"I never mix business with pleasure Mr. Parker, it makes for bad business and then that turns into bad relationships and that is one thing I don't need."

"No pressure, I just want you to know that I'm here for you in any capacity that you may need me to be and please call me Tyler."

"Mr. Parker is far too formal."

"As far as I'm concerned, the stage is yours if you want it, it can be just business if that's all you're looking for."
Meanwhile, Carolyn had returned to the bar where she was greeted by Calvin and William.

"Wow, where did you learn to play the piano like that, you sound like one of the fellas."

"Cousin don't be silly, we know that it was a woman that taught most men how to play, I'm just not one to sit in the back drop as a musician is all."

"Hello Calvin, good seeing you again."

"Hello there, great show and Queen, wow that was breathtaking, no words for that one."

As the girls and Ma'me started their small talk Calvin looked over across the club and noticed Queen sitting with a gentleman at a large table in the far corner.

"Hey Wil, who is that guy sitting with Queen?"

"Oh, that's Tyler Parker the owner."

Adrienne Lynn Rutherford

"Real weird type dude, don't do much around here but count his money, always in and out of town a lot."

"Mom usually runs the bar her and Gloria the other bartender.

"Never really understood his angle though, but as far as I know he's harmless."

Calvin on the other hand didn't see what William saw, what he seen was something far more complex than that. Since he'd left home many people who drifted into Greenwood District came because of its reputation and comfortable way of life. Most were good people who contributed to the economic prosperity of Tulsa's the north side and some were not so good dragging their past as well as their pre-meditated ideas of evil dealings, but it was something very different about this guy. To him, Queen didn't exactly look like she was having a great old time with the character so Calvin decided to pay them a visit. Calvin fought his way through the crowd and went over to the table where Queen and Tyler were sitting.

"Good evening."

"Ohh…Calvin what a surprise, good evening."

"I would like to introduce you to Tyler Parker"

"Tyler this is Calvin Watkins."

Both shook hands, but Tyler feeling quite intruded upon while in the company of Queen soon let it be known without reservation.

"Pardon us fella, but we are having a private moment here, now be the gentleman that I know you are and allow us this space."
Calvin, quite amused by the tough guy stance the Tyler fellow was failing at miserably humored him by backing up with his hands up in the air.

He then tipped his hat at Queen.

"Hey man, no problem here, just congratulating your lady on a job well done, very entertaining from voice to body."
As he walked off Queen turned to Tyler angrily.

"That was so very rude of you, that is a friend of mine and you had no right."

"Save all that nonsense, we have money to make, you see the full house you got tonight, when word gets out it will be twice that, you will need to do two shows."

"I know you need the money."

"Excuse me!"

"What do you mean, I never said anything about working for you."

"You got a lot of nerve talking to me like I'm some sideshow act, you don't know me and I don't appreciate you disrespecting my friends."

Queen then got up and walked off headed toward the bar with the rest of her family and Calvin while Lewis sat back and watched her. Now he felt that he had been truly disrespected, after all that he had done for her to make the night a success. She had the nerve to talk to him that way. Lewis snapped his finger at one of the waitresses and she brought him over a cigar and lit it for him. Queen watched him from afar as their eyes met. She then rolled her eyes with distaste and he returned the gesture with a smile.

"I'm ready to go!"

Carolyn looked at her sister and could see that she was uncomfortable."

"What's wrong sis?"

"I'm ready to go, can someone please take me out of here now!"

"Come on I'll drive you home."

Ma'me then got up as well.

"Calvin, you mind taking me too."

"Go on Calvin, I'll hang back with Ma and the girls, you go on man, we'll catch up later at John's place."

"Carolyn can you get my things from the dressing room please?"

Sure sis, no worries."

Tyler watched as Queen, Calvin and Ma'me exited his club. It was at that moment he realized he had bigger plans brewing outside of Greenwood and that Queen was a distraction that would be far more trouble than she was really worth. In a few months, he would no longer have to live in the bowels of this god-forsaken country as he thought about his plans to rejoin his crew and venture far away to the other side of the Atlantic Ocean for good. Investing in Greenwood was probably one of the smartest things that he'd done in the past and now that it was a seller's market, he was ready to cash in. Tyler had some very interested buyers back east not your typical businessmen, but businessmen still the same that were interested in moving into Greenwood and taking over the Paradise Club. He smiled as he imagined himself on the coast of Africa relaxing in his ocean front palace. His train would leave for Memphis Tennessee first thing Monday morning.

****

The night was still young as Calvin, Queen and Ma'me made their way back to the big house. Tonight, had been a very surprising treat for Calvin, as he became aroused thinking about Queen and the stunning outfit that she wore while performing. She on the other hand was quite amused by the quiet demeanor Calvin was currently displaying and made no attempts to make him feel uncomfortable. Queen had been in this predicament many times before with suitors who were speechless after seeing her create such a stimulating illusion on stage. Although her encounter with many of them was an innocent cup of coffee and sweet cake after her performance, they all seemed to escort her out the Club with the same look of astonishment on their faces and Calvin was no exception.

Ma'me sat in the back seat looking up at the millions of stars that covered the clear spring night.

"My, my, my Ma'me sure did enjoy that evening out, I'm surprised I stayed up as long as I did."

"Ma'me gonna sleep good tonight, the night air is breezy, I know just what it's gonna feel like coming through my bedroom window too."

Queen smiled.

"What did you think of the performance Ma'me?"

"Well I must say that was one of the oddest things I've seen in my time of life, I can't say I ever seen a woman move like you Queen."

She then began to laugh.

"Yes suh."

"If I would have known all that moving along that you done tonight when I was yo age, I probably would have had a far different life than the one I have today I can tell you that."

Queen was shocked by her comment.

"Ma'me!!!"

Dance of Angels

"I'm just telling you the truth, but the one you should be asking is mumbles here, he ain't said a word since you left off that stage tonight."

Queen looked over at Calvin as he made attempts to pay close attention to the road.

"Calvin, what did you think of my performance tonight?"

Calvin surprised Queen as he took one hand off the steering wheel and reached over to grab her hand off her lap."

"Again, I will say before I was rudely interrupted earlier."

"I think it was a most artistic expression of love and life and you displayed it quite eloquently in voice and body."

"I must say I haven't seen anything like it before."

Queen began to blush trying to hide the joy she felt inside from his compliment.

Ma'me smiled.

"Calvin my niece den been here before you know, but she was a little girl, now she all grown up and beautiful with some smarts to go with it too.

"Yeah, I know and I was wondering if she would ever catch on."

"I knew her the first time I saw her back in downtown Tulsa, the twins kinda threw me off at first, but she had no clue."

Queen hit Calvin on the shoulder.

"You mean you knew all the time and didn't say anything, how did you know me and I didn't know you?"

"That is a question you will have to answer for yourself my love, but I recognized you by that very exquisite heart shaped birthmark on your left cheek."

Queen then put her hand up to her cheek.

"That is a very detailed observation Mr."

Before they knew it, they'd arrived at Ma'mes home.

Calvin helped Ma'me out of the Automobile.

"Thank you, son are you guys coming in for coffee?"

"I'll put some on before I go to bed."

"No thank you Ma'me, we will be fine, gonna hang out here for a spell and talk a bit."

"Okay then, Calvin sweetheart, thanks for everything and tell

Adrienne Lynn Rutherford

your mom I said hello when you get a chance you hear."

"No problem Ma'me you know you my favorite gal and I will let mom know."

"I used to be your favorite gal, but right now I think somebody is pushing old Ma'me right on out the way."

Calvin went out to the porch with Queen and looked out into the grove. The moon was three quarters full but its illumination truly told a different story.

Calvin"

"Yes"

"Why are you being so nice to me, I haven't been the easiest person to get along with since I arrived you know."

"Because I adore you."

Queen was startled by the comment that Calvin made and she could hardly put a sentence together after hearing it, so she began to laugh to hide her lost for words.

"Umm adore me?"

"Don't be silly Calvin, you hardly know me."

"Ahh, but your wrong my sweet, I know you very well, I know that."

Calvin pointed to her heart.

"That is what I know about Queen."

Queen feeling herself sinking deep in to what she considered a very vulnerable place attempted to combat the strong energy that seem to pull at her very existence.

"Well sir I'm not that same little girl from long ago."

"No, you're not, you're quite the woman now and a beautiful one I may add, but the heart, the heart is the same."

"I don't understand what you mean Calvin, I am changed, and I am a woman not a child." "Well it's just that simple, rarely do we ever really change we do grow up to become adults true enough, we may have life experiences that take us through many different twist and turns, ups and downs, but the core, the core of who we are it's rarely ever lost."

"We just need someone from time to time to come into our life to remind us is all?"

Queen looked over at the dark beautifully made man that sat next to her. Never in Queen's life had she felt what she felt tonight. It was all too surreal for her and she wanted to hold on to this moment in time forever. She gently placed her fingers over the large scar that traveled down the entire right side of his face and traced it with her fingertips from his temple to the side of his chin. Calvin closed his eyes and gently placed his hand on top of hers.

"Calvin, what happened?"

"It's a long story, I will tell you about that another time."

Queen took both her hands and placed them on each side of his face.

"You know what?"

"I think I adore you Mr. Calvin Watkins."

She then softly placed a kiss on his lips. Calvin was caught by surprise and it was the first time that Queen saw a glimpse of shyness befall this intelligent man of the world.

"Would you like another my Prince Hannibal?"

Calvin then began to laugh aloud.

"You remembered."

"Yes, it took me a minute and a few family pictures, and eventually it dawned on me."

"My Prince, you were the one who rescued me."

Queen kissed him again, but this time he gently grabbed her and laid her across his lap with her head inside his chest and returned the sensual gesture. In that moment, Queen found solace in the arms of her prince. Finally, she was in a peaceful place in her life and she felt secure in Calvin's arms.

"Will you stay with me Queen?"

Queen said nothing as she stood up over Calvin's large masculine frame and reached for his hand.

"Come with me."

Calvin took hold of her hand and she led him off the porch to the side of the large house. The flat wooden doors that lead into the shelter below were far too heavy for Queen to open alone, so Calvin stepped up and Queen moved aside.

"Stop my love, let me."

Calvin then grabbed the large metal handle and pulled one of the doors wide open.

"Shhhh, easy Calvin, you'll wake up Ma'me."

He held Queen by the hand as she carefully stepped down into the cool cellar. Next to the door entrance she grabbed a large lantern and Calvin grabbed the large match box off the shelf. As he struck the match stick it briefly lit up the entire room and gradually dimmed as Calvin placed the fire inside of the lantern. He did a brief scan of his surroundings and was very impressed.

"Looks like Wil, has been putting his work in, this place is solid."

Calvin walked along the wall as he took his hand and touched the neatly laid bricks that covered the entire inside of the cellar. He was impressed with the finely carved wooden table and chair set that sat neatly over in the corner. On the other side of the modestly made room was a square wooden bed frame that held a soft down mattress inside of it. He walked over to the tall narrow wooden pantry and opened it to his surprised there were shelves filled with can goods, soaps, sheets, towels and Wil's famous jug of homemade red wine. Queen began to smile.

"I couldn't believe it either, Wil calls it his man cave."

Calvin nodded with confirmation.

"Very nice, very nice indeed."

Queen then went over to the pantry and grabbed two tin mugs and the jug of wine.

"Would you like a swig?

"Don't mind if I do."

Calvin sat at the small but sturdy table and watched Queen as she poured the wine for them both.

While in thought, he contemplated all that had happened to him since coming home. Overall It had been a joyous occasion seeing his family and even his father. However, this moment in time he felt it a gift from the heavens to be able to cross paths with Queen once more. As hard as it was not to reach for her and to show her how much he wanted her, Calvin patiently contained himself.

"Umm you like, this is pretty good."

"Yeah, Wil has been making batches like this since we were

kids, we always had a stash out in the grove unknowing to our parents."

Queen shook her head.

"You guys, were so mannish."

After a few moments of swapping their childhood memories, Calvin got up and extended his hand to Queen.

"Please come to me."

Queen didn't hesitate as she got up from her chair and went over to Calvin. He kissed here gently on the top of her head and lifted her face to his, while gently placing a kiss on her lips. Queen closed her eyes and received his unrestrained desire, as he exposed his eagerness to bear witness to the magnetic sensuality that haunted him since first seeing her perform that night. With each touch and each kiss, he caressed her softly. Queen closed her eyes and received his mannish invitation and before she thought her limbs would give out, he swooped her up into his arms and gently laid her across the soft featherbed. This was all so very new to Queen compared to the passive rebellious nature she had mastered so well back home in Memphis. All her life, she had always been in control, the master manipulator of her suitors and her weapon of choice was a successful lack of emotion. However, this experience was much more than what she was expecting. Tonight, she would be caught off guard and the fact that it felt so good made the experience that more inviting to her. So, she gave in to his touch, gave in to his kiss, and gave in to his professing his love to all that she was. Surrendering was a new thing for Queen and tonight it felt liberating and she embraced it. Calvin on the other hand was full of joy deep in the inside and the void that he'd felt for the past eight years had been filled the instant that he laid eyes on her at the station that day. However, tonight he realized this would be the beginning of the rest of his life.

Queen smiled as this wonderful man in all his tenderness gave off such a magnetic vibration of sensual manifestations of intimate bliss, she could hardly speak. So, she said nothing as he laid down next to her and began undoing her dress. Calvin knew all too well the importance of pleasure and gently caressed her until reaching her most inner core while enjoying her moan with erotic insatiable delight. Queen did not know if it was the wine or if it was the strong

Adrienne Lynn Rutherford

energy of this man that left her speechless and wanting any and everything he had to offer her. He placed his lips softly on her nipple and suckled her until her spine arched and tingled in pure delight. She grabbed him tightly as he slowly, with her help removed her dress. He was amazed to see that she wore no under garments and closed his eyes and smiled at another sensual fact he had gathered from his Queen. He gently rolled her on her side and she was more than willing to allow his strong hands to softly trace the frame of her body. He started at the shoulders then gently caressed her arms and then over the hill of her hips until he reached to tip of her toes. Queen facing the other way with her eyes closed smiled at the game that he played with her. Calvin then got up and removed his clothes and returned to her side. As then gently kissed the back of her neck and her shoulder and turned her over, Queen smiled as her eyes met his.

"What a gift of a man."

She thought to herself.

Calvin, gently grabbed her on top of him and she straddled him placing his manhood perfectly in her center. She smiled down at him as she felt it slowly rise to greet her. Queen laid her chest against his and begin to kiss him with all the passion she felt. He anxiously grabbed her hips and massaged her softly as he returned the same sensual kisses to her. Gently he went into her moistness and she moaned with pleasure, Queen began to dance sensually moving in the motion of her own heartbeat. With every single stroke, Calvin returned the favor and they danced this way for hours. Neither wanted to leave, but both had promised to meet the others at John's place for a night cap.

What time is it Calvin?

Calvin reached for his pants and removed his Brequet pocket watch and handed it to Queen as she got out of bed."

"Ten after twelve."

She then handed the watch back to Calvin as he took the two large pails out to the water pump.

Although Queen had not mentioned it to Calvin, she was aware of the value of such an exquisite pocket watch. She'd seen this same extravagant gold encased time piece once before back in Memphis.

Owned by a friend of Greta, a very wealthy businessman that was passing through town. He'd stopped by to see what unique talents his longtime friend had come across. He'd approached Queen, intrigued after her performance and offered her a drink. Queen remembered him educating her on the hand-crafted time piece that he was quite fond of and it was an almost exact replica of the piece that Calvin now carried.

So oddly enough she knew such extravagant were treats of the wealthy and she now wondered what fortunes in his travels would have afforded him such an expensive time piece. Calvin returned from the old water pump with fresh water. He poured one of the pails into the larger one for bathing and modestly for a time watched Queen as she bathed. Afterwards she would do the same enjoying the view just as he. After spending such a sensuous time with Queen, it didn't matter to Calvin one way or the other whether they made it to his brothers or not. If he'd had his way, he could have stayed down in that cozy cellar forever. However, after many more intimate kisses and a promise to dance again, Queen would eventually get him on the road.

Tonight, both would had professed their love to one another, below the surface neither was willing to speak about the current context that were contents that were crowding their lives. Queen and Calvin held secrets and they held them from one another. However, each had the same intention, promising themselves that they would share soon with the other. Nevertheless, in all that it was neither spoke a word of that which they kept to themselves. A careless deception that could soon transform into a guilty as charged verdict for both and possibly even taint the grace bestowed upon their lives to meet again. Soon after the two arrived at the air strip and Queen was amazed to see so many airplanes lined up one after the other, each with its own personal design. The area was spacious and well-lit. When they entered, Queen was amazed at the large scraps of metal that covered an entire area of the building as they walked through. She couldn't help but be amazed at what these talented black men had put together just a few miles from downtown Greenwood.

Adrienne Lynn Rutherford

"Calvin this is absolutely amazing, I mean I would have never thought something like this ever existed."

"Yeah, it is quite the jewel we have, airmen fly from all over as far as from California to hang out with John and visit Greenwood. Some stay nearby and do a lot of crop dusting too."

"Wait until you see the home, John started on it when he returned from the war."

Queen had never seen such privileges afforded to black folk in her part of the country. Yes, there were many who had become successful and wealthy, but to branch out like this economically was unheard of. Tulsa's northside Greenwood community was truly a unique place for black folk. A phenomenal blueprint for more advancements economically for black people across the country. After a brief tour of the airplane hangar, Queen looked over at the house and was amazed at what she saw. There was a crowd of black people, laughing, socializing and dancing on the large cemented patio. There were tall wooden poles neatly placed strategically around the cemented area that gracefully held large antique oil lanterns all which illuminated the patio area. In the distance were beautiful handmade wooden lounge chairs with soft cushions that allowed the guest to stretch their legs out comfortably, giving off a tranquil ambience as they listened to the sounds of Scott Joplin. Queen gave witness to such a harmonious gathering of happy and beautifully dressed people and for the first time in a long time in her life she felt the same.

Calvin looked at Queen.

"You like?"

"Very much."

Suddenly out of nowhere the twins came up behind Queen and Carolyn put her hand over her eyes.

"Guess who?"

She and Connie both began to laugh.

Connie however knowing her sister all too well observed the sly look on her face. She then looked at Calvin.

"Where on Earth have you two been?"

"We've been waiting for you?

"What happened at the club?"

"No worries about that girl, I'm good."

"Hey Calvin."

"Hey Connie, Carolyn."

Queen interrupted

"What are yawl up to?"

"Enjoying yourselves?"

Connie noticed a different aura on her sister and she smiled.

"Sure, we met some real nice folk out here, I tell you this place is paradise."

Carolyn looked at her sisters and grabbed them both by the hand.

"Calvin we'll be back, c'mon girls lets go to the ladies room."

Before he could respond the girls were gone.

When they got to a quiet place inside of John's home near the restroom. Connie squeezed Queen's hand.

"No, you didn't?"

Queen while looking in the tall glass mirror, checking her attire smiled.

"Yes, I did."

Queen knew she could not lie to her sisters, so the best thing was to just come clean. After all, they were her sisters.

Connie covered her mouth and Carolyn gasped into laughter.

"Chile, you glowing, you should see yourself."

"You in love with him?"

Queen smiled.

"I think so, but I gotta take my time with things like this, I don't really know much about him, I mean it's been a long time."

"And besides, we were kids."

"Queen what are you talking about, you see how that man look at you?"

"You're going to need a crow bar to get him off your hip."

The twins begin to laugh, but for Queen it was a habit to be precautious, it had become second nature to her after all these years and it had served her well in many cases. Also, after being spooked by the heartbreaking love of her parents, it didn't make this thing called love that much easier "Love is a very sticky situation, it can leave you in a bad way if you're not careful, I just want to stay

124   Adrienne Lynn Rutherford

focused and take it slow.

"Enough, enough about me, what's going on with you two?"

Connie smiled,

"Well I have been invited on a date next Saturday to the premier of the great Micheaux newest movie right here in Tulsa, can you imagine that a premier. I'm going with Sebastian.

"Who is that?"

"The train engineer, the one who brought us into Greenwood, He's a dream."

"And what about you Carolyn?"

Connie as always spoke for her sister.

"John's invited her out to his friends place next weekend and they're flying."

"Carolyn, you wanna fly?"

Carolyn smiled. "I thought I would give it a try."

"It's his friend Alvin's turn to host, he gets second Friday."

To Queen it was obvious that the girls were making well in their situation. However, she knew they still had unfinished business in Memphis and as much as she would have liked to forget it was far impossible to do so right now. Queen made a promise to Ma'me that she wouldn't bring any danger upon her doorstep, but she also refused to leave Jonas holding the bag. His loyalty had been solid over the years even up until the death of her father. She needed to know how he was panning out after leaving him in the hell's fire that night. Somehow, she knew the Medusa was on the hunt and had probably already visited his doorstep. Queen would not mention any of this to her sisters, she wanted them to stay in a comfortable space. As far as Jonas was concerned, she didn't want him to think they had abandoned him. So, she made a mental note to visit Downtown Tulsa and get a telegram to Greta.

Meanwhile, back on the patio were the men who had fallen head over heels for these fearless independent women. Sabastian the train engineer joined Calvin, John and William while they each enjoyed a Cuban cigar.

"Man, where did you get these fresh twisters?"

"Their smooth as silk."

"If I tell you I'll have to kill you, just say it pays to have friends that travel in the airways."

The men begin to laugh.

"I asked Connie out to the Oscar Micheaux movie premiere at the theater next week."

Calvin began to laugh

"Oh yeah, I ran into Damita and her family at Maggie's."

"I was going in and they were leaving."

William took a long drag of his cigar.

"I still don't know how that square guy nabbed her?"

John smiled.

"C'mon man you know Damita was always planning and plotting for status, even though he's not her type it doesn't matter to her none."

"She played that situation like a grand piano."

"The man hadn't been here a month before she put her claws into him."

"He didn't even see that predator coming. Between her and that mother of hers, he didn't have a chance."

William nodded in agreement.

"Yeah but we all know who she was really after was Calvin, she would have lived in a one room shack with him if he would have married her."

"Yep ole Cal here was the one guy that she would have threw all her dreams away for and that I know."
Calvin shook his head.

"Sebastian you're taking Connie, I wasn't going to go, but I will ask Queen to be my date and we can all go together."

William interrupted as he took a drag off his cigar.

"All these fancy invitations going around, how come I don't get invited to nothing?"

"Calvin just got here and he got two tickets to an event"

"I been here all my life I can't even get one."

Calvin begin to laugh.

"You are spending too much time across the tracks brother, you need to hang out in your own neck of the woods sometimes. You just might stumble up on an opportunity."

Adrienne Lynn Rutherford

All the men laughed as William just shook his head and took another toke of his fine Cuban cigar.

Later, as the evening came to a close John made arrangements for them all to stay at his place. When the ladies retired for the evening, Calvin found this a good opportunity to talk to his brother and William while they played a game of billiards about his trip back home.

"Calvin I'm really tired of the whipping you are putting on your boy William here."

William shook his head as he passed Calvin another C note."

"I'm done with you man."

John could not stop laughing.

"You look pitiful man."

Calvin slid him back his cash and went to the bar to pour himself another shot.

"I was wondering what plans you guys have after next Saturday night, I want you to take a trip with me."

John curious, was the first to respond.

"Where you trying to go?"

"Montana"

William interrupted

"Montana?"

"What's up there?"

"Well, a little bit of this, a little bit of that."

John, knowing his brother also knew that meant opportunity.

"Oh yeah, sure I'll go"

Calvin then looked at William.

"What about you Wil, you have any plans?"

"Naw, but how long you are talking about staying?"

"A few days."

William interrupted again.

"A few days, what do you mean man?"

You just can't tell a working man, come on let's take a trip, we'll be gone a few days."

"Man, I have a job a J.O.B."

"You gotta provide me with dates man and times."

He then looked at John.

"You hear this guy?

"A few days."

Calvin laughed aloud.

"We are going to have to pry this man out of Greenwood, or else he's never going to leave here."

"Man, you need to get out and see the world, its bigger than Greenwood."

William knew his friend was right, but just like many in Greenwood, he felt no reason to leave. Everything that he thought he needed or wanted was an arm's length away. Many times, he thought about jumping out there into the world, but for William the world outside of Greenwood district seemed far larger than his current ambitions.

"Aww man come on it's not like that at all, I would love to join the brothers, but I've been working on an investment across the tracks and I'm just about ready to cash in real soon."

Calvin didn't push his friend, he respected his need to be his own man. It would have been nice to surprise him with an opportunity that would require him to never have to work across the tracks again, but for now he would take this opportunity to make up lost time with his elder brother.

"Man, okay it's cool."

Chapter 15

Queen met with Damita briefly in the early afternoon to complete the final touches for the surprise after the film premiere. Since her performance at the Paradise it wasn't long before word had gotten out about the gracefulness of what was a new form of artistic expression in Tulsa's Greenwood Community. Unknowingly to Queen she'd quickly become a local star, so she was quite surprised when Damita asked her to perform for the great *Oscar Micheaux*. Thanks to Connie, she and her sisters had been fans of his work for quite some time. She'd secretly planned with Ma'me to have her costume picked up at the house and delivered to the Reynolds place for her performance. Queen decided to shake things up a bit and chose her favorite costume to wear this evening. A beautiful African inspired piece shipped from Sierra Leone. It was a gift from Madame Greta for her twentieth birthday. She also requested the Reynolds provide two drummers. Tonight, she would pay ancestral homage to the resilience and strength of those who'd crossed the great Atlantic divide many years ago. Queen could think of no better way to honor the accomplishments of the people in Tulsa's Northside Greenwood district. It was a testament to this same resilience and the strength of a people, who like a phoenix rose from the ashes of adversity time and time again, only to reclaim their God-given greatness.

Queen, couldn't wait also to see the expression on Calvin's face when she stepped out into the light from the darkness. A stage was set up in the patio area of Damita's home. Queen would perform after a late dinner and just before the discussion of the film. The performance would be a surprise and no one was to know anything. Not even Mr. Reynolds who enjoyed surprises and Damita thought this was the best one yet. Although happily married to James Lee and the hostess of such an extravagant affair, Damita's slight envious curiosity could not resist bringing Calvin up as a topic of discussion.

"You are quite the eye catch Queen I must say."

"The performance you gave at the Paradise Club was absolutely intriguing. My own dear husband couldn't even close his mouth, it was very creative. "

"I am all about the arts you know and I give compliments where they're due of course."

"I'm also always eager to please my husband so, I thought your artistic expression would be an excellent addition to such a magnificent night don't you agree?"

"Of course, I would not have expected you to work for free. I'll pay you your price as I agreed."

Queen smiled at Damita.

"Well thank you very kindly, your words of encouragement are well taken and I will hope that I am able to perform up to the expectations of the very, um should I say posh crowd this evening."

"Oh, I'm absolutely confident that you will be fine, I will have everything set up for you when you get to the house. We just have to stick to the plan."

Both women begin to laugh at the thought of pulling the plan off to perfection

"Queen, I do know one thing."

"You must have some secret love dust on stash, because I have never seen Calvin cling to a woman like he was to you the other night."

"Well Damita, I don't know about any love dust, but I will say I'm quite fond of him as well, he's a good guy."

Damita shook her head.

"Yeah, he's a good guy alright, honey every young woman marrying age in town, when they found out Calvin was back was in an uproar."

"He was the catch then and he's the catch now. Shoot if I wasn't happily married myself I would've been a part of that circus as well."

"Chile, I promise you, there were many ladies crying in their pillows that night."

"You know me and Calvin were an item once, did he ever mention me?"

Queen looked at Damita quite awkwardly as if to try to understand why she needed to share that with her.

"No, I don't recall him mentioning any of his past relationships."

Adrienne Lynn Rutherford

Then she caught herself.

"Not that we are in any relationship of course."

Damita countered her gaze suspiciously with a slight grin on her face.

"Yes of course."

"Well you just be careful and hold on good and tight to that man."

"Calvin, I've known all my life and believe me he almost always and I mean always has something up his sleeve."

He didn't just come back here for nothing."

"That much I do know."

After the ladies completed their plans for the evening, they bid one another farewell, there was much to be done in a short amount of time.

****

Becky stood in the bedroom doorway watching her new-found family. Never in a million years did she believe her boring mediocre life would ever have any real adventure until Queen and the twins showed up.

"Stop with the fussing yawl you two look absolutely grand."

Connie smiled as she continued fixing the bobby pins in her hair.

"You sure you don't wanna come with us Becky?"

"Gloria did promise she would work the bar herself tonight, she does owe you one you know."

"Humph, she owes me plenty, but you two go ahead, I don't wanna be no fuss."

Queen turned from the mirror and looked up at her eldest cousin.

"What do you mean girl?"

"Get over here, I know I got something for you."

"No Queen you two are going out on a date, I don't want to be a third leg or should I say a fifth one for that matter."

"Becky, that's nonsense and anyway we insist."

"Yeah Becky, what do you want to do?"

"You are not about to sit around the house tonight, especially on one of the most talked about events in town going on."

"I do get out, at the Paradise Club."

Connie put both her hands on her hips.

"Now Becky, work don't count."

"We have to get you out on a real date."

Becky started laughing.

"A date, girl ain't nobody got time for a date."

"I have enough on my plate, I got Ma'me to look after."

Queen smiled.

"Well Becky what are you looking for in a man."

Becky begin to blush as she looked up into the ceiling as if gazing into some unknown place.

"Well let's see, he must be kind and strong, and he has to be educated about the world you know, because I like to talk about what's going on in the world."

"He has to have a work ethic for whatever it is he chooses to do."

"Most important he must be God fearing, honest, loyal and loving to me."

"Oh, and not afraid to show me his most tender side without feeling vulnerable or weak."

"I want him to be a protector and I want him to have family values, because family is the foundation of all that exist of any value in this world."

"You ask what it is I want in a man, I want these things, I want my man to be a man."

The two looked at Becky smiling at how passionately she shared what she knew to be true love. Queen smiled, knowing in that moment that they truly had the same blood running through their veins. Connie took her fan and began waving Becky.

"Goodness Becky, you sure putting the pressure on a uh brother."

Queen began to laugh at Connie's comment.

"Connie, when a girl knows what she wants, she knows what she wants, isn't that right Becky?"

"That's right, I'm no spring chicken anymore, I got no time for games girl."

"I've had plenty of time to think about what I want all these years, I want to be honest. If I can find a man to love and cherish me and is hardworking I'll take him."

Connie listened attentively at her elder cousin, all her life her wisdom had come mostly from her eldest sister Queen. However, now she could receive another wise perspective of life from her cousin Becky.

"You know Becky, all jokes aside I totally respect your values."

"I mean, if you think about all that you said it's not really a lot that you're asking."

"I too must re-evaluate what it is I want in a man as well."

"I know I am still young, but hearing you say the things that you have said makes me feel another five inches tall in my big girl shoes if you know what I mean."

Queen looking at the time, interrupted the ladies.

"Don't you dare give up on any of those things Becky because anything is possible, but please dear let's just start out with getting you in an evening gown and out of the house first."

"So, come on Becky let's get you dressed because the fellas will be here in a few and we want you looking as stunning as ever."

Queen then walked up to her cousin and smiled

"Because, tonight my dear cousin is going to be the beginning of the rest of your life.

****

Calvin and Sabastian stopped by his parent's home before picking up the ladies.

"Wait here man, I'll be right out."

"No worries man, but hurry up I can't wait to see Connie."

"Man, you'll see her soon enough."

He was dressed in the finest of many suits tailor made to fit. This was one of the many positive things that resonated with Calvin about his father. He'd taught him everything he knew about the finest in dress code and the fabrics, the good ones that would hang perfectly on his genetically acquired muscular frame. Although his father preferred a sophisticated top hat to compliment his finely tailored suits, his son would settle for the contemporary Ferdora instead. Inside, Mrs. Watkins was sitting in her favorite rocking chair by the fire place knitting another one of her award winning beautiful afghans for a senior in the community. Mayor Watkins was seated in the chair across from his dear wife holding his hand carved tobacco pipe enjoying his habitual after dinner smoke by the fireplace. For Calvin, the aroma brought back memories as he inhaled the fresh smell of cognac soaked tobacco leaves. Mayor Watkins put his paper down to see his son standing in front of them, a reflection of them both. "Good evening mother, father."

Mrs. Watkins put down her knitting needles.

"Oh, just look at my boy, I mean my young man, you look absolutely stunning tonight dear."

"Doesn't he Henry?".

She stood up and gave her son a hug and embraced him with all the love that she had in herself to give. However, for Calvin tonight wasn't about mother it was about father. All he and his brother ever wanted was Mr. Watkins blessings to go out into the world. Nevertheless, Mr. Watkins felt it to be a contemptuous thing. So, Calvin and his brother John made executive decisions regarding how they would experience life outside the Tulsa Greenwood District. Therefore, out of respect this time he felt a need to receive a proper blessing for their journey North.

Mr. Watkins granted his middle child a well to do and took another pull of his pipe and sat back down in his chair.
You look sharp their son."

"Why thank you pops, I'm headed out to that movie premiere with some friends."

"Yeah, I heard the classiest of the classiest are in town tonight for that gala."

"Blackman making moving films, that's good stuff, really good stuff."

Calvin noticed the tone in his father's voice had grown solemn since the last time he'd spoken with him, the light he'd once had seemed to have also diminished. Mayor Watkins had regretted passing such harsh judgement on his sons for so many years. They had turned out well enough he thought to himself and he'd realized that he'd made a big mistake. Mrs. Watkins looked at her husband and in that moment, she could see the gentleman she'd married long

Adrienne Lynn Rutherford

ago resonate above the disingenuous man that he'd become.

"Pops I stopped by to talk to you."

Surprised Mayor Watkins sat up curiously in his chair.

"Pops me and John are going away tomorrow for a time, right now he has flown his airplane to his friend Isom's place in Colorado.

He will leave it there and take the train back this way."

"He will meet me at the main train station in downtown Tulsa on Sunday and from there we will head up state for a time."

"He asked me to bring his keys over to check on the place for him."

Calvin then handed his father the keys to his brother's place and his father stood up.

"Oh, no problem son, I've done it before."

"Me and your mother will go out, I know how he is about that darn cat."

"Uh Calvin, will you be returning with your brother when he comes back?"

Calvin was taken aback by the question and for a moment experienced a loss for words. Never did he think his father would say these words to him again, especially after the terrible disagreement they'd had the first day he arrived home. He then grabbed his father and they embraced. Mrs. Watkins could not hold back her tears as she watched the men of her life embrace one another in family and love. There were many things that Mayor Watkins wanted to share with his son, but because of his past behavior he didn't know if his son would take the time out to listen to what it was he had to say, so he kept things as simple as possible. Calvin then looked at his father.

"Yes Poppa, I'll be back."

Keeping his tears back Mayor Watkins backed away from his son.

"I don't want to wrinkle you."

"You go on have a good time and have a safe trip we will see the two of you when you get back."

"Oh, and Calvin."

Calvin turned back toward his father before exiting the room.

"Were sending out prayers for a safe journey there and back."

Calvin nodded his head at his father's words and put his hat on his head, in that moment his heart was healed. All he ever wanted was his father's blessing in any capacity. Yes, he will be back the thought to himself, but not to stay. He would return to gather all those that he loved who was willing, and take them far away from Tulsa. He bid them both farewell and headed toward Ma'me.

Calvin and Sabastian arrived to see Ma'me was sitting on her porch looking out into the beautiful green meadow that stretched for acres in front of her home. They both got out and greeted her. Calvin greeted her with a kiss on the cheek.

"Hello Ma'me"

Sabastian gave her a big genuine hug.

"How's it going Ma'me

"Well, look at the two of you, looking mighty fine I say, mighty fine."

"Folks been in a hissy fit about this Michael man from the east coast."

"The girls been carrying on all afternoon trying to get themselves together and I must say they are looking right mighty fine too."

"Ma'me where is Wil?"

"Chile, don't ask, he out somewhere across the tracks being hard headed. I told him to stay away from over there this late, but he won't listen. It's gonna catch up with him soon enough I tell you, it breaks my heart to see him risk his life for some woman."

"It's just too much hate over there, it's bad enough he gotta work over there too."

"Lord knows I've prayed over that situation for quite some time, it's bound to get fixed pretty soon."

Calvin shook his head, he knew if Wil knew how heavy his actions had weighed on Ma'mes heart he would reconsider some of the choices he'd made regarding hanging on the Southside of Tulsa after hours. Wil was always living on the edge even as a kid. Nevertheless, the childish tendencies had grown with him into manhood and now they were life threatening. He was playing with fire and now Calvin knew that Ma'me knew it.

"It will come a time Ma'me he'll come around, but in the

Adrienne Lynn Rutherford

meantime, you can't let yourself worry so about him."

"I'm not son, I've given it to God"

"Pastor Joseph always says"

"If you gonna pray why worry, if you gonna worry why pray."

Just as Ma'me finished her sentence the front door swung wide open and one by one the ladies came out of the house. They had all been waiting anxiously for Calvin and Sabastian to pick them up. Queen was dressed in a beautiful embroidered strapless all satin green party dress. It was covered below with a beautifully flowing accentuating green chiffon. Her hair was pulled back into a simple French roll that was supported by beautifully embroidered hair comb full of emerald green crystals. Her shoes where the finest of French couture thanks to the likes of Madame Greta displaying the latest in women's three-inch heels. Carolyn preferred the modest color of Cream revealing a stunning pearl embroidered and laced dress that she'd been saving for a night such as this. Her shoe boots where also cream in color. Both her favorites, were two of the first things she'd packed in her carpet bag upon leaving Memphis. The crystal head piece she managed to craft on her own from the items found in the attic of the Paradise Club were equally astonishing as they hung admirably to accentuate her face. Last to come out of the door was Becky, and when Ma'me saw her she could not help but comment

"Mercy, Mercy is that my child?"

"Yes of course that's my child."

"Becky, you look so pretty."

"Thank you Ma'me."

Queen smiled.

"She looks absolutely stunning, doesn't she?"

Becky wore a beautifully embroidered coral party dress that hung just below her knee with a deep V cut in the back. Her shoes where a beautiful coral as well and the heel was as equally as high as Queen's.

Queen did the honors of giving her cousin a beautiful set of party waves in her hair while Connie did the honors with the makeup.

The gentlemen were speechless and Queen smiled.

"Hello fellas you look very handsome this evening."

Both thanked the ladies for their compliments

"Calvin, I hope you don't mind Becky joining us tonight, I insisted that she come with us."

No not at all there is plenty of room for you to join us, this is going to be a spectacular night, definitely wouldn't want you to miss such an historical evening."

"I hear people have come in from out of town, the bed and breakfast and the hotel are completely full."

"They have done a wonderful job with this, I hope that everything goes well".

Ma'me smiled.

"Yawl are going to have a night to remember, there ain't many nights like these that come through old Greenwood, I can tell you that."

"But be careful of your surroundings you here, I smell a rat and its stench is bad."

Becky looked at her mother.

"Ma'me, stop that, we in front of company."

"I told you about that, you stop it you will ruin their evening."

Ma'me put her hand on her hip.

"You shush, I know what I know and I'm telling these folks here to keep their eyes open, you know my visions are real, so why don't you stop acting like that."

Becky then turned to Queen.

"I don't think it's a good idea to leave Ma'me home alone, I better stay back."

Ma'me hit the wooden porch with her cane."

"You stop that, you just stop that now."

"Ma'me, gonna be fine you hear, you go on out and enjoy yourself, Ma'me gonna be just fine and besides if I have any problems Honey and her family are just next door, go on now take some time for yourself."

Becky hugged her mother tight and then turned to Calvin.

"Thank you, Calvin, I appreciate you letting me tag along."

"Well, we're happy to have you."

****

When Calvin pulled into town, Greenwood Avenue was full. There where automobiles, horse drawn carriages and wooden plank wagons all in line waiting to park and valet for the event. The town's clock struck eight times as the people, while laughing and talking made their way into the theater. The entrance was grand as the Reynolds did not leave any rock unturned. There was a red carpet for all those who would enter the building for the special occasion. Some of the locals stood outside and watched as the movie goers marched in with their escorts on their arms greeting them with whistles and shouting out compliments. Tonight, was going to be a beautiful evening Queen thought to herself. The past couple of weeks had almost catapulted her into believing the world that she'd left back in Memphis had never existed. She knew that eventually she would have to tell Calvin what happened. Although Queen had sworn her sisters to secrecy, she knew after hearing Ma'me this evening she had to accept the facts, as long as the Medusa had breath, she and her sisters would have no peace.

Now, she only waited patiently for a response from her telegram to Jonas. Sending it to Madame Greta was the safest thing to do. She hoped that he was safe and had not been punished for the mess that she and her sisters had left behind. Queen's thoughts were interrupted as it was their turn to pull up to the front entrance. Her door was quickly opened by the valet, he extended his hand to her and she took it as he assisted her and the other ladies out of the automobile. Becky looked at the lights amazed as she read the Marquee

"*Oscar Micheaux Presents, Within Our Gates*"

"Then she then turned to Carolyn and Sabastian.

"Wow, would you look at that."

Carolyn was excited as well as she and Becky led their small group down the red carpet and into the lobby of the theater. Once inside the world had changed. Everyone looked beautiful as they enjoyed the light refreshments that were served. Alcohol was not allowed in the building. Tonight, prohibition trumped any risk of ruining such a spectacular evening. James Lee Reynolds refused to

Dance of Angels   139

allow anything that would trigger the authorities to ruin his. When James Lee recognized Calvin and his group he didn't waste time to greet them. He extended his hand to the gentleman and greeted the ladies."

"Good evening."

"Good evening

"So, glad you could join us."

"Absolutely, thank you for the invite you know everyone here, so there is no need for introductions."

"Yes, yes of course

"I must say Calvin you clean up well."

Calvin smiled as he understood quit well what James Lee meant by his comment even on a night that practically made him look like king for a day, he somehow still had it in his mind to make a common remark. Soon Damita came over to join the group.

"Oh, ladies you look absolutely beautiful."

"Uh Becky. is that you?"

Becky smiled condescendingly

"Yes Damita, it's me."

"Well I just want you to know that you look wonderful, I'm glad you were able to come out this evening, we are making history you know?

"Why thank you, and of course, there hasn't been anything like this in Tulsa Greenwood District that's for sure."

"Good evening ladies and gentlemen."

A voice came from behind Becky and as she turned around the gentleman smiled at her."

"Hello."

Damita interrupted in disbelief.

"Everyone this is Mr. Isaiah Franklin, Mr. Franklin I would like for you to meet Calvin his friend Sabastian, Queen, her sister Carolyn and their cousin Becky."

He greeted them all while shaking hands with Calvin and Sabastian

"Good evening ladies and gentlemen it is a pleasure meeting you all."

"Cousin Becky, is it?"

Adrienne Lynn Rutherford

Queen and her sister Carolyn looked at one another and smiled and then looked back at Becky,"

"Yes, I guess I am cousin Becky."

"Mr. Franklin, is it?"

He then began to laugh.

"Please call me Isaiah."

"Okay, Isaiah."

"Well first cousin, I would like to compliment you on how beautiful you look tonight, I saw you when you walked in."

"Why thank you very much."

"Secondly, I'm never usually this straight forward, but I noticed that you do not have an escort and just so happens I don't have anyone to escort'"

"Would you be so kind as to give me the honor to escort you this evening?"

Becky was speechless as she considered the proposition of this very handsome gentleman.

"Of all the beautiful women in this lobby tonight why would this man come and embarrass me."

Everyone stood by and waited for her response.

"Please, I promise you I will be a complete gentleman."

Becky then gently placed her hand inside of his."

"Okay, but on one condition, you have to sit with us during the show, this is my family and I came with them."

"It just wouldn't be appropriate for me to go wondering off with some strange fellow you know."

Isaiah laughed aloud.

"Point taken, I don't mind at all."

"Good."

As Calvin took Queen's arm inside his and Sabastian took Connie's arm inside his they all went in to find their seats in the theatre.

Chapter 16

Memphis Tennessee

Tyler made his way from the train station to the eastside of Memphis, it had been almost two years since he'd seen his friend. Coaster had been a good business associate over the years using Tyler's Caribbean rum to entertain at his afterhours on the eastside of Memphis. He was glad he'd stayed in touch with him, even after losing the fatal shipment that drastically changed his life. Now, Coaster would possibly be his saving grace and first-class ticket out of the country and back to the life that he treasured. As he approached the large framed home he was greeted by a gentleman who walked up at the same time. Suspicious by his appearance, with his hat pulled down far enough to hide his face, Tyler was hesitant to speak.to the stranger. Suddenly, the door swung wide open and in the vestibule stood Manuela.

"Jonas?"

Manuela was startled to see the other gentleman standing in the door way as well

"May I help you?"

"Yes, I'm here to see Coaster."

Manuela quite inquisitively dug deeper."

"Is he expecting you?"

"Yes ma'am, I do believe he is."

Soon, Coaster came to the side of his sister and when he seen both of the men he was pleasantly surprised. He extended his hand as a salutation and Tyler reciprocated he gesture.

"Wow man, you made it, it's been a long time please come in. He then greeted Jonas in the same manner.

"Hey man how's it going?"

"Things are good man, I can't complain"

Coaster, then introduced Jonas to Tyler. The men shook hands and followed Coaster into the parlor.

"Manuela, don't just stand there can you bring these gentlemen something cold to drink.?"

Once they were settled in, Manuela returned with a tray of cool lemonade and as she sat it on the table she slowly looked over at Jonas, as if to ask what was going on. Jonas himself was clueless to why he was invited to this meeting.

"How was your trip man?

Tyler shook his head and pulled out a cigar

"May I?"

"Sure, man go ahead."

As Tyler lit his cigar he took a long drag and then spoke with unconcern as he acknowledged the dust on his pants from the long trip by baggage car.

"The ride, it was easy, no worries, I expect what I expect when riding in the south by train."

"Hopefully after this, I won't have to worry about such ignorance anymore."

"How's business Coaster?"

"Slow man, love the business, but the people are changing. Beale street is really the happening spot now, been that way for a few years."

"It seems there is more to offer there for everybody. New acts coming in every night, famous folk too!"

"But, as far as a black man owning any establishment in the area, that's on ice."

"I have to expand my options, so that's why I'm considering your offer."

"I'm always planning ahead, so let's not waste time and get down to business."

Coaster took a long sip of his cool drink and then looked over at Jonas.

"Jonas, I invited you here man, because Tyler here has a piece of property out west that I am considering for purchase."

"If things go well, I will be taking over his club business."

"It's a two-story brick building and I know you know buildings, so I would like to hire you to go and check it out."

"I've heard some strange things about that twister weather out west."

"If I'm going to put my life savings up, I just want to make sure I'm getting my monies worth."

Coaster then looked over at Tyler jokingly.

"I don't need no buildings crumbling on me, you see."

Tyler then returned the humor.

"Man, I been there for over eight years and seen only one twister and it's still standing, that place is solid as a rock."

"The masonry in the town is top shelf, but if it makes you comfortable to send your guy out, do what you must."

"This way, all parties will be completely satisfied when the deal is done."

Jonas took a sip of his drink and then interrupted the two.

"Coaster, where is this place you're talking about sending me?"

"Tulsa Oklahoma, Greenwood District, or should I say, Black Paradise."

After hearing the location, it took everything in Jonas not to lose his composure. He couldn't believe what he was hearing

"It must have been in the stars."

Jonas thought to himself.

It had been nearly a week since the girls had left, and still no word from Queen. Now, he knew for sure a universal plan was unfolding by a higher power. How this was going to end, only the universe knew.

"Sure, I'll go."

"I could use a get-a-way, when do we leave?"

"In a couple of days."

"Solid, I'll get my things together."

Coaster stood up cueing the men that the small meeting was pretty much over.

"Yeah Jonas, go out for about a week or so to look over the building and the business traffic."

"Be my eyes and ears to determine whether it's worth me and the family packing up and leaving this place for good.".

"Wow! that's huge man."

"Okay, just give me the details for departure, I can always use a few extra notes in my pocket."

Jonas then stood up and extended his hand to both men.

"Fellas I have a little business of my own I must attend to, but I must say this has been pleasure.

"Coaster thanks for the opportunity. I'm looking forward to it."

"Tyler man, I'll meet you at the train station."

When Jonas walked out of the parlor, there he found Manuela standing waiting for him.

"Jonas, what is my brother talking about leaving Memphis?"

"I don't want to leave Memphis, this is my home."

"Shhhhh Manuela."

"It's not etched in stone, he wants me to check things out, try to look at it as an opportunity."

"I got to go, I'll catch up with you later."

Jonas put his apple hat on his head, pulled it down real tight and headed swiftly out the door.

Chapter 17

Georgea sat a many of days in her rocking chair reminiscing on her life. However, this afternoon was different and after meeting with Jonas and hearing all that had transpired, she could no longer wait. Georgea's mind had somehow been transformed and the longer she sat rocking back and forth in that chair, the more disturbed she became. For as long as Georgea could remember, she allowed he eldest sister Viola to indirectly manipulate her life.

However, even in her quiet strength of making the bold move to marry Bufus Sawyer, Georgea longed for her family. Therefore, she made one last attempt after he mother died to reconcile with her only sibling sister Viola. To Georgea they were blood and nothing else mattered, not even the ill treatment she'd experienced in the past. Little did she know at the time, Viola had no plans to acknowledge what she deemed the tainted bloodline that Georgea had produced. Viola vowed to keep the promise she made to her mother on her death bed, even until her death.

Georgea was known to have a gracious heart for seeing the good in all those around her. These sensitive ways of viewing life had made her vulnerable to the cruelest intentions of both her mother and her only sister Viola. Nevertheless, that day her life would change forever and Georgea could think of nothing but her dear children. The ultimatum that came to her doorstep that early morning after seeing her family off for the day was nauseating and to her it seemed like only yesterday. If it wasn't for meeting Jonas near the stream that day in the mountains, she would have probably driven herself mad with guilt long ago. The Captain had made it very clear that morning he would not have any control over the nightriders that randomly came into the segregated area of Memphis. Many times, she and Bufus would witness the terrorism of the Ku Klux Klan as they targeted selective households. Many of these households were friends that they would never see again. Therefore, she had to decide or face the consequences, so Georgea without a second thought decided she loved her family more than fighting with her sister.

Adrienne Lynn Rutherford

The greed and jealousy that possessed Viola all her life had festered into a cloak of darkness that covered both her and her son. She used her dark power and wealth to remove Georgea permanently out of their lives and the lives of her husband and children. It was because of this, Georgea had given up life as she knew it and everything she loved. Now, looking back she thought of her mother and the deceptive hate she instilled in her once loving sister Viola. In that moment Georgea slowly got up out of her old rocking chair, the place where she mourned sometimes almost endlessly. She opened her front door and looked up into the sky and to her surprise the moon was out earlier than usual this evening. With the sun barely settled in its evening resting place, the fullness of the moon was eager to show its illumination high above the tall pine trees. Georgea thought of her daughters, how they too had become prey to her sister Viola. She then screamed at the top of her voice

"SHE WILL NOT DESTROY MY SEEDS!"

Georgea returned inside of her modest log cabin home and went over to a lonely trunk that sat in the corner near the fireplace. She held her lantern close as she opened it. Inside was a variety of beautiful yet weathered women's clothing, make up, shoes and a few photos that she had taken many years ago at what was now the abandoned Sawyer home. Georgea wiped her brow as she gazed down into the picture of her beloved husband Buford Sawyer.

"The Sawyers will never have to run, ever again!"

She then softly placed a kiss on her deceased husbands photo and began preparing for her return to the city. As Georgea continued to ramble among her belongings she came across the Bible that her husband had given her. She opened it up and read the inscription Buford Sawyer had written many years before.

"In this life, we will have many trials and tribulations, but through love and faith and holding the hand of the Lord we will always have peace surrounding us."

She embraced it and held on tightly as she regained her strength in the comfort of beautiful memories. Georgea smiled as she thought of the many scriptures her husband shared, she flipped the pages to read his favorite, Romans 12:19-21 and afterward, she looked to the sky.

"Dear God, I'm stronger now and I'm ready for this battle."

Georgea didn't shed a tear, she'd already cried far too many nights. She then pulled out a cloth satchel and placed her bible and a few items inside. While traveling down the mountain carefully and patiently, Georgea realized that she'd created a prison of her own. All these years thinking she was protecting her children, but now she would come to the even more painful realization that it had been fear all along that controlled her life. In that moment, Georgea vowed to bring Viola to her knees for all the misery she imposed on their lives and in doing so sought to reunite with her daughters, her goal was to seek forgiveness and an attempt to salvage the love that once brought peace and joy to the Sawyer Family many years ago.

Georgea soon arrived on Beale Street, she noticed that things had changed a great deal since her last journey. She took her time from memory as she passed by the many entertainment spots and restaurants to identify the exact location of Venus Alley. When she finally came across the uniquely French inspired building she knew she'd arrived at her destination. In the front of the building and inside a large glass framed where pictures of the entertainment that performed nightly. She looked closely at the photos and smiled when she recognized the face of her daughter Queen among the other entertainers. Georgea checked her appearance through the reflection of the glass. She fixed her hair and rugged mountain attire before entering. Georgea with all the grace that she learned in finishing school walked through the front door. When she entered, Georgea was quite intrigued by the beautiful décor of Venus Alley. The black velvet chairs and crisp white table clothes accented by the large beautiful crystal chandeliers all gave an alluring ambience. Every table was full and the waiters and waitresses where moving around servicing tables as if in a well-rehearsed routine. Georgea could smell the lingering scent of cigars as the live band performed in front of the empty stage floor. Georgea suspected that it had been intermission and her thoughts were confirmed as the master of ceremonies took the stage. His humor encouraged Georgea to smile, but was soon interrupted.

Adrienne Lynn Rutherford

"May I help you?"

Georgea leaned on the bar.

"Yes, Greta Funchess Please."

The young barmaid looked over Georgea with curiosity for a brief moment.

"Who should I say is inquiring please?"

"Tell her it's a friend of Queen's."

The young woman looked startled for a minute and then waved at a waitress to meet her at the end of the bar. She whispered in the ear of the waitress and she disappeared into the crowd.

The barmaid then returned to Georgea.

"Would you like a drink while you wait ma'am?"

"Yes, thank you."

"I will have a shot of your best rum dear."

Before Georgea could finish her dink, JoJo greeted her at the bar.

"Good evening, Miss Greta will see you now."

Georgea turned up the remainder of her shot, spent around on her bar stool and followed Jojo through the crowd into the back of the club. Soon the sounds resonating from the front would become only a distant echo. He took her up the tall spiral staircase until they reached a large cedar wood door and then he knocked.

"Come in please."

Jojo pulled the handle down gently and pushed the door open, he didn't step in but opened it wide enough so that Georgea could enter.

Greta then smiled.

"Welcome, a friend of Queen's is truly a friend of mines, Jo leave us please."

The large giant of a man nodded as he gently closed the door behind him and when it was clear, Greta smiled at her long-life friend and they embraced.

"Oh Georgea, what a surprise."

The two met many years ago as teenagers in the South of France. Their families would gather with many others from around the world to address the atrocities that where a threat to human rights. Their fathers became ally's in this cause and collaborated with

Dance of Angels   149

others to address its negative impact in the United States and abroad. The Quickman family spent many summers in France and as a result the girls would become close friends. However, while speaking out against the German occupation of France and the up rise of anti-Semitism, Greta's father was killed. With the help of Mr. Quickman, she and her mother would flee to London and it was here that Georgea would visit and watch her friend perform. However, after the tragic death of her father, Georgea would lose contact with Greta for several years until reuniting again in New York at the World's Fair.

It was here for the first-time Greta was introduced to Queen when she was just a child. She would share her plan to move to Memphis Tennessee to open a Burlesque House on the famous Beale Street. At the time Georgea had no idea that Greta's decision would be her saving grace. However, their paths would not meet as soon as she would have otherwise expected before he fled to the mountains. The time she spent in the mountains, away from the life that she missed so dearly was softened after meeting Jonas. He kept her informed about life in Memphis. So, after she found out about the death of her beloved husband Georgea wrote a letter to Greta. In the letter, she explained the terrible events that had manifested in her life. Georgea vowed Jonas to secrecy and sent him to present the humble petition to her dear friend Greta. Her request, that Greta position herself in the lives of her daughters and make sure they were safe.

At first, Greta did everything she could to gather more information from Jonas and she was both infuriated as well as impressed by the loyalty he displayed for her dear friend. Overtime, she stopped inquiring and did as her dear friend asked of her. She would have to be creative by not giving away her intentions to Queen, otherwise it could be a catastrophe for all those involved. Overtime, Greta would successfully position herself with the intent to fulfil the promise she made and as a result, things had worked out well considering the dire circumstances. However, but now seeing her dear friend after all of these years brought her overwhelming joy. Greta lit her a cigarette and poured them both a drink.

"Things are a bit coarse right now with Queen and that evil

Adrienne Lynn Rutherford

sister of yours."

"The woman is mad, mad I say."

Greta began pacing the floor.

"You know she had the nerve to come and visit me here with that old crooked cop?"

"As if me of all people would give her any type of information."

"Foolish woman, if I did know anything, I mean anything, I would never betray you."

"She also knows she can't harm me, she's in far too much debt to not only my husband but the *Banks of Old*."

"She's a terrible business woman, she's running your father's legacy into the ground.

"Oh, and that nephew of yours, he was a sick man, sick I tell you.

"It's almost unspeakable the things that he has done in the community and your twisted sister, she would turn a blind eye to it all."

"He got what he deserved."

When she cooled off, Greta sat down next to Georgea who appeared to struggle with digesting everything that had transpired since she had abandoned her life and her family. Greta had kept her promise all these years that she would not retaliate against Viola. Although she wanted to make her accountable for all the pain that she had imposed upon the timid Georgea, Greta could only pray in hopes that she would come out of hiding and take her life back. Today her prayers had been answered and she waited patiently to hear what Georgea had to say. She would walk this walk with Georgea to the very end, even if it meant eliminating the likes of the Medusa for good.

Georgea in her new-found strength then spoke to her dear friend.

"Greta, I just want to thank you for all that you have done, your loyalty is far beyond words."

"There could not be a better friend in this life."

"Oh, my dear Georgea, how could I not be there for you."

"I must admit, I honestly thought I would never see you again."

It was if one day you were here and the next, you just fell off the face of the Earth.".

"Georgea smiled briefly."

"I do believe I did for a spell, but I'm back and I'm ready to deal with my sister."

"I refuse to allow her to destroy the lives of my daughters, they deserve a decent life in this world and she has no right to interfere with that."

"Well your sister has been quite the monster in this town for a while and everyone fears her."

"The power that she holds has driven her mad just mad!"

"I think she has gone mad, they have nicknamed her the Medusa."

"Well thank God you're here now and I'm sure you heard the details of what has happened to the girls."

"I have thanks to Jonas, love him like my very own son."

"I have put a terrible burden on him all these years, but from now on I have to face my life myself."

Chapter 18

Meanwhile, Coaster and Tyler relaxed at his spot on the eastside of Memphis. *"Fat Cats,"* was located in the basement of a large brick tenement building. It was a modest place with several tables and chairs, a small bar and a piano in the corner. Coaster also managed to have a small stage built for performers and local talent who auditioned weekly to catch his attention. Tonight, there was a small local band playing with a woman singing a rendition of *"Aint Nobody's Business If I do."* Tyler and Coaster sat down at his table near the stage and they continued their discussion. He looked around the small humble establishment and once seeing it, he knew that coaster would be more than grateful for the opportunity that he was offering him back in Tulsa. He excused himself from the small group to go to the restroom Tyler, on his return noticed wanted sign" sign stuck to one of the large wooden poles that supported the foundation of the building. Out of curiosity went over to the picture when he got up close on it he almost choked seeing the faces of Queen and her twin sister. Tyler continued reading the description and was even more shocked to see that they were all wanted for murder. He looked at the reward for them all and grabbed his handkerchief to wipe the sweat off his brow suddenly broke out in a cold sweat. When he returned to the table and sat down sat down his previous worries lifted like an early morning fog. He could think of nothing but the handsome reward that was offered for the capture of these three women. He then inquired about the wanted sign to Coaster.

"Hey man, what's that all about?"

"They look harmless."

Pointing to the picture of the ladies."

"Oh, those three are far from harmless, more like heroines"

"They got rid of one of the worst scum bags here in Memphis, running around attacking young women at night."

"From what I heard in the streets, he attempted to attack one of them in the house and they got the best of him."

"The sheriff's department would turn a blind eye, until those three laid him to rest, stuck him one good time rumor has it."

"Here's the catch though, his mother is Viola Quickman of the

Quickman coal mines."

"Filthy rich man, but one evil woman, who I might add you don't want to cross."

"Those three were in their right mind to skip town, they had no chance for any kind of justice, none!"

Tyler was quite amused at the discussion that had surfaced from his inquiry and attempted to explore the situation even further.

"They fled the town and no one had heard from them since. As you can see the reward is quite tempting."

"Of course, none of the folks around here would even consider it and their father was a good man, a really good man."

"The sheriff insist that we post their picture, but to us it is a sign of solidarity to the girls and their brave attempt to seek their own justice."

Tyler was amused at the events that transpired and would be the catalyst for his encounter with the girls back in Greenwood. He pulled out his cigar and began to light it, but before he could the crowd began to scream as the police strong armed their way down the stairs with Billy clubs and revolvers. The captain shot in the air and the room went into silence.

"You all are under arrest"

"I hope you people have bail money, because you all are going to jail tonight."

"Who's in charge here?"

The room remained silent.

"I'm going to ask one more time, and then I'm going to start giving out additional accounts to everybody."

"I am sir, I'm in charge."

The Captain pulled Coaster to the side and walked him to the bar area.

"Routine run man."

Coaster whispered back.

"What do you mean routine run?"

"I pay you guys not to get raided."

"Well, things have changed."

Before Coaster could respond the captain pushed him into the crowd with the others. He then went behind the bar and underneath

154

where two cases one of tequila the other Caribbean rum. The captain pulled out a bottle and grabbed a glass and poured a shot. He took the glass and shook it up and then lifted it to his nose.

"Ahhh you got the good stuff too."

He then turned the glass up taking the shot and sitting it back on the table.

"Book'em all."

"Captain I assure you this is all a misunderstanding once we get to the police station I think we can settle this with no problem."

The captain looked over Tyler in his finely dressed clothing and narcissistic demeanor.

"Who the hell do you think you are?"

The captain had no time to educate him on how things were done in Memphis and swiftly threw his hand up.

"Take'em all."

As promised, everyone was loaded into the two paddy wagons and taken to the police station.

Tyler and Coaster along with a few others were still sitting in the cell waiting to make bail. Tyler knew there would be no one coming for him, but after the events that had transpired at Coasters place, he found himself in position for an opportunity. So, he waited in hopes of speaking to the captain alone.

In least than an hour the Captain showed up with two other deputies.

"You two get up someone made bail."

Surprised at the comment made by the captain, Tyler got up and dusted his pants off, grabbed his suit jacket and followed Coaster out of the cell. As they walked down the hallway the captain the large door opened and Coaster went through, however the captain would hold Tyler back. Coaster turned around curiously as he watched the door shut behind him as his sister Manuela greeted him in the waiting area.

"Coaster, what happened?"

"Don't want to talk about it right now sis, how'd you know we were here?"

"Alta told me, she came by the house."

"Something wrong Coaster?"

"No, everything is fine."

Suddenly the large steel door opened again and it was Tyler.

"Hey man, what's going on what did the captain want with you?"

"Nothing man, he just asked me a few questions is all, where I was from, what I'm doing here, and how long will I'll be here."

"You know the standard harassment tactics."

After collecting their confiscated belongings Coaster and Tyler agreed to meet for more discussion about their business venture. The night had obviously been cut short and both were in much need of rest. Coaster and his sister took Tyler to his room and they headed home.

After the disturbing events, Tyler had been up all-night thinking about the picture that he'd seen. It had amazed him that the situation had fell so smoothly into his hands and all he could think about was the reward. Still quite surprised, he would have never suspected those beautiful women he met back in Greenwood would be capable of murder. Nevertheless, it was this same thinking that had got him in the situation that has haunted him for the past eight years. Tyler knew that he could in no way discuss the possibility of pursuing the reward money with Coaster, it was obvious he was far too loyal to the family. He then thought of the priceless opportunity for his egotistical pride, to see the look on Queen's face after making him look like a fool in his own club.

The following afternoon Tyler joined Coaster for breakfast.

"Damn last night was crazy man, I sure hate you had to experience that."

"No one wants to go out of town and end up in jail."

"What are the chances of that?"

Tyler laughed.

"Those chances are high and likely for a black man."

Coaster smiled.

"You know, you are right about that."

"So, now man you see my dilemma."

"The folks don't want to come into my place anymore because of that crooked captain and his croons."

"Do you know I paid him this month and he still reneged on the agreement and took the money, man I can't take it no more?"

"It's taking everything out of me not to do something real desperate up in here, he's trying to run me out of business man, this is my livelihood and he won't us alone."

"When I first seen the likes of Tulsa Greenwood District in the papers, I said that's the place for me and my family." "Greenwood is a Blackman's utopia and a lot of folk's dream of going there."

Tyler, although entertaining the conversation wasn't really interested in the small talk about Greenwood. He felt it a comfortable prison sentence and was now ready to move on and the only way he could do that was with money. He had no loyalties to Coaster or the city of Greenwood district. Tyler longed for a future that resembled the past. IT was because of this he had a deep longing in the depths his soul, and was willing to do anything to retain it. Coaster on the other hand was no fool, the small talk was only a smoke screen for the thought that he really had about the Tyler fellow, after leaving the station last night he thought about the expression that was left on Tyler's face when he walked out of the holding area. Tyler had spent too much time in the back with the captain and his extended stay behind that big steel door brought Coaster to one conclusion, he was a rat and he could not be trusted. However, Coaster would not become distracted by the questionable character of Tyler Parker. He had decided that he would concentrate primarily on getting this business deal finalized, so that he and his family could start a new life. After breakfast the men parted ways, Coaster headed to the Billiards hall for his meeting with Jonas and Tyler returned to his hotel room to wait for the opportunities that would soon change his life for good.

Tyler was never one to put all his eggs into one basket. His thoughts where to play the situation like a good game of chess. Coaster's intuition was correct. Tyler had spoken to the captain and after the conversation at 'Fat Cats, it was far too obvious that Coaster would have no parts in turning the women in for monetary gain. So, later in the evening after dark Tyler found himself being picked up and driven into the darkness of the night. The ride was the most uncomfortable ride he ever felt in his life. Never in a million years did he ever think he would voluntarily get into the automobile with two white police officers and be driven out into no man's land on two lane road in the south. As he sat in the back seat of the car, his obsession with Queen seemed to resonate as well as the cynical thoughts of her being hauled off like the criminal she was. He would unapologetically claim the enormous reward for himself and never set foot on American soil ever again.

Tyler's thoughts were interrupted by two sets of headlights that illuminated brightly through the front window. When the automobile came to a complete stop, the two policemen got out and then hit the passenger door with a bully club signaling Tyler to get out as well. As he followed them over to the other automobiles there was the Captain accompanied by an elderly stern-faced woman.

"Tyler Parker, I would like to introduce you to Madame Viola Quickman."

Tyler extended his hand to Viola, only to have it lingering alone in space as she looked at it with distaste. He then slowly retrieved it and rubbed off his trousers. Viola looked him up and down and gave him a smile of mockery. "Let me be simple and brief, we are not friends, we are not associates, nor are we buddies…nothing. I don't know you, I don't care to know you."

"That I have found out however is that you have some very valuable information for me and that is the only reason, I mean the only reason that I have taken the time to ride out her to even entertain this meeting."

"Once you provide me with what you know, I will decide whether or not it is valuable enough for me to act on. If I decide to act on the information you providef and it serves to give me what I expected, then and only then will you be rewarded."

"Do you understand?"

Tyler gazing into the hatefulness that laid dormant in the Medusa's eyes, nodded a speechless affirmative. He could not believe what he saw, as an evil darkness he had seen in all his life. This woman's energy was cold and dismissive and filled with an indescribable hate, but also pain. Tyler also sensed pain and loneliness beyond anything he'd ever come across in all his travels of the world. Although surprised, he was not intimidated by the attitude and demonic energy this woman displayed. His persistence would not be overshadowed, especially not now. Tyler had made plans and

158   Adrienne Lynn Rutherford

he would see them through if it meant the death of him, so he simply responded properly.

"Yes ma'am"

"Okay boy, tell her what you told me."

Tyler greed, but before he spoke it didn't take long for another idea to settle in, especially with the opportunity that had presented itself tonight."

"'Now if they wanted to kill me, they would have done so a long time ago, the information that I have must really have some value, maybe even more value than the reward she is offering."

What's really going on with the Madame Quickman and Queen, he thought to himself.

"Okay, I will simply tell you what I told the captain, I know where the girls on the wanted poster are."

Becoming impatient with the whole situation, Viola popped her fan out and began to wave it the humid night air.

"Yes, we know that much, Mr. Feldman told me that much."

"Where are they?"

Tyler straightened out his suite while eyeballing the other police that stood on both sides of him.

"Well let's just start off with one fact, they are not in Tennessee."

Viola walked up to Tyler and put her face in his displaying frustration due to the turn of events.

"Captain where did you get this scumbag?"

"My time is far too valuable for this, this magnet."

She then turned her attention back to Tyler who grimaced because of the remarks she had made toward him. It had been way to long since he would have a face to face conflict with the likes of Viola Quickman and it was obvious that she had not taking long to get up under his very thin skin.

"Let's just be straight and to the point, you are playing a game with me."

"I didn't come all this way to play games with you boy. I have a train to catch in exactly two hours and if you value your life, you will give me the information that I need this instance!"

Tyler spit on the ground.

"You won't kill me you need me."

Viola grinned at what she thought was absolute madness.

"Captain this man doesn't know anything, get rid of him."

Once Tyler realized just how expendable he was he frantically stopped the captain.

"Okay, Okay, Okay."

Viola then cynically smiled again.

"See, he's full of foolery captain, take him out into the woods and string him up high and let the vultures have their way with him."

Viola then walked away and Suddenly out of desperation Tyler screamed out to the *Medusa*.

"She has a birthmark the shape of heart on the side of her cheek, her right cheek, her eyes are a hazel brown and her skin is the shade of a ripe walnut."

Viola swiftly turned around.

"Turn him loose."

Tyler fell to the ground and Viola stooped down and took her gloved hand and squeezed Tyler's face tightly.

"I'm going to ask you again, where are they?"

Tyler smiled at the skill that he had mastered since a youth. He had hustled Viola Quickman right into the palm of his hands. He laughed to himself as he watched her frustration cloud her dark cynicism. Tyler reeled her in nice and easy and she would be his biggest catch yet.

"You get your hands off me!"

"You think I would risk my life to come out here in the middle of nowhere if I couldn't deliver you the goods."

"Let's be clear Madame Quickman, I'm a different kind of nigga, don't let this European suit fool you by any means."

"I got what you want and I'm willing to hand them all over to you on a silver platter, or hey you can kill me now."

"I have nothing to lose only to gain, but you, you on the other hand you I do believe have a lot to lose."

Viola with a stern look of contempt on her face, released Tyler from her grasp. As he straightened out his suit wiping it off with his hands he looked around at the shock look on the faces of the

Adrienne Lynn Rutherford

officers. Apparently, it had been a first for them to see someone handle the Medusa in such a way, especially the captain. No one spoke a word while they waited for the next move from Tyler.

"Your reward is generous, but you and I both know that it's not a lot for someone like myself, who knows how serious this matter really is to you. I want double what your offering for the twins and triple for Queen."

Viola said nothing, as much as she would have liked to give orders to the captain to take the life from this man, she had to respect his ruthlessness. It was obvious he knew what he was talking about. It was difficult for anyone to see such details in the black and white photo that appeared in almost every corner of Memphis.

"Okay Mr. Parker this is what I am offering, you can take it or leave it, its solely up to you."

"This hefty reward you're asking for is steep, so you will of course have to work for it. Therefore, you will have to bring them to me."

Tyler was stunned, in his mind this arrangement was going far better than he could have imagined.

"I will take it, but you must come to Oklahoma once I get her to the border you can take them from there and the money must be there. I want cash all c notes please. We both know this thing won't work without the money.

"Mr. Parker, we are all too clear on the fact the money plays a primary role in the situation you need not remind me of that."

"Also, please know if you do not deliver, let's just say your head on a platter is of equal value to me"

"Do you understand?"

"Of course, Madame."

"Okay then it's settled, you will give the captain the details."

Viola returned to her chauffer driven automobile and was swiftly driven off into darkness. The captain walked up to Tyler scratching his head.

"You are one lucky son-of-bitch, you know that?"

"I thought you were done, but you found a way slither out of that one son, just know you're playing a deadly game of Russian Roulette with that one."

"You will not get another chance like that one, I can promise you that."

The captain nodded to the others as they grabbed Tyler and shoved him in the back seat of the captain's car. During the ride Tyler gave the Captain just enough information to get them to downtown Tulsa. Afterwards, he was let out along the roadside almost half a mile, but could see the well-lit district of Greenwood in the distance. Tyler leaned against the weeping willow alongside the road and took a deep breath. He was not moved by the events that had taken place to night, he had been a fool to risk his life. However, as he marched in his dusty suite back to town, he lit his cigar thinking to himself

"Soon this will all be a memory".

Adrienne Lynn Rutherford

Chapter 19

Greenwood District Tulsa, Oklahoma

Cody was excited when her big brother took time to teach her how to drive his shiny C.R. Patterson Automobile. She had been the talk of the town among her peers. Although her parents had not approved at first, like always she was able to convince them for the opportunity that all teenagers dreamed of. Today, her brother would give her the ultimate test and she waited anxiously on the porch for his arrival.

Mayor Watkins also waited for Calvin, he needed to talk to him. It had taken him quite some time to build up the nerve to do so. He'd had some questions for him and not withstanding his past behavior, he knew that it was important that he spoke his peace before his departure. The last family dinner, he'd broken his wife's heart and on that same night he promised to never do it again. So today, he would be a listener and do what he should have done from the start. Mayor Watkins would respect his son as a man and not a child. Time had stood still for Mayor Watkins, he was quite proud of the economic success of Greenwood District. It had surpassed all his hopes and provided a haven for his children to have a far peaceful childhood than he could ever remember. However, he also could see the tension growing, it had been doing so for quite some time. When Calvin arrived to confirm what he had been denying for the past few years it struck a chord in him and he acted out of fear and hurt. Mr. Watkins would have a firsthand encounter because of the flourishing economic freedom for black folks in Greenwood District.

Less than six months ago he had been literally kicked out of the very bank that he held his money in across the tracks. It left him confused and disheartened trying to withdraw his funds while being mocked by the locals inside. How could they treat him in such away taunting at him and calling him out of his name? After speaking to the bank manager, he demanded to close his account and collect his funds. He put his head down while sitting on his front porch thinking about the disrespect he had encountered. He never told his wife what had transpired at the bank, including the fact that the manger informed him it would take thirty days for him to withdraw his funds. This brought a sense of anger and discontent that did not sit well with Mayor Watkins. As a result, he knew only one man could straighten out his situation, the real mayor of Tulsa. His primary objective was to collect his funds and then he would resign as administrator of Tulsa Greenwood District, allowing him to sever his ties with the southside of Tulsa for good. However, upon arriving to the Mayor's modest Mansion he received the surprise of his life. Mayor Evans was hardly interested in the issue that Mr. Watkins would bring to his doorstep, instead he was more concerned with what he thought a very pressing problem in the political business of Tulsa.

"Watkins please come in and have a seat, I was just about to send for you."

"Great minds think alike I guess."

"Please sit down."

Mr. Watkins sat down across from the mayor and the distance between the two of them was much farther than he had remembered. The events of that day seemed as though he was now looking at the world through a microscope, everything seemed to be more magnified in his mind. Reality had created in him an awakening from a sleep he'd been in far too long.

"Mayor Evans, before we get started, I have an issue."

"I do as well, if yours is personal we can deal with it later, mine however is about the people Watkins."

"The people are getting quite agitated by the negras and their uppity ways."

"The negras don't come and shop on this side of town like they use to anymore."

In that moment Mr. Watkins heart fell in his lap, because he could not believe what he was hearing. All this time he felt that he and the Mayor were on the same page regarding the progression on the northside of Tulsa. Mr. Watkins thought he'd did a mighty great job encouraging economic growth and providing opportunities for successful black entrepreneurs and professionals on the Southside. It had ignited a sense of pride and dignity in the community as well as a foundation for generations to follow.

Adrienne Lynn Rutherford

"Mayor Evans, I beg your pardon sir, but I don't understand how the Negros money can affect the economic stability of the Southside."

There are plenty of wealthy white folks over here to sustain the base, far wealthier than the people of Greenwood."

"True, but they don't spend in the community as much, they shop European, Italian, French you know that."

"I here they pay their maids and butlers a pretty decent coin."

"It's the hardworking white business owners that I'm concerned with, they feel that Greenwood business is destroying their stability and they're upset about it."

"They fear for their children's future."

"I just want you to encourage them to share the wealth just a bit is all?"

Mr. Watkins shook his head as he felt like a fool, he was also a republican, but how could he could have ever thought Mayor Evans would be concerned for the best interest of his people. As he continued to rock in his chair, he took a long toke from his pipe, remembering that day as if it was yesterday.

"This ass hole has lost his damn mind, what in God's name did he think the Negros where concerned about, did he not think we were concerned about our future and the future of our children as well. Had he not been paying attention to our concerns all these years, didn't he know that's why I took the damn job, to better the position of my people too!"

"Why does it always have to be us or them?"

"Sir I must say that it's very difficult for the negroes to patronize your businesses if they're working all day and have to be back on the northside before dark."

"As for the weekend, well there is no need to cross the tracks unless they're working in the homes, so they stay on their side and mind their own business just like you wanted them to."

"Remember Mayor that was the arrangement, that was the main priority when you appointed me over twenty years ago.

"Well Watkins, now things have changed and times are changing."

People are on the edge about their futures, so agendas as well as strategies must change as well."

"That is why you were afforded some of the opportunities that you have had, you're supposed to take care of things like that."

"Take care of things like what?"

"Excuse me?"

"My apologies Mayor, but what do you expect I do?"

"I want you to think hard Watkins, you're a smart man, be real creative about it."

"I mean after all they do call you the Major over there, don't they?"

"With all that had been said in those few moments nothing burned the spirit of Mr. Watkins like the last comment made by Mayor Evans."

"Well don't they?"

"Yes Sir."

"Well, I chose you to oversee the business of Greenwood and you've done a mighty fine job, but I just want to let you know my folks on the northside been having a difficult time seeing negras walking around uppity in their fine clothes and driving their fine cars."

"It's just not normal behavior and it's not something I think the folks on the northside of town could ever get used to."

"Do you understand where I'm coming from Watkins?"

"Watkins, it's just not appropriate, it's not the American way."

"Hell, if anyone would have told me that there would be a negra community with self-owned businesses, educators, airplanes, trains and automobiles and such, well I have to just come right out and tell you."

"I'd have to tell them, they have lost their goddamned mind."

"All I'm saying Watkins is I can't be responsible for what happens, don't get me wrong I even enjoy coming over to that Maggie's Place for that good down-home cooking, like my mammy use to make back home in Alabama."

"But, my folks her on the northside wanna see a little of that prosperity on this side of the tracks is all and I'm sure you can convince them all the same."

"What do you mean?"

Adrienne Lynn Rutherford

"I mean I'm an elected official and being an elected official, I have to appease the people who put me in office, I can't be responsible for what happens, I can't stress that enough."

It was apparent to Mr. Watkins that there was nothing he could say that would resonate with the Mayor. It appeared that a meeting had already taken place and he had not been invited. Although feeling defeated he'd walked with his head high. He would not internalize the hatred the Mayor of Tulsa displayed penetrate his spirit, even as disingenuous it was. He was still a very prideful man and rightfully so, However, he'd put much too of his trust in a very complicated and bias system. It was a disturbing conclusion to what Mr. Watkins thought was a civil arrangement. His thoughts were soon interrupted by the sound of Calvin's automobile pulling up to the house. As he greeted his sister, Mr. Watkins was thankful of the fine job Mrs. Watkins had did with instilling so much love in their children. He was proud of his children and now understood their need to find their own way, even in the mist of his criticism. They were strong confident human beings of purpose in this world and this he proudly accredited to himself.

"Hey pops."

"Hey Calvin"

Calvin gave his father a nod and went directly into the house. Mr. Watkins had expected as much, he'd been hard on his son the first day he arrived back to Greenwood. Calvin reminded him of the foolish and prideful idealism he would have come to embrace and how that same idealism would portray him and leave him penniless. His thoughts were interrupted by is his daughter.

"You alright papa."

"Yeah."

"You don't seem like it, you know I know you."

"Cody always remember, when you are young, you are invincible, nothing can harm you and there is no fear."

"As you grow older and wiser you realize the world can be a dangerous place and it will run you over like a train if you are not careful with the choices you make."

"Behind every choice is a consequence, remember that."

"I don't want you to have any regrets like your father."

"Yes papa."

Mr. Watkins, as much as he wanted to could not bring himself to have the discussion that he had so anticipated with his son, he was too ashamed. Soon Calvin returned to the front porch and Mrs. Watkins and they could see Mr. Watkins walking toward the stables in the distance.

Mrs. Watkins went up to her son and put her hand on his shoulder.

"Be patient with him dear, I feel he's coming around."

"Yes Ma."

"You wouldn't believe it but you are a lot like him you know."

"How do you think we made it out here to Oklahoma, his intuition and a desire for a better life."

She then hugged him tightly.

"Please, watch after your brother John and you tell him I said to be careful. I know you both are grown men, but you can still look after one another."

"Absolutely, and it was a pleasure meeting you as well."
Calvin cranked up the automobile and then signaled to Cody.

"Cody, your gonna drive us to pick up a friend."

"Who?"

"You'll see soon enough."

After picking up Queen they made their way to the train station. Her presence had changed the way he was seeing his life. Before returning home, Calvin had everything all planned and had no intentions of settling down. He reminisced on his previous thoughts about his next great adventures, he would tackle the Canadian terrain. The mountains of Canada where vast and he'd heard rumors of the abundance of minks and beavers that made fine coats for the winter months. Not that he needed the money, he thought it would be intriguing to explore. Nevertheless, his bright idea was shattering by the day, thanks to Queen.

Now, he would have to settle this business in Montana. Calvin had no idea what this big meeting was about because they all had agreed to a certain percentage of ownership in the contract. Calvin assumed Roger Quickman's percentage would just go to his mother. However, his intuition told him there was something else brewing

Adrienne Lynn Rutherford

and he wasn't looking forward to it Regardless of the circumstances it would not ruin his plans, Calvin was looking forward to the highlight of his trip and hated that William wasn't able to come along with them. He was looking forward to sharing with his brother the life he'd lived for the last five years. While in Montana, he would take him would take him to his ranch in Montana and show him the one-hundred-acre ranch we're he'd made his fortune with cattle and breeding mustangs for his investment in horse racing down in Central America. He smiled to himself as if he could see the look on his brothers face when he would explain that the family would no longer have to work again. Not only did he want the company of his family at his ranch, but he also wanted the company of Queen and hopefully for the rest of their lives. Queen had shared with him the most intimate part of her existence, but deep down his intuition told him she struggled with much more. Also, the entertainment business was her life and many who chose this type of lifestyle very rarely settled down. He smiled again, thinking it had not been until now that he considered settling down himself.

As they reached the train station Cody spotted her older brother in the distance.

"Look there's John and a lady, who's the lady?"

"That's my little sister Carolyn."

"She doesn't look so little to me.'

Queen laughed.

"You're right she's all grown up and I have to remember that."

Cody then looked over at her brother.

"Tell me about it, between the two of them, they still try to treat me like a little girl and I'm almost grown."

"Shoot I couldn't even mention a fella's name around my brother John until my sixteenth birthday, imagine that."

Calvin pointed his finger at his younger sister.

"You just be just be glad it was John who was home with you, because if it was me you would not have been able to mention a fella's name until your twentieth birthday."

"Oh, stop it see what I mean Queen."

Queen greeted her sister.

"How was the trip?"

"It was really fun, I spent the night on an Indian reservation and I smoked a peace pipe."

"John knows so many different people, I brought you guys something back."

"How about you, how was the big film bash?"

"'It was wonderful, the film was remarkable, I was asked to perform and...."

"Wait hold up, you were asked to perform, for Oscar Micheaux?"

"Yes."

"Oh, my goodness, Queen that's amazing."

"Wow, if I wasn't with John I would say that I hated to miss that."

Queen then put her hand on her hips.

"Ohh is that so huh.'

They both laughed amongst one another as Calvin pulled his luggage out of the trunk. And Carolyn then looked over at Cody.

"Who is this beautiful young lady?"

"Howdy, Cody is my name."

"I'm Calvin and John's younger sister and I'm driving."

Carolyn eyed her elder sister then looked back at Cody.

"Are you riding with us?"

"Well I suppose so."

Soon the loud sound of the train whistle could be heard and it received the attention of all that were waiting its arrival.

Calvin sighed

"Ah, right on time for a change, you ready John?"

"Yep, haven't rode the train this much since the war."

John walked over to Carolyn and gave her a kiss.'

"Take care of yourself I will see you soon."

Calvin did the same and Queen smiled, blowing kisses to him as they departed.

"See you soon."

"Yes, see you soon."

John and Carolyn both looked at the two of them oddly. Once the men settled in the baggage car John didn't hesitate to address the situation with his younger brother.

Adrienne Lynn Rutherford

"Man, what was that all about."

"Open displays of affection, that's not the Calvin that I know."

"Man, what's gotten into you in the last forty-eight hours, did I miss something?"

"It appears I missed something."

"You didn't miss nothing, it was just a hug man."

"A simple hug."

"Naw man, that wasn't just a hug that was a huuuggg."

"You love that girl, don't you?"

John waited for his brother's typical combative response when it came to his feelings about relationship in the past.

"Man, it is, what it is."

John hit his brother on the back and laughed.

"Wow, who would have thought this day would come, leaving home either did you some good, or where you were the air was really thin."

Calvin started laughing.

"Man, your foolish, eh what about you and Carolyn?"

"I have to admit, I'm digging her."

"We had a great time out at the reservation."

"Something strange is going on with her though man."

"Like what?"

"I don't know, like she's guarded and she doesn't talk much about her past."

"Really?"

"Well I got that same feeling with Queen, real mysterious like."

"Man, when they first arrived I was at the station."

"All of them looked a little uncomfortable, especially the twins. I don't think they had ever visited Greenwood District before."

"They looked uneasy you know"

"Queen, well it appeared it had been a life time ago since she set foot in Greenwood, because she didn't even know who I was."

"Which is kinda strange to say the least, come to think about it."

John began to laugh at his brother.

"Oh really, kinda bruised your ego uh?"

"Yeah sorta man."

"Well, let me be the first to say I'm not too cool with secrets and I don't like surprises either."

Calvin stretched out and laid back on his luggage.

"Yeah bro, I know what you mean."

****

Queen and Carolyn made their way down the country dirt road bracing themselves while overseeing Cody at the wheel of the car. To Carolyn's surprise, she was doing pretty good. Cody was not like most young ladies in the area, since she had to grow up in the shadow of two alpha male brothers.

"So, ladies, what brings you to Greenwood?"

"Visiting our aunt Ma'me."

"Miss Ma'me?"

"I love her, I use to take her chocolate all the time when I was a little girl."

"She loves chocolate you know."

"We used to sit and talk for hours on her porch, she has the gift you know."

Carolyn was quite amused by Cody's revelation.

"The gift?"

"Yeah sure."

"I remember when I was a little girl, people would come by the house all the time and they would pay her to tell them things."

"She never took money from me though, all I had to do is bring her a little chocolate sometimes."

The sisters exchanged a look of discretion, as Cody without suspicion continued to enlighten them.

"But one day she just stopped and told folks she wasn't reading no more."

"I asked her why."

"She told me, sometimes if you're not careful certain things can drain the life force right out of you."

In that moment, Queen realized she wasn't the only one who was keeping secrets. The ladies dropped Cody off at home and Queen took the wheel as they made their way back to the house. When they arrived, Ma'me was in her favorite place peacefully rocking in her chair on the porch. The ladies greeted her with kisses of love, but Queen had more on her mind and Ma'me knew it.

"Baby is there something wrong, you want to talk to Ma'me?"

"Ma'me, why didn't you tell me you had the gift?"

Ma'me was silent for a while and then she spoke.

"Who told you that?"

"Cody Watkins."

Ma'me began to smile humorously.

"That little girl always had a big ole mouth, but I love her."

"Well you gonna tell Ma'me what else she said?"

"I'm a little rusty you know, it's been a while."

"Well, she said you use to read for folks."

"Why didn't you tell me, I was open and honest with you about everything and I didn't hesitate?'

"You sure about that Queen?"

"You didn't think to look through that drawer for my address all those years until you got yourself in trouble."

Queen gasped, while Ma'me looked at her over the top of her spectacles. The twins looked at their sister as she bowed her head in shame.

"We had nowhere else to go."

"Did I turn you away?"

"No."

"Alright then!"

Ma'me continued rocking in her chair looking out into the beautiful green grove that had been her view of the world since even before the establishment of what was now Greenwood District Tulsa, Oklahoma.

"Ma'me please tell me about my mother and father, I know you know."

Queen got up and begin pacing the long porch back and forth and she then turned to Ma'me again.

"The time father left us and went away for over two weeks, he was, here wasn't he?"

"He came here to see you."

"He knew, didn't he?"

"He knew you had the gift."

"Papa wanted you to tell him where my mother was didn't he?"

Ma' me suddenly stopped rocking in her rocking chair, but continued to gaze out into the meadow.

"You know what dear child?"

"The world that I came up in, you either lost your mind or you got stronger and that was it, wasn't no in between or no time to get yourself together. You better had come out the womb running with good strong legs and arms and a sound mind to work them."

"Folk had to be strong enough to deal with some of the most unimaginable things, things you had no control of whatsoever."

"And, when it got bad, you had damn well better figure out a way to block it out of your mind."

"That was the only way to ease the pain of things of my time."

"Now, this is something hard for average folks to do."

"But, imagine these same experiences for folks with the gift of second sight."

"See, second sight has no filter baby, you either see it all or nothing and the terrible visions I've seen in my lifetime would sometimes make me sick in my mind, body and spirit."

"Can you imagine, just imagine seeing the visions of a young woman being raped and watching her scream for her life and then seeing her young son confront the man who did it. Then seeing a mob in the middle of the night take this woman and her only child and lynch them from a bridge."

"Ma'me started wiping her eyes with her handkerchief.

"I saw all of this."

"One of the worse visions I ever had in my adult lifetime, it almost took my breath away. That same woman and I can call her by her name from the papers, Laura Nelson and her son L.D. Nelson was found hanging at the bridge that crossed the Canadian River up in Okemah Oklahoma. They had been lynched by a mob of white men."

"At that moment, I asked the lord to remove this gift from me, cause to me it had been a curse on my life, but he didn't."

Because we all know, when the Lord give you a gift he doesn't take it back. It just ain't his way."

"Instead, I had to practice remembering to forget over and over again."

"Your father and my dear brother, God bless his soul."

Ma'me continued to wipe her eyes while the ladies listened with attentive ears. All their lives, each in their own individual way had a deep yearning to gain clarity about the history of their broken family.

"Buford came here days, I mean days after that."

"I could see he was broken, just so terribly broken. I didn't know what to do, because I was so broken too."

"I couldn't help him, as much as I wanted to I just couldn't help him. I was afraid of what I might see."

Becky stood in the front doorway listening to her mother through the screen.

"Queen, it takes too much out of her and that is why I have to watch her."

Queen kneeled in front of Ma'me and placed her head in her lap, then she looked up at her dear old wise aunt.

"I'm sorry, I'm so very sorry if I'm being selfish, but me and my sisters need to know."

"We lost both of our parents and we never ever really knew them, their spirit or their heart. We knew our father loved us, but his heart had been so broken for so very long."

"We never got to know his true complete heart.".

Ma'me then placed her hand on Queen's head.

"You don't lose baby! You don't lose!"

Ma'me then grabbed her cane and gradually eased her way out of her chair, when she got her balance she slowly walked over to the front door and went inside.

Queen sat there quietly with her sister now at her side.

"Come on Queen, get up."

Queen didn't move, she sat there gazing off into the beautiful green meadow, hoping to get a glimpse of what Ma'me saw while spending endless hours there in her rocking chair. Becky grabbed Connie and took her in the house to console, while Carolyn continued to encourage her older sister.

"Queen please, let's go inside!"

After Carolyn sat with her sister for a few more minutes, Queen finally stood up and straightened out her clothes and went inside.

Dance of Angels   175

Chapter 20
Memphis Tennessee

Georgea awoke early in the day, she looked around the beautifully decorated guest room and snuggled deeper into the confines of the softest down comforters she felt in a very long time. On the table was breakfast and a lovely silver coffee holder with beautiful French decor and coffee cups and saucers to match. It was a huge change compared to the life she had grown use to in the mountains all these years. Georgea had almost forgotten the feel of soft cotton sheets and soft satin pajamas. After relaxing for a few more minutes she decided to get up, since there was much to be done. She sat on the side of the bed to find the most beautiful embroidered house slippers placed strategically at her bedside. Greta had not changed, as Georgea remembered she had always took pride in the finest of home living. She had been a woman who truly believed in every home amenity being conveniently at her finger tips. Greta would always remind Georgea that coming home should be like a queen returning to her castle and the ills of the world should be left at the doorstep, where one should always be greeted with peace, joy and especially love. It was obvious she still lived by this code and Georgea was grateful. As she attempted to remove herself from the huge king size bed, she took advantage of the step stool. It wasn't until then she now felt the aches and pains that settled in her joints from her travel down the mountain. Before taking any more steps, she took the time to rub her knees as if she could ease the slight pain she felt. She had truly overworked herself yesterday, but she'd made it. She slowly walked over to the porcelain face bowl and gently picked up the matching porcelain water pitcher and poured the warm water. She dipped both hands in the water and gently placed her hands over her face. Greta had arranged everything for her all the way down to a tooth brush. Georgea smiled at her dear friend's meticulous nature and went about her self-care business. After she was done, she then looked in the mirror as she picked up the soft cotton towel to dry her face. In that moment, she looked closely after almost twenty years. Now, she was home and ready to face her destiny. Georgea grabbed the robe from the end of her bed

Adrienne Lynn Rutherford

and put it on. As she poured a fresh cup of coffee, there was a slight knock on the door.

"Georgea, are you up?"

"Yes, come on in."

Greta walked in with a beautiful purple satin house robe and slippers to match.

"How do you like your room?"

"I love, love my room, thank you Greta.

"For everything."

She hugged her dear friend and she then relaxed on the sofa with her cup of coffee while admiring the view from the balcony glass doors.

"You mind?"

"Not at all."

Greta then got up and lifted the latch on the fine double doors and opened them as wide and the sunlight eagerly fell in as if waiting patiently for permission to do so.

"How did you sleep?"

Georgea laughed.

"Like a newborn baby."

"It's been a long time since I had the luxury of a mattress as comfortable as this one."

Greta looked at her weary friend.

"I'm sure."

"I have a surprise for you later, but for now we have much to talk about dear."

Both of the ladies stayed at *Venus Alley* most of the night waiting for Jonas and to Greta's disappointment he never showed up. It was not like him to stand her up, especially business regarding Queen and the twins. Greta promised Georgea that she had gotten word to him to meet them at the Funchess Estate sometime in the early afternoon, hopefully just in time for lunch. In the meantime, they would make plans and calls to find out more about the status of the family business and stop Viola for good.

****

Earlier that morning, just a little after midnight Jonas received a knock on his door. As usual he looked out his peep hole only to see the large framed man. Right away he knew who was calling.

"Shit."

He opened the door and just as he'd expected it was JoJo.

"Madame Greta request your presence at her home tomorrow at noon."

Jonas with his arm leaning on the door, nodded in confirmation.

"Okay, tell her I'll be there at noon."

Jonas then slammed the door shut and thought to himself.

"How much more complicated is this thing gonna get?"

"What the hell am I supposed to tell her?"

Jonas knew Miss Greta wanted to see him about the girls and it appeared that by default had become the source that everyone pointed too. First the discovery of their mother, the sworn silence, the murder, and the visit from the captain and Viola Quickman. Now, it was Miss Greta seeking out some type of information from him. Jonas then tried to think about the request for his presence in a more positive light.

"Maybe she's gotten word from the girls?"

Jonas sat on his bed and reached underneath pulling out his jar of white lightening. He turned it up and then wiped his mouth with his sleeve. He then went into his draw and pulled out a tray and on it was the remnants of dried marijuana leaves that he'd taken from the mountain. Finally, they were good and dry, he lifted the tray to his nose and smelled the aroma and closed his eyes as if savoring the long-awaited scent of the strong leaf. He took the tobacco papers and meticulously placed the dried plant in side and rolled it up. Jonas took another swallow from the jar and then twisted the top and placed it back I under his bed. He laid down and turned on the radio to hear the big band music that he enjoyed so much. Jonas lit his homemade cigarette and deeply inhaled and closed his eyes. Slowly he blew it up into the ceiling. He opened his eyes and repeated the routine until it was halfway gone and placed it into the ash tray. Now relaxed, he drifted off into a deep sleep and that is when the nightmare began. All Jonas could see was fire as he reached out for

Adrienne Lynn Rutherford

his mother and father, he fought as hard as he could but the hold that Chief Lone Wolf had on him was much too strong for the young boy.

Jonas began calling out to his parents as he heard the unidentifiable screams in the uncontrollable blaze. His last visions before passing out from the smoke was a man running in slow motion behind them through the flames completely a blazed screaming in agony as he fell to the ground lifeless. Suddenly, Jonas jumped up and sat straight up in the bed, with his shirt soak and wet with sweat. He wiped his brow and looked at the clock, it was now ten o'clock in the morning. He sat at the side of the bed and put his face in the palm of his hands. As time passed, he thought the dreams would get better, but they hadn't. It had been fourteen years since the big forest fire in the mountains. As much as he fought it, he couldn't get the visions out of his mind. Jonas got up and washed his face, bathed and got himself together. After he was done, he reached under his bed and grabbed his jar opened it and took another swallow. Jonas thought about Coaster and this new character Tyler who coincidently was from the same place that Queen had fled to. What were the odds of that, he thought to himself.

Soon there was a knock on the door.

"Who is it?"

"It's me man, come on open up you know it's me, it's almost noon."

"Alright, okay man, I'll be down in a sec."

Jonas grabbed his bee bop and pulled it deep down on his head, he looked around his one room palace. The narrow bed he'd slept on for almost 4 years, the small table and chair set that sat off in the corner and the coal stove that he used for cooking and keeping himself warm on those winter nights. Also, the squeaky floor that sounded off every time he took a step and the ceiling that leaked continuously when it rained. Somehow today, Jonas felt his life was changing. Maybe the recent opportunity with Coaster was the universe was letting him know that what he was doing wasn't just for Queen and the twins, but somehow also for himself. Jonas opened the door and looking out into his future, slammed it shut behind him.

****

Jonas arrived at Madame Greta's on time as requested. He was led to the parlor where Greta and Georgea where starting a late breakfast. When Jonas walked in and seen Miss Georgea he couldn't believe his eyes. Although there was a big resemblance, the person that he was looking at today looked nothing like the woman that he'd left on the mountain several days ago. Jonas was speechless seeing the two women together. Greta took a sip of her coffee and seeing his surprise, helped him collect his thoughts.

"Please dear have a seat and don't waste your time trying to figure out this situation here, it's far before your time dear."

"Are you hungry?"

Jonas had not heard a word Greta spoke, as he continued staring in disbelief at Georgea. She looked nothing like the sad broken woman that he'd met on the mountain. He took off his hat and held it in his hand and Georgea got up from the table and gave him a hug.

"Jonas, I know this looks really strange to you, but once we explain everything you will understand."

"Miss Georgea, pardon me but I almost didn't recognize you."

"Miss Greta then waved her hand out to Jonas."

"Come now please have a seat we have tons to discuss."

"We've been waiting for you, Chole can you please get Jonas here some breakfast."

"What would you like dear."

Jonas was still feeling flighty from his personal; therapy session and as a result his response time was delayed and Greta shook her head.

"Never mind, Chole can you bring him some pancakes, eggs and a glass of orange juice please?

"Thank you dear."

After Jonas had gotten over the initial shock of it, all three spent hours talking about the turn of events. Jonas had also told the ladies about the man who stopped by to see Coaster. Madame Greta made a note to have the gentleman thoroughly investigated. What they did not see coming was the fact that Coaster had requested that he join him for a trip to Tulsa. After hearing all that had transpired Greta handed the telegram to Jonas, he took the paper from her hand and looked at the contents and to his surprise it was addressed to him.

"I believe she thought it would be too risky to have the telegram sent to you so she put it in my name Jonas."

Jonas pulled the thin paper out of the envelope and began to read the contents slowly.

Dear Jonas,

First, I want to apologize for the length of time it took to contact you. Me and the girls are fine, I hope things are well at home as I left you with such a mess to deal with.

Your loyalty is beyond words and we so love you for that. When you get a chance, I would like for you to come out this way, we need to talk. I have asked Madame Greta to purchase you a train ticket, please except it.

Sincerely Queen

Once Jonas finished reading the correspondence he was happy know that the girls were safe.

Nevertheless, he knew his friend all too well. Queen wanted to know everything that had taken place back home and the only way to do that was he somehow get to Tulsa.

If Viola got wind of her entering the borders of Tennessee she would diffidently have her detained. Therefore, the trip to Tulsa for Jonas was a mandatory journey, and either way he had to go. Georgea found it important and in the best interest of the girls that Jonas not mention her whereabouts just yet. Jonas would however, go to Oklahoma as planned and wire Queen when he would arrive.

"What will you two ladies do in the meantime?"

"Well son, first I have to find out what my sister has been up to, it's been almost twenty years and I'm sure she's made a mess of things. She has never been good with the family's money; her gift was spending it."

"It would be dangerous for both me and the girls if she had any information about our whereabouts, right now they are in a good place. It will give be time to address a lot of things regarding my family's business."

Georgea then shook her head thinking about the sadness that had come over her sister many years ago.

"You know, I don't know what happened to Viola."

"My sister is possessed with a spirit of evil and now, it has completely consumed her. She has no love for others or life itself. She only exists for control, manipulation and intimidation."

"Somewhere in this life I lost her, somewhere long ago."

Georgea, even with the pain and suffering that her sister had caused the Family she was somehow still able to have compassion for her. Jonas passed her his clean napkin and she wiped the tears from her eyes.

"Do you know what happened Miss Georgea?"

"I don't, I always wondered how she could have become so hateful, we were so close."

"Now, those days are gone forever."

Greta smiled at her dear friend and held her hand to comfort her.

"It's so good to have you back Georgea."

"It's good to be back."

Jonas shook his head.

"So, you two really do know each other?"

Georgea took a sip of her coffee and then smiled at Jonas.

"Although the girls and Bufus have been the most absolute joy in my life, there was another wonderful life I had long ago."

"The walks in the streets of Paris, coffee shops and the best pastries."

"I loved Paris."

Jonas could see the joy overflowing in Miss Georgea, there was life in her again. The mountain had become a haven for her over the years, but in reality, it truly wasn't where she belonged. Jonas continued to listen while finishing up his breakfast, it had been the perfect remedy for the early morning abuse he'd given to his body.

"Are we clear on everything Jonas?

"Yes, Miss Greta."

"Good we will get a telegram out to Queen right away on your behalf"

Miss Georgea felt a need to reiterate her concern to Jonas one more time.

"You must not breathe a word to no one."

"In the meantime, Madame Greta and myself have some traveling of our own to do."

Chapter 21

Morgan Montana

Unlike Tulsa Oklahoma, Morgan Montana was a cattle town. Far different from the hustle and bustle of the Oil town of Tulsa, Oklahoma. Montana's ideal of a normal environment consisted of constant herds of cattle sweeping through town almost ten hours a day every day except on Sunday.

The children played with ropes attempting to emulate the cowboys herding cattle by lassoing the towns tall wooden poles. The city was far more rugged and displayed the true eminence of the wild west. Montana was a town that was full of diversity more so than back home. Here was were Calvin had been exposed to many types of people not just black or white, but also Canadians, Frenchmen, Native Americans and Chinese all who were a part of the Morgan Montana community. The small upcoming town centered around the construction of the railroad that would support the expansion of the oil business. Although Calvin enjoyed being home the variety of cuisine in Morgan was something that he enjoyed. John took it all in smiling at the children running in and out of the corridors of the buildings with their play hand guns made of dry twigs and tumble weed. Up above he saw the ladies smiling and waving for him to join them for a more sensual entertainment, this humored him very much as he smiled back and tipped his hat to the working girls. He spotted the saloon just beneath and made a note to come, interested in knowing who was their supplier the moonshiners or the Canadians. John hoped it was the moonshiners because although he enjoyed Canadian whiskey, white lightening was always nicer to him the next morning.

"Not today ladies. I'm here strictly on business."

One of the ladies opened the top of her bustier and shouted below.

"Sweetie, I am your business."

John laughed aloud at his brother and shook his head as they continued to trot through the cities dusty main road. Soon they came to a store front.

"We're here."

Calvin parked the wagon out front."

John looked at him confused.

"Eh Calvin, are we going to just leave our bags out here unattended?"

"Calvin opened the front door and two giant canines came running out at full speed."

John didn't hesitate as he leaped like a cheetah into the bed of the wagon, while the canines jumped up on Calvin showing their affection.

"Down Senegal, down Sudan."

In an instant, they followed his instructions.

"Come out the wagon brother.".

"I'm not getting out, those dogs are huge, they look like horses, man."

"They're Rhodesian Ridgebacks, dog of the Hottentot Tribes of South Africa."

"They are known as the *Lion Hunter*, I've had them since they were pups.

"They're well trained come on get out."

John cautiously got out of the wagon and walked his brother near the front entrance of the building. Calvin snapped his finger and pointed to the wagon, the dogs then leaped into the bed and had a seat.

"There, see, no one will bother our stuff, come on in and meet the man of the hour."

When Calvin and John entered the little shabby office, there was Ira sitting down at the table looking over a chessboard. John looked over in the other corner and there was another table but this one had two chairs and a table with a chess board on it as well. When he noticed their presence, Ira appeared pleasantly surprised.

"What's up man?"

Ira grabbed ahold of his friend and they exchanged their unique handshake of brotherhood.

"It's good to see you son, I didn't think you would need to get back this way so soon, but business is business."

He then extended his hand to John."

"How are you son, pleasure meeting you."

"Ira, this here is my brother John."

John returned the handshake.

"John, I've heard some phenomenal things about you son, say you can build one of them aero-planes from scratch huh?"

"Yes sir, I do be believe I'm capable."

"Well son I may have an opportunity for you if you're interested."

Before he could go any further Calvin stopped his trusted friend.

"John, you have to pardon him, Ira is always got business on the mind, you guys can talk about that later."

Ira waved his hand at Calvin.

"Alright, alright."

He then walked over behind his desk and pulled out a bottle of Mexican tequila that was half full. Calvin smiled.

"Where did you get that from?"

As Ira poured them all a shot he explained.

"Here, take a swig."

"Best regards from Honcho and Poncho."

Calvin grabbed his forehead.

"Aww man, I completely forgot, when did they leave?"

"Yesterday morning and they were looking for horses, I told them you were out of sight for a few."

"They said it's our turn to cross the border this time."

"Man, I completely forgot about them coming up, I gotta make it up to um, they traveled a long way."

Ira took a shot and tightened his face.

"Yea man they are ready to make a huge investment, they've made some serious cash betting the horses down in Honduras."

"They showed me the pictures and everything."

"I know they were looking for breeders and I already had them picked out for them."

"Now, I've got to take them down myself, but after I finish up my business in Greenwood."

John looked at his brother.

"Horses man, you're selling horses?"

"Yeah something like that."

Adrienne Lynn Rutherford

Ira smiled.

"Hah, something like that, believe me them fellas didn't come all the way up here from Central America just to play a few rounds of chess."

"John your brother here has some of the best mustangs on this side of the Mississippi."

"Calvin, you haven't taken him to the ranch?"
John turned and looked at his younger brother."

"The ranch?"

"What ranch?"

Ira, knowing Calvin's modesty about the wealth that he'd acquired enjoyed getting under his skin and sarcastically kept it going.

"Man, you didn't know?"

He then turned to Calvin

"Calvin my boy, he doesn't know about the ranch here in Montana?"

Calvin knowing his friend's cynicism, folded his arms and looked over at him.

"Well I guess he does now, doesn't he old man."

"Aww shucks Calvin it's your brother, I'm surprised at you."

Ira continued to talk and by this time he'd turned up far too many tequila shots. He was then interrupted by John.

"Calvin man what's going on, you have a ranch?"

"Why didn't you tell me?"

"Well It was going to be a surprise, but I didn't count on the old man being boozed when we came."

"There are a lot of things I need to tell you brother."

"There are a lot of things that I must tell you brother and I'm hoping you and the rest of the family will be a part of it."
John sat down in the chair trying to grasp what he was hearing; his brother had left home and did amazing things.

"Man, this is something a Ranch, can it hold my airplanes, how many acres you got."

Calvin scratched his head, while Ira continued.

"Well over two hundred acres, this fella got two hundred acres of beautiful green and a fine white picket fence that travels all around those beautiful meadows and grassy lands."

It's enough room for the whole family, you gotta see it man, you just gotta see it."

Calvin threw his hands up and looked at his brother.

"Well there you have it."

John got up out of his seat full of excitement.

"Man, this is great, when will we see the place."

"It's not far from here."

"What made you settle out this way anyway Calvin?"

"Greenwood is such a prosperous place and it's home. You could have made your living there with no problem and been around family."

"I did have plans, I actually purchased a small farm in Oakhurst but soon my plans caught a few snags."

"I didn't feel so good about Greenwood anymore, there is a lot of tension rising on the north side of town."

"What would make you say that Calvin?"

"When we attended the film premiere, I didn't feel safe anymore."

"Those train tracks had always been like an invisible fence separating Greenwood district and Tulsa's northside."

"I carried both my pistols while I was home, I've never felt that way about Greenwood District, ever."

John, confused could not believe what he was hearing from his brother.

"Calvin, what do you mean Greenwood is not safe?"

"That's absurd."

"We don't have to go outside the community for anything it is completely self-sufficient, except of course for some of those who work on the south side of Tulsa, but outside of that Greenwood is fine."

"That's my point John, you are right Greenwood district is very successful, maybe a little bit too successful for some."

"I realized it the night of the film premiere. It was something I observed that night that didn't sit well with me."

"Do tell brother."

Adrienne Lynn Rutherford

"After the premiere was over it was late and there where a group of young hooligans from the southside hitting sticks on the train tracks when we were leaving."

"Everyone saw it, but chose to ignore them because they were kids."

"They were just standing there taunting and shouting disrespectful comments."

"But for me, just the fact they felt that comfortable to do that, well it raised a few questions with me." "There has always been an invisible line between the two and everyone on both sides have always respected that line, but that night, that night they made a huge statement for everyone to witness."

Ira then sat back in his chair behind his desk.

"Well son, what are you gonna do?"

"I'm gonna hitchem up."

"You sure son?"

"Yea, I'm sure."

John threw his hands up.

"Okay, okay, wait, wait, wait, can someone please tell me what's going on here?"

Calvin turned to his brother with a serious look on his face.

"We're leaving Greenwood, Mama, Pops, Cody, and you too hopefully brother."

John looked at his brother in disbelief.

"Leaving Greenwood, brother what are you talking about?"

"I can't leave Greenwood, and you know mom and pop aren't going to leave either."

Hell, it's safe there, it's the only home they know, it's familiar there and their friends are there."

"Damn Calvin their whole lives are there."

"They have a home, you have a home, it's not safe brother, trust me when I tell you, I know trouble when I see it brewing and it's going to be trouble really soon."

"Man, this is crazy."

He then looked at Ira.

"My brother is crazy"

He then looked at Calvin

"You know this is some crazy shit man."

Calvin continued.

"John, it's getting too dangerous and the more successful Greenwood District gets the bigger target it's gonna be. You think them white folks on the other side of the tracks enjoy watching the economy grow in Greenwood."

"Do you really think they're going to let Greenwood District flourish.?"

"We no longer need to shop in their stores or buy food from their restaurants out of the kitchen backdoor."

"There are no white only or colored only signs in Greenwood District."

"We have our own impressive business district."

"Our own bank, hotels, restaurants and retail stores."

"Think about what we have accomplished man, thirty-four plus blocks of successful businessmen and women who were the decedents of slaves."

"That's what you call prosperity man, and it's dangerous."

"Think about it man, what other black community you know has an airplane landing strip in the community, we are a catalyst for other communities like our own in this country and you better believe there are many adversaries that come with this success."

"Don't you know those young kids that were attempting to intimidate us that night didn't come up with those ideas on their own, they had a whole lot of influence."

"That behavior is condoned and you know that."

John listened to his brother as he mentally processed everything that he was saying.

"Let me get this straight, you want me to leave my airplane hangar, that I built with my platoon brothers with our bare hands because of the shenanigans of a group of silly young coward -white boys playing on the tracks."

"C'mon, brother, meet me half-way here man."

"Where will I go with my engines and all my stuff."

Calvin took a shot of tequila and tightened his face from the strength of the distilled liquor and sat the small shot glass down."

"Uh, with me."

"Calvin, you're my brother and I love you dearly, but you have to admit you've been gone a long time and besides if things were getting that serious don't you think me and William would have seen it coming, especially William because he spends a lot of time across the tracks anyway."

Calvin poured himself another shot and addressed his brother.

"John let me ask you, how often are you really in town, better yet how often are you really home?

"You do no business in Tulsa, you travel all the time."

"Now William that's another story."

"That's my friend and I love him like a brother, but we both know he is delusional sometimes and he doesn't even value his own life."

"He knows what will happen to him if they ever catch him on that side of town after dark, but he will risk it every chance he gets."

"Do you know he stays nights over there with that woman and what do you think they are going to do with him if they catch him in that woman's house?"

"We can't help him if he's over there."

"People talk you know, and they won't be calling the sheriff either, because he won't be wearing that badge on that night."

"You get my drift?"

Ira thought it was time to give some light on the subject.

"John, your brother is right, I must admit he has a sense about certain things. If he's feeling that strongly about it take heed son, he saved my life and that boy."

Ira pointed to a picture on his wall of a young boy and a woman standing next to him.

"Did he tell you how he got that long nasty scar on the side of his face?"

"He didn't want to talk about it."

Calvin placed his hand on his face and traced the long scar with his fingertips.

"This is my rites of passage and that's all I'm going to say, but it changed my life forever."

Ira patted him on the shoulder as he headed toward the front entrance.

"Not only your life son, it changed a lot of lives."

John looked at Ira.

"Well old man, you gonna tell me the story or what?"

"I'll let Cal here tell you the story, let's just say he's full of surprises."

The men's conversation was interrupted by the barking dogs out front and Ira turned and looked at his friend.

"Looks like our guest have arrived."

As John took a seat on the sofa against the wall, Ira went back to his desk and opened a wooden box filled with Cuban Cigars.

"Here, take one son, this is going to be a very interesting meeting I assure you."

John took the Cigar and Ira lit it as Calvin greeted Viola Quickman and her escort Mr. Garrison at the door. Calvin shook his hand and gave him a peaceable hug.

"Good to see you man."

He then nodded at Viola Quickman."

"Miss Quickman."

"Mr. Watkins."

John sat in the corner quietly, he felt it unnecessary to introduce himself after observing the woman who had entered the building. Viola as always displayed a cold look of contempt, something that John of all people was never fond of. It reminded him of his travels in Germany during the first World War. Calvin appeared to share his brother's sentiments as he addressed her again.

"Please come in and make yourself comfortable, how was your trip Miss Quickman?"

Ira opened the box and offered Viola a cigar, the look on her face was priceless as John turned his head to hold back the urge to laugh at the witty gesture.

"No thank you Mr. Ira, the trip as usual was long and hot."

"We are very sorry to hear about your loss."

"Yes, it was a terrible thing those girls did to my son, but they will surely pay, I may have a lead and I have a handsome reward for anyone who will bring them into custody in Memphis dead or alive."

Adrienne Lynn Rutherford

Calvin became quite curious.

"Them?"

"Yes, it was three young mulatto women two of them twins, but the eldest, well she is an evil one and she orchestrated it all. I do believe that I may have a lead, but right now we have business that must be dealt with."

Calvin looked over to his brother John and he said nothing. He then took a long drag from his cigar and continued flipping through the newspaper as if he hadn't heard a word. They didn't need to communicate right now, but he knew he and his brother would surely talk later. Viola without reservation, continued her quest.

"Well Gentleman I'm sure your wondering why I asked you to come together today. I'm sure you know that I have lost my son in a terrible brutal way. Since then I am very concerned with my business dealings here in Montana and the direction that it would be going if I decided to continue with this partnership."

"The reason behind my venture out west in the beginning was to secure the future of the Quickman Estate and of course my heir."

"Since that time and the change of events that have taken place, I have decided to sell my portion of our oil investments to the Cornerstone Bank out east in Boston. In doing so, I would then relinquish all rights to them."

"I have the papers here."

As Viola began pulling out her contractual documents, Ira stood up in disbelief.

"What bank in Boston?"

"We don't know anything about any Cornerstone bank in Boston, we had an agreement and your reneging, you came to us."

"You can't do business like that it breaks the code."

He then looked over at Calvin

"Cal, she's breaking the code."

Viola then interrupted.

"Yes, your absolutely right I did come to you and look how much money you have made because of it."

"Do not fool yourself Mr. Stovall."

"Please let's be clear, in the real world you are not the ideal business partner, so the childish tantrum that you are displaying is useless. I will relinquish my portion of the partnership to the bank, there was nothing in the contracts stating that I could not sell my portion to whomever I choose."

Ira Stovall did everything he could to compose his temper, he'd had enough of Viola Quickman's insults about him and his race.

"The real-world Viola?"

"You mean your world, don't you?"

"Why don't you just sell your portion to us?"

Calvin shook his head in disbelief.

"Because she's strapped, Cornerstone Banks of Boston huh?"

"Well Miss Quickman If I'm not mistaken the Cornerstone

Bank back in Boston must be here for some sort of agreement can take place, that portion of the contract is written clearly as well."

Calvin then picked up the contract from the table and read it aloud to Viola.

"As stated, if such any partner decides to sell their portion of the investment to another party outside of the original party established, a onetime agreed upon meeting and I do stress one time, of all investors including and I may stress again the word including the intended investor must be present."

He then looked over at his two other partners.

"You guys see any representatives from the Cornerstone Bank of Boston?"

They both nodded a negative as John shook his head behind the newspaper.

"Well I don't either"

Viola growing angrier by the minute interrupted.

"That's ridiculous."

Calvin shot back.

"No, what is ridiculous is you, my time is very valuable Miss Quickman and this was a waste of my time."

"If you want to sell us your portion of the investment we will accept your offer and negotiate a price, but as of today this is the first and last meeting regarding this matter.

Viola Quickman turned beet red as she stood up and began to gather the paperwork that she'd laid out so neatly on the desk, along with a new contract presented from the bank.

Adrienne Lynn Rutherford

"Who do you think you are?"

"Do you know who I am?"

"I can make your life very miserable, how dare you speak to me that way."

"You're just a negra."

Calvin shook his head, not out of disbelief but out of pity for this woman.

"Miss Quickman like I said, I'm speaking on behalf of all of your partners here and if you're willing to sell your portion, we can have the papers drawn up as soon as this afternoon."

"You don't give me orders, I will not be strong armed into anything."

Viola then grabbed her purse.

"You think your something, don't you?"

"Out here in no man's land and lucky enough to pick up a few coins for yourself, let's be clear my wealth is old and powerful son and you have crossed the wrong one."

"Humph! This won't be the last you hear from me."

Before she left Ira passed Calvin an envelope.

"Uh Viola before you go, here are this month's profits there was no need to mail them to you since you came this far."

"And actually, Miss Quickman for the record, we all draw our wealth from the same wells."

Viola stopped and turned around with all the rage in her and walked over to Calvin and snatched the envelope from his hand.

"You know nothing of my wells Mr. Watkins."

Then she stomped out of the door and Calvin turned around looked at his friends and begin to laugh.

"That lady is out of her mind, I mean who does she think she is coming in here throwing her weight around about some bank in Boston, hell I've never even heard of the Cornerstone Bank of Boston."

John closed the paper and looked over at his brother.

"That's because Cornerstone is a private institution, for the wealthy of old. It was established during the 1700's backed by *Great Britain's Llyod's of London World Renowned Insurance Company* who backed the Boston Bank of the New World with gold as an insurance policy to support the institution of slavery."

"They loaned money to finance slave trading fleets and early colonist who were interested in becoming potential slave owners. Once they were established they were to pay back the debt they owed to Great Britain. Each slave was literally backed by their weight in gold. Only a selected few colonists were granted this one-time opportunity, it seems your Miss Quickman comes from a very old and quite interesting bloodline."

"So, you see the Cornerstone Bank doesn't need to invest in anything. Their more of a sophisticated loan shark for the aristocratic wealthy and elite. If she is selling to them, she my brother is up to her neck in debt."

Ira and Lou where quite amused by the knowledge that John had shared with them, however Calvin was not surprise. His brother John was quite well read and being over in Europe afforded him the opportunity to read things that he would not otherwise have access to in the states.

Calvin shook his head again.

"Yeah, I guess the rumors about her financial problems are true, and I'm sure they're offering her a lot more than what we are willing to buy her out for too."

"Your right Calvin, there obligation is to help them to keep the wealth that they have, it's a security blanket so to speak."

"A revolving door, once she is able to provide a means to get out of debt they will return her investment back to her, but hears the tricky part. It doesn't have to be the exact investment, but something of equal value, so instead of the oil wells of Oklahoma and Montana.

"It could be diamond mines in Angola you follow me?"

"Yeah, I understand, but believe me, I have heard some very evil things about that woman, she preys on weakness, you can be sure we will not hear the last of her."
Lou Garrison interrupted the conversation.

"Enough about her, Calvin what's your plans while you're here."

"Well, I'm going to take my brother up to the ranch, it's about time he sees what his little brother has been up to for the past 8 years."

John smiled.

"Believe me, I'm quite amused so far and there's more?"

Ira patted John on the back.

"Well, let's just say it will surely be a pleasant surprise."

"Your brother here, is a fine business man and he has done a great job out there."

"Well I hope so, because if he's planning to get mom and pop out of Greenwood this had better be good."

Calvin begin to laugh.

"Yeah, I'm hoping so John."

"But, you will have to keep it under wraps because I'm not quite ready to share everything with them just yet. It may be too overwhelming and plus I have a few more things I have to do first."

Chapter 22

Tulsa Oklahoma: Greenwood District

Queen laid across her bed looking up in the ceiling thinking about her life, she thought of the good times and she thought of their most recent struggles. Calvin also crossed her mind and it made her spirit dance, never had she even considered opening her heart up to this man. The complications of her life had left her thinking that she probably would never find the love that she'd heard Miss Greta speak of so many times. However, little did she know the complicated circumstances that interfered with her life back in Memphis would be the very thing that would catapult her into the arms of a man and Calvin showed her nothing but the epitome of love and kindness. That small piece of hope and joy radiated in her heart and she promised herself she would continue to seek it. Nevertheless, the darkness that lurked in her past left her equally weary. Queen knew eventually she would have to tell him everything and how she would do it at this point, she did not know. She figured the easiest thing to do was to give all her worries to God, it was what had gotten her through thus far. She had become mentally exhausted from the turn of events and she continued to be haunted regarding the mysterious circumstances regarding her mother. It had really taken a toll on her faith. Queen struggled to come to grips as she thought of the tragedy that had broken up her home many years ago.

She then thought of her father Bufus, even in some of the weariest moments of his life, he was still able to instill a spirit of resilience in she and her sisters. It was this same drive that took him back to Greenwood. Queen thought the way things had played out in her life would have made any ordinary woman question her sanity. She shook her head and tried to make logical sense out of the three words that resonated with her so strongly, murder, secrets and love. They had been the most recent and accurate description of her life thus far.

"Am I crazy?"

These were the thoughts of a young woman who seemed to carry a strength for her family that far exceeded the strength she had

Adrienne Lynn Rutherford

to fight her own internal battles. As she began to weep softly in the still of the night she heard the solid steps of a soul approaching.

Soon, the squeaky hinges slowly swung her door open. Queen sat up in her bed waiting to see who was behind it.

"Whose there?"

"It's Ma'me baby."

"I felt your spirit stirring in here, put on something and meet me on the front porch."

"Ma'me?"

"Hush girl, and do as I say"

"Tonight, is a good night yes suh, a good night."

As she quietly closed the door and headed for the porch, queen leaped out of the bed only to stumble and hit her foot to on the wooden leg of the nightstand. She sat on the bed and grabbed it until the pain left. After putting on something warm for the early morning air, Queen headed outside. When she stepped out onto the porch she could not believe her eyes as the bright stars danced around and around. It was the most beautiful thing she'd ever seen in her life. She then turned to Ma'me full of wonder and Ma'me smiled.

"You like that?"

"Come here and sit next to me."

Queen sat in the swing chair next to Ma'me in her rocking chair and continued to gaze at the magnificence.

"The stars are so beautiful Ma'me."

Ma'me begin to laugh.

"Those are no star's girl, them are Angels dancing to the rhythm of the universe."

"Queen laughed, that's silly Ma'me."

"Angels?"

"That's what I said, one thing Ma'me ain't got to do is lie."

"Shoot, most folks don't really pay attention to the universe at all. Don't slow down for nothing but to just try and find an even quicker way."

"Those creatures up there they dance all the time, it's such a wondrous thing. God really put this here thing together I tell you."

"He's the master artist you know." "They just dance and dance worshipping him in all the Glory that he is. This is how I knew that

Dance of Angels   199

I had something special even in all of that evilness of being held in bondage."

"I been watching them all my life, they got me through some terrible terrible times I tell you."

Queen listened attentively to her dear aunt as she shared some of the deepest parts of who she was. Ma'me was truly a complicated woman and rightfully so, she'd survived one of the most terrible historical atrocities in the world.

"You know when I was a little girl and my mama left me, I thought my world had surely ended, I mean there was nothing nobody could do for me. Then my daddy left me too. That was it, I was done and my heart just broke in a thousand pieces you know."

"Your daddy, my brother Buford he took care of me and gave me all the love that I needed to get stronger in this life. Then I got a visitor, a strange visitor the most beautiful winged creature you could imagine. It spoke no words it was bright as the sun, but had the face of my mama. I couldn't understand it, I thought I was losing my mind, but I wasn't.

"She said:

"Don't be scared dear child, I have been sent to you from all that is good and merciful. You will see a different world from that which you live in, you will see beyond the shadows of people, places and things. You will give revelation and through a spiritual sight high of discernment."

"I never forgot them words, I didn't know what they meant at the time, but it was if they were stamped into my heart. As quick as she came she left. I jumped up from my cot and I looked up into the sky and there they were hundreds of them just dancing round and around moving farther and farther away from the Earth."

"I was so wide eyed and excited I couldn't even go back to sleep, so I just sat on that old porch watching them dance and dance until they became like the stars you see there tonight. So, you see my dear child things are not always as they appear. God is at work tonight and there is a prophetic word."

Adrienne Lynn Rutherford

Suddenly what looked like stars shot out toward one another and created the most brilliant light in the sky that Queen in awe. Ma'me started to smile.

"See their showing off now, it's a spirit filled night tonight yes suh."

Queen remained speechless as she basked in the wonders of the universe and the opportunity to share in Ma'mes great gift, to see the world from her eyes. Ma'me continued to rock in her chair and before Queen could blink the sky had returned to its normal state.

"Chile, I have been her in Tulsa all my adult life, I come here as a young woman thanks to your papa. It wasn't more than a rinky dink ole wooden planked depot then. Your father was my everything and I looked up to him and we were the only family we had. Your papa was a mover and shaker and a risk taker. When he left I was sad, even though he'd married me off to a strong, kind and loving man."

"I still missed my brother.

"When he came back with you and Georgea, oh that was such a great day. She pretended that she was a Jewish woman so that the locals would not bring harm to your father, because you know they don't take kindly to mixing. My soul just danced and danced because I had just lost my husband to a terrible accident. I thought my life would be complete again and we all would be a family again."

Queen continued to listen attentively to Ma'me as the sky began transforming into in early daybreak.

"You know, life is like a deck of cards, sometimes you know you can shuffle and shuffle them cards over and over again, but sooner or later if you play long enough the deck will turn around and those face cards you were looking for will pop right up in your hand again."

"Your mama is alive, she has been all along."

"I have to tell you, there has been so much evil suffocating her, has been for a while. Your papa did come here, but he didn't tell me much."

"I didn't even know about the twins, but I could feel the pain that he was carrying. But the love, the love he had for your mother that is what I remembered most."

Dance of Angels

"I told him what he wanted to know, that she was alive."

"I also had to tell him that she had a curse on her life that would bring his entire household down if he went looking for her."

Queen interrupted Ma'me.

"Curse?"

"What curse?"

"Your mama's family has generations of torment and pain."

"My mother's family?"

"She never knew anything about her family, papa either."

"What are you saying Ma'me?"

"I'm saying what I'm saying girl, you were so very young, just a baby and you were a threat from the start and then two more after that."

Ma'me began shaking her head and then extended her hand to Queen.

"Give me your hand dear child."

Queen placed both her hands inside of Ma'mes.

"Close your eyes."

Queen closed her eyes and suddenly she began to see a vision illuminate in her mind as if she was dreaming. It was as clear as a moving picture as she watched a woman crying while leaving the Quickman mansion with a newborn baby in her arms. Queen then suddenly snatched her hands from out of Ma'mes and quickly stood up.

"Ma'me, what is going on? Who was that woman with the baby?"

"What's going on?"

Ma'me looked up at her niece with all the love that she had for her and reached for her to sit back down.

"Be still dear heart, I told you that this wasn't going to be easy. I told your father the same thing. You got his blood and mine too girl, use your gift and figure it out."

Tears began to race down Queen's face and she wiped with both hands.

"Talk to me Ma'me, how?"

"Chile, you gotta be strong for the both of us, Ma'me ain't as strong as she used to be, it just takes too much out of me."

Adrienne Lynn Rutherford

"Go on now."

Queen then uttered one word.

"Quickman?"

Yes girl, that's it, keep talking to Ma'me."

Queen then put both hands over her mouth and began to wail.

"Oh no, Oh my God no!"

"It can't be Ma'me, it can't be!"

Breathe girl, take it easy, it's alright the spirit is with us and he is so mighty in his works."

"There has been a prophetic word lingering for such a time as this, the cards have turned around girl."

"My mother is a Quickman?"

"How could this be?"

"Papa knew that all along?"

She covered her mouth again

"Oh my God, that baby, that baby was me?"

"Jesus Ma'me this is too much."

"Breathe baby breathe, stay with me.

"Who then is Viola Quickman?"

Ma'me continued to rock in her chair.

"You're asking me a question again that you know the answer to."

Queen's shoulders then slumped and she put her head down.

"Dear God, she's my mother's sister and oh God that sick man was my cousin."

"I killed my cousin."

"You had no idea about that at the time, and it doesn't matter who he was, you saved your sister's life."

The two heard a quiet stirring on the inside of the front screen door.'

"Who is there?"

Slowly the twins eased their way out of the door and Ma'me looked them over.

"Hasn't anybody ever told you that eavesdropping is a sin."

Thy spoke in unison.

"No Ma'am."

"How long have you two been standing in that doorway?"

Neither said a word and Ma'me shook her head

"I suppose long enough, come on out here."

The two stepped out onto the porch and then both went over to hug their eldest sister and Ma'me smiled.

"Yes, that's it and you all are gonna need that love to get you through this."

All the emotional drama of her family had exhausted Queen. Now, she understood what Ma'me meant when it came to matters of the spirit. She had become a little lightheaded, but before she could stand they noticed the headlights of an automobile coming up the road. It didn't come up to the house, it was hard to see who exactly it was that was getting out of the car, the morning fog had barely lifted. As the two bodies, had gotten closer it was obvious that it was William and he was carrying someone. He was bleeding profusely from the head. In his arms was a young white woman who also looked as if she'd been beaten. Carolyn opened the door and they all followed him into the dining room. He then laid her on the couch.

"Dear Lord William, what happened?"

"Don't worry about me mama I'm fine just a few blows upside the head is all. Help Sarah please, she's carrying my baby."
Becky ran down the stairs swiftly after hearing all the commotion on the first floor. When she got downstairs and seen the condition of her son she didn't hesitate to go up to him and check him thoroughly for injuries to his body. When she took off his jacket she noticed a stab wound in his side.

"Dear God, he's been stabbed, and he's lost a lot of blood."

"Queen please go get Mrs. Watkins, she can help with this, please hurry."

Becky walked her son over to the sofa in the family room and slowly helped him lay down."

"Dear son, what were you thinking, how long did you think you were going to get away with this madness."

"You could have been killed."

"What happened?

Before he could speak William passed out cold and his mother then returned to the front room.

"He's lost a lot of blood, I don't know if he's gonna make it."

Adrienne Lynn Rutherford

Becky began to cry.

"I told him that sooner or later his actions were gonna catch up with him."

Queen returned from upstairs dressed along with Connie, she went into the room and looked William over, to her it didn't look good. Nevertheless, she thought to herself stranger things had happened in the lives of their family and she quickly dismissed the worse.

When she returned to the front room looked at Becky and she could see the hurt in her eyes.

"Everything is going to be fine, he just hit a little bump in the road is all, see what you can do for his girl, it looks like she will be with us now. I'm going after Mrs. Watkins I'll be back in a few ticks." Becky nodded her head and then gave Queen a long hug.

"I'm so glad you are here."

"Me too cousin, me too."

The ladies left out the front door and no one had noticed that Ma'me had returned to her chair on the porch. The sun was halfway between the earth's surface and the sky when Queen looked out into the meadow. Ma'me looked at Queen and Connie as she continued to rock slowly in her chair.

"There's a storm brewing, yes suh, life as we know it real soon will be no more.

Queen didn't have the time to inquire about what exactly Ma'mes word meant, but somehow, she felt no solemnness behind her words. She went over kissed her on the cheek and held her hand tightly.

"You said it yourself Ma'me, we don't lose, we don't lose."

Chapter 23

Manhattan, New York

Georgia and Greta arrived in New York in the early afternoon. Both enjoyed their time together and neither hardly were interested in discussing the circumstances that had brought them on this journey. The last time the two had traveled together they were overseas. They had successfully completed their summer studies in France and to celebrate they traveled along the Rivera Coast of France. Therefore, to make light of a very serious matter they decided only to talk about growing up together in pleasant times. Greta made sure they were provided with all the luxuries of a comfortable ride as they enjoyed all the first-class amenities of her husband's private railcar.

The Waldorf Astoria had been the place of choice when their families would meet in New York for the Christmas holidays. Mr. Astoria himself had been an astute protégé of Greta's father, so it was not a question they would reside there for their short business visit. When the train finally arrived at Grand Central Station the ladies were assisted off the train car by the porter.

"Hello, sir what is your name?"

"The name is Ulysses."

"Pleasure to meet you Ulysses, my name is Greta and this here is Georgea."

Ulysses tipped his hat to the ladies.

"Pleasure to meet you both, how can I be of service to you today?"

"Well we are here visiting and need our bags transported to the Waldorf Astoria."

"That's no problem, I will load them on my cart and then you can follow me please."

The ladies followed Ulysses along with their luggage through Grand Central Station. It was mid-afternoon and the station was busy. People were moving briskly in all directions attempting to get to their destinations as the sounds of the loud overhead voice spoke times of departures and arrivals. Ulysses guided the ladies to

Adrienne Lynn Rutherford

transport desk and it was here they were greeted by another Porter.

"Hello, how can I help you."

The ladies greeted the gentleman and then Ulysses spoke.

"Afternoon Victor, these ladies just arrived from Tennessee in their private railcar. I have their bags here, they will need to be taken to the Waldorf Astoria Hotel."

"Well Ladies, that shouldn't be a problem at all. I can have a carriage for you in no time. The gentleman attempted to pick up the phone, but Greta interrupted him.

"No, I don't think that will be necessary, we will walk a few blocks instead, it's not far and plus I want to show my sister here around a bit."

"That is quite a distance away miss."

"You know, you may be right, it's been awhile for me, any hoot if we get fatigued we'll catch the trolley"

"As you wish Ma'am."

Greta generously tipped the gentleman for his services and the ladies made their way through the corridors and into the busy streets of Manhattan. Things had changed a lot since the last time Georgea had been to New York. Union Square had transformed almost completely with trolley cars and the newly growing number of automobiles that now dominated the new and improved paved city streets. She smiled as she observed still a few horse and carriages that trotted by reminding her of her youthful days, a time that was now far behind her. Georgea had a re-awakening and she smiled while exploring the thoughts of finally closing a very long and tormenting chapter in her life. She'd felt miserable for a very long time. Georgea had failed herself, but she would not fail her children. Her thoughts were interrupted by her good friend Greta as she pulled at her arm.

"Look."

Georgea smiled at her dear friend as she led her across the street to the sounds of swinging jazz. They both looked up high at the marquee and Georgea immediately recognized the name "Marion Harris and W.C. Handy's Saxophone Quartet.

Greta pulled at Georgea.

"C'mon."

The ladies went inside the large opened wooden double doors and glanced around the extravagant, dimly lit main dining room. There where round tables everywhere and all were covered with crisp white table cloths. The waiter staff were assembling fresh flowers on each table as the big band rehearsed on the stage. The ladies smiled as they watched their longtime friend W.C. Handy perform a solo rendition of his famous "Memphis Blues" on his saxophone. Greta could recognize that sound anywhere as she reminisced of the times she listened to his band perform back home on Beale street. When he seen the ladies, he stopped.

"Greta is that you?"

"What a wonderful surprise?"

He made his way off the stage to greet the ladies and Greta smiled as he approached.

"Hello Darling."

"Georgea this is a good friend of mine W.C. Handy, also known as a genius of course."

Georgea shook his hand as they continued their conversation

"W.C., I could hear the sounds of that sax from all the way across the street."

W.C. shook his head and smiled.

"Tess must've left those double doors open again?"

"Well thank goodness for Tess, or we wouldn't have seen you."

"Yeah, she does that just before opening night."

"I believe she likes teasing the folks who stroll the street hoping to get them interested, but little does she know we don't need that."

"The people always wanna hear a hot blues set, if you know what I mean."

"This here Sax is my baby, and she ain't failed a crowd yet."

"Anyway, what brings you here all the way to the big city?"

"Oh, just a little business."

"Well after your done the set starts here around eight o'clock this evening."

"As much as we would like to W.C. We have to pass."

"Greta here has a meeting and we don't know how long its gonna take."

"Oh okay, but I just think it's insane to come all the way to

New York City and not indulge in a tad bit of the night life."

"I tell you what, you take care of your business and then later tonight after the sets close downtown, I want you ladies to come join me uptown."

Greta smiled.

"Harlem?"

"That's right ladies got a gig at midnight at this nice little after hour up on 125th and Lenox."

"Ma Rainey is performing too, but for one night only."

"She's headed out to on her Juke Joint stroll along the Gulf first thing tomorrow morning."

Greta thought this would be a good time for Georgea to get her mind off the events that had recently unfolded in her life. She knew she had been sick with worry about her girls. Although she had not been present for most of their lives, she had made it up in her mind to do everything that she could to make sure they were safe. Greta looked over at her dear friend.

"What do you think Georgea?"

"I guess we can stop in for a few."

"Great, then its settled I will let them know that you're my guest this evening, Harlem is a very sacred place if you know what I mean."

"Georgea and I are staying at the Waldorf Astoria."

"Just ask for me and leave a message with the address and information and we will join you later tonight."

The ladies gave their farewells and returned to the busy street. As they continued their stroll, they noticed the Hotel in the distance. Just like Georgea had stated, the walk was not that far at all. While they continued their stroll, she found herself gazing in the windows of some of the most exquisite boutiques that she had seen in a long time. However, there was one particular store front window that reminded her of the couture dress shops her mother would frequent while they enjoyed their summers in Paris. The store front was of French Décor, beautifully draped with some of the most beautiful fabrics the ladies had seen in a long time. Inside the window was a lovely display of fashionable women's dresses and beautifully made hats to compliment the modern look of the day. Georgea stopped in her tracks and gazed into the window as Greta looked up at the sign.

"Chanel?"

Greta was excited to share a brief history about one of the most influential fashion designers of their time with her dear friend.

"Chanel, oh this is the fabulous designer that everyone is buzzing about, I didn't know she had a store front in New York."

"I've been in the south far too long honey."

"There just too slow, look how we are so behind on the latest fashions and you know we use to always keep up."

"This young lady Coco Chanel speaks to the elegance of French Couture you know, that's what I heard."

"Her accessories are the buzz, so this is what Chanel looks like.'

"Come on let's go in."

The ladies walked into the little modest store front and were amazed at all the sophisticated handmade materials that reminded them so much of France. They roamed the two-story boutique inattentive to the time admiring the amazing dresses and uniquely made accessories. They both walked in to the storefront and roamed the small two-story boutique filled with beautiful accessories.

"Georgea will you look it feels like Paree, such beautifully crafted pieces, only a consumer of true French couture would truly appreciate this place.

Soon a young beautiful lady came from the back of the store.

"Bon Jour"

"Bon Jour, we were just admiring your beautiful pieces and the boutique is absolutely beautiful."

"I see."

"You are from France no?"

Greta smiled and took her comment as a compliment, grateful to have still retained her accent after all these years.

"Yes, I am, but I've been in the states for a very long time though."

"Yes, but still I can hear Paree in your voice so very clearly Mademoiselle."

Greta smiled.

"Are you Coco Chanel?

Adrienne Lynn Rutherford

The young lady returned the gesture.

"No, I am not."

"Coco is in Paris preparing for her spring line, she will return in the summer months."

"Oh, I see,"

"I will make it a note to come by and compliment her on such an elegant display of the finest of *Par'ee,* or I may even take a trip to France, who knows with these things."

While the two were talking Georgea returned with three beautiful broaches that she had seen while roaming the store.'

"I'll take these please."

Greta looked down at her friend's choice.

"Those are quite lovely."

"Yes, I'm getting them for the girls."

The young lady looked at both women and then down at the broaches.

"I'm sorry mademoiselle, but those are very expensive."

Georgea frowned at the young lady.

"Oh, and I only thought they were pure gold with a mother pearl encased in each and let's see, hmmm Greta can you take a peak are those chipped diamonds."

Greta looked over the broaches.

"My dear, it appears that they are, to accent the pearl of course."

The young woman said nothing as Greta pulled out a note and wrote it for Thirty-Five Hundred Dollars. After completing the transaction, the embarrassed young woman attempted to apologize for the insult, but it had been far too late for that. On their way out, Greta felt it necessary to give her a live lesson in that moment. The young lady still standing their wide-eyed with embarrassment.

"Let this be a lesson to you, my young up and coming Mademoiselle."

"Never, I mean never judge a book by its cover."

Soon the ladies arrived at their Hotel. They were quickly serviced and escorted to their suite. When they entered they were not at all surprised at the service that had been provided. Fresh flowers along with fresh fruit and a beautiful glass bowl field with chocolates were all the signature features of the Waldorf Astoria that was engraved in their memory.

Their first visit would be to her Godfather, Mr. Clarence Seward Darrow. He was a famous U.S. Lawyer and leading member of the American Civil Liberties Union. Mr. Darrow was also the best friend and lawyer to her belated father. Georgia remembered how her father would always tell her that if anything ever happened to him to find Mr. Darrow. However, after the traumatizing event that had occurred in the past she had not thought of the saving grace of her father's instructions until recently. Georgea hoped that her Godfather was still alive and well, because without him it would be almost impossible for their plan to work. Greta opened the double doors that led out to the balcony that looked out over downtown Manhattan.

She took a deep breath and then released it slowly, and then screamed at the top of her voice

"I LOVE Life so much."

She then invited her dear friend to join her.

"Come on Georgea, say it, say it like you mean it."

"Oh no Greta, that's not necessary."

"C'mon, do it not for you but for the girls."

In that moment Georgea walked up to the balcony and looked across the sky and seen a cloud and behind it illuminated the sun. It had been the first time in twenty years she would witness a cloud with a silver lining. She then looked down at the busy street of people in their everyday life, each walking into their very own destiny. She grabbed a hold of the rails and at the top of her voice she screamed the words.

"I LOVE Life."

She looked back at Greta and smiled.

"That did feel good."

"It was supposed to feel good, how blessed you are to have a second chance. If the first time around is a gift, well the second time around is surely a miracle my dear friend."

"I know every time I think about the girls I get butterflies in my stomach. I can't wait to see them Greta, I hope they will understand."

Adrienne Lynn Rutherford

"My sister is filled with so much evil, I don't know where it started or why she became that way. I could see the evil in my mother long before I understood exactly what it was. I would have never thought that Viola would take after her."

"Well Georgea, she may be the evilest but she sure isn't the smartest."

It's a shame how she's running your families fortune into the ground."

"I've never seen someone so careless and so filled with hate that she can't manage to see its destroying everything around her."

"It's quite disturbing, your father must be turning in his grave."

"C'mon Georgea, let's get ready for the rest of your life."

After freshening up the ladies had a light meal and headed over to Darrow Law Offices Esquire. When they entered there was a young woman at the front desk filing her nails. Georgea looked around the office waiting room noticing that It had not changed. On the wall was an oil painting of her father's dearest friend Mr. Clarence Darrow. Of all the people that had been a part of their lives, she was sure that he would be able to assist her in what she needed to claim her portion of the Quickman estate and hopefully save her family's fortune.

"Mr. Darrow please?"

"One moment."

The young full-figured woman got up from her desk and disappeared behind the large wood stained door. After a few minutes, she returned accompanied by a much younger man. She then returned to her desk and continued to file her nails.

The tall handsome gentleman smiled at the ladies.

"May I help you?"

"Yes, I'm looking for Mr. Darrow."

"I'm Mr. Darrow."

"Mr. Clarence Darrow?"

"I am he."

Greta then interrupted.

"No son, senior Clarence Darrow, the man who made all of this around us happen."

The young man blushed.

"Oh, you're speaking of my father, he has retired from the practice and I have taking over the family business."

"I want you to know, I am highly qualified for whatever services you will need."

"I have learned everything from my father and……"

Again, Greta interrupted the ambitious young man.

"Pardon me son, I want to first congratulate you for stepping into your father's footsteps, I'm sure he is very proud of you, but there is a matter of history here that you may not be able to verify for us."

Georgea then interrupted

"Nothing against you dear."

"I'm sure your very capable, but we must speak to your father."

"Can you please tell him Mr. Quickman's daughter Georgea is here?"

The young man looked astonished and then excused himself. This time he did not exit back through the large wood stained door, but exited out of the main office door and after almost fifteen minutes he returned.

"My apologies, please follow me."

The ladies followed the young man out of the law office and through the door next to the street entrance. He turned the key and opened the door which led to a stairwell. After climbing the stair case they came to another door and the young man turned the key. When he pushed it open for the ladies to enter, right away both Greta and Georgea could see the street front from the large wooden window pane. The apartment had a modest décor with minimal furniture and beautifully buffed hard wood floors. There were quite familiar hand-woven runners along the floor neatly positioned, Georgea knew they had come from India. The lengthy coffee table was filled with framed pictures that must have been the generations of Darrow's over the years and above them all on the wall were awards and recognitions in the name of Clarence Darrow Sr. Esquire. In the far corner was another room and in a glimpse, could be seen a wall encased library with many leather-bound books. However, it wasn't long before the ladies turned their attention to

Adrienne Lynn Rutherford

the large breathtaking oil painting. The picture caught both Georgea's and Greta's attention. A rather mysterious paradise with a beautiful scenery of mountains and white washed cottages neatly arranged facing a breath-taking ocean front.

Below the picture in a maroon colored high-backed leather chair that was fit for a king, sat a frail but jolly Clarence Darrow.

"Come in, come in ahh what a surprise."

George went over to the gentleman and gave him a hug she would have given her very own father if he were alive.

"Please, please have a seat, son send Jesse in here to me and grab Georgea a handkerchief please."

Although Georgea had tried with all her will, she could not hold back the tears that filled her eyes once seeing Mr. Darrow. The memories came in like a flood and it was as if she were seated in the presence of her father. There was no other person she knew on the Earth that knew about the lives of her and the family like this great man and she respected his wisdom.

"Well, well, look at you two."

"Time has served both you young ladies well."

Greta noticed the young woman enter the room and stood at the side of Mr. Darrow"

"Jesse, please bring these ladies something cool to drink, I presume this will be a very interesting meeting that is about to take place."

The young woman did as she was told and upon her return served them all.

"May I be excused papa."

"Yes, dear you may."

"The young lady then disappeared into the room that Georgea noticed filled with shelves of books.

"My mind may escape me but aren't you Pierre's daughter Greta?"

Greta surprised at the old man's memory nodded in affirmation.

"I thought so, heard some interesting things about you, free spirited in all, done well for yourself too, that's good."

"Thank you, sir."

"You're a good friend coming all this way with Georgea, I didn't think I would ever see her again."

"Time is a funny thing you know, it's a revolving door of memories and sometimes with a little bit of hope it will manifest in the physical."

"It's all relative you know."

The ladies listened as Mr. Darrow talked about old times, things that only he could understand and then he confirmed something that Georgea had already known.

"Your sister has grown to be a very cynical woman, I never thought all those things that had been spoken would come to pass, but I tell you after seeing all the evil that she has done and the boundaries she would cross to get what it is she wanted, I would sadly say it was true."

Georgea was quite curious about the comment.

"What was true?"

Mr. Darrow then changed the subject and knowing the answer to his question addressed the ladies inconspicuously.

"What brought you ladies all this way to see this frail old man?"

"Well, I wanted to talk to you about my family, about my life, my inheritance, is it still there?"

"My father told me, if anything were to ever happen to him for me to come and see you, but so much has happened over the years. Many things I regret, I'm here to fix things and make them right for all of us if I can."

"Uncle Darrow, my sister Viola is destroying everything that my father worked for."

"She is mis-managing the finances of the business and from the looks of it, she has practically sold most of the families shares to the Cornerstone Bank in Boston."

"She's been reckless since I've gone away and she needs to be stopped, before it is too late."

"Greed and hate have consumed her and she is threatening the lives of my children."

Darrow attentively listened to Georgea as she explained everything that had transpired in her life over the past twenty years.

216   Adrienne Lynn Rutherford

It had saddened him that everything that had previously been spoken had come into fruition. At the time he wasn't quite sure, but now in his feeble old age he was a believer.

"Georgea, your inheritance is not in danger. It is just a matter of retrieving the proper legal paperwork and proof of times and places to support them." Mr. Darrow then took a sip from his coffee cup and continued.

"I must warn you, your sister may be legally liable and could face prison time for her mindless behavior."

She signed documents stating that you were no longer living and that she and her son were the only living heirs of the Quickman Estate. She never mentioned the girls and now that you are here, I can pull some dusty old timer strings to get done what your father always wanted."

"But Uncle Darrow, I asked you about what you thought was true?"

"What happened to my sister?"

"What made her so evil and hateful?"

"Well, my dear I don't know everything, but I do know some things."

"One thing I do know, when she came to me with the information of your death I knew there was no truth in it, but the legalities she presented were concrete and she'd left no stone unturned after your mother's death."

"And besides, I hadn't spoken to you myself so I couldn't prove it."

Mr. Darrow shook his head. "It's amazing how deceitful and manipulative people can get when it comes to matters of money and power. It was really disheartening not being able to get any information about you from her."

"That Viola thinks she is smart."

"But what she doesn't know is before she could even walk, me and your father had many conversations up until his tragic death regarding you and your sister's future."

"He wanted to make sure you were taking care of and I made a promise to do just that."

"Regarding why your sister is the way she is, well I must say it has a lot to do with your mother."

"Being the eldest child, she took a lot of the burden of being paraded around by your mother."

"She had Viola's life all planned out, she would be the debutant wanted by every wealthy young man of European descent, she would marry Aristocrat and nothing less.

"Your mother, she loved the aristocratic life she valued it more than anything. You were too young in the heyday of it all."

"Not so much your father though, they were quite opposite to say the least."

"Your father, like myself had experienced a different life and as a result we saw the effects that greed and power had on much of the world. So, we put our lives on the line many times for liberties sake."

"We were threatened by some of the worse bigots in this country and around the world I might add, I will tell you no lie."

"So, the circles that he'd known all his life, he no longer had a desire for anymore. Your father was a just man and he believed in the liberty of all men."

"Your mother resented him for that and began to treat him distastefully and on many occasions in front of guest."

"She made a mockery of him, and he slowly year after year began to distance himself from her. When your father was home from his travels on business, he spent all his undivided attention with you and your sister."

"Your mother and sister would travel quite frequently in the summer months to Europe when you were younger, while she paraded your sister around like a trick pony." "Because you were so young at the time, she left you home with the nanny and this made your father very angry."

Georgea briefly reflected on the life that she remembered with her family.

"But, Viola was nothing like she is today when we were coming up, never!"

"It was after father died that I was able to see the dreadful change in her."

"When we are very young, very rarely do we see the true troubles of this world."

Adrienne Lynn Rutherford

Mr. Darrow slowly lifted himself out of his chair while holding on to his cane. He turned around to face the large oil painting, grabbed the frame and pulled it toward him. Behind it was a safe in the wall and after several turns the ladies heard a click and Mr. Darrow pulled the small door open. He reached his hand inside and pulled out an age worn leather satchel and closed it shut. He then handed it to Georgea.

"My dear girl I want to will tell you a story, but before you open that."

Georgea looked down at the satchel in curiosity and as the ladies made themselves comfortable, Mr. Darrow shared a piece of the past that he experienced with her father and his loyal friend.

"Georgia, your grandfather Mr. Dupree, was a very ambitious man in his time. He had become very wealthy during the slave trade investing in ships to transport cargo back and forth from the west coast of Africa and arriving on the coast of Charleston South Carolina many times."

"Well after the importation of slaves became illegal here in 1807 he insisted on continuing his business along with many of his business partners. So, your grandfather hired mercenaries to sail his ships and illegally continued to return to the lower regions of the western coast of Africa kidnapping and bringing more African people across the Atlantic Ocean.

"Since these ships were no longer allowed to dock on the coast of the North American colonies, he instead shifted his business to a small island by the name of Guyana on the coast of South America. This small island was indeed a very different inhabitant because, although it was surrounded by many Spanish influenced countries it was controlled by the British. At the time slavery was still one of the major sources of wealth for *Great Britain's Lloyd's of London World Insurance Company,* a powerful broker with influence in India, the America's and Caribbean. It made things that much easier to conduct his business because you see, he'd already been doing business with them before the 1807 law was passed."

"Your grandfather would take his cargo to this Island were many times he made a profit doing business deals with the Spanish who would purchase and then transport his captured cargo to other parts of South America."

"Mr. Dupree, although sinister was a very smart too and he always knew the value of land. He purchased a very sizeable amount of land on Guyana and developed his very own plantation, far away from his home and his family. "He lived a double life for a long time, but he did the unthinkable, he fell in love."

"On one particular shipment from the African continent a beautiful high priestess along with her tribe were captured. He was intrigued by her beauty, wisdom and how her people revered her even in the darkness of their servitude." "It was rumored by many that for your grandfather, it was love at first sight and it was because of this it would go down in history as one of the largest bidding wars ever witnessed on the small island of Guyana."

"He built a house for her and made her overseer of his properties in Guyana. Those slaves who lived life there wanted for nothing. They farmed the and ate from it. Your grandfather did make money off the sugar cane and traded coconut oil and such, but the land pretty much was a solitude for this woman and her people. She bore him three children two boys and a girl and no one ever knew of this until many years later."

Georgea sat back in the couch with her mouth wide open, she couldn't believe what she was hearing. The secrets and the lies that had haunted both sides of her family were a powerful declaration of generational dysfunctional choices and circumstances that eventually had destroyed her happiness. It angered her that the pitiful lies and deceptions that wreaked havoc for generations in her family had managed to extend its tentacles into the lives of her daughters, and destroyed what little happiness she tried to salvage in her own life. She continued to listen falling on every word that Mr. Darrow would speak. Greta listened as well, trying to grasp this very complicated and emotional situation as Mr. Darrow continued.

"Many years later after your grandfather's death, your mother came to me with a letter and a deed that she'd found in your grandfather's things back in Memphis. She was pregnant with your sister Viola at the time."

"She found the documents in the library where your

220   Adrienne Lynn Rutherford

grandfather would conduct the company's day to day business in a secret drawer under the bottom of his desk. She was sure your grandmother knew nothing about the contents. So, she asked your father to bring it to me to investigate what was going on and to check out the legalities of it all."

"When I told him about the property and profits that generated out of this secluded place she was livid. She recalled your grandfather going out of the country from time to time for most of her life on business of course. So, to hear this information was quite disturbing to your mother. She asked me to her your father to this place called Guyana. We went by boat and when we arrived It appeared to be a very rural place, hardly even touched by the modern world.

"But, I must tell you it was one of the most beautiful places we all had ever seen. It was a paradise and at that time there were still a hand full of wealthy British land owners, most who managed hold on to claims made by their family's years before. But, the Island itself was culturally dominated by the decedents of African slaves and they made up most of the population. "Overtime, many of these descendants were able to claim small plots of land because the descendants of the British landowners gradually abandoned or sought to rid themselves of the hassle because it was no longer as profitable or considered a safe place after the Civil War. So, by the time we arrived there was a culturally strong African presence. Guyana now had become a popular port and rest stop for traders headed to South America."

"Your mother couldn't understand how he could keep such a secret from her and her mother all that time. I must tell you she was a bit upset, your father had to remind her that she was with child, but there was no calming her. We were escorted to the property by a very articulate fellow that was quite familiar with your grandfather, shared that he was a great loss and how kind he had to him and his sisters, sometimes bringing them gifts from the mainland. He took us by horse and wagon to the road that led up to this huge beautiful White washed home. Your mother, with the help of your father got out of the wagon. It was hot, yes, I remember it was very hot that day. She then asked the young man what portion of this land belonged to her father, he told her all of it. We all gasped, he

Dance of Angels   221

confirmed that it as far as the eye could see behind the iron gate belonged to Mr. Dupree."

"And that's when it all began."

"Your mother asked who lived in the large White house."

"The young man told her that the mistress of the land lives here. He called her the High Priestess, well that didn't sit well with your mother at all and she told him."

"Take me to this high priestess."

"We all then got back up onto the wagon and he took us down the long dirt road just beautiful palm trees lined the side of the road, the closer we got the wider the path became. There were children playing outside and neatly well-kept cabins that lined the side of the road. The people were staring at us as if we were trespassing. It looked more like a small village than a plantation once we got inside the iron gates. We then passed a beautiful vast lake where a few of the men were fishing along the bank. It was like nothing you could even imagine. No one said a word as we continued up the road. Soon we went up hill and then when we got to the top we could look down. As we got closer, that's when we saw the house in its entirety.

"It was a mansion, a very solid beautifully built Mansion I may add."

"It had a very large front porch with beautiful tall cemented pillars, beautiful large cement flower pots filled with the most beautiful exotic flowers simply just astonishing. I mean, this place was mind blowing and your grandfather left no table unturned. When we pulled up to the front entrance of the house. He then young stepped off the wagon bowed to the tall slender, yet beautiful woman. Her skin was the color of dark chocolate and her hair of locks were white as snow. Her presence was profound, I mean you knew that this woman was of a royal lineage. She said nothing, it was as if the people that were around her could read her mind. She wore a beautiful long purple dress, nothing like I had ever seen and a beautiful purple head scarf to match. If I didn't know any better I would have thought she was a queen. Now your mother, she didn't like it one bit and after your father helped her out of that wagon the walked right up to that woman."

"*Who are you?*"

Adrienne Lynn Rutherford

"It is I who should be asking you that question, I believe you have come upon us, but I am Mantu."

"And you?"

"Beatrice, Beatrice Dupree-Quickman, daughter of Benjamin Dupree III."

"This is my husband Mr. Quickman and our close friend Mr. Marrow."

"Your mother then went into her satchel and pulled out the deed and the legal document stating that the land belonged to the family. After she presented the papers to her the woman said nothing about them, instead she was very warm and kind."

"Yes, I do believe we both have suffered a great loss."

"I see you're with child my dear."

"Please, join me in the garden so that we can be more comfortable, rest a bit as you have traveled a long way I am sure."

"She then handed the paperwork over to the tall gentleman that stood next to her."

"I will have my lawyer look over these things for me, in the meanwhile please join me and when he is finished looking them over, he will present them to me and we all can then talk with equal understanding.

"The house servants escorted us all to the garden in the back of the house. It was just as beautiful there as it was in the front of the property, I mean your grandfather had out did himself. There was a small lake out back and we all admired the beautiful Swans. It was an amazingly peaceful place almost hypnotizing I might add"

"This woman then told us that she in fact was the mistress of the house and it was pretty much obvious at that point."

"Even then, long after your grandfather's death.

"When the young man returned with the papers he joined us and then he began to speak in what we presumed her native tongue."

Then after several minutes she addressed us."

"My lawyer has explained these documents to me and I find it to be nothing that I am interested in discussing after all."

"Me and my people have toiled this land for the last 65 years. Are you not satisfied with what your father has provided your family?"

"I know you want for nothing in your world do you not?

"There is nothing here attached to you."

"Although maybe it was merely only curiosity that brought you here?"

"It is not likely that a woman of your status would travel all this way carrying child, if not for curiosities sake."

"Your mother slowly got up from her chair holding on to her stomach and she was very adamant when she spoke to the woman. I mean even I was blown away by the comment she made."

"Let me tell you something, you know nothing about me or my family, my father obviously lived a double life for a very long time and it's obvious that he created this fantasy of a life here on this God forsaken Island for whatever reason."

"So Mantu, don't you dare be mistaken, I am his family not you."

"My mother gave my father everything of her, every breath, every thought, every emotion for as long as I could remember, and it never seemed to please him. She would cry nights when he was away for months on business, when he returned he didn't so much as look at her. I saw all of that and I couldn't understand why he could treat her that way."

"Until now and I must say I am quite disgusted!"

Mantu slowly got up from her chair.

"What do you really want with what we have down here, your father was just a man, who overtime understood quite well the error of his ways of course."

"Oh, really is that how you see it?"

"Well the view is quite different from up here!"

"I suppose you are the one responsible for showing him the errors of his ways!"

"You were his little secret, his little whore that he follied with, you were the reason that my father couldn't seem to stay home, you where the reason that he lied to my mother."

"It was you a mere ignorant slave woman who single-handedly destroyed the foundation of my family."

The lawyer grabbed the hand of the elderly woman as if he were calming her and she held his hand tightly, I could have sworn she looked straight into the soul of your mother.

"That is enough, I didn't ask to come here, our children were also not asked to be born on this land."

"The greed of white men brought us here. "

"The greed of white men killed my king, my true love."

"This place around you is merely a sordid reminder of the atrocities that had befallen upon my people.

Adrienne Lynn Rutherford

"Have you ever had your life stolen from you Beatrice, the lives of your people and the generations that were to inherit your legacy stripped of their birthright forever?"

"Yes, your father spoke of you all the time, I know you all too well it cured my stomach, each time he mentioned you and your spoiled selfish ways."

"I am Mantu rightful owner of this land and you have no right to come into our home and display such disrespect, the ways of the real world are truly cruel and it's obvious with such privilege, you have not had the opportunity to live in it as I or my village"

"The paper work that you bring to my front door is of no consequence to me"

"It is from your world and it carries no power here, not anymore."

"Your world left when your father left. We have no reason to acknowledge any threats you present."

"A mere receipt from a bill of sale for this land from your fathers over crowded desk"

The tall gentleman then addressed your mother.

"I am Sou'ke Dupree the son of Benjamin Dupree III and I carry his blood and his gene, just as you."

"You see these people around here, they are my family, we are a free community caring for one another."

"I am a lawyer, my father sent me to the finest schools in Paris France. My brother Tafari Dupree is studying medicine abroad as we speak. He is currently in the amazon valley right now doing research on healing plants for the body so that we can continue to thrive here."

My twin sister Su'kai, she speaks four different languages fluently and she teaches at our school over on the other side of the creek that our father built for her. Do not be mistaken there is no ignorance here Beatrice, none at all."

"We have established something here that most white men in your country would ultimately fear, economic freedom without them."

"After your mother heard this, there was no way she would be able to leave that place with any peace on her heart. I could see the shame and hurt festering in your mother and I watched it resonate quickly to hate. This was a strange and awkward predicament that we were in. Out in the middle of nowhere with a people none of us were familiar with. Me and your father knew that we needed not make any waves we were obviously out numbered. We needed to get back to the docks the same way that we had come."

"Your mother, she was a fire cracker you know. She didn't back down one bit."

"Well, since you are a lawyer, you read the documents and everything you're sitting on belongs to my world, it was all willed to me."

"I could see that the elderly woman's patience was running thin with your mother, we tried to stop her but she wouldn't give in. These people were only living their lives is all, just like you and me. But it got worse for your mother, especially when she found out about your grandfather's other grown children."

"There is nothing for you here, leave us. We only want peace."

"This is our home and we are not leaving. You see this young man Sou'ke and he spoke of my other children as well, they all belong to Dupree. You are not the only heir to that will.

"So, you see Beatrice we belong here and understanding these conditions will make this life easier for us all, but you are welcomed to come here as much as you like, you are my children's sister, you are family."

Greta interrupted Mr. Darrow.

"I can't believe what I am hearing. You mean Mrs. Quickman all those years thought she was her father's only child and she found out there were other children by this mysterious African woman."

Mr. Darrow nodded his head in confirmation while Georgea sat motionless taking everything in.

"You have to understand; the Civil War was a turning point mostly between northern and southern whites over the U.S economy on and slavery was a huge casualty for the south losing that war. They never intended to give ex-slaves in the U.S. forty acres and a mule or

"The situation with the British and Spanish who'd owned plantations in the Caribbean were faced with a quite different dilemma, the increase in the slave population outnumbered slave owners and this created a civil unrest and fear that drove most of the British, French and even Spanish out of many areas of the Caribbean"

"That is what the lady Mantu and her son was trying to relay to your mother Georgea."

"She really had no power to push those people off the land."

Adrienne Lynn Rutherford

"And why would she want to, I asked her?"

"I tried to get her to see the bigger picture."

"Where would they go?"

"We were talking about almost four generations of a village, this was the only home they would ever know."

"Your mother wasn't trying to hear any of it and she became very irate, cursing the island and the people, she wouldn't stop she was so consumed with hate and pain, it was hard to watch."

"Your father tried to talk her into leaving, but she refused to listen and then she grabbed a hold of her stomach."

"That's when the woman Mantu spoke words to her that always stuck in the back of my mind, that woman spoke of much, much more than what your mother needed to hear Georgea."

"You're carrying a daughter; your evil heart and ways will transfer to her and her seed if you do not release the hate that you have for me and my family. This is not a good thing this hate you carry."

"All the riches in the world will not be able to sooth the discontent you will have in your spirit, release it at this instance or you will be terribly sorry."

"Your father was holding your mother and she was quite frantic, trying to get her to the wagon while she cried out in anger at the woman"

"You have no idea of who you're dealing with."

"The woman continued to watch her as we were finally able to get her to leave."

"Sou'ke, son please escort these people back to their wagon, this discussion is over and I shall not expect to see you again, as it is you who has no idea with whom you are dealing with."

"Your mother's anger then turned to rage and your father did all he could to calm her down but she promised to return. As we loaded her up onto the wagon, she stopped and turned to look back and Mantu stood on the porch holding on to the documents. She then tore them up in our faces and the pieces of paper fell to the ground. Her son then escorted her back into the house and that was the last time any of us laid eyes on Mantu."

"When we finally got your mother home, she was sick for a long time. She'd become hateful and emotionally detached. Your father could no longer communicate with her anymore. She blamed him for not speaking up for her and standing up to the Mantu woman. It had become all his fault. When your sister Viola was born she cried for months. It was terrible, no one knew what was wrong with her. Until one day suddenly she stopped."

"For a time, your mother and father were distant from one another, but they eventually made amends and she became pregnant again with you. You brought your mother and father back together again. Your father made sure that this pregnancy would be perfect for your mother. She received the best of care and was pampered beyond belief. When you were born, your father was the happiest man in the world. He thought he'd done right by your mother, but soon after she turned back to her old ways."

Georgea interrupted.

"This Mantu woman that you speak of in Guyana, did she put a curse on my mother and my sister, is that what your trying to tell me"

"I'm only telling a story, one that I have witnessed, one that I know."

"I know nothing of curses or such things, I do know that when we left that Island your mother was not the same."

"So, my mother never went back to that place?"

"No, I'm afraid not, your father forbade it."

He insisted that she leave those people be."

"I think that's what put a wedge between her and your father. It was quite ironic though, I think your father as well as I was quite intrigued by what these people were able to accomplish on their own."

"After we returned home, your father and I began to support organizations that supported the liberties and freedom of all people. We became quite dedicated to that, we lost a lot of business contracts because of it. Almost put us in the red, but we gained more loyal base of business partners and genuine friendship in folks like your good friend Greta's father."

"Before your father's passing, he took you everywhere with him.

He tried to shield you and your sister from what he thought was a great evil."

Adrienne Lynn Rutherford

Georgea smiled, as she figured this was why she and Viola could spend so much time with Greta in France.

"I know and for many years too, that's how I met Bufus. My father approved, but my mother and Viola were so upset with me. They refused to show up at events with us, but not my father. They didn't even give him a chance."

Mr. Darrow shook his head.

"Your father's dedication to philanthropy catapulted his aspirations for a political career and people gravitated to him."

"We knew the experience that your mother had would be the wedge between him and his political career and she was turning your sister against him."

"The staff in your home would share very disheartening information with your father. Your mother would remind your sister Viola, that she was her only hope and that she must maintain the family legacy and values because your father had brainwashed you."

"Never in a million years did I think that after your father's death, she would do everything to destroy what your father built, even despite it all."

"Although she could not do anything about the property in Guyana, Beatrice took back all the financing that he'd provided for many of the schools and medical facilities throughout the south as well as Central America."

"She fired me and I watched both she and your sister strip those people of everything, it was terrible just terrible to witness."

"When word got back to the U.S. Press she made a statement that shocked us all. It was printed in the New York Times an absolute disaster. Many of the stockholders in the company where previous abolitionist and philanthropist just like your father. They insisted on speaking with her, and because of so many requests she invited us all over to dinner. When we arrived, she was stone cold drunk and It was just a terrible time. She stood up in the middle of dinner and made the speech that changed the course of Quickman Mining Corporation forever."

"*I have two brothers and a sister and they are all niggers, can you believe my father. Educated niggers at that, he didn't leave a stone unturned in his life, did he?*"

Dance of Angels   229

"He had to explore everything, even at the expense of his family's happiness."

"You see that man up there, that is my father Benjamin Dupree III he built this legacy and a proud confederate by right, so I thought. I hope he is turning in his grave to know I'm letting the world know that he failed his family. Over there is a portrait of my late husband Mitchell Quickman IV. Who would have ever thought I would marry someone like my father, because he too was also a failure."

"Long live the confederacy".

"The guests were appalled, those who'd invested in the company expressed their distaste and vowed to take their investments elsewhere. Any political ties she had to the union supporters, thanks to your father were completely destroyed."

"Investments went down considerably and even though she and your sister managed to keep the company running, it is hardly where it used to be."   "

"Your father mentioned it many times, the events that transpired on Guyana that day and how he truly felt the words that the Mantu women spoke were powerful enough to make a difference in the lives of his family. After your mother's public mockery of your father, Beatrice returned to wallowing in her misery and no one was there financially anymore except her loyal and greedy friends at the Boston Commonwealth Bank. They had been trying for years to get their hands on your family's coal mines. Although your father had considered selling, he refused to be low balled."

"Only weeks after you moved out on your own, your mother and sister left for France, with little focus on the company. Beatrice's primary goal had never changed, she was going to marry Viola off to a prominent European family."

"All that had changed when your sister became pregnant while in France, and I was told your mother was so upset with Viola that she brought her home kicking and screaming."

"To pacify her hurt and pain, she gave her complete control of the Quickman Mining Company and for the last fifteen years she has been gradually selling off the company to the Boston Bank of the Commonwealth the very people whom your father despised."

"So, you leaving when you did was a good thing, regardless of the circumstances that surrounded your departure. They created a web of evil and pain and because of it, your sister's son was born of it as well."

Chapter 24

Tulsa Oklahoma Greenwood District

Queen knocked hard for a few minutes on the cellar door before William decided to open it up. When the sun hit his face he immediately blocked it with his hand.

"Wil, did I wake you up, I brought you a cup of coffee."

"No come on down, I was about to get ready to come up and check on Sarah.

"Oh, she's stirring and she still a little shaken up though."

Queen then sat at the small corner table.

"William, what on earth happened the other night, things were far too intense to talk to you about it and you know your mom was furious."

The events begin to stir at William's emotions as he remembered that evening and he hit his chest with his fist.

"It's them, the hate!"

"Me and Sarah Jane are in love, have been for a while."

"And those sick people, all they see is the color of my skin."

"As long as we are shucking and jiving for them, working for them, cooking, cleaning and saying yes suh or no suh, it makes them feel superior, they need that."

"They want us to shop in their stores and spend our money in their businesses on their terms and we are supposed to be okay with that."

"That's a sick way of thinking Queen."

"Their hearts are so full of hate, if not the lot of them, but most of them."

"If it wasn't for her brother Billy Jo yawl probably would be taking both of us down from a tree this morning."

William then went over to the table at sat down with Queen to finish his coffee.

"You know, every time I cross them tracks to come back over here on this other side and see all the prosperity in the community of Greenwood, it gives me a sense of pride knowing that we are not the people they try to make us out to be."

Adrienne Lynn Rutherford

"We are strong, resilient, intelligent and most of all creative and loving."

"Even in the mist of all the hell we've endured we still prosper."

"Queen, I wanna show you something"

William got up and went to the cabinet and brought out a large black box and opened it. Inside where many types of tools and gadgets, all which were foreign to Queen. William went underneath and pulled out a drawer and laying neatly on a black velvet canvas were several handcrafted time pieces. They all were attached to leather straps, femininely made, some with beautiful embroidery. He pulled out one and handed it to Queen.

"Oh Wil, these are absolutely beautiful, you did this."

"Yep, been working on this for about three years now, trying to get the designs proper you know."

"Well you did a lovely job."

"Well, you know, I'm good at what I do."

Queen began to laugh as William reminded her that he never lacked self confidence in something he could do very well.

"I'm going into the watch making business."

"I sent several pieces back east, New York you know."

"I got a few investors that are interested."

"I didn't want to say nothing until I was sure, you know I've been working across the tracks for Mr. Gurley for over ten years now learning the trade.'

"It's about time I start up my own business."

"Wow I'm impressed, good for you Wil."

"Thanks, that's the upside of all that's been transpiring."

Queen took a sip of her coffee as William went over to place his future back into the cabinet.

"Wil, what happened?"

Wil sat back down while shaking his head. As much as he wanted to forget the encounter, he knew that it would be imbedded in his memory for the rest of his life.

"Well, I closed up the shop at 5pm and just like clockwork I waited in the cellar in the rear of the building until way past dinner time. By then most of the business district on the Northside are closed and the alley is almost always empty by then."

"I wait for a signal from Sarah Jane and she picks me up with the wagon. She's a seamstress at the cleaners a few doors down, but she works from home. So, in the afternoon she comes by and with a key she opens the cellar to drop off the alterations from the day before and pick up new ones left for her to fix."

"When she slams the doors shut, that's my cue and I come out where she has the wagon blocking the cellar door and then I just slide under the floorboard and she takes me home."

Queen could not believe what she was hearing all of this for the woman he loved, as crazy as it sounded to her it also was quite intriguing. The things that people would do for love, even if it meant risking life and limb. In that moment, she thought of her mother and father. She wondered what they had endured for loves sake. She then focused her attention back to William.

"Man, but this time when we get to her farm, I hear her brother Billy Jo arguing with his girlfriend, some chick he just started dating. Our routine was solid up to that point."

"Something told me to stay in those floorboards, but when she pulled out the gun on Billy Jo and he raised his hand I knew at that moment that our lives where gonna change forever. I was concerned about Sarah Jane. I slid out on the other side of the wagon where she couldn't see me and I came around the side of the house and I just walked up like I'd been there all the while."

William began to laugh.

"You should have seen the look on her face when she saw me."

"What is that nigger doing on this side of town after dark?"

"You know it's against the law for you to be over here."

"Queen when I tell you whatever it was that pissed her off about Billy Jo, hey that was completely out the window and by that time he'd taking the gun right out her hand."

"He then asked her, what the hell was wrong with her and that, she could've killed him. So, he took the gun and told her bring to her father's house in the morning."

William began to laugh again, but contained himself.

"At the time, it wasn't that funny because she had not heard anything that was said by Billy Jo. She kept inquiring about me, *the nigger*."

Adrienne Lynn Rutherford

She then looked over at Sarah Jane.

"Is this your doing Sarah J?"

Sarah Jane kept her cool and she didn't say nothing, but I don't know if that was the worst thing or the best thing, because she just would not let up off of her after the silence.

"What's it like Sarah J?"

"Sarah Jane, she ain't no coward and she didn't back down."

"She asked her what she was talking about. But, this angry white girl, she didn't give up, she was obsessed with the mere presence of me."

"She then turned to Billy Jo, and asked him if he knew, but Billy Jo didn't say a word either."

"She then walked over to me and then started walking around me as if she was inspecting me or something and I told her they had taken niggers off the auction block years ago."

She looked over at Billy Jo waiting for him to defend her honor and when he didn't he screamed at the top of her voice."

"I hate you Billy Jo, I hate you."

"Billy Jo came from the porch and snatched her up, *what's wrong with you?*" She snatched back, your what's wrong with me Billy Jo."

"*I hate you Billy Jo, you will pay for this I promise you that, I'm telling your Uncle Clyde about you and your sister and your nigger loving ways.*"

"She hopped on her horse and she took off like lightening."

"I then ask him why did he have to go and get some head case."

Queen interrupted.

"Wil, why didn't you leave?"

"Man, I don't know."

"We went in the house, didn't think much more about it and that was the mistake that I made. I got too comfortable with the situation, just too comfortable."

"Before we knew it their Uncle Clyde and three of his sons came to the house with that head case. He looked at me, and then he looked at Sarah Jane and said nothing. She hopped out of the wagon going on and on, I told you so, I told you so. A nigger, he ain't got no business on this side of the tracks after dark.

"She kept talking."

"Are we gonna hang em?"

"Are we gonna hang em?"

"Queen when I tell you that was one time I feared for my life, I swear I thought it was the end for sure for me. I didn't say a word. He walked up to me holding that rifle at his side with his finger on the trigger.

"What's your name boy?"

"I said William Black".

"You Ma'mes grandboy?"

"I was shocked."

Queen looked on in disbelief

William continued.

"Yeah, and then he told me."

"You know the rules boy. I would normally call the sheriff up here to lock you up, but we both know you wouldn't see the light of day."

"He then looked over at Sarah and asked her what was her business with me."

"Queen, when I tell you Sarah Jane didn't back down and she stood her ground. She told them she loved me, but before she could finish the sentence his hand went so swiftly across her face. It took everything in me not to come to her defense, she held her hand up to me while she got up from the ground and waved her hand at me to leave it be, she knew that we both would die. He then asked her.

Is this the way you wanna live your life, like a nigger?

At that point, I couldn't take it and I had to step in."

"Wil no you didn't."

"Yeah, I did."

"I would have been less than a man not to say what I had to say, if he was gonna kill me, he would have done it already."

"His sons rushed me and started beating me, I could hear Sarah Jane screaming for them to stop, I couldn't say nothing it was as if I was having an out of body experience as if I was looking down on them boys kicking and punching on me. After a few minutes, I could hear Billy Jo.

"Uncle Clyde please, please tell'em to stop, they'll kill em."

"I looked up at Billy Jo, he had his head down, wouldn't even look at me, but I knew he was angry too, but his hands were tied and he couldn't help me. Their Uncle called them off of me and I laid in

Adrienne Lynn Rutherford

the ground so sore, I knew I was gonna look like Jo Jackson the boxer in the face come sunrise.

"Sarah Jane came to my side to help me up and looking at the expression on her uncle's face, we probably looked pretty pathetic to him at that point. He told us we had five minutes to leave off the farm he and then looked at Sarah Jane."

"Your father is turning in his grave right this moment."

"You get your ass in that wagon with this boy and take yourself right over them tracks, you don't belong here anymore. If I ever see you this way again, you're my niece and I love ya, but I will kill ya.

"What you have done is a blasphemy to our god giving name, but imma spare your life and boy you have your grandmama to thank on this day. If anybody else would've caught you, the both of you would be hanging right now."

"Go on git outta here."

"Deep down me and Sarah J both knew he was right."

"He then spit his tobacco on the ground and took his rifle and sat it on top of his shoulder and then turned to Pauline.

"If I hear any word about this in town while having a beer at the saloon, or during a hand at the poker table. If I hear anything even getting a scoop of my favorite chocolate ice cream on Sunday afternoon, girl I will kill you."

"You hear?"

"Revenge can sometimes end up backfiring and you put yourself in a pretty mess with that mouth of yours, stirring up the shit pot in my family business. I will warn you just this once gal."

"Queen you should have seen the fear in that girls face and afterward she left, and if you know me I don't leave well enough alone that well. I had to ask him how he knew Ma'me and he turned and looked at me."

"Ma'me saved my life as a child, she came to our home with an elixir for the small pox, it was wiping out many families. I remember her coming into my room. I was sweating and I had a fever, but when she opened that door it was as if a bright light came into the room and the house stirred like an earth quake, these were days of old here in Tulsa.

"She ain't no nigger."

"Couldn't no nigger carry that kind of power, I spared you because she spared me, so now you know."

Dance of Angels   237

"After that we didn't waste no time, we left, Sarah Jane was in a bad way. I know it hurt to hear what her Uncle said to her about her father. Sarah Jane's spirit was broken and my body was broken."

"After that Billy Jo brought us to the house in his pick up and I knew after that I couldn't go back to the watch shop no more."

"I know we eventually gotta leave, her uncle just bought us some time is all."

"It's not going be safe for us here anymore, I tell you Ma'me saved my life."

"I mean even when she ain't trying she is doing good in the world, I'll never tell her what happened though."

Queen smiled.

"Something tells me you don't have to."

Queen looked at her eldest cousin and appreciating him to trust her enough to share the details of his circumstances, after all it had been years since they'd seen one another. So, to know that he trusted her made her feel as equally trustful of him. William then turned up the last of his coffee and grinned at Queen.

"Well, cousin Queen, when you gonna come clean?"
William then got up and went to the pantry opened it up and pulled out the homemade wine.

"Something tells me that your story is gonna require something a little bit stronger than a cup of coffee and now that I'm out of a job, I guess I'm back in the grape business."

Queen nodded in confirmation as he brought two glasses to the table. William poured them each a shot, he turned his up his up quickly and then poured another.

"Ahhhh, that's good."

Queen took a sip and then started to slowly spin her glass with her fingers on the table.

"I guess you're wondering why we're here huh?"

"Yeah, because it was so sudden."

"Don't get me wrong, I was glad to see you it's been a long time and it's good to meet the twins too, but I was a little suspicious."

"What happened to aunt Georgea?"

"To be honest Wil, I don't know."

"Things are so complicated for all of us now."

Adrienne Lynn Rutherford

"I haven't seen my mother in damn near fifteen years and the twins hardly even remember her besides the pictures we have."

"I remember she made us breakfast before school like she did every morning. I remember coming home that day looking for her. Daddy did everything he could to comfort us, but I could see he was just as confused about her disappearance as I was."

"She never came home, I cried myself to sleep for a year every night, then for some reason one morning I woke up and knew that I had to look after my sisters."

"It's so complicated."

"Yeah sounds like it, but we both know that's not the reason why you're here."

William looked at Queen waiting for her response, she then turned her drink up as he'd done and he poured her another glass.

"Spit it out girl."

"He tried to hurt Carolyn and I couldn't allow that to happen."

"I'm supposed to protect them, that's my job."

"It happened so fast there was the knives on the counter and him on the floor on top of Carolyn trying to take advantage of her."

"You gotta understand William I'm not a murderer, I had no choice."

"He was evil, just an evil man"

William was in shock, he didn't expect to hear the story that Queen was telling him. Although he looked on attentively all he could see was the little young shy girl who was afraid to come out of the tree. What had changed her life so drastically, what had destroyed the family bond that his uncle had worked so hard to have. He'd looked up to that bond a blueprint for his future, but now he felt saddened by the events that Queen so honestly shared with him, a decision that had obviously changed her life and the lives of the twins forever. Queen continued.

"I tell you his Mama she is far eviler than him. I let him on the kitchen floor of my father's house."

"I found Ma'mes address in one of his phone books, thank God because I don't know where we would have gone."

Queen got up out of her seat and started pacing the floor.

"If she finds us she will kill us, I don't think there is no worse enemy than Viola Quickman, she's a monster of a woman to say the least."

"You have any cigarettes William?"

"When did you start smoking."

"I don't actually, it helps to calm my nerves."

"Look over in the pantry."

Queen scanned the pantry and pulled out a single cigarette from the pack and lit it. She then took a long drag off it and exhale as the smoke filled the air. That woman is plagued with hate and she has no heart and if she finds us Wil, she will kill us."

Wil was speechless never would he have ever thought what brought Queen and the twins to Tulsa would be murder, and he knew as well as Queen that murder was definitely by law a reason to hang.

"What's your plans?"

Queen took another drag and smashed the cigarette on the cement wall.

"Right now, it's basically to just stay low and figure how we can put the pieces of our lives back together."

"Does anyone else know that you're here?"

"No one beside my father's assistant Jonas, he was loyal to father for years and still now to us. He was the reason we could get out of Memphis safely. I sent him word that we were safe. He'll contact me when he can and by then he will be able to fill me in about what's going on in Memphis.

"Queen, this Quickman woman is she's as powerful as you say, it won't be long before word gets out this way. Believe it or not people here in Greenwood District spend lots of time on the railroad going east for one reason or another."

"I know Wil, that's been on my mind a lot too."

"Well, I gotta be frank with you, you can't just be thinking about this stuff any longer. We must come up with some type of a plan. You ain't got a whole lot of time, especially if she got a bounty on your head."

Queen had not thought about a bounty, but it made perfect sense to her. Viola was capable of anything and a bounty would be the best way to get results. With her wealth, she had the power to send anyone looking for them.

This time it was Wil's turn as he went to the pantry and lit himself a cigarette.

"I'm expecting Calvin and John to return soon and when they do we gotta tell them."

"No, no please Wil, I couldn't"

"What do you mean?"

"Queen this is serious, it's just not about you anymore we all maybe at risk, so we need to make plans just in case we all may have to leave this place."

"You understand, its bigger than you now, hell its bigger than me and we can't go at this alone, can't you understand."

"Calvin and John, they are like my brothers and they will help us, but you gotta promise me no more secrets you hear?"

"Yes, I promise."

"I mean it Queen, no secrets."

"Wil, I told you everything."

"Have you spoken to Ma'me?"

"Yes, but not in so much detail as we have today."

"Okay good, what's your plans today."

"Well me and Carolyn been working on this performance at the paradise tonight. It appears Tyler is trying to sell the paradise to some big-time investors from back east, but no specifics just yet."

"Well, in the meantime you girls be careful."
William could not hold back his frustration about the events that had transpired in the lives of his family.

"Damn, I will be so happy on the day we can live in some type of peace."

Queen got up from her chair and patted her cousin on the shoulder and returned to the brightness of the sunshine on the other side of the cellar door. In many ways, she was relieved that she'd shared the events that forced her in search of solitude in Tulsa. Nevertheless, it would be a far different experience when she had to share her story with Calvin, that she was sure of.

Later that evening, Queen prepared the last costume that she'd brought from Memphis. For Queen, performing gave her a sense of peace if only for a brief moment and when arriving to Tulsa she would have never thought she'd be able to continue wooing crowds with the talent that came to her so naturally. Queen's burlesque act now had rumored as far as California in just a few weeks. Nevertheless, she was not as anxious to embrace the popularity knowing the consequences that it could have on she and her sisters. So far, no one appeared suspicious about their presence. The Greenwood District of Tulsa was a busy area and people were coming in daily to seek out opportunity and establish lucrative businesses within the community. The Sawyer sisters had been successful in their transition to Greenwood thus far and Ma'mes house being on the outskirts of town was truly a bonus. However, Queen harvested a lot of resentment for her mother over the years. She remembered spending many nights inside of their garage while her sister was asleep. Here, she wrestled with the anger and frustration of her mother's absence. Queen's thoughts were interrupted by her sister Carolyn.

"Sister, you hear me?"

"What are you thinking about."

Queen looked over at her sister and smiled.

"Nothing, just the performance."

"Are you ready?"

"Of course, I'm always ready."

Carolyn knew her sister too well and as much as she tried, Queen could not hide her feelings. Carolyn joined her as she sat down in the rocking chair in the bedroom.

"Queen, is this were we will be?"

You know where we will live permanently, don't get me wrong it's a wonderful place amazingly different from back home to say the least, and Ma'me and Becky are such a treat."

"I don't know, I really can't say now, we just have to take it one day at a time, and yes, it is an amazing place and Calvin told me a little about the rich history here in Greenwood District."

Queen was startled that Carolyn had asked such a question.

"Queen c'mon, I've seen the way he looks at you, the way you look at him. I truly believe it all started at the train station too, although I know you won't ever admit being smitten by a man, let alone a rustler.

242   Adrienne Lynn Rutherford

Queen said nothing, she knew her sister was right, but she would never tell. Yes, she did have feelings for Calvin and she knew that under the current circumstances it would be impossible for him to feel the same after finding out that she'd deceived his trust. At the time, she didn't know if it was the best thing, as a matter of fact she really didn't know how to tell him that she had murdered a man and was now a fugitive. Dancing had been the one thing that soothed the anxiety she experienced in her sleepless nights. Although she displayed a hard shell to the world, inside her spirit longed for solitude and peace. Becky knocked on the door.

"Hey, c'mon you guys I got work to do."

"You know every time Queen and the band perform I get a full house."

When they reached the lower level of the house the ladies said their goodbyes. However, before Queen could get out of the front door William took her by the arm.

"I don't want you worrying about nothing, you hear?"

"We're going to get through this thing, we're a family and family stick together"

Queen grabbed her cousin and held him close.

"Thank you, thank you so much Wil."

He opened the screen door for her and she hurried out to join the other ladies.

****

The ladies arrived early at the Paradise and Becky was relieved. The band had just come in all the way from California and setting up for the evening. Carolyn went to check the tuning on the piano and Queen made her way to the dressing room. A few hours later Queen was ready as finished her makeup and did the final check on her beautiful Pink ensemble in the mirror. In that moment, she realized tonight was far different than any of the others. Somehow, although she and her sisters were not out of the danger of the unthinkable, she knew with faith and hope she would see the other side of the mountain. The stage manager walked pass her dressing room once more.

"Last call Queen, you're up next."

Queen made her way back stage. As the band played she could hear the clapping of the crowd, always had a way preparing the crowd just before her introduction. When the master of ceremony stepped out on the floor he had on a very outrageous outfit, one that reminded you of a ringmaster of the Barium & Baily Circus. He gave the crowd a few minutes of comic relief before introducing her. Queen waved her hand from side stage as she heard whistles and cheers from the audience, but briefly paused when she looked over at Tyler's table. There was Jonas, waiting patiently to see his friend on stage.

"What is he doing here?"

Queen's nerves started to get the best of her, but Carolyn tapped her on the shoulder.

"You about ready?"

Queen turned around and looked at her sister and right away she knew something was wrong.

"Queen you okay?"

"Look over there casually at Tyler's table, what do you see?"

Carolyn took a look at the table

"What?"

"Look closer."

Carolyn looked closer and then gasped.

"Oh my God is that Jonas?"

"What on Earth is he doing here?"

"I know, but I don't know, I mean."

"Why is he with Tyler?"

"There must be some outrageous reason why he's at the table with Tyler, shake that right off Queen your about to go on stage."

"You go out there and do your thing and I will find out what's going on."

"I will have Pete play Piano for me tonight okay, meanwhile I'll help Becky at the bar and do a little mingling in the crowd."

As the curtain closed on the first performer Queen prepared to take the stage. Jonas had never seen Queen perform, it was something that he'd vowed not to do out of respect for her late father. When their eyes met in that moment as she took the stage, Tyler watching him carefully was unable to detect anything. As far as he was

Adrienne Lynn Rutherford

concerned, Jonas knew nothing about Queen or her sisters personally. Nevertheless, he was sure after getting a closer look at her he would know that it was the woman posted all over Memphis. Jonas would be the proof he needed to cover his promise to Viola Quickman and his first down payment for the personal bounty.

Tyler took a long drag of his Cuban cigar

"Every seen that dame before?"

Jonas was careful not to speak so quickly, but took his time.

"No."

Tyler was relieved, if Jonas could identify the girls it could possibly ruin his plans. Soon the curtains opened and Queen looked over as she strolled out on stage. She wore in her beautiful satin pink lounger and her beautiful feather covered heeled slippers. She'd done a beautiful job on her headpiece as it sat high atop her head secured with the support of almost an entire box of bobbi pins. She then dropped her lounger and the crowd exploded into cheers. Queen begin to sing her song strutting her stuff until she made it to the center of the stage as the drummer complemented each step, soon the entire band joined in.

"She met him on a Monday, gave her heart to him on Tuesday and lawd by Thursday, his good days were now his bad days. Cause she was a sly fox in the lion's den and she showed him up for the time he spent on Beale street."

Queen begin to slowly pull off her long satin gloves and with the removal of each she through them into the audience, now the room was standing room only and Queen smiled. As she guided her way to the corner of the stage were Jonas and Tyler were seated she smiled again. Jonas paid close attention to Tyler, and he could see that he' d had a thing for Queen. He looked back up at her and she gave him a wink and then strolled back to the center of the stage and gave her audience the final chorus.

"Now to lose in love was not her thing, and what he thought was a fling would keep his mind at ease. But not before he begged. Ohhhhhhh mama please, I'm giving up the ladies on Beale street."

During the performance Tyler was summoned to the front of the house to deal with an issue at the front door. Moments after he excused himself from the table and made his way through the standing room crowd he soon disappeared. Carolyn took the opportunity and made her way to the table with a tray of drinks.

"Carolyn?"

"Jonas?"

Both wanted to embrace, but under the circumstances it wouldn't be a good idea. She sat the drinks on the table.

"What on Earth are you doing here?"

"Coaster."

"Coaster?"

"Yeah, he sent me here."

"He wants to buy this place and move here to Tulsa."

"Are you serious?"

"As a heart attack."

"But Carolyn, there is more and there is no way we can talk now."

"Is there somewhere we can meet."

"Are you sure, how will you be able to slip away from Tyler, what will you tell him."

"Tyler will be no problem, I'm sure he will be leaving here with a lady tonight, I'm staying at Mattie's Bed and Breakfast can you meet me there tonight."

"Yes, I know the place."

"I'll be waiting for you guys, I'm on the first floor the side window facing east."

"Okay, okay I gotta go I will see you tonight."

Queen watched Carolyn and Jonas from stage also noticing, while Tyler's attempt to fight his way back through the crowd toward his table. Queen gave off a sigh of relief as Carolyn disappeared into the crowd heading back toward the bar. Tyler returned to the table unaware of the events that had taken place.

"She's something else, isn't she?"

"Yes, she is very talented."

"So, you have never seen her in Memphis?"

"No, I'm sorry to say, I don't usually hang out at the clubs."

"Would you like to meet her."

"Umm sure why not, I never turn down an opportunity to meet a beautiful lady."

Adrienne Lynn Rutherford

Tyler got the attention of one of the bus boys to get word to queen to join him and a special guest at his table who would like to meet her. The young man did as he was instructed. He toked on his Cigar one more time and leaned back into his chair.

"So, what do you think of the club"

"Coaster would be satisfied don't you think?"

"Jonas nodded his head in approval.

"Nice, very Nice."

"I must say I'm quite impressed, more so with Greenwood District."

"I've never experienced anything like it."

"Such a prosperous town of black folks, it's really amazing."

"The people here are beautiful."

Tyler nodded in agreement.

"Yes, Greenwood District is a wonderful place a black utopia if you will."

"This is what hard work and resilience looks like."
Tyler lifted his drink to Jonas.

"Toast to black folks everywhere."

Jonas lifted his glass.

"Here, here."

Jonas was not for one second buying the act that Tyler was putting on. Tyler was a different breed, an opportunist who fed off o greed and deception. When money was involved it didn't matter to him one way or another and Jonas knew he'd do anything to get ahead. Jonas deep down despised Tyler because he was a con, the lowest of the low. Jonas had been in the streets far to0 long, a con was a con and he didn't have to travel all the way to Greenwood District to know the likes of him.

By the time she'd finished the chorus, Queen held her arms out and she took a bow and the crowd went wild. She then strutted across the floor. After the curtains closed the gentleman covered her with a lounger. She could hear the whistles and cheering of the audience as they shouted for more, and that's exactly what she gave them. Queen stepped out graciously, but this time when she curtsied and blew her routine kisses to the audience somehow after seeing Jonas she knew Memphis had finally caught up with her.

Dance of Angels   247

Tonight, it would be her final curtain call and she knew it was a farewell to the "Paradise Club" and Greenwood District Tulsa.

When Queen got to her dressing room Carolyn was waiting for her.

"What'd he say?"

"He's here for coaster.'

"Coaster?"

"Yeah that's what I said, seems he's been talking to Tyler, he wants to buy the place and move to Tulsa."

"Are you serious?'

"Yes girl"

"That's not good Carolyn, not good at all, that means he's been to Memphis, how else would he have met Tyler."

"Coaster won't leave Memphis because he doesn't trust anybody with his money, this I know."

"So, he sent Jonas."

"Carolyn agreed."

"Oh Queen, it gets better"

"Jonas wants us to meet him tonight at Maggie's place, apparently he's staying there,"

"What about Tyler?"

"He said don't worry about him, he is supposed to be tied up with some woman over in Oakhurst until the morning."

"No, that's too risky."

Suddenly there was a knock on the door.

"Who is it?"

"Miss Queen, Tyler wants you to come to his table when you come out, he says there's someone he wants you to meet".

"Yes, dear thank you kindly, tell him I shall join him shortly."

After their discussion, and a change of clothes she headed to Tyler's table. Queen walked up to the table and both gentleman stood up to greet her.

"Madame Queen, I would like you to meet Jonas Simon from Memphis Tennessee. Jonas extended his hand to Queen as Tyler watched her carefully for any expressions she would display and neither disappointed him. As he breathed a sigh of relief, Queen extended her hand to Jonas

"Pleasure to meet you."

Jonas also not wanting to seem suspicious took her hand and kissed it.

"It seems we've met someplace before."

"Well Mr. Simon it seems since performing here at the Paradise I get a lot of that, unfortunately, I can't say the same."

"No mind, I must say though, that was quite a performance"

"The last skit was hilarious; did you write it yourself."

"Yes, I actually did."

Both noticed Tyler, it was obvious that he had somewhere more important he was trying to go as he continually checked his pocket watch. Jonas looked over at Tyler.

"Is everything okay man."

"Oh sure, sure I have some business over in Oakhurst and I promised I'd get there tonight.'

"Remember I discussed it with you earlier Jonas."

"Oh, sure man, I don't want you to stay on my part. I can get myself back to Maggie's place."

Tyler then looked over at Queen and although he had no idea that they had known one another it didn't prevent his inherent insecurities from re-surfacing.

"Did you want to leave with me Jonas."

"Since I'm going that way, I can drop you off."

"No, I think I would like to stay around here for a while, it's still early for me man you go ahead on."

Jonas then turned his attention back to Queen. Tyler grabbed his cigar out of the ash tray put it in his mouth and lit it, he then got up from the table. It was hard for him to hide his irritation.

"Well I guess I will be going, Jonas enjoy the rest of the evening as I am leaving you in good hands."

Tyler tipped his hat to Jonas.

"I will contact you by noon tomorrow."

"Queen."

Queen nodded as she watched him depart from the table and into the crowd. When they both thought it was safe they both squeezed the others hand.

"Jonas what the hell is going on, how did you......"
Before she could finish, Jonas began to over talk her."

"Queen it's been crazy back home, the Medusa has lost her mind trying to track you down, we have a plan and it will work.

"We, who?"

Jonas in all his excitement had slipped up, he'd promised George that he would not say a word until she made it to Tulsa."

"Ummm Miss Greta, she is on the case back home, making some moves for you guys, things are going to be alright I promise you."

"What's this thing about Coaster coming out to Tulsa, everybody knows he isn't leaving Beale street.

"I don't know Queen, he sounded real convincing, he paid me to come out here to be his eyes and ears."

"I must say I'm quite impressed myself with Greenwood District."

"Yes, it is a beautiful place, I've come to like it a lot."

Queen felt heavy in her heart and even though she knew Jonas had not known her thoughts, she apologized for them.

"Jonas when I saw you, I must admit I had mixed feelings, I know we had discussed you coming this way, but not this soon and with Tyler."

The two were interrupted by Carolyn as she sat down to join them.

"Jonas, what's going on back home?"

"You guys are what's going on, the Medusa isn't leaving a rock unturned to find you, I'm a little suspicious about this Tyler fella, he did a lot of snooping around back home when he was there".

Carolyn shook her head in disbelief.

"You know that is what confuses me to Jonas."

"What even made him go to Memphis in the first place and how does he know Coaster?"

"Well it appears he has shipping connections of some sort and one of the connections happens to be a friend of Coaster."

"They met some time ago and he'd mentioned this place to Coaster, after a while Coaster called him up to set up a meeting to

250   Adrienne Lynn Rutherford

talk about the possibilities for the place and here I am."

"How long are you here?"

"Well a week, then I'm headed back to Memphis to report what I saw."

The three spent the remainder of the night talking about the events that of the time. Jonas, as much as he wanted to share the good news about their mother. He'd given his word back home to Miss Georgea and Miss Greta. Now Jonas feared he was risking his friendship with all the girls, but their wellbeing was far more important to him than anything in the world. He could live the rest of his life with himself if they decided to go on with their lives without him. Being there for the girls had given him the ability to feel again after the death of his parents so long ago, he was starting to see feel a change in himself. He smiled at the girls, feeling good to know they were in a good place

"Where is Connie?"

Now a little tipsy the ladies began to laugh.

"She's back at Ma'mes, learning how to cook."

"To cook?"

Jonas laughed aloud, Connie can't cook."

"Yeah, we know and tried to tell Ma'me she was wasting her time, but you don't know with Ma'me."

"Well, it seems as though you girls are getting along pretty well with your aunt, I'm glad to hear it."

Carolyn smiled.

"Oh, she is absolutely wonderful, you have to meet her."

I would like that very much."

Becky walked over to the table to join the three.

"Who's your new friend."

Queen smiled.

"He's not new, this is Jonas, Jonas meet my cousin Becky."

Jonas, got up and extended his hand."

"Oh my, and a gentleman too, nice to meet you Jonas."

"The pleasure is all mine."

"He's here for a possible investor for the club."

"An investor?"

"Yeah."

"Wait a minute, Tyler is thinking about selling the club?"

"It appears so."

"He didn't mention anything to me about this, that low-down dirty bastard."

Queen looked over at her cousin, she knew how much she enjoyed managing the place.

"Don't worry about this place, no one else can run it like you, you know that, Jonas here is really good friends with the fella that is thinking about purchasing the place."

Becky knew what Queen was saying was right, no one knew the people or the business like her.

Becky could see that the three of them had a tad bit too much to drink.

"Gloria is closing and I'm off the clock, maybe we should call it a night, Jonas you need a ride?"

"Don't mind if I do."

****

Tyler made his way to Oakhurst and the meeting that he was scheduled to have this evening would determine his future. He was running out of time to get the money he needed to pay off Captain Francoise. Selling the Paradise Club would not be enough so Tyler knew he had to make the deal happen with Viola Quickman. As he pulled up to the one level log cabin house he grabbed another Cuban cigar and got out of the car. Outside the porch was brightly lit and there were a group of women laughing and talking while they played dominos. When Tyler went inside the small cabin and smell the residue down-home cooking that he was so familiar to his nose. There he would find the man who had saved his life

"Well Tyler, welcome, I was wondering when you were going to show up, how is everything?"

"Everything is good, what about you father?"

"Good, things are good, please have a seat, you hungry. Mable cooked some dinner."

"Sure, why not".

Tyler got up and made him a plate, and then went back to the table to join his father."

"Who are those ladies out front?"

"Oh, those are friends of Mable's they live in the area, she takes really good care of me when I'm here

"I'm glad you remembered the place."

"How could I forget this place, we spent a lot of time up here counting a lot of money.

Captain Francoise laughed.

"Yes, that's right son we did."

"How's business with you son?"

"Business is good, I think I have a buyer."

"Oh really, that's good, that's really good."

"You know our agreement, you pay off the ship and you can get another shot, if you can't pay it off, you got to work it off son."

"It's been eight years Tyler, your debt would be almost paid off by now, you're wasting time."

To Tyler these words ripped through him like fire, he enjoyed his freedom too much. He couldn't see going back on the ocean for months at a time as a ship mate. He'd paid his dues, long ago. He had his own ship and his own men, so was and still is simply out the question.

"Yes, father I understand, how is business for you by the way?" Captain Francoise grabbed his cane got up slowly.

"Business is business, that's all I can say about that, it's the same it doesn't change."

"Money coming in and money going out, you either make money or you don't, it's just that simple son."

Tyler loved Captain Francoise for everything that he'd done for him, however when it came to money they saw things far to differently. Right now, Tyler was desperate. After experiencing the opportunities that wealth had afforded him and have it taken always was tormenting. However, now things were about to change for the good he thought. Viola have given him new life and Queen and her sisters would may the price.

- -

After dropping Jonas off at Mattie's Bed and Breakfast, the ladies arrived at Ma'mes house, everyone noticed in the distance that the house was fully lit. Becky turned off the paved road onto the dirt road that led to the house.

"What in the world is Ma'me doing up this late?"

The ladies pulled behind the beautiful shiny convertible and got out of Queen was the first to step inside and once inside she froze in her steps. As they came in one by one she didn't move. The room got completely quiet and Queen as much as she wanted to speak nothing came out as her mother stood up.

"Queen, it's me, our mama."

Queen looked around the room as seconds felt like minutes and minutes like hours. She and covered her mouth with her hands in disbelief. Suddenly everything became an echo as the voices and sounds collided in her mind to her, it felt like a dream or maybe even a nightmare. Then, a clear voice spoke to her, it was Ma'me.

"Queen, baby you okay, are you okay?"

"Say something, dear child."

Queen, although hearing Ma'me speaking to her, could not find her voice. She then looked at her mother who was standing in front of her. She stared at her for a few minutes and touched her face to see if she was, Queen then looked over at Miss Greta. Queen put slowly lifted her hands as if surrendering to the drama of the moment. Everything was confusing and had been just way too much. Everyone was happy and smiling, everyone but her.

William walked up to his cousin.

"Q, are you okay, say something."

Ma'me got up from her chair and walked over to Queen and stood next to her mother.

"Queen, baby this is your mama, she's here now.
Greta got up to join them.

"Queen I know this is a bit much for you but it's okay dear, it's okay now, were hear, were hear, everything will be fine you don't have to do this alone, not anymore."

In that moment, Georgea grabbed a hold of her daughter and held her tight, Queen responded and held her just as tight and began to wale.

Her sisters got up to join them and they hugged and loved on one another, something they hadn't done for over fifteen years.

254   Adrienne Lynn Rutherford

Overwhelmed by all the excitement Queen passed out cold. William picked her up and took her up the stairs and Becky followed behind to help her get to bed. Ma'me then took Georgea by the hand and held it tight.

"Give her a little time, let her get some rest, this is a lot for a young girl to swallow you know."

George nodded in agreement.

"Okay we'll go into town and come back tomorrow."

"That would be good dear that would be really good."

William returned downstairs and sat on the couch next to Sarah

"She's okay, Becky is making sure she gets to bed, this has been a lot on her."

"I just want to say, it's good to see you aunt Georgea."

Georgea smiled, it's good to see you too Wil."

Connie Spoke up.

"Mama, can I go with you?"

Georgea stretched her arms wide open and Connie went to her.

"Sure, sure you can come with me."

She then looked at Carolyn"

"Would you like to come too."

Carolyn now distant, was concerned about her sister

"No, I'm fine, I think someone should be here when Queen when she wakes up."

The ladies bid everyone farewell and returned to the city. Queen woke up in her bed the following morning, the sun shined brightly through the window. She quickly jumped up in bed as she remembered the events that had taken place the night before. She grabbed her housecoat slid into her house shoes and made her way downstairs. When she got to the dining room Ma'me, William and where sitting at the table. Carolyn came out the kitchen with a large bowl of grits and sat it in the middle of the table, Becky came out behind her with the remaining entrees and they both sat down. Everyone greeted Queen as she sluggishly made her way to the table holding her head.

"Boy what a night."

Carolyn looked at her sister.

"Your telling me, I thought I was dreaming when I saw our mother"

Queen looked around and noticed that Connie was not present. "Where is Connie?"

Ma'me looked over at Queen.

"She stayed in town with your mother and her friend Greta." "Oh."

After Becky said the blessings, Queen grabbed a piece of bacon from the center of the table. However, she said nothing. William attempted to break the ice hoping it would cheer her up.

"I got a call this morning, Calvin back."

"I was thinking maybe we can have a little get together out here today you know a little bar b que."

"How about it Queen, what you think?'

Queen hunched her shoulders as she used her fork to play in her grits. Then in all her frustration she finally spoke.

"It's mighty funny to me that folks acting like this what's going on is a normal thing."

"We haven't seen our mother in almost twenty years, I thought she was dead, myself."

"Where the hell has she been, where she been all these years?"

"My father looked everywhere for her until his body eventually gave out on him and he grew tired from grief and heart ache."

"Where has she been?"

"That's what I want to know."

Queen then got up from the table and walked out the front door. Carolyn cried out to her and Ma'me then put her hand on Carolyn's shoulder.

"Let her be sweetheart, she's got a lot to digest, she'll come around."

"She will be fine, it's going to be a little more difficult for her."

Queen ran out into the meadow and rested herself up against the large trunk of the oak tree that she'd watched from Ma'mes front porch. Tears begin to run down her face as the feelings that she'd learned how to suppress all those years began to resurface. In the distance, she could see the same car that she'd seen the night before

Adrienne Lynn Rutherford

when they pulled up from The Paradise. She watched as Connie, Greta and her mother got out of the car and went inside the house. Queen was quite confused as to how Greta and her mother had known one another. Soon Greta came out of the house and Queen noticed that she was coming in her direction. Greta stood over Queen.

"May I join you?"

"Sure, why not."

"It so good to see you, we were so relieved."

"We?"

"We who?"

"Me and your mother."

"How do you know my mother?"

"It's a long story dear, one that would take a lifetime to tell."

"Well seems as though I have nothing but time."

Soon Georgea made her way out to the meadow.

"May I join you ladies?"

Georgea looked over at her eldest child, who was pulling grass and refused to say anything. Greta took her by the hand and she sat down next to her. Georgea looked at her daughter, she was so beautiful she'd thought to herself. Also, her strength, that had very well come from her father.

"Queen, dear heart I know this may seem very hard to understand and a lot of time has passed, but I need you to know that..."

Before she could finish Queen interrupted her.

"Very hard to understand, my God."

"Where have you been?"

"We thought you were dead."

"Don't you know that was the only way we could go on with our lives, although father knew different, but that's how we dealt with it.

"Father died from grief looking for you, and now you come here like it was yesterday telling me how difficult it must be."

"Who are you?"

"I don't even know you, you're a stranger and to the twins only a memory, one mostly I provided for them."

Greta interrupted.

"Okay Queen that's enough."

"You must listen to what your mother has to say, you must know why your mother did what she did."

"Your mother loves you and your sisters very much and she loved your father just as much but..."

Georgea then interrupted her dear friend.

"Thanks Greta, but this must come from me, she deserves to know it from me."

"Queen, life when I first met your father was wonderful, my father, your grandfather was a very honorable and wonderful man, one who valued the lives of all people regardless of the color of their skin. He allowed your father to escort me to many of the events that supported his way of thinking. Then father decided to run for the Governor's seat of Tennessee, when folks found out they were furious, because he conducted business with many of the black men who were apart of the Prince Hall Masonic Order and men of the Black Greek Fraternal order.

"He was establishing a solid political base in the black community of Memphis and throughout Tennessee. Well, this enraged a lot of people, people who wanted to keep the old confederacy alive. One day they found my father's car on the side of the road, he'd had a crash the car was totaled. They said it was an accident but I knew better. After that I ran to your father and we got married. Your grandmother was so angry, oh she was so angry. But I didn't care, because I had a beautiful baby girl and a wonderful husband. Well, after your grandmother died, I thought things would be different between me and my sister Viola. So, one day I took a trip to see her and I took you with me, so she could just see you."

"I thought if she would just laid eyes on you she would understand how good things were for me and we could be a family again. When I arrived with you, she refused to see me. I saw her looking at us out of the window and she had grown evil over the years just like my mother. Eventually I got over it and by the time the twins came I'd forgotten all about that life. Until one day, when your father took you all off to school and he went to work, there was a knock on the door. When I opened it, it was the Memphis Police

Adrienne Lynn Rutherford

Captain and two more men, I wasn't familiar with them, but they were not lawmen. They busted in the house and shut the door. I didn't know what to think in that moment. I was afraid for my life and I hoped that your father didn't come home, because I knew they would kill him. They told me that I had two options, to leave and spare my children or stay and they find me dead on the side of the street and afterward, you would die one by one."

Georgea begin to cry, but she found the strength to continue and she didn't stop. Queen looked on fearlessly as she finally heard the story that she wanted to know all her life. "I asked them what was this about, what did we do. One of the men told me it was my sister; my sister had sent them for me. I insisted on seeing her, but one of the men he pulled out another gun and he put it up to my head and told me I have five minutes to get what I needed and to get the hell away from my home and away from Memphis. I gathered as much as I could carry. They took me to the state lines near the bottom of the Mountains. So, I climbed, and I climbed until I got to the top. I hadn't realized that I'd passed out. When I woke up I was in a small cabin of the elderly medicine woman of the mountain. She and her son had helped me. I thank her for my life. When I told her, what had happened she said that Viola had acquired an iron fist and that I should be careful."

"So, I didn't come back, I spent almost twenty years on that mountain running from fear, it was fear. After a while, I ran into Jonas in the mountains."

"Jonas?"

"Yes, and after he told me his relationship with you all, I was so grateful. I had already contacted Greta to watch over you. I know it sounds crazy and backwards the way I reacted, but I couldn't imagine anyone harming you or your sisters."

"Please don't be cross with Jonas either, it was all my fault."

"I am taking the blame for all the people that I used to see into your lives, because I had lost my will to fight"

"I made him swear not to tell you where I was because I knew you and your sisters would come looking for me and I just couldn't risk it, not with Viola.

Queen could not believe what she was hearing.

"What, wait"

"What are you saying?"

"You know Jonas?"

"Our Jonas?"

Georgea gave a long sigh.

"Yes, I met Jonas about six years ago, while I was fishing at the creek in the mountains. That is when I found out that your father had died. He didn't know me, and after we talked I realized he was in your lives. He was an angel sent.

Queen shook her head and Georgea could see that she was getting more upset.

"Please, sweetheart, don't be angry with him, it me you should be angry with, for hiding all these years, wallowing in my self-pity. Fearful of what my sister was capable of, scared what she might do to my children."

Queen then looked at Greta.

"And you knew, all this time my mother was alive and you said nothing."

"Queen, wait!"

Queen got up and she ran, she ran so hard she left her slippers in the grass. She made it to the main road and continued to run until she was exhausted. Queen then started walking, too angry to cry she laughed instead, she laughed at the entire escapade. The joke was on her she thought to herself.

"Viola Quickman is my mother's sister."

"Viola Medusa Quickman is my aunt."

"The Medusa's son is my cousin."

"The woman Viola Medusa Quickman is the mother of my cousin Roger, the one I murdered."

"I murdered my cousin."

In that moment Queen noticed people passing by looking at her. She soon realized that she'd been walking almost an hour in bare feet and a house robe and was able to see the clock tower in the Greenwood District Square. Queen heard another horn blow and without turning around she moved to the side of the road out of the way, but the horn blew again. When she turned around to her

Adrienne Lynn Rutherford

surprise it was Calvin. He continued to roll slowly along the side of her.

"Can I give you a lift?"

"No, I'm fine, thank you."

"You don't look fine, you're in the middle of the road in your bare feet and a bathrobe."

Queen looked at him and rolled her eyes and stopped in her tracks.

"Well, you wouldn't believe what I've learned in the past twenty-four hours."

"First, my mother is not dead, she's alive."

"Oh, and it gets better."

"I murdered my cousin, my aunt's son, my mother's sister."

"Who I might add is a very ruthless woman and the wealthiest woman in all of Memphis."

"Did I tell you I was from Memphis?"

"The man who attacked my sister in my kitchen only a month ago is also my cousin."

"Oh, did I mention, my aunt is also Viola Quickman the heiress to the West Virginia Coal mines the same woman who has a bounty on me and my sisters head for killing her son. Who I might mention again attacked my sister."

Queen began to laugh sarcastically again.

"She turned and looked at Calvin as he continued to drive slowly along the side of her.

"Can you believe that?"

"Now you know all about my sick life."

"Queen please, would you just get into the car, let me take you home."

"Home, where is home?"

"I don't have a home."

"Hell, my whole entire life has been a lie."

"A moving film that others know more about than me, and they watch me live out this life knowing things about me that I don't even know about myself."

"Queen please, get in the damn car."

Queen looked at Calvin, she knew if he didn't care he would not have come after her. So, she decided to get in. When she got in, Calvin handed her his handkerchief, she then realized how ridiculous she looked walking in the middle of the road barefoot, with her hair all over her head in a house robe.

"I guess I look kind of crazy huh?"

Calvin said nothing as he turned the car around and headed back toward the meadows and looked over at her.

"What's gotten into you woman."

"I was having a moment?"

"Oh, you were having a moment alright."

"Calvin don't take me back to Ma'me, I don't wanna go there, not now."

"Well, we gotta get you cleaned up somewhere."

****

The spring breeze hit Queens face softly as she began to think about the conversation she had back at Ma'mes with her mother and Greta. Everything was so complicated, even with Jonas, who hadn't said a word about her mother coming to Tulsa last night at the Paradise. She made it her business to speak to him very soon. Calvin pulled up at his mother and father's home and turned off the engine.

"We're home."

Queen then smiled with gratitude.

"Thank you, Calvin."

"Ahh son, your back."

Mr. Watkins looked over Queen and then at his son, as if waiting for an explanation for her appearance.

"Morning pops, this is Queen, you remember Queen, don't you?"

"Ma'me niece and Buford Sawyer's daughter."

Mr. Watkins took another look at her, my goodness your Buford's baby girl, Jesus I haven't seen Buford in almost twenty years."

"He was sure good with his hands, could design a house and lay that brick with expertise."

"You know he built a lot of the buildings here in Greenwood

Adrienne Lynn Rutherford

District."

"How's he doing these days?"

"Um, my papa passed away, it's been about eight years now."

"Wow, I'm so sorry to hear that, good man a really good man."

"Where you guys coming from?"

"Well, Queen here got herself into a pickle and I was hoping mama still had those clothes she planned on taking downtown to the Church."

"Well you're in luck, I was just about to pull the car around and take her into town. Then we were going to have some lunch and do a little shopping."

"Mrs. Watkins, come on out here, your son is home and he's got company with him."

Mrs. Watkins stepped out the house and Cody was behind her and carrying the large box, she then sat it on the porch. Cody looked at Queen.

"Hey Queen, what happened to you?"

"Hey Cody, It's a long story."

"Oh."

"Papa, mama said you're supposed to be bringing the car around, this box is kinda heavy."

Calvin then introduced Queen to his mother.

"Mom, I would like you to meet Queen and Queen this is my mother Mrs. Watkins."

Mrs. Watkins extended her hand while looking Queen over, she was reluctant to even ask and so she didn't, instead she greeted her with a smile."

"Hello Queen, nice to meet you."

While shaking her hand she looked at her a little closer and just like her son, she noticed right away the heart shaped birthmark on her cheek."

"Queen, Buford's baby girl?"

She then smiled and gave her a hug.

"Oh, my goodness, Calvin didn't tell me you were in town."

"I almost didn't recognize you."

"It's been such a long time."

"How are you?"

Queen smiled and without hesitation took in the kindness to replace the feelings of melancholy from the events of the day.

"I'm fine thanks and you."

"Oh, I'm doing good, same ole same ole."

She then pointed at Mr. Watkins as he pulled in front of the house with the car.

"Keeping that one out of trouble."

"How's your Mama, and your papa?"

Well, my papa has gone on its been about eight years now and my mother's up at Ma'me house."

"Is she really?"

"I guess I'm going to have to get up there to see her then."

Mrs. Watkins gave her a hug still reluctant to address her appearance."

Calvin then interrupted.

"Ma, I was wondering if we could get Queen something to wear out of the box of the donated clothes you collected for the church."

"Uh sure, absolutely."

"Cody, can you please open the box and let Queen look through it, will you please dear."

"Queen rumbled through the variety of clothing that filled the box. There were children's clothes as well as overalls and a lot of dresses that appeared to be quite large for her frame. Queen looking at Mr. Watkins in all his impatience seated in his automobile, finally settled on a pair of overalls and a bright orange shirt. Queen continued to rummage through the box and came across a pair of ladies tie up boots and grabbed them.

"There, I'm so sorry to keep you guys waiting, thank you so much Mrs. Watkins."

"No problem dear, I'm so glad we could help."

"Cody come on, let's not keep your father waiting any longer."

"Calvin dear, can you bring the box to the car please."

Calvin did what his mother said and returned to Queen's side on the porch. After his family pulled off he opened the screen door for Queen and walked in. Inside the Watkins home was like a museum displaying hand sculptured African inspired mask and statues of tribesman and women. There was a grand piano that sat

Adrienne Lynn Rutherford

in the living room and next to it, in the corner was a large beautifully hand crafted wooden elephant. Queen looked up behind the piano and hanging high above was a picture of W.E.B. Dubois himself. The fire place was large with a brick mantle and above it, an oil painted portrait of the Watkins family.

"Calvin is that you, you were so young on that picture."

"I was thirteen years old on that picture, that was the last year you were here in Tulsa."

Calvin then grabbed the overalls from Queen and held them up."

"What will you wear under these overalls."

She then smiled.

"Nothing I presume."

Calvin returned the smile.

"That suits me just fine.'

He then grabbed her and placed a kiss in center of what he thought were the most lustful lips he'd ever seen. Queen responded with her greatest intentions, as her feelings resonated while holding him close to her. Until now, she had not realized how much she'd missed his touch in the after leaving for business up North. Nevertheless, the unfamiliar erotic tenderness that Calvin had once unveiled within her had resurfaced once more. Today it would not take her by surprise as she welcomed it as returned the sensual kiss that he'd placed on her lips so tenderly. As she opened her eyes, Queen observed him watching her and he smiled.

"You like that huh?"

Queen smiled blushingly.'

"Yes, very much."

"C'mon with me."

Queen followed Calvin up the large wooden staircase to the second level of the home. Calvin opened the second door which led to his bedroom and inside was a large bed with a soft feather mattress on top. The bedframe was professionally hand crafted out of a mahogany wood. Queen ran her fingers alongside the bottom of the bed frame.

"This is a very beautiful bed."

"Oh yeah, you like that too?"

"Yes, I do very much."

"Come here."

Queen walked over to Calvin and he placed a kiss on her lips once more. He gently removed her housecoat and underneath was her night gown. With each button, he placed a kiss softly on her lips teasing her as she began to moan for more.

"Calvin?"

"Yes, my love?"

"Oh, my."

He then slid his hand inside of her gown and softly caressed her breast and then teasing the tips of her nipples, giving each the equal satisfaction as the other. Queen pulled him closer to her pressing her lips against his. Gently he laid her down on the softness of his bed while holding her close and moved his large hand along her now famous sensual body, tracing every curve. Calvin closed his eyes, now playing for keeps imagined her just like this in his life permanently. Queen opened her legs wide as he laid down in between playing with her with every stroke of his muscular frame.

She could feel his manhood rise, even inside of his jeans, as she moaned with each stroke. Both had missed one another and neither wanted to admit the love they'd found in each other. To say it for Calvin would be a sign of weakness, something he could not allow himself to succumb. However, Queen had spent most of her life perfecting the skill of keeping her heart hidden far away from any man. As she gently traced the long scar that traveled down his face, in that moment true love for Queen was no longer a mystery.

"Will you ever tell me your story."

"One day, perhaps I shall."

As he removed himself from the bed, he grabbed ahold of Queen's hand and assisted her up as well.

"Can you please show me to the lady's room?"

"Well of course."

As Calvin instructed her down the hallway, he gave Queen a nice pat on her backside

"Are we done?"

Queen then graced him with a smile as she made her way into the bathroom. Inside was a large ivory bath tub and Queen smiled

Adrienne Lynn Rutherford

at the surprise. She began smelling the variety of oils and was thankful for Mrs. Watkins and she took a warm relaxing bath. After spending time thinking of the events that had occurred, she decided that she had acted quite immaturely. Queen had been a role model for her sisters all their lives up until now. Although seeing her mother was hard to do after all those years, she should have been thankful that she was still among the living. After finishing her bath, Queen stood up in the tub and as the bath water rain down the frame of her body, Calvin watched in the doorway holding on to her towel.

"What a beautiful picture, the body of a Goddess."

"I thought you might be needing this."

Queen smiled as he took the thick towel, wrapped it around his lover and slowly helped her out. When her feet were safely planted on the floor, she intentionally allowed it to fall to her ankles. She then began kissing him while vigorously unbuckling his pants. Her moans excited Calvin and he prepared to give her exactly what she longed for. When his pants fell to his ankles he picked her up and sat her atop the bathroom sink and slowly he entered her. Queen's head fell backward as she loosely wrapped her arms around his neck. Calvin began where he'd left off, tenderly kissing her at the base of her neck. Gently and rhythmically he went in and out of her stirring the love only she could provide for him. The warmth of her softness took Calvin to a heaven he'd could never have imagined. He savored every moment of this new adventure embracing the passion that she displayed. For Queen time had stood still with each moment like this she had with Calvin. Queen had never expected this man to be so loving or any man for that matter, so protective of her emotionally and soulfully. Calvin slid his feet out of his pants legs and quickly lifted his lover up as she wrapped her legs around his waist. As he walked her back to the bedroom in all their nakedness, neither cared about the world around them, only the world they shared in this moment together. She moaned not wanting him to remove himself from her and he obliged her with ever step he made until he reached the softness of the bed. As he laid her down, he continued giving her soft strokes that almost left her breathless. As the climax sweetly manifested between them, Calvin let out the roar of a lion, while tears filled Queen's eyes. The feeling was so overwhelming and in that moment Queen made a vow. Calvin was and would be the only man that she would give her essence to. However, she would never tell him because she had no idea what his future would hold. People change all the time and in her life, love had not been the cure for unhappiness. Nevertheless, one thing she did know for sure, life without Calvin would never be the same.

Adrienne Lynn Rutherford

Chapter 25

After spending, most of the early afternoon at the Watkins' residence Calvin and Queen made their way into town. Calvin's suggestion to Queen to have an early dinner was music to her ears. It was a compliment to the beautiful morning they had spent together. As much as he didn't want to depart from her company, Calvin promised John that he would help him with one of his customers tractors out in the plains.

When they entered Mattie's place to Queen's surprise there was Jonas having his breakfast alone. She had not spoken to him as much as she would have liked to at the paradise, so she briefly excused herself from Calvin's side while they waited to be seated.

"Jonas."

Jonas stood up from his meal.

"Queen, what a pleasant surprise I didn't think I would see you here again, I saw the ladies this morning for breakfast, please have a seat."

"Jonas, I have someone with me, a longtime friend."

"Do you mind if he joins us?"

"Not at all, please invite him over."

Queen waved her hand toward Calvin and he joined them at the table, right away Precious came by to provide two more table settings."

"Afternoon Calvin and Miss Queen."

"Afternoon Precious, I'll have the usual extra sauce."

"Okay, and you Miss Queen?"

"Hmmm let me see, I'll have the roasted chicken and green beans please."

"Sounds good, that's my favorite, okay be up shortly."

"Jonas, I would like you to meet Calvin and Calvin this is Jonas,"

Both men extended their hands to one another. Jonas sat and waited for Queen to take the lead in the conversation, he wasn't quite sure who this man was to her or what type of role he'd played in her life since coming to Tulsa."

"Jonas, I just want you to know that we can talk openly in front

Dance of Angels   269

of Calvin, he is a longtime family friend and I trust him very much."

"Does he know?"

"He knows pretty much everything."

"Well I know that your cover is blown out here in Tulsa and I want you to know I don't trust that Tyler guy."

"I think it's time for all of us to get up out of here."

"Right now, I got to find out what my mother knows, do you know what my mother knows Jonas?"

"It appears your mother and Madame Greta have plans of their own for the Medusa."

She has some pretty bad accusations on her and her business dealings, things that can put her away for a very long time. I don't know if you have spoken to anyone just yet."

"No, I have not, seeing my mother was a lot to digest Jonas, I'm sure you know that better than anyone, including my sisters. I just think it was awfully weird that she would spend her life in hiding all those years."

"Well Queen, sometimes we can't question why people do what they do."

"Your mother walked away from a life of privileged, for love too, remember that."

"Not many folks have the balls to do that, trust me I know. They sit around and become a glutton for punishment being controlled by others all for the sake of status, wealth, or anything that will make them feel less inadequate. Even with knowing in their hearts and minds that they're living an absolute lie."

"They began to slowly dye inside."

"Hell, just look at Viola Quickman, just a sad miserable woman, so full of hate and pain."

"Could you imagine anger being the only freedom you have?"

"I couldn't imagine that."

"Queen, I hope that you are not angry with me for not telling you about your mother, but I made her a promise and looking back on things it probably was for the best at the time. When I first saw her, she was a wounded woman, spirt gone from her. But when she found out about everything that had happened, it was as if she had gained a new breath of life, like she was born again.

Adrienne Lynn Rutherford

"You and your sisters did that for her Queen."

"When I saw her again it was in Madame Greta's parlor at her home and I told them everything I knew about Captain Feldman and

"The Medusa". I told them you were here, I couldn't lie to her nor could I betray you either, but I knew that you were in danger and I knew she could help."

Queen looked at Jonas solemnly and grabbed both his hands across the table.

"Of course not, you're my family and you saved our lives."

"Thank you, Jonas, Thank you."

Queen ten looked over at Calvin.

"I told you about Jonas, strange turn of events huh?"

"Please chime in whenever you feel a need about this Calvin.

"I think the best thing for you is to get you, your sisters and your mother out of town as soon as possible, the sooner the better.

"I have a place up north and Jonas you are also welcomed to come and stay as long as you like. Any family of Queen's is family of mine."

Queen looked over at the man that she knew was the love of her life and he gave her a wink and returned his attention back to Jonas.

Calvin then looked over at Jonas.

"Jonas, this business you have with this Tyler guy, is it finished?"

"Not quit, he left late last night headed to Springfield had some business to take care of, said he would meet me back here today. In the meantime, I'm just waiting to hear from him. Once I do I will return to Tennessee."

Queen looked over at Jonas.

"You're going back home?"

"Yes, Coaster is waiting to hear from me."

"Queen, did you forget?"

"I came out here to also do a job, I can't leave my man out to dry."

"I understand Jonas."

Jonas looked over at Calvin with curiosity.

"If you don't mind me asking, where are you taking them?"

"Montana."

Jonas slouched back into his seat, It had already been difficult enough not having the girls around in Memphis. They were the only family that he had for most of his life, outside of Lone Wolf and the Cherokee Mountain People.

"Oh, I see."

Queen looked at Jonas.

"Jonas, don't worry."

"I will contact you soon as we get there and we will all see one another again really soon, I promise."

After everyone finished their meals Jonas bid them farewell and Calvin took Queen back to Ma'mes house. When she arrived, the ladies were sitting on the porch. Queen said nothing as she looked at her mother, her pride had again got the best of her. She excused herself and made her way into the house, up the stairs and into her bedroom. Carolyn, not long after came to see about her.

"Ma'me wants you to come downstairs Queen, she wants to speak with you."

"Carolyn, I'm really not in the mood to speak to anyone right now."

"I just have so much to think about, this situation is really taking an emotional toll on me and I'm just trying to really wrap my head around it.

"Plus, while at the same time plan for us to leave."

"Leave, what do you mean?"

"I saw Jonas at Mattie's place, me and Calvin.

He thinks Viola Quickman may know that we are here, so we can't stay."

"Well, we spoke to him too, and mother says she's going to make things better."

"Mother, make things better?"

"Wake up Carolyn, she doesn't even know us."

"Don't you get it."

"She can't help us Carolyn."

"How do you know?"

Adrienne Lynn Rutherford

"Your so head strong right now, you won't even give her a chance, she's trying. She says that things are going to be different from now on, we don't have to run anymore Queen."

"Did she guarantee you that?"

"Did Greta guarantee you that?"

"We have been in this together from the beginning, if you want to stay, you stay."

"I'm leaving here."

"Calvin has a place in Montana, we can start a new life there, and we can stay as long as we like."

"He said that?"

"Yes, he did today, all of us."

"We had dinner with Jonas in town, we talked about it."

Carolyn sat down on the bed next to her sister okay.

"Queen I will go with you."

"I don't want us to be separated, whatever plans mother has they can be planned around us heading north."

"Now will you come downstairs?"

Queen dragged herself off the edge of the bed and followed her sister downstairs. When they stepped out on the porch Ma'me was laughing aloud. In the time that she had been there, she had never heard Ma'me laugh so loud. She was very much enjoying the conversation that she was having with Georgea and Greta. Greta was bidding her farewells as she prepared to return to Memphis to handle business back home for Georgea. The others were amused by the stories that both shared when they were younger. Queen sat down next to Becky on the swing chair and said nothing.

Ma'me stopped her conversation with the ladies and turned her attention to Queen.

"Well young lady, are you through pouting with yourself, because Ma'me don't take to that kind of nonsense in the house."

"I should have known your father spoiled you the minute I laid eyes on the likes of all of you."

"Yes Ma'me, I am, but this has nothing to do with being spoiled, there is a lot of emotions stirring around inside me and rightfully so. There is no excuse that my mother can give me that would explain her need for leaving us all those years."

Georgea tried to speak.

"Queen I ….."

Ma'me waved her hand to stop her.

"Dear child, are you in one piece?"

"Yes."

"Did the Good lord keep you all those years, made sure you were safe, sent people to make sure you had everything you needed to go on in this world."

"Yes, but at times it did get hard Ma'me."

"You just sit there and tell me who haven't had times that were hard?"

"What makes you so special, even Jesus had burdens child, your mother loves all of you very much."

"Yes, she made some bad choices and who knows maybe they weren't so bad."

"What if she would have stayed not left like them men told her to?"

"What would have become of you and your sisters?

"You ever think about that?"

"Dear child, sometimes we just have to take notice to the good things that we have today, the past is gone, not forgotten but gone forever."

"Your mother is here right now, what you have is right now."

"So, let's just let's dwell in that and besides It's time to build your life get a fresh new start."

"I sure do wish my mama was here."

Queen feeling ashamed bowed her head.

"No need of feeling sorry for yourself girl, that's another thing we don't do around her is pity parties, only birthday parties."

"So, get up come over here and hug your mama, come on now get on up."

Queen got up and her mother greeted her with a hug, they held each other tightly until the tears fell uncontrollably down Queen's face. Her sisters also witnessing the embrace began to cry as well. It was an emotional day in Greenwood District one that for only a brief time overshadowed the darkness that was brewing. Viola Quickman and Captain Feldman would be arriving in Tulsa soon and she had adhered to Tyler's request and coming for blood.

Chapter 26

The Riot Begins

Early in the afternoon the Watkins family had returned from Oakhurst, Mr. Watkins was feeling great about life as he smiled at his beautiful wife. Although he'd been criticized by his own people and humiliated by those across the tracks, Mr. Watkins felt that it all had been worth it. If nothing else He was so thankful for these two special women in his life. His daughter had grown into a beautiful young lady anxious to attend college and learn as much as she could about the world. As he parked out front of the house he helped Mrs. Watkins and Cody bring in the fresh fruits and vegetables they picked up on US 70. Suddenly, they heard a loud explosion and Mr. Watkins stepped out onto the porch and Cody followed. They walked out into the middle of the grasslands trying to get a closer look at the dark cloud of smoke that lingered over their neighbor's property. In the distance Mr. Watkins could see his son's airplane coming toward them. He lifted his hands and waved back and forth to get the attention of who he thought was his eldest son John. However, to his surprise when the plane swooped down low, there was a strange white man behind the controls. The plane soon turned around and when he realized that it was heading toward him and Cody he shouted to her at the top of his voice.

"Run, Cody run."

Cody dashed out toward the barn as fast as she could with her father following behind her. As the air plane passed by the house, he noticed there was not one but two white men in his son's plane. Mr. Watkins had his eyes fixated on the two and noticed a large flame in the hands of the rear passenger, and as he released the cocktail from the sky it blew up on side of their home. The flames and dark thick wasted no time consuming the recently beautiful day that the Watkins family had claimed. Mr. Watkins and his daughter made their way to the house, but the heat was much too intense for them to reach the front door, one side of the house had gone completely up in smoke. Mr. Watkins feel to his knees in the front of the house as the flames continued to consume it. There was so sound at all

Adrienne Lynn Rutherford

from his dear faithful wife. Suddenly he heard a faint call from her in the rear, Mr. Watkins and his daughter Cody immediately went to her aide has she cried out in shock.

"Our home, our dear sweet home is gone, gone forever"

"Dear God, what shall we do now, everything is gone, just gone."

Mr. Watkins did what he could to calm his wife as they all listened helplessly to the crackling wood burn to a cinder. He looked up and to his surprise in the distance he could see the plane coming back for another turn. They could hear the horses in the stable hysterically awaiting to get out of the barn.

"C'mon hurry, C'mon."

"Cody, help your mother, take her to the wooded area near the gully"

"Papa, where are you going?"

"Please don't leave us papa."

"Do as I say, hurry."

Mr. Watkins, in all his faith ran into the barn and released the horses. As they stormed out the wide opened field frantically and with the gift of instinct, they followed Cody and her mother into the wooded area to safety. Soon the airplane made its third round and Mr. Watkins noticed the same large homemade cocktail being held by the back passenger and he began to run for safety, but before they could make it to a safe area the next cocktail was dropped and hit the ground less than five feet away from the barn and lay burning in the grass. The plane then disappeared high into the dark clouds until it could not be seen anymore. Mr. Watkins then began looking around at the properties of his neighbors in the distance and with great grief had noticed the same familiar smoke stacks. He ran out in to the wooded area and was soon able to hear his wife and daughter attempting to calm the horses. When Mrs. Watkins realized her husband was safe, she grabbed him for dear life and began to weep. All the memories of love and life they had known for the past forty-five years were in that house. Mr. Watkins held on to his dear wife and daughter in a state of shook trying to wrap his head around everything that had transpired.

"How where those white men able to get a hold to his son's airplane and use it to terrorize the northside?

Dance of Angels   277

"Where was John?"

"Where were the authorities?

"What the hell was going on in Tulsa Greenwood District?"

His next thought was Greenwood district's town square and his heart grew even more heavy. He then returned to the barn and grabbed his back up shout gun. Several minutes later, he saw John and Calvin arrived as they ran to Cody standing in the distance among the trees. Calvin quickly grabbed Cody and inspected her for any wounds or burns.

"Where is mother?"

"She's okay, she's in the trees with the horses."

Both Calvin and John ran into the wooded area to their mother and embraced her tightly and she returned the gesture.

"I'm fine, I'm fine, but I thought we were done with this madness, we left Mississippi for this exact same thing."

"The evil, the envy, and the jealousy when does it stop?"

Cody consoled her mother and Mr. Watkins shook his head knowing this was a pain that he could not take away from his wife of fifty years. In his face was a deep pain as he attempted to catch his breath to speak to his sons.

"They came from the sky, they came from the sky son."

Mr. Watkins then looked over at John.

"They were in your airplane; how did they get to your airplane son?"

"How could you be so irresponsible."

Calvin spoke up for his brother, while trying to hold back his tears.

"Pop that's not fair, you can't blame John for this."

"It's not his fault."

"You want to place blame?"

"You place it where it should be, on that evil across the god-damned tracks."

John ran out of the woods and looked out into the meadow, witnessing the destruction that had been imposed on his family. He looked over at what was once one of the most beautiful homes in all of Greenwood district. It now all laid in cinders as the hurt pierced deep into his heart in. As he looked up at the thick smoke making its way into the sky, he realized smoke was coming from the homes

278   Adrienne Lynn Rutherford

of lifetime friends and neighbors that he had known all his life. Soon, he could hear his father's words resonate in his mind and the darkness of guilt overcame him. In that moment John ran as fast as he could to his brother's automobile. Calvin attempted to catch up with him but he was too far away

"John, wait, John, John wait."

John hopped in the car and sped off. Calvin looked back at his father who said nothing, he shook his head, although he was furious about the comment that his father made. He had to keep a level head and tend to his sister and mother. He began to untie two of the horses from the tree.

"Cody, I want you to get on that horse and follow mama as fast as you can, to Ma'mes.

Just like the wind, you hear me."

Don't you look back for nothing.

"I want you to tell them what happened and I want you to stay put."

Cody could not stop crying, the experience was far too traumatic for her young heart to bear."

"Cody!"

Soon the nearby neighbors came to help.

Mrs. Watkins in an instance attempted to calm her youngest child

"You have to shake out of it, now, Mamas here with you, we will be fine."

"Now let's do what your brother has told us, yah hear?".

"I need you to get on that horse and ride with me to Ma'mes as fast as you can you hear me?"

"Yes mama."

Cody wiped her eyes, climbed on the horse to do what her brother told her to do. She rode as fast as she could and didn't look back. As the tears pressed against her face, Cody rode like the wind beside her mother, while wondering if she would ever see her dear brothers or her father again.

When they approached Ma'me home she was exhausted, surprisingly also from the backroad Billy Jo pulled up stirring dust with his pickup shaking and rattling uncontrollably. Ma'me got up

Dance of Angels   279

out of her rocking chair to meet her two guests and It was evident that something had gone wrong. Billy Jo hopped off the wagon and ran up on the porch toward Ma'me

"It's a riot in town, they're coming across the tracks in droves killing folks in Greenwood District, yawl gotta get out of here now, right now."

Hearing all the commotion outside Georgea, Queen and, Becky along and the twins came outside to find out what all the commotion was about. William and Sarah came up from the cellar. Cody climbed off her horse and helped her mother down. When Becky came out the house and Cody grabbed her and held on to her tight.

"Cody dear, what's wrong, Ms. Watkins you okay?"

"They dropped a cocktail on the house and it caught on fire, and they dropped one after another on every farm."

William walked up on the porch.

"What did you just say?"

"The house is gone, the airplane from the sky dropped cocktails on all the farms."

Everyone listened in awe and disbelief of the recent events explained by the Watkin's ladies.

"It's true me and papa heard a loud noise and it was John's airplane."

"I would know that sound anywhere, we thought it was John and I started to run closer and that's when I saw them, saw them two white men. The one in the rear he dropped the cocktail jug on our house. I saw it with my own eyes and before I could scream my mama's name the entire front of the house exploded into flames."

"Me and papa, we thought we had lost mama, but she made it out the back way."

"It was awful, but we managed to make it into the woods near the gully. They circled around again tried to hit the barn where the horses were. Papa was able to get them out and came after us so we ran as fast as we could, they tried to hit the barn too, but they missed."

Becky held on to Cody tight as she began to cry uncontrollably.

"It's okay, your safe now."

Queen tended to Mrs. Watkins as the reality had finally set in.

"My home, lord, I ain't seen nothing like that not even in Mississippi, horrible everything just gone in the wind."

William interrupted.

"Cody, where are your brothers and Mr. Watkins?"

Papa and Calvin, they're back at the house gathering the horses."

"Some of the other folks came down to check on us."

"What about John?"

"Papa blamed him for the fire, asked him how they got hold to his airplane, he got upset and took off in Calvin's car."

William punched the pillar on the porch.

"Damn"

Billy Jo shook his head in remorse, but reminded the family how serious the situation was.

"I'm trying to tell you we have to go, you can't stay here."

"I've been through town it's a bloodbath, they been probably watching John's place for a long time waiting for the opportunity to go in and steal that plane."

Queen went to Cody and held her by the hand.

"What did they tell you."

"Only to ride here as fast we could, I don't know what they are doing, but papa grabbed his shot gun."

"Are we at war Queen?"

William shook his head, these words resonated for him, because he and Calvin had contemplated this most of their childhood life. He then walked over to Cody.

"You don't have anything to worry about you hear?"

"Becky take Cody and Ms. Watkins on in the house and help them get cleaned up while we chit chat a bit out here, I'm going to buy my brothers and Mr. Watkins some time to get out this way to us."

Billy Jo continued with William and the others.

"Yesterday, it was a rumor going around that a black man tried to rape a white woman in the elevator at the department store on the Southside."

Both Queen and Georgea shook their heads in disbelief and Georgea shouted."

"That is a lie if I ever heard one."

"In an elevator in the middle of town?"

"I don't believe it, I just don't believe that."

Billy Jo continued.

"Well it appears the locals do and they are on the warpath, they been hurting folks. I had to come out and tell you."

"I wanna help yawl any way I can to get outta here."

"Connie looked on in terror, what do you mean help us get out of here?"

Carolyn then looked at her dear sister.

"He wants to help us escape so we don't get killed silly."
Connie gasped.

William went to his cellar and grabbed his shot gun and ammunition. When he returned he tossed a box to Billy Jo.

"Where you plan on riding to?"

"I don't know, just away from here."

Queen spoke up

"Calvin has a farm, he told me in Oakhurst, we can go there."

That's good place, its far enough to be out of danger and by that time, I'm hoping the government should be her to intervene."

Becky spoke through the screen door.

"How are we all gonna get in that pick up, Billy Jo ain't got enough room for all of us".

"Ms. Becky those crates, they're just a camouflage."

Billy Jo walked over to the truck and unhooked the latch of the bed when he opened there was a large baseboard underneath padded down that could hold at least four adults.

"I know I can get you through, they won't be suspecting nothing with me."

"Me and my sister can ride up front with Miss Georgea."

"No one will know the better."

"Yawl will be safe until will get to Oakhurst"
Becky spoke through the screen door.

"What about Ma'me?"

"She can't lay down there."

Adrienne Lynn Rutherford

"Watch it now Becky, you can't go speaking for ole Ma'me you hear."

"I know what I can do and if he gone save our life from this place Ma'me don't have no problem laying down in that pickup truck."

"There was plenty more before me that have done far riskier things for their freedom from the south all the way north. It ain't gonna hurt none for me to go a few miles to the next town."

Queen's thoughts were running rampant, the turn of events had become so much more complicated than she would have ever imagined. She couldn't help thinking about Jonas, he was in town. She hoped that he was safe. Queen also knew he was a survivor, but the depth of this violence made her second guess her intuition about her dear friend. She also wished that she could be there for Calvin, she knew that it must have been devastating for him to walk up on such a horrific incident involving his family and she mourned for him. Although Queen knew the best thing was to follow William over to Oakhurst so that they would be safe. Deep down she did not want to leave without Calvin. Before she could finish her thought, she seen a wagon coming down the road and behind it was Calvin's automobile. Cody busted out of the front door and stood on the porch pointing.

"That's my papa's wagon, that's my papa and Calvin."

Queen breathed a sigh of relief as she placed her hand over her heart knowing a portion of her prayers had been answered. William then looked up into the sky and saw one of John's airplanes fly pass at full speed, the wind made the leaves of the tallest trees of the grove dance uncontrollably. Behind it was another, going at equal speed on its tail. Everyone looked up astonished at the cat and mouse air chase as the two flew high into the sky and then low. Calvin got out of the car shaking his head, he and Mr. Watkins tried to catch John at his place, but it had been too late. John got into his other airplane and took off after the thieves who violated his family, his home and his property.

Calvin and Mr. Watkins knew the second plane was John chasing the rouge plane on his own. In that moment, a silence came over them all as they watched the John complete a donut that placed

Dance of Angels   283

him face to face with the rough airplane in an instant the collided in the sky and both burst into flames. Mr. Watkins fell to his knees once again as he watched the flaming pieces of debris land in the large meadow. Mrs. Watkins came out the house screaming hysterically as the other ladies consoled her while gasping in disbelief. William and Calvin wasted no time as they ran toward the sight as if their lives had depended on it. At that point, there was nothing either could do, their where no remains. Calvin shouted out to his brother and William pulled him away from the flames as the smoke traveled high in the sky.

"Calvin, we have to get out of here, it's not safe man, we have to go now!"

****

Jonas went deep into his carpet bag and pulled out his revolver, he pulled the curtain back to see the uprising below. He couldn't believe his eyes as he watched the angry white mob coming across in their pickup trucks and on foot. They were carrying everything from farming tools to rifles and they had their rage set on the northside of Tulsa. Suddenly there was a hard knock on the door, Jonas slowly walked up to the door and lean in to hear as he cocked this gun with an eager finger on the trigger.

"Open up man it's me Tyler, open up."

After hearing Tyler's voice, Jonas cautiously opened the door. Tyler came in with his gun at his side.

"Man, we gotta get the hell out of here, I just killed me a couple of crackers they all over something got them all riled up man. They're killing innocent and unarmed black folk out here man."

"That Mob is headed down this way, we gotta go man."

The men made their way downstairs and able to look out the store front window of Miss Mattie's place, the angry white mob was heading their way. The men ran to the back of the building and while attempting to make it outside the back door they realized in that moment that they had no place to run. The mob had taken over the Northside, and they could hear the chaos on the other side of the backdoor as well. Both Jonas and Tyler prepared themselves for the worst as they lock and loaded their revolvers ready to go out fighting for their life. Jonas looked at Tyler and they both knew what the

Adrienne Lynn Rutherford

other was thinking. They would fight to the death and if they had to go, they would take a few with them. Suddenly Jonas heard the voice of Miss Mattie.

"Down here, quick hurry."

Mattie lifted the wooden floor board and looked up at both Jonas and Tyler. What you are standing there for get down here. Without a second thought of the matter, both one after the other joined Mattie and her daughter Precious underneath floorboards. She then sealed the latch on the floor board from below so that it could not be moved. It would be only seconds later they could hear loud talking and cursing above their heads as well as the sounds of gunfire and destruction. No one spoke a word as they listened to the hate and resentment for the hard work of the business owners of Greenwood Tulsa's northside. Suddenly, there was silence above and they could smell smoke and Precious looked over at her mother in tears.

"They set our home on fire."

Miss Mattie, didn't waste time as she pointed to the large round hole that led into darkness.

"Move quickly, that's our way out."

One by one each bent over under the low ceiling of dusty cobwebs and earthly clay making their way further into the darkness. Miss Mattie went into her apron pocket and pulled out candles and handed each of them one and lit them. Tyler looked at Miss Mattie in awe.

"Is this an underground tunnel?"

"I've heard rumors of them around here, but I thought that's what they were, just rumors."

"Well folks around here don't talk much about them, there are plenty around here from the old timers. My father was an old-timer."

"In the old days, my father and other men in town would use these tunnels to travel at night to protect themselves from the twisters and Ku Klux Klan. But I will tell you I have never in my lifetime seen nothing like what just happened here today. A Blackman couldn't be caught out at night it was just a plain old death wish around here. So, my daddy and other men made tunnels underground and used them for shelter and a way to exchange

Dance of Angels   285

supplies, tools and medicine whenever they needed, even outside of Greenwood District."

Jonas was amazed at the story that Miss Mattie had shared.

"Will we be able to breathe?"

"Do you know where it ends?"

Precious spoke before her mother.

"She doesn't but I do, it ends near the creek just outside of Oakhurst."

"And yes, you will be able to breathe just fine, I promise."

Tyler interrupted

"That's almost three hours away."

"Well, underground, it might take all night, so I suggest we get to moving."

Precious pointed to the wooden roller that sat at the edge of the opening with a can of lantern oil on top.

"That will help us."

Jonas pointed his candle toward the wooden flatbed, it had four wheels and an iron rod placed strategically in the rear with an oil lantern secured on its hook.

"Your grandfather didn't miss a beat did he."

"No, I guess he didn't"

She then took her candle and lit the lantern on the flat bed and grabbed the rope attached.

"Follow me."

While traveling through the darkness Jonas couldn't think of anything but the girls. He hoped they were safe. The last he'd spoken to Queen her friend Calvin was taking them out of harm's way of Viola Quickman. Tyler on the other hand couldn't wait to get to the nearest phone line, although they had been exposed to such terrible unforeseen circumstances he was still determined to finish what he started. Will underground they could hear the trampling of feet above them.

"We should be safe here."

After almost three hours they finally made it to the end of the tunnel, but the entrance was covered. Jonas placed his hands on the soil wall.

"Its soft soil."

Adrienne Lynn Rutherford

They all began to dig deep into the soil to make their way out and when they reached the other side the day had turned into night. Jonas, could hear the stream just like Precious said and one by one each stepped out into the night air. The silence was almost too eerie and a far fetch from what they had experienced only hours ago. They all washed their hands in the creek and Miss Mattie sat on the edge of the bank and began to cry.

Mattie thought about her family, the legacy of her father, the hatred, the meaningless and senseless deaths that racism had brought. But more importantly, the thought that no one cared for the lives of the black folk of Tulsa Greenwood. She could only imagine the horror that many had faced. She thought of friends and family that she could not save as she wept grievously. Precious went to join her mother on the bank and comforted her. She knew all too well what her mother was feeling because she felt the same way. After a time spent of mourning Precious helped her mother up.

"We're under the road, once we go up the side of that hill that's the road, we gone cross it and it will take us to the outskirts of Oakhurst to my Cousin Harwood's farm"

However, back in Greenwood above ground the terrorism of hatred from Tula's southside continued to make its way across the tracks, claiming the lives of many in the most successful and wealthiest Black community in the nation. In a rage, it's white counterparts burned down buildings and randomly killing in cold blood as many as they could. Black folks fought back in this act of terrorism that happened on May 31, 1921. Although many fought back the casualties of death where in the hundreds with no initial sign of help from local, state or national authorities. The next day, Tulsa Greenwood District also known as *"Black Wall Street"* a thirty-six-square block radius and economic blueprint for self-made, self-built and self-sufficient Black America now laid in cinders.

Chapter 27

Oakhurst Oklahoma

Calvin was relieved that he decided to buy the old homestead in Oakhurst as he made the call to Montana. Ira Stovall was relieved, after hearing what happened what he and a couple of his hands were preparing to ride out. Calvin convinced him otherwise and informed him that he and his family would instead be joining him in Montana. After speaking to Ira Stovall and braking the news about John, he went to a quiet place and grieved his brother. Not seeing him again would be one of the hardest things he would have to live with. Calvin was glad that he could share his dream with his brother. Never did he imagine he would not make another trip north Calvin knew once this nightmare was over he would have to go back and check on things at his father's farm and his brother's place. Once he got himself together, he went outside with the others. Calvin went put his arms around Queens waist and held her from behind tightly as they all watched from afar Greenwood District of Tulsa. The smoke and fire could be smelled and seen for miles. Becky put her face inside of her son's chest as she cried for a lifetime friends left back home. People she'd known all her life and people she would probably never see again. Ma'me was being consoled by the rest of the ladies on the porch as she sat on the rocking chair swing and reminiscing on life and all the experiences that she'd had. Suddenly she spoke out and everyone turned to give an ear.

"In all my life, nothing has been more consistent I tell you than the disruption of white folks in our lives."

"I don't care what we do, where we do it, or how we do it, they gonna find a way to somehow get they hands on it or in it"

"It reminds me of a jealous child you know, don't never want to see you have nothing, nothing I tell you."

"You can never be friends with a child that is jealous of you, no way I tell you."

"No matter how much you show them that you can be friends, that child even though they play with you at times and yawl share memories and such while always when the opportunity presents

Adrienne Lynn Rutherford

itself they will hurt you."

"I know, because that happened to me."

"It ain't been so long that I was on the plantation you know, I looked that hatred square dead in the face every single day of my life."

"I tell you it can be a sho nuff ugly thing. I've seen things in my life that you probably couldn't even begin to imagine."

"But this here is a lesson to you all, you are seeing things for yourselves."

"How you gonna move around in this world now that you see things for yourself?"

"This aint nothing you heard or read in a newspaper, you seen it for yourself."

"I'm praying for the souls of my folks this time."

"Even being the Christian woman that I am, I can't pray from them white folks, not this time."

"They're on their own in all this evilness."

The front porch was silent, Ma'me then slowly got up from the chair and grabbed her cane.

"I'm tired and I'm going to bed, when I wake up in the morning the sun going be shining on my face, but in my heart, it's still a storm raging on."

Only Ma'me went to bed that night, while many told their story of how they escaped. Those who made it to the Oakhurst and Springville borders had a voice, a voice to tell what they had seen. The evilness they had witnessed was so profound that it could only be described as an act of terrorism. The fight didn't stop there, as they set up traps for the white mobs that attempted to chase Greenwood families who managed to escape into the darkness of the night. The families of these mobs would also remember this day, as they too were silently struck by the force of those who took the opportunity to fight back. Each truck load of south siders that dared to go into the darkness were strategically captured and made to pay for the atrocities that they had brought into the lives of the people of Greenwood District. Soon those back roads to Oakhurst became silent as the loud cries and gunshots faded into the darkness of night.

Back in town, the mob continued to pour in from the

southside with one thing on their mind death and destruction. It was a terrible massacre that went on for hours as men, women and children of the northside lay in their homes and in the middle of the streets dead. Their lives gone forever as the white mobs stepped over their lifeless bodies looting stores and businesses of these once resilient descendants of slaves who toiled for almost four generations to make something out of this dusty unwanted and unsettled northside of town. A people who were passionate in their vision, with unity and purpose had successfully built an economically prosperous community in Greenwood District Oklahoma. Even with all the odds against them, those who settled here on the northside had done quite well. However, because of the outward jealousy that festered like a cancer on Tulsa's southside of town, the northside would be short lived and destroyed at the hands of hate and bigotry. It was a travesty and a sad day in the city of Tulsa, Greenwood and the smoke could be seen and smelled for miles. The United States Government sat in silence until the next day, but by then the damage had been done and Tulsa Oklahoma's northside lay in ruins. This vibrant district that was once revered as a beacon of hope and economic freedom for the black people all over the country, affectionally called Black Wall Street was gone forever. It had openly been a testament to the resilience of a people who had the tenacity to rise far above the circumstances and chains that dragged them to this country and up from slavery

The following morning, Queen and her sisters were awakened by the loud noises of trucks passing by on the road. It was the national guard and they were headed in the direction of Greenwood. William came out on the porch and shook his head.

"They are far too late, the damage is done now, where were they when we needed them?"

Trailing behind was the Red Cross and while some pulled over on the side of the road just a few feet away from the house the others continued toward Greenwood District.

People in the area came out and helped as much as they could. Queen and her sisters spent most of the day assisting the Red Cross caring for the wounded and disarray that came from the wooded areas after a night of hiding. Queen was unable to get in touch with

Adrienne Lynn Rutherford

Jonas and thought she would never see him again, until she seen her mother in the distance assisting Tyler and Jonas. When she found out how they had escaped the riot she knew it was nothing but fate that had spared her dear friends life. Tyler upon seeing Queen and her sisters thought this the perfect time to get word to Viola Quickman. With all the recent turn of events and the tragedies that had come to the people of Greenwood, Tyler made sure that his plans would not falter. He would deliver the package to Viola that he'd promised one way or another.

"Jonas?"

Queen and her sisters hugged their dear friend."

"We thought we would never see you again."

"Hey, have a little faith will you."

Jonas Smiled, while rubbing his head with a sigh of relief himself.

"Yeah it was a strange turn of events."

"Thanks to Precious and Miss Mattie, me and Tyler here made it out safe.

"We were headed to Ms. Mattie's brothers farm, when I saw Miss Georgea up the road with the Red Cross."

Tyler walked up to Queen and Jonas.

"Be careful with her man, that Calvin is a crazy one."

Queen said nothing, but only looked to Jonas."

"It's good that your safe, I'm going over to help with the others, maybe we can talk later."

"Yeah, sure."

Tyler shook his head.

"Man, you never cease to amaze me, not hear more than a week and you all cozy with the residence, makes me wonder about a lot of things."

Jonas looked at Tyler.

"You need not wonder about a thing, I'm just what you call a nice guy and people take a liking to nice guys, but wise guys well let's just say they tend to not be liked as much, if you know what I mean buddy."

Jonas patted Tyler on the back and left him standing alone while he made his way over to the twins. Tyler decided not to take the offer of hospitality offered by his fellow escapee's family. However, being the snake that he was, quickly slithered his way out of everyone's sight. Due to his unwanted company, his presence would hardly even be missed he thought to himself. So, he decided to set up camp at Captain Dorian's cabin not far from the inner city of Oakhurst. It was a good place to hide and there was a working phone line that he hoped was not affected by the recent events, that way he could contact Viola Quickman in private. When he arrived, the cabin was empty just as he had suspected. This was racing season down in Central America and he was sure Captain Dorian and his entourage where there placing their bets on the horses and enjoying the weather of the tropics. For a brief moment, he felt a tad bit envious, but soon came to his senses and realized that he too would have the opportunity to relish in the luxury of being at the tracks again soon. Tyler had been looking forward to this moment for over eight years, receiving approval from Captain Dorian about paying off his debt and more importantly he fantasized about returning to his ship.

Adrienne Lynn Rutherford

Chapter 28

Southside Tulsa

Viola and the Sherriff arrived in Tulsa as planned, but as the train pulled into the station they were astonished at pandemonium around them. Viola looked out the window and in the distance, could see part the town's south side laid desolate in ruins as smoke covered the sky like a dark cloak. The frantic screams and cries of the black families could be heard as they chaotically stood in line surrounded by the national guard to receive a pass for the next train to take them out of Tulsa.

"What the hell has happened here?"

The Sherriff escorted Viola off the train and they were both stopped by a tall burly red-bearded gentleman in a uniform.

"Please step to the left."

"Step to the left, what is going on here?"

"Do you know who I am?"

"I need my luggage, wait, wait a minute I said, I have reservations in town."

Viola's request fell on death ears, while she and the captain were herded along with the other passengers into a modest warehouse that sat less than eight hundred feet from the train station. Inside where locals from the Southside and other travelers all who apparently had been there all night.

Viola screamed back at the guardsmen

"What about my luggage?"

"What is this madness?"

The captain attempted to console her, but Viola snatched away from him and with her clothing disheveled and her hat twisted ridiculously on her head she screamed at him.

"You're a lawman, find out what the hell is going on here, and get my things so I can get the hell away from this God forsaken place."

Unbothered by her consistent and irate disposition, the captain did what he was told. Viola walked over to one of the large wooden benches while talking to herself.

"That damn Tyler better come through for me, because he's been far more trouble than he's worth."

"I've come much too far to go home empty handed."

She then grabbed her large satchel and held it tightly.

Viola found a place on one of the benches with the others and could over hear the rumors floating conspicuously between them.

"They say a black man raped a white woman in the elevator at the department store on the southside, the locals apparently got furious and because of it they went rioting on the northside of town where the niggers live."

Viola shook her head at the ignorance displayed by the people she was forced to keep company with, and being the narcissist that she was could not resist to respond.

"That is absurd, it makes no logical sense at all."

"What Is the real reason for this subhuman behavior, let's be honest with ourselves why don't you people."

"I mean, I don't care for the nigras any more than anyone else, but we all know, nobody raped a white woman, especially in an elevator in a white department store on the white side of town."

"I may have been a fool in my lifetime, but never a damn fool."

In Viola's mind, her generational wealth superseded any of the people that were sharing the unstable bench with her. She displayed her thoroughbred aristocratic ways as she pointed her finger at all of them, while scolding the group like children.

"I've heard a lot about the northside of town where the nigras live, and it appears they have done quite well for themselves in a matter of a short time." "Hell, I have to admit, I've even conducted business with the likes of them myself. I can't say I wanted too, but it turned out to be quite a lucrative investment for me.

"Self-sufficient is what I see"

"Isn't that what you all wanted for them to be, self-sufficient and not looking for governmental handouts or that forty acres and a mule promised?"

Everyone on the bench with Viola became silent as they turned their noses up and rolled their eyes in the air. Viola, however seeing the responses thought it amusing that these people with all the privileges they had been afforded in this great country, would find it

Adrienne Lynn Rutherford

necessary to mess up a good thing on the northside.

"Started getting a little envious, didn't you?

"We have to do better people, okay so let me give you a lesson in acquiring wealth."

"So, for the last sixty years nigras been attempting to come up from over three hundred years of slavery and now they appear to be doing just as good or if not better than you. How could you even be intimated by such a thing?"

"On the other hand, not knowing any better, I can see your frustration clearly. I've had my share of nigra troubles in my own family believe me. But, you all must look at the bigger picture, you're throwing the baby out with the bath water. If no other wealthy white man or woman ever tells you this, let me be the first, this is the most ignorant thing that I have seen by far, much too impulsive. This city will never thrive the way it has in the past, even with the northside all torched up now. You all shot yourselves in the foot yesterday. These wealthy whites who can afford to move will move and those of you who do not have the wealth to do so, you're stuck. After this dreadful massacre that I have witnessed, others like myself will never risk investing a dime in the city of Tulsa. The economic base is what creates wealth and right now you all do not have one anymore."

Soon the captain returned with a private from the national guard who was struggling with Viola's luggage. She got up from her seat, pulled her fan from her waist vest and popped it open to cool herself."

"See what I mean, good day to you all."

As they walked out into the streets, the sounds of the train whistle began to blow. The pandemonium that consumed the small little ticket box had almost diminished. Viola, climbed onto the wagon with the help of the captain and the private and disappeared into the dust.

After being escorted by the National Guard to the pressing areas of concern, Calvin and William made their way back to Oakhurst. It was no need for them to speak about what they had experienced, their faces said it all. Queen went to Calvin and held him tightly, the pain for them all had been too much to mention. Never would she had thought that when leaving Memphis, there would be far more travesties of heart ache and pain than what she'd left behind. The feelings were almost surreal as she also thought of the connections that she'd made with her mother and her family. She vowed that she would never let anything come between them ever again. Calvin was eager to share the news that he'd received from the national guard.

"Some of you will be leaving here today, they have opened the railway back up and people are making their way for railroad passes. The National Guard is posted at all the train stations in the areas so, let's just say the worse of it is over, but we have lost a lot. Far too much to imagine. The race has taking a serious economic blow and Greenwood will probably never be what it once was. No one will ever realize how much love and pride were between the mortar and brick of every one of those buildings"

"The pride and dignity of black folks making a way out of no way, perseverance was what Greenwood represented to many in this country, she was a beacon of hope from the atrocities that our ancestors have faced in this God forsaken country."

Meanwhile, Georgea had also gotten word to Greta about the turn of events and had received confirmation that their plan was I place. Georgea hung up the phone teary-eyed. With all the terrible events that had transpired, she would do what she had promised. Georgea would have her life back with her daughters to start anew. Becky however, received a pleasant surprise thanks to Queen. Soon after Calvin's return Becky was greeted by a visitor, not just any visitor but Isaiah Franklin. He stepped out of his chauffer driven automobile and smiled at Becky. In all her shyness she turned her head, as she truly thought she would never see this man again. He walked up to her and embraced her and she held on to him for dear life.

"Are you okay?"

Becky looked around and nodded to her family as if looking for confirmation.

"Yes, Isaiah I am okay, but how'd you….?"

"Queen called Damita last night, thanks to her they made it safely to my place in Springville. I was concerned and since I was still in the area I didn't want to miss this opportunity again."

Adrienne Lynn Rutherford

"I was worried about you all when I heard the news, I shouldn't have never left you without telling you how I felt about you Rebecca."

"What do you mean?"

"Well I haven't been able to stop thinking about you since the night of the premiere."

Becky was speechless as she turned to look at Queen with a smile and then back at Isiah.

"I... I... I don't know what to say."

"I did think of you as well, but obviously you can see that we are in a very serious situation and we will be leaving soon with Calvin to a safe place. Right now, were figuring out who will be leaving out today on the train, right Calvin?"

Calvin nodded in confirmation and Isaiah took Becky by the hand.

"Please come with me, just for a little while to Canada, I don't want to lose you again. I promise you I will take you to Montana in a couple of weeks."

"I don't want to miss out on this opportunity again, there is so much I want to show you."

Becky smiled and then quickly thought of her mother.

"What about Ma'me and William, I can't just leave them, they need me especially now."

She then looked over at her son and mother as her eyes filled with tears. Just the thought of having to choose was unfathomable. William then walked over to his mother.

"Ma, it's your turn. This Isaiah seems to be a good guy and he obviously loves you or he wouldn't have come all this way back for you."

"That says a lot about his character as a man, and besides anyone who is a friend of Queen, is a friend of mines."

Isaiah extended his hand to William and he grabbed it and they exchanged a strong brotherly embrace and he felt gratitude for the trust that William had bestowed him.

"Thank you for that man, I appreciate it. I did not know how you all were going to receive me and you all have my word I will take good care of her and will be up in a couple of weeks, that's a promise"

Calvin extended his hand as well.

"We will hold you to that, I have friends everywhere."

William then looked at his mother who had cared for both he and Ma'me most of her life.

"Don't worry we will take really good care of Ma'me."

Rebecca still unconvinced now was hugging her mother.

"Ma, I said don't worry, I will look after Ma'me."

Ma'me laughed out loud.

"Ma'me don't need nobody to look after me, I've been doing a good job all by myself."

Becky smiled at her stubborn mother and shook her head. Ma'me then smiled at her only child living on earth.

"That's a fine man you got yourself there."

"Don't you go fretting over me, you hear?"

"Ole Ma'me is going to be just fine, anyway I can't wait to see this place we going to, my my my."

"You go on and have some time to yourself baby, we'll meet up with you real soon.

Becky went over to Queen and the twins and they exchanged hugs, laughter and tears.

"Thank you, Queen."

"Thank you for seeing me."

Queen in her efforts not to get emotional encouraged Becky to be safe."

"Go one now girl, it's getting late around her."

For the first time in Becky's life she felt light and after she embraced and revered in the solitude of family, Becky took a leap of faith. With encouragement and love Becky for the first time in her life did something self-fish. William smiled as his mother embraced him, he then looked over at Isaiah again.

"You look after my mama you hear?"

"I wouldn't have it no other way my man, no other way."

"I am going to put a permanent smile on that beautiful face, you wait and see."

Becky began to blush as Isaiah escorted her to his automobile, while Calvin shouted to the driver.

"Be safe on those roads my man"

After seeing Becky off, Calvin reached in his pocket and gave his father the keys to his ranch in Montana.

"An older gentleman by the name of Ira Stovall will be waiting for you at the train station."

"Waiting for me, what are you talking about

"I'm sending you all on the train to Montana you, Mama, Cody and the twins."

"Ma'me you too."

I will make sure for you to get everything you need and Ira will take good care of you. For the first time in his life Mr. Watkins sincerely displayed humility in the presence of his family. It had been one of the hardest things for him to do as he made every effort to set an example of pride, however it had been misplaced and misunderstood most of the life of his children. Nevertheless, as time stood still he realized in that moment that he'd lost more than he'd gained all those years. Carolyn glanced at her eldest sister and her mother with a confused look on her face."

"What is he saying?"

"Montana, I don't want to go to Montana, I want to stay with you."

Connie nodded her head in agreement with her sister. Queen walked over to them both.

"Calvin has made arrangements for you all to leave Tulsa, it is important that you are safe."

"We'll be right behind you I promise."

Queen and Georgea gave them all a big hug and Queen smiled at her sisters.

"Don't worry I will be fine, you guys will get the awesome view of the countryside."

"We are coming directly, I promise."

Although reluctant at first eventually the twins agreed.

Ma'me stood up again from the swing on the porch.

"Ma'me won't be riding no train today or any other day, I will be traveling with the rest of yawl on the road."

After much fuss from William and Queen they finally gave in to her wishes. Ma'me slowly sat back down in the swing chair and closed her eyes to get a tad bit of rest, a storm was soon to come and she had to get ready.

Calvin escorted Mr. Watkins, his mother and the others to the train station. Before arriving, he reached in his pocket and handed his father an envelope. Mr. Watkins looked inside and to his surprise it was filled with a handful of banded twenty-dollar notes and with financial experience it wasn't hard for him to figure it was well over two thousand dollars. He then looked over at his son and attempted to speak, but Calvin spoke first.

"Everything will be fine from now on papa, you don't have to say nothing and you don't have to worry about nothing."

"Not anymore."

"You are going to have a lot of work to do Mr. Watkins when you get to your destination."

Mr. Watkins proudly smiled at his son as Mrs. Watkin wiped the tears from her eyes, although she'd struggled a deep heart for the lost her eldest child, she was able to find some peace in the union she'd witnessed in this moment. After a short journey and several detours thanks to the national guard they finally arrived at their destination. Calvin was grateful that the others did not have to witness the terrible remains that laid in cinder at his brother John's place, all his dreams up in smoke. He would never tell them how they raided and looted his home trashing his prestigious honors from and destroying his blue prints and his life's work to his most prized airplane designs. Calvin did all that he could to hold the tears back.

When they arrived at the train station it was swamped with people trying to leave Tulsa. Both young and old who had an opportunity to leave stood by waiting for the pass for any train route that would take them far away from the tragedies they'd witnessed. Calvin made his way through the crowd leading all that were in his company. He was grateful that he had already picked up passes earlier that morning when they first began issuing them out. He didn't want to take any chances so they were all prepared to board the next train in route to Montana before night fall. Since Ma'me would not be joining them, Calvin realized that he had an extra ticket in his possession. He looked around hoping to find a soul that he could bless with a new beginning. As the others made their way to the front of the board walk for the next train coming through and in the midst of the crowed space Calvin could identify a small framed young black boy. His clothes and face were covered in sot and appeared to be alone, as he sat on the stoop next to the fire station. Calvin out of curiosity walked over to him.

"Are you here alone?"

"Where are your parents son?"

The young boy with his head down hunched his shoulders as if not to know.

"How did you get here, to the train station?"

"Them ova there."

The young man pointed to the large green National Guard Truck that stood in the center of the street blocking the entrance from the most northern side of town.

"I don't know where my Papa is, my mamma she dead."

"What's your name son?"

"Solomon"

"Solomon Morgan."

"You got any family around hear son?"

"Not that I reckon sir, my mama and daddy brought me here from Mississippi when I was just a little boy."

Calvin extended his hand to the proud young man.

"Get up son."

"How old are you?"

"I'm twelve years old sir, my birthday is tomorrow, be thirteen."

"You a hard worker?"

"Yes sir, very hard worker, I want my own business one-day racing horses."

Calvin smiled.

"Is that so, can you ride a horse Solomon?"

"Yes, sir I been riding horses with my daddy since I was five years old."

Calvin reached down in his overcoat and pulled out the last remaining ticket, handed it Ulysses and pointed him the direction of his father and the ladies on the boardwalk.

"You see the people there, you will be traveling with them today, Happy birthday Ulysses you just got yourself a job.:

"I will be joining you all in a few days where you're going, there are plenty of horses to ride, but I'm going to need your help caring for them you hear."

Solomon looked up at Calvin with a huge smile across his face.

"I remember when I was a little boy and we left Mississippi my mama told me we were going to place where all our dreams would come true, thank you sir thank you."

"Call me Calvin, Solomon."

Calvin pulled out his pocket watch as he heard the loud sound of the train whistle. He then walked Ulysses over and explained the plan and right away Carolyn began taking her napkin and wiping the sot off his face. Although Solomon hadn't welcomed the attention, he took it in stride as he was more grateful in that moment than anything else. Soon the chaos at the station house began to cease as the National Guard began to escort those off the boardwalk who were unable to obtain tickets or the next train. The citizens without tickets stood impatiently behind the barricade as they witnessed the dark smoke from the train push high into the sky. Calvin affectionately and without any malice in his heart embraced his father.

"You take care of Mom and Cody, I'll see you all soon."

Mr. Watkins nodded as Calvin said his good byes to the others. Eventually, after little under an hour everyone was on board. He watched as they all waved good bye, even Solomon whose life he'd changed forever. Today would be the beginning of many days of mourning for the once vibrant Greenwood District of Tulsa Oklahoma and the people who lived there. Soon many would tell their stories to the world about their disingenuous neighbors of the southside with all their jealousy and hate destroyed one of the most successful self-sufficient economic communities of Black America. The train wheels began to turn on the track the steel to steel motion could be heard in its swiftness, as it continued gaining momentum for the long journey. Mr. Watkins and his wife looked out the window as the they traveled through Greenwood District. His eyes teared up as they rode passed the what was once his most prized

302   Adrienne Lynn Rutherford

jewel, the clock tower which now laid crumbled in ruins. Nothing but ashes and debris were left from a once vibrant Greenwood District. Mr. and Mrs. Watkins like so many others had lost so much that it would forever leave a void in their hearts and souls for as long as they lived.

Calvin made his way swiftly back to the house. If they were going to leave he wanted to be far north of Oklahoma before sun down. When he returned he was surprised to see Tyler sitting on the porch with William and the ladies.

"Ah, Calvin, we were just talking about you."

"Oh really, hope it was good."

Calvin walked over reached down and gave Queen a kiss.

"What brings you back around these here parts Tyler?"

"I thought you would be long gone by now, there is nothing to keep you here, I seen the paradise, its burnt to cinders."

Inside, Tyler cringed at the cynicism from Calvin as he twirled his hat in his hand and quickly changed the subject.

"Well I actually came to see all the beautiful ladies, but I noticed there are a few of them missing, but it appears most of them are traveling and Becky has left for the east coast, that's quite interesting enough.

"Who would have known after all these years she would be able to get out of Greenwood there are all kinds of blessings in curses I tell you blessings in curses I tell you."

Queen looked at Tyler and said nothing, the look alone spoke a thousand words. The only reason they even entertained his presence was Georgea had high suspicions of him because of her conversations with Jonas.

"So, Mr. Tyler, what are your plans now?

Ma'me glanced over at Tyler and at that moment she shouted, while continuing to rock in the wooden chair.

"Merciless, you are the merciless one, you will self-destruct because of it, yes suh."

She then began to laugh out loud and Tyler looked at her as it he'd seen a ghost for the first time.

"I didn't give you permission to speak over my life."

Ma'me laughed again.

"You call it what you like Mr. Tyler, but you will be cold and wet soon, really soon."

William returned to the porch with the map that Calvin requested before he'd left.

"I found the route Calvin US 70 it's narrow, but after that the road should be pretty much wide open.

"I imagine we should be leaving sooner than later, I don't want to run into any knight riders, Ira will meet us at the border."
Calvin looked the map over.

"Distance wise, it looks like we should be out of Oklahoma by the Twilight hour, let's get loaded up and prepare to leave before night fall."

Tyler glanced over at Queen and whispered.

"Going somewhere my beautiful one?"

Queen got up.

"Yes, far away from here."

"Ma'me, mama let's go inside and pack food for our trip."

As the ladies went into the kitchen, Tyler's thoughts now focused on the conversation between Calvin and William. This would be far easier than he thought. There was only one road with a bridge that took you to the border of Oklahoma, they were going north. Now, he had to get in touch with Madame Quickman. It would be now or never for him, today was the day of reckoning, today was the first day of the rest of his life. Never mind the comments Ma'me made, they were just the words of an old frail woman. Today would be the day he would reposition himself. Tyler tipped his hat and thanked Calvin for the grand hospitality as he escorted himself out. Calvin looked out the window and shook his head as Tyler strolled down the dusty road happy as a lark. William curious at what his friend was looking at joined him at the window.

"Wil, man I don't trust that guy."

"Eh, we don't have to worry about him, we are going to be leaving here soon, we may never see that character again, besides he's lost everything, the Paradise is nothing but ruins.

Meanwhile in the kitchen, Queen and Georgea where listening to the wise words of Ma'me while managing to pack enough food

Adrienne Lynn Rutherford

for the journey thanks to the kind folks of Oakhurst."

"Ole Ma'me would not have thought in a million years even with the good gift of sight, I would be sitting here with the two of you."

"You better watch yourself in this life, because God will surely give you the business of reminding you who is really in charge. Lord, this has been such a terrible time. I ain't seen nothing like this since I was a young girl coming off the Greensboro tobacco plantations in North Carolina."

"Yes Suh, they burned that place to the ground and I can still see Massa Conrad standing there weeping like a little ole woman. I couldn't understand where all that had come from. I'd never seen him do nothing but hurt other folks to get what he wanted."

"And his wife that was a tuff ole lady, she had a standoff with them army men holding her rifle to keep them from taking any of us children out the house. I thought to myself, this lady in all her evil ways had been beating on me since I was a young child, gonna risk her life for me now. I never could understand the strange ways of white folks."

"They ended up dragging her along out the house with us, I reckon they could have punished her for even having the nerve to point a gun at them, or maybe they put her to work for the union, who knows. No matter if its northern white folk or southern white folk when it comes to this country, they're going to stick together. I found that out early on after that so-called reconstruction."

"I talk about all these things because when they marched us off that plantation, I thought the pain would be over. I thought that after those big tall white men came in and rescued all the children off the plantation, we were that free thing. That free thing everybody around me spoke about all my life. What my mama and daddy left us for, I was finally going to experience that free thing for myself."

"What I didn't know at the time, I was still had to work just that much harder for it."

****

Tyler consistently paced the floor going over his plan and up until now, he had not thought about the devastation he felt about the events that occurred on Tulsa's south side. While at Calvin's farm house with the others, he could not show his true feelings. However, now alone in the cabin he displayed a deep regret. The Paradise was destroyed, he had gambled by putting his life saving into that club to turn a heavy profit. Never in a million years did he think a race riot would destroy one of the most successful and lucrative black communities in the country. His plan to sell to Coaster was no more, so now his only recourse would be to finish what he'd started with Viola.

Tyler tried not to think the worse, after leaving several messages at Viola Quickman's hotel to contact him when she arrived in Tulsa. Nevertheless, he could not resist thinking that maybe there was a slight possibility Viola Quickman would make her way back to Memphis after hearing about the riots in Tulsa. He then began to think of Queen and her consistent disdain for him. Tyler thought for certain his charming ways would seduce her right into his arm. Afterwards, he could hand her over, collect his bounty and be on his way to Honduras. Unfortunately, his plans would fall short as he gritted his teeth thinking about Calvin and his pompous heroism. He knew to get to Queen he would have to face him, and facing him would mean a fight to the death. At this point it made him no matter, because now he had nothing to lose. He then smiled as he remembered the herb Captain Francoise always kept stashed in the pantry. Tyler, sat down at the table and began to roll himself a spliff. When he was done, he pulled his lighter from his pocket, lit it and took a long drag. He held it in a few seconds and slowly blew smoke up in the air. Soon his body began to relax and he could feel the herb taking effect. He took another drag and this time a lot slower as he thought again of Queen and how he was going to change his life forever.

Meanwhile, Viola looked out the hotel window as she watched the National Guard trucks roll through town. From the view, she had from her hotel room, the place looked like a war zone. The sheriff knocked on the door,

"Come in."

"Madame Viola, I just spoke to one of the National Guard and the ranking officers think it's best that we stay inside until further notice.

Adrienne Lynn Rutherford

Viola through her hands up in disgust.

"I could hardly believe that any black man would be that stupid to do such a thing"

"In the middle of an all-white segregated community?"

"I didn't believe it then and I don't believe now."

"Just look how they tore up that beautifully built place. It's just disgraceful

Viola then poured herself another glass of whiskey.

"Have some?"

"No thank you."

The sheriff's trust in Viola had run thin after spending more time than he had wished with her. He never expected to be dragged across state lines. Viola in her almost drunken state began to rationalize the situation to the sheriff.

"Let me be the first to explain to you the reason behind all of this rabble rousing. "Economics my dear, pure and simple."

"Those poor whites have no clue what they've done you know, no one is ever going to invest in this pitiful God forsaken place again, it's cursed, by wealthy white folk's standards"

She then turned the glass up and finished it off and poured herself another.

"Have you spoken to the Tyler fellow, he had us come all this way to have to deal with this nonsense."

Viola then looked over at the large carpet satchel and smiled.

"I'm sure he wants his reward."

"Captain, I feel like a criminal, not allowed to leave the hotel"

"It's for your safety, Ms. Viola."

"For my safety?"

Viola, let out a loud burly laugh

"That's absurd, I have no worries at all."

"It's those people across the tracks who need safety not me."

Soon the Phone rang.

"Captain please get that."

Captain Feldman picked up the phone and not to his surprise it was Tyler, he then handed the phone to Viola.

"Good evening Tyler, I must let you know I am quite annoyed with this situation that he have gotten me in, you failed to mention that I would run into a race riot once I got here, actually I'm surprised that you are alive yourself. It appears these people have quite a disdain for self-made black men here in Tulsa."

Tyler had no time to exchange sarcasm with Viola, his time was running out, his primary focus was getting Queen in the hands of Viola before she and the others headed north.

"Viola, there has been a change of plans and we must move quickly, I just left them all and they are planning to leave tomorrow the whole lot of them. They are moving north. It appears this man Calvin Watkins fellow has a place up there for them all."

"Calvin?"

"Yeah, you know him?"

Not willing to share her business holdings with either the captain or Tyler she rescinded.

"I've heard the name."

"Well they're making plans as we speak."

"Who may I ask?"

"Queen, her sisters, old aunt and her mother, the whole lot of them."

"They're leaving first in the morning, it's a family affair."

The comment took Viola's breath away, she was speechless momentarily before she was able to catch her breath again.

"What do you mean her mother?"

"Her mother, they called her Georgea."

An uncontrollable rage ran through Viola, never in a million years did she think she would see her sister again. She dropped the phone and began impulsively pacing the floor. She then grabbed the flowered vase and smashed it against the wall shattering it into pieces. The captain looked on in shock at the behaviors that raged in Viola. He'd seen her emotional reactions before, but nothing as violent as this. He then picked the receiver up off the floor and continued speaking with Tyler himself.

"What is your location?"

"I'm near the western border of Oakhurst, route 70 it's a log cabin with a red chimney you can't miss it."

"I will be waiting for you."

Adrienne Lynn Rutherford

Afterwards the captain hung up the phone. In the corner sat Viola her mascara running down her face, tears rolling down her eyes.

"They all will die, all of them, I warned her, I warned her to never show her face again."

Viola then stood up, straightened her dress and went to the table and poured water in the basin to wash her face. Afterwards she displayed no emotional expression to the captain.

"Do you know Tyler's whereabouts?"

"Yes, he says we must move fast, it appears they are planning to make their way North."

Viola walked over and poured herself another whiskey and turned it up once more.

"Gather the men, we are leaving."

"As I explained before Ms. Viola, the national Guard..."

Viola threw her hands up.

"Silence."

"I don't give a damn about any of what you are saying to me right now, Captain do as I say or you will not make it out of this God forsaken place, I promise you."

Viola then reached for a small pouch in her luggage and placed several gold pieces inside, she then went to the door and opened it up for the captain.

"Do not come back to my room until you have arranged transportation for all of us to ride out of here."

Chapter 29

The Journey North

Captain Feldman and his men stood at the bridge crossing all armed with rifles in hand as the rapids underneath created a mild cool mist that moistened their faces. The day of reckoning had finally come and after it was all over, he would no longer have to bow to the whelms of *The Medusa*. The captain would never admit in a quiet since of relief his gratitude for Queen and her sisters for taking on the task of getting rid of Rodger Quickman. His job had been on the line, because he could no longer make excuses to the Mayor of Memphis regarding the unrest that was rapidly festering on the eastside of Memphis.

Even now, he still wallowed in his own sense of greed not with having understood the consequences of it all. Greed was a two-edged sword and one way or another it would surely wreak havoc in the lives of those who would succumb to it. If he could go back to that day in the kitchen of the Sawyer home, he would have handled things far differently. However, it was too late and now he had to play this thing out to the end. Just as he had planned, the captain would finally have the wealth that he desired all his life. Nevertheless, it would leave a permanent scar on the integrity of his name and the many generations that would follow. He had seen the repercussions of this as he looked over at Viola and Tyler, who both of waited patiently for this catalyst of greed to secure their future.

Inside the automobile, Tyler attempted to engage in light conversation with Viola. However, since meeting up with *The Medusa* and her so called mercenaries he saw that she was far too preoccupied in her own thoughts. Tyler looked over as Viola gazed off into the distance clutching ahold to the satchel that would be the one and only thing that would change his life forever. Inside was a new beginning and his mouth watered just thinking about it, suddenly his thoughts were interrupted as Viola shouted out to the captain.

"We have been here for hours, what is taking them so long?"

"Do you see anything?"

Adrienne Lynn Rutherford

"The heat out here is dreadful, if they don't come soon I will have to leave."

Tyler attempted to encourage Viola, but she held her hand up to his face in contempt.

"You have been way more trouble than you are obviously worth."

She then patted her satchel, reminding him who was the superior in the situation and smiled. Tyler returned the smile, but inside he felt contempt for the dreadfulness for *The Medusa*. The mere existence of this evil woman reeked of disgust. Although Tyler had never had a real family of his own, his greed had always been his desperate motivation to fill that void in his life. It had left him cold and callus and he was no better for it. However, looking at Viola he knew he could never find himself able to ransom out his own flesh and blood for murder. As he attempted to light his cigar, Viola quickly expelled him from her presence and he got out of the automobile whipping off his dusty suit with relief. Tyler looked down and checked out his shoes and shook his head. Not long after, in the distance the captain was able to see a small convoy. The closer they came to the bridge the more recognizable they were.

"It's them, It's them."

Viola got out of the car and Tyler in all the excitement never took his mind or eyes off his future for one second. In a matter of minutes, he would walk away with a new life and a wealthy man. Captain Francoise would forgive him without contempt and he would sail off as he always planned. Viola watched Tyler's uncontrollable thirst for the contents of her bag.

"You won't get a single dime of this until I have my hands on those murders."

Tyler said nothing as the convoy moved in closer to the crossing. Leading was Calvin in his automobile with Queen, her mother Georgea and Ma'me in the back seat. William, Sarah and Jonas pulled up the rear with the horses and the pickup truck.

The Captain and his men turned their guns toward the front of Calvin's automobile and he slowly stopped once they were on the bridge. When Georgea could recognize her sisters face in the distance she called out to her.

"Viola, is that you?"

Viola was stunned as if she had seen a ghost. Even after the time that had passed between them, she was unable to set aside the pain, the hurt or the jealousy that had raged on in her all these years.

"Don't you take one step toward me, or I will have my men send you to your maker."

"My business is not with you, it is with that one right there, she knows what she did."

Georgea attempted to rationalize with her sister.

"Viola, what are you saying, that is my daughter your talking about."

"Did you hear what I said Georgea?"

"She killed my son."

Viola, shook her head in contempt while the others stood by waiting for further instructions.

"Is that Calvin Watkins, the magnificent black cowboy tycoon?"

"What are you doing slumming with the likes of these people?" Calvin countered her light humor.

"Looks like you're the one whose slumming Viola, considering the company that your keeping these days."

Viola looked over at Tyler in his run-down suit and the other weather-beaten men that had taken the long journey with her, and found that what Calvin said had been true.

"Well, do you know you're sitting next to a murderer, she killed my son and I came to collect her and take her back to be prosecuted."

"Where are your accomplices?"

"Oh, never mind, you will do just fine, you and that one over there."

As she pointed to Jonas.

"I knew the day I walked out of that god forsaken one room den of yours you were lying, now I have you on aiding and abiding."

"You have me on nothing old lady, over my dead body will you take me anywhere, unlike you, I have nothing to lose, nothing!"

"Hah, oh really, well that will make it all the better."

Adrienne Lynn Rutherford

Queen then stepped out the car, she'd had enough. All the fear and intimation tactics that this woman had imposed on the people that she cared about the most had taken its final toll.

"That is enough, enough, you evil miserable witch."

Calvin looked over at William and gave him the sign to do nothing. If they were going to kill them they would have done it by now. William knowing the ways of his friend, could keep the others at bay as well. This situation would have to play itself out and Ma'me closed her eyes and said nothing as she listened to the vision that she had already witnessed some time ago.

"Your son was a monster he tried to rape my sister, in our home, so you need to get your facts straight, it was self-defense and you know it, the captain he knows it too."

"He should have been locked away a long time ago for the crimes he committed and you allowed it, you allowed him to do those unspeakable things that he did. No young woman on the east side of Memphis was ever safe as long as he roamed the streets."

"Captain, and you, you are supposed to protect and serve and you continued to let it go on, with a watchful eye."

The captain feeling ashamed took a brief second and then ordered his men to put their guns down and everyone became silent. Viola then dropped the satchel and turned around to the men.

"What the hell do you think you're doing?"

"Captain order your men to take her, take her now."

While no one was paying attention, Tyler ran over and grabbed Viola's satchel and leaped over the bridge into the rapids of the river. He held on tight and screamed a sigh of relief and with loud demented laughter as the current took him swiftly away. The captain ordered his men to fire, but no one was able to get a good shot. Viola screamed at the top of her lungs out of frustration.

"Kill them all, kill them all."

Ma'me opened her eyes, it had been some time since she would take on such a presence, but for the sake of her family she would do anything. In that moment, a raven landed on the branch of the tall oak tree that carried that one fragile memory for dear Ma'me. See, she had not shared the very first vision that had shattered her to the core, the one she would never mention. Here was the place that she

Dance of Angels   313

and Mr. and Mrs. Watkins would cut her dear husbands limp body down. She and her dear friends found her husband at the bridge after he'd challenged a man from the south side for the money he'd owed him for an honest day of work. She remembered how Becky was just a baby. Although she never spoke a word, this place never left her mind or spirit. Today however, she would break every chain and end the generational curses that chased her family for good. Ma'me knew with the power that she possessed, it was likely that she would also make her peace here in this same place. The life that she lived had been a complicated one, not by her choice or by her doing. Many times, in her circumstance resulted in her fate being in the hands of others. However, today she would determine her own fate and in this freedom, she would rejoice in victory. Meanwhile, Viola grabbed the rifle from the hands of one of her men and aimed it at her sister

"If I die today, so will she."

Calvin opened the door and got out to try to make sense with Viola, he also signaled William who had his hand on the draw for his Holster.

She turned around in circles frantically observing everyone around her and was feeling quite alone. Viola wondered how it all had come to this. She was a Quickman, the one with the power. Queen attempted to reach for her mother to get her out of arms way of the loaded rifle pointed at her chest

"Stay back, don't you come any closer none of you get back I said. Queen you too, stay away from her before I pull this trigger."

Viola wiped her face of the sweat and tears that ran continuously down her sunburnt face

"None of you will ever understand my pain never"

"I was my mother's child, her first born and bred to lead. I was trained to do whatever was necessary to protect the family legacy and that was my job as the eldest child."

She then looked over at her sister with an unfathomable sense of hatred and irreparable pain.

"Who was she to live in peace while I was forced to take on the responsibility willed by my mother."

"How dare she live in love and kindness, while I was forced into this, this pitiful life. You think I wanted this for my life?"

Adrienne Lynn Rutherford

"Father always did those things for you too Viola, he never played favorites"

"You made the choice to detach yourself from him, he loved you no less Viola."

"You liar, he loved you more, he spent more time with you while I was forced to live the life that mother made for me, I was never happy doing those things. I wanted to travel to the south of France and Rome to study the arts, I wanted a life of joy and happiness."

"I felt like I had a ball and chain on my life. But you, you walked right out the front door and into the life that you wanted. You are far stronger than you think little sister."

"Viola, I didn't know, I didn't know that you had these feelings."

Viola begin to cry and wale.

"It's not fair, it's not fair, then you took my only son your daughter she murdered him in cold blood."

"Viola, he was sick in the mind demented in his ways. His actions were unacceptable you know that."

"It didn't matter he was mine, my flesh and blood, she had no right to take his life. I know he was ill but she had no right to take his life".

Ma'me then stood up and stretched out her arms into the sky and spoke in all the gifted power that she had aloud.

"Dear Lord forsake this child, forsake this evil spirt that has brought pain and agony to the spirit of the this once sweet child. Release her from this generational curse of evil, hate and guilt."

She then pointed to Viola.

"You release this child right now, remove yourself, you have no place here anymore."

Viola screamed and cursed Ma'me at the top of her voice as she moaned in pain. She eventually dropped the gun and fell to the ground turning and twisting vexed with and obvious struggle that laid far deeper in her spirit than any natural eye could see.

Ma'me continued her battle with unwavering strength to finally release her family for good.

"You can't win, you can't ever win."

"Out I say, Out and return to where you came from."

"You have no place in this family."

"Ma'me will never let you have any peace in this family, out I say"

Viola continued to jerk and moan and the others watched in disbelief. Then suddenly, her body laid limp on the bridge road. Georgea ran to her sister side while Queen and her sisters covered their mouths in disbelief, never had they witnessed such a thing. Georgea shook her sister repeatedly, but she never awakened. Ma'me walked over to Georgea, shaking her head.

"Your sister is gone from this world, she chose death over life"

"Viola, although deceived by your mother, had completely given in to the darkness of hate long ago my dear child."

"It's out of the hands of the living now."

Ma'me then looked over to the Captain.

"She should have a proper burial."

The Captain and his hired henchman were astonished at what they had just witness. None spoke a word as the Captain instructed his men to pick up Viola's body.

The Captain then looked over at Queen.

"You need not worry about anything, live your life, live your life."

****

Queen awakened from a deep sleep and looked over at the love of her life. She was grateful and very thankful that her family was safe and sound. Although tomorrow would be their wedding day, Calvin could not bear spending a night without her, they all had been through enough. Queen, was never one for tradition and as a result accommodated his request. It had been almost three months since losing Ma'me, and it was one of the hardest things for anyone of them to accept. Ma'me had been their rock of ages and even in the short time she was able to spend with her, Queen felt blessed. Ma'me provided them all with an unforgettable legacy of love, faith, spirit and strength. As she gazed out the window, she noticed the peculiar illumination of the moon and was compelled to go outside and appreciate the greatness of its fullness. As she walked out onto the large porch she gazed out into the distance and could see in the moonlight the beautiful horses that grazed freely in the pastures. She

Adrienne Lynn Rutherford

also thought how Ma'me would have appreciated such a porch. However, as she looked up into the sky she almost stumbled and fell as tears began to roll down her face. Then with a wide smile Queen sat down in the fullness of the moon and just like aunt Ma'me she watched the *Dance of Angels*.

Impelling African American History facts and people that inspired "Dance of Angels"

Queen Sawyer, entertainer and writer: Black Women of Burlesque
Inspired by: Baker, Josephine, and Jo Bouillon. Josephine. ANESA, 1988.

Calvin Watkins Automobile
Inspired by   C.R. Patterson & Sons Company (1893-1939) | The Black Past: Remembered and Reclaimed, www.blackpast.org/aah/c-r-patterson-sons-company-1893-1939.

Buford Sawyer father of Queen and, protégé to Robert R. Church, first black Millionaire in Memphis Tennessee
Inspired by: Robert Reed Church of Memphis - the First Black Millionaire,www.historic-memphis.com/biographies/robert-church/robert-church.html.

Origin of the Sawyer and Watkins Family Legacy: Greenwood District of Tulsa Oklahoma (a.k.a) "Black Wall Street"
Inspired by: Beneit, Stephen Vincent, and Tim Madigan. The Burning: Massacre, Destruction, and the Tulsa Race Riot of 1921. Thomas Dunne Books/St. Martin's Press, 2001.

The Fisk Jubilee singers, a favorite of Ma'me Black
     In 1866 the Fisk Free Colored School was established in Nashville, Tennessee by the American Missionary Association. Housed in abandoned Union hospital barracks, Fisk set out to educate former slaves with the support of donations from former abolitionists. As those donations declined over the next five years, Fisk fell on hard times.
     To save the institution, Fisk's treasurer, George Leonard White, decided to gamble on the extraordinary voices of the young black singers who had begun to share with him the songs of their ancestors. Over the objections of his colleagues and sponsors, White and his assistant, a frail young African American pianist named Ella Sheppard, led a choir of nine young former slaves (now called the

Dance of Angels   319

Fisk Jubilee Singers) up from Nashville to perform for congregations in the North along the route of the Underground Railway.

The Jubilees, as they were eventually called, struggled through a schizophrenic world of liberal ministers and adoring audiences, but also poor receipts, and segregated hotels, restaurants and trains. They made their way to New York, where they chose for their debut *Steal Away, Swing Low, Sweet Chariot and Deep River*, the secret hymns their ancestors sang in fields and cabins and brush arbor churches, the spirituals they were about to introduce into the universal canon of Christian worship.

"Fisk Jubilee Choir." Tennessee | The Black Past: Remembered and Reclaimed, www.Blackpast.org/tree/Tennessee/Tennessee /.

Ma'me traumatic vision of Laura and L.D. Nelson
Inspired by: The Lynch Quilts Project, LaShawanda Crowe Storm, www.thelynchquiltsproject.com/laura-nelsons-story#!

Ira Stovall a "Freedmen" and friend of Calvin Watkins
Inspired by: "AFROCENTRIC CULTURE BY DESIGN."
Sarah Rector the Richest Black Girl in The World, 1 Jan. 1970, afrocentricculturebydesign.blogspot.com/2010/05/sarah-rector-richest-black-girl-in.html.

John Watkins, Black Pilot of World War I.
Inspired by: "First African American Pilot Fought Racism (and Enemy) in World War I." www.militaryhistory.com

Greenwood District Oscar Micheaux Film Premiere
Inspired by: McGilligan, Patrick. Oscar Micheaux, the Great and Only: The Life of America's First Black Filmmaker.
Harper Perennial, 2008.

Dear Explorer,

First, I would like to thank you for your curiosity, because it is curiosity that first ignites the desire to explore. There is such a rich and vibrant history of the African American community in this country. No story can be told on this great continent without it. It has been my motivation to creatively; through love, romance and adventure to write such stories. Although a fictional novel, "Dance of Angels" will amuse and entertain you, while acknowledging some of the most profound historical events in African American History.

About the Author

Adrienne is a native of Detroit Michigan, she holds a Bachelor's degree in Business with a minor in Africana Studies from Wayne State University and a Masters of Occupational Therapy from Eastern Michigan University.

She was introduced to the literary world at an early age, thanks to her mother and enjoys writing poetry and screenwriting for short films. History has always been an intriguing subject for her and has inspired her imagination and desire to write about the human experience.

Adrienne is an advocate for community outreach and a member of Sigma Gamma Rho Sorority Inc. (1990) She enjoys traveling and spending most of her time with family and friends.

www.ingramcontent.com/pod-product-compliance
Lightning Source LLC
Chambersburg PA
CBHW031107030726
47496CB00002BA/420